# The Search

# For

# Shannon

*To Tina*
*Enjoy!!*
*Vicki Allen*
*9/23/01*

## Vicki Allen

Published by Magnolia Publishing Company, Inc.
P.O. Box 770514
Oklahoma City, Oklahoma 73177
www.magnoliapublishing.com

ISBN  0-9674880-5-2

2nd Printing March 2001

Manufactured in the United States of America

**Also by Vicki Allen**

*For Molly*

*For Mama,*
*Donna,*
*Katharine*
*and*
*Jo*

## Acknowledgements

My eternal thanks goes out to:

My family: for loving, supporting, and putting up with me during this long and sometimes grueling process. I love you!

My boss and coworkers: for patiently indulging my midlife crisis and for trying to understand why I gave up all tangible forms of income to pursue a dream.

My close friends who double as first readers: for pointing out the flaws and praising the good parts.

And to my editor, Maria: for tireless hours of wading through hundreds of pages and doing a fabulous job — all while holding my hand and cheerleading. I appreciate you!

# Prologue

It was happening again: The bright lights, the frantic bustle of activity, the guttural screams of a young girl. Amid the shadowy figures and muffled voices, the girl thrashed and moaned, desperately clutching the cold metal rails on either side of her. She didn't think she could endure much more. She grabbed the hand of a passing figure, her voice hoarse as she shrieked in pain. "Please, please, make it stop! Please." The torture seemed to last forever.

At last, it was over. A baby came into the world, kicking and screaming, her terrified cry like sweet music to the girl's ears. She fell back against the bed, an exhausted smile on her face, accepting the baby with ready arms. "My baby," whispered the girl, gazing down at her with tender eyes.

She was beautiful — a perfectly shaped little face, pink cheeks, rosebud lips. What mother could ask for more? The girl stroked the baby's cheek. She cradled her close and pressed her lips to her soft skin, gently whispering her name. "If only your father could see you," she said.

A figure in white appeared next to her, looking down with a frown. "It's time," she said, reaching for the child.

"Please," protested the girl, holding the baby tight. "Just a few more minutes."

"No. It's time." She ripped the baby from the girl's arms, ignoring her tears, and darted swiftly to the door.

"No!" The girl let out an anguished wail, lunging weakly for the side of the bed, only to be stopped by another set of hands. "No!" she screamed. "Don't take my baby! SHANNON!"

The woman awoke with a start, cold beads of perspiration standing on her brow and upper lip. Trembling, she looked around the room, running a nervous hand through her hair as she tried to figure out what had happened. Then she remembered.

"The dream again," she moaned, pulling her knees protectively into her chest. "Will it ever go away?"

She'd heard that time heals all wounds, but she didn't believe it. Time had not healed her wounds, nor had it taken away her pain. She lay back against her pillows, miserable tears streaming down her face while memories stabbed cruelly at her heart.

She had never recovered, nor would she ever be the same. Years had passed with little reprieve. Her soul still ached as though it had been yesterday. She would never be content until she found Shannon.

# The Search

# For

# Shannon

# Part One

## Andie

# 1

The wheels of the 727 touched down with a bang onto the hot concrete runway at Dallas-Fort Worth International Airport, bouncing Andie roughly in her seat. Her face paled, her stomach churned, and she gripped the armrest, holding on for dear life, her knuckles turning white. She stared out the window, keeping her eyes focused on passing buildings and patches of green and brown landscape, trying to ignore the miserable flip-flop of her stomach and wishing she had reconsidered her mode of transportation.

*What on earth ever possessed me to fly?* she wondered. She despised flying and couldn't decide what bothered her most — her extreme claustrophobia or her god-awful motion sickness.

"You know what they say, don't you?" Andie's seatmate spoke up, touching her gently on the arm. "Any landing you can walk away from is a good landing."

Andie glanced at him doubtfully. "If you say so," she said, fighting the awful taste of bile rising in her throat. Unsteadily, she leaned forward and pulled her tote bag from beneath the seat in front of her. She watched the other passengers scramble into the aisle, eager to exit the plane into the welcoming arms of loved ones. She waited, letting

2

Vicki Allen

the bustling crowd clear. She was in no hurry. There would be no one here to greet her.

She finally deplaned and walked through the busy airport in a daze, collecting her luggage and renting a car, then left the busy airport for an hour-long drive. Traveling the jammed roadways, Andie eyed the once-familiar Dallas skyline, staring at shining architectural monuments rising high into a hot Texas sky. "What am I doing here?" she asked. The overwhelming déjà vu of the city and its memories were depressing, and with each block, she grew increasingly blue. At last, she came to her exit and heaved a sigh of relief, steering the rental east onto Interstate 20, heading away from Dallas toward home.

She sped down the four-lane highway bordered by tall dry brush, lost in a nostalgic trance. How strange it seemed to be traveling this road again — the very same stretch of road that had been so dark and lonely on that August morning long ago.

Andrea Shepherd LaRue may not have been the most beautiful woman in the world, but she had been the loveliest girl to grace the halls of Eisenhower High School. Tall and blonde with long slender legs and eyes of ocean blue, at one time Andie Shepherd was the talk of her tiny Texas hometown. She had been a head-turner, sure to stand out in any crowd.

As smart as she was pretty, Andie was the owner of Crème de la Crème, a flourishing catering business. She had married once, but was currently single, having no desire to find husband number two. She had not had much luck with men and felt it best to honor the old philosophy: don't play with fire if you don't want to get burned.

*Twenty years.* It was hard to believe how much time had passed. At one time, she'd had it all: loving parents, a devoted big brother, a bubbly best friend, a high school sweetheart she adored. Life was good and her future looked wonderful, but it all disappeared one summer, gone forever in an instant.

Andie rolled down the window, letting in the morning sunshine and pulled the barrette from her shoulder-length hair, allowing it to whip around her face, carefree in the wind. *I hate remembering*, she thought unhappily. Blocking it out was so much easier. Remembering only made her heart ache, and lingering too long in the past was not healthy.

Her parents were gone. All that remained of her happy childhood was David, and even he was not the brother he used to be. Their relationship was strained at best. They were cautious, struggling to overcome a twenty-year rift.

Receiving the reunion announcement had been a fluke. It arrived in David's mailbox six months after Andie made the call letting him know she was alive. David forwarded the engraved invitation to her home in Biloxi, writing on the outside of the envelope in bold letters, "*You should go, Andie. Go to Texas, clear the air and let go of it once and for all.*"

And now she was going back — to face her past, confess her sins, right the wrongs and come face to face with those she had left behind.

Andie exited the interstate onto a dusty two-lane road, recognizing the main streets of her tiny hometown as they came into view. Pine Prairie, Texas. Nothing much had changed. All the landmarks were in their proper places. The same houses, the same mom and pop stores downtown, triggering fond memories of a young girl. Reminiscing, Andie grinned broadly and drove slowly toward the edge of town.

She pulled into the gravel driveway and stopped in front of the house, going back in time as she surveyed the old Shepherd homestead. The two-story frame house sat on a grass-covered hill, shaded by ancient weeping willows and oaks. David hadn't been able to let the house go any more than Andie could have, and had asked their old neighbor, Mr. Whitmore, to look after the place. He'd done a good job. The lawn was immaculately manicured and the weeded flowerbeds full of blooming daylilies, marigolds and petunias. The old house was freshly painted crisp white and the familiar wooden swing on the veranda swayed gently in the faint June breeze.

Killing the engine, Andie got out of the car and pulled her garment bag from the back seat. She hesitated, viewing the front door reluctantly, then fished through her purse for the key David had given her. She hated the gnawing loneliness welling inside her.

*How I wish Mama were here to welcome me. I could really use a hug right now.* But her mother's embrace would forever elude her. Doris had been gone for years, and Andie hadn't even gotten to say goodbye.

She slowly climbed the front stairs, her legs trembling, and sank onto the top step, too overcome with emotion to go any farther. *This is so hard*, she thought desolately, holding her head in her hands. *Much harder than I anticipated.*

It was this place. This house brought it all back, tearing down her defenses. All the events she had so stoically repressed returned swiftly from the dark recesses of her mind, bursting their shackles and flying at her full force. She winced, her temples throbbing from the images racing at lightning speed through time. And the images were not happy ones. Her last days in this house had not been pleasant.

*No*! she thought as her protective mechanism kicked in. *I can't think about this now. I have to get inside.* Raking her hair from her face, she rose wearily from the stoop and crossed the porch to the front door. Slowly she turned the key and the old door opened, its hinges creaking loudly.

The familiar scent of vanilla candles and rose-petal potpourri drifted faintly above the musty smell of the closed-up room, rushing to Andie's nostrils as she stepped over the threshold. She inhaled deeply, letting her senses take her back to eighteen, remembering with each breath how wonderful life had been for Andrea Shepherd.

She draped her garment bag over the banister and wandered down the hall, the sound of her footsteps echoing through the empty house. It felt strange to be there alone. Subconsciously she waited to see David appear from the kitchen, or to hear her parents call out to her from the den.

She entered the living room, plucking the drab white drop cloths from the furniture, and then opened the Venetian blinds, allowing bright sunlight to filter into the dark room. She stood very still, gazing slowly around the parlor, entranced, taking in every detail: the pale creamy walls, the antique lace drapes across the front bay window, her father Jake's prized oil painting of the Alamo. Her eyes rested on photographs atop the ancient piano, encased in shiny silver frames, lovingly displayed by Doris. She walked lightly across the hardwood floor to admire them, taking one in each hand, smiling fondly at the grinning images of David and Charlotte's children. Her mind drifted to her own son and daughter, the grandchildren Doris had never known.

Jerry and Dana. Her babies. They were so beautiful, each with smooth, flawless skin, dark hair and dark eyes. They were so much like their father. Andie could see very little of herself in her children. It was as if they were Freddie's, and Freddie's alone.

She hugged the pictures to her chest, sitting on the piano bench as tears flooded her eyes. "I was so stupid, so very stupid," she sobbed, lifting her face to the ceiling. "Why is it that everything I do is wrong and every decision I make so foolish? How many times can one person screw up?"

She rocked back and forth, holding the pictures tightly, imagining the faces of her children as she cried. If only she could take back all the things she had said and done.

With a heavy heart, Andie returned the pictures to the top of the piano and left the room, collecting her bags and mounting the carpeted steps as she moved upstairs to unpack. She trailed her fingertips along the smooth wood of the banister, leaving a light path in the dust. Her eyes followed the textured walls of the stairwell, noting with wonder how very little had changed since the last time she had been there.

David's room at the top of the stairs remained untouched, as did the pristine suite of Jake and Doris. Even her own bedroom had been caught up in this curious wrinkle in time. Andie paused in the doorway, viewing the eerie still frame from her past. Despite the hard feelings between them, Doris had left the room exactly as it was the day Andie left home. Beneath the picture window was her large brass bed, topped by a sunny yellow and blue quilt, her tattered old Raggedy Ann and Andy resting on pillows at the head of the bed.

The maple dresser was cluttered with hairbrushes, glass bottles of perfume and an assortment of framed photos featuring Andie and her best friend. She picked up the one closest to her, laughing when she saw the photo of two muddy nine-year-old girls captured one long-ago summer at Girl Scout Camp.

"Good old Tammy," Andie said, holding the frame in her hand, staring at the freckled-faced girls in the snapshot, their snaggle-toothed grins returning her smile. Tall and lanky with a shock of bouncy sable curls, Tammy Whitworth had been Andie's best friend since first grade. She was a basketball-playing tomboy with a life-long dream to coach, and she left Pine Prairie after high school to attend the University of Texas and major in secondary education.

"*God only knows what I'll teach*," Tammy had said, gruff and cynical. "*Although I don't really care. My only ambition is to shoot hoops and pass my talent on to the deserving youth of Texas.*"

Grinning, Andie returned the picture to the dresser and moved toward the closet to hang her garment bag. Until now, she hadn't been sure whom to contact first. Seeing the photograph made the decision easier. Tammy would be the first to learn the truth.

After another sentimental journey through town, Andie located Tammy at the YMCA, coaching summer basketball camp. Leaving her car on the far side of the parking lot, Andie strolled casually across the hot blacktop toward the basketball goals, watching Tammy referee a pack of preteen boys.

Time had been kind to her best friend, leaving her unwrinkled and youthful in gray jersey gym shorts and white T-shirt, her muscular legs shapely and lightly tanned as she ran up and down the court, clapping her hands and bellowing encouragement to her players.

"Shoot, Danny, shoot!" Tammy screamed, her mouth twisting into a grin as the scrawny young boy tossed the ball through the net. "Good job, boy, good job!" She clapped her hands and lifted her silver whistle, blowing it shrilly. "Take five, everybody, take five."

Andie paused beside the basketball court, hooking her fingers through the chain-link fence. Smiling broadly, she watched as Tammy grabbed her water bottle and whipped the kelly-green cap from her head. She shook her tousled brown curls wildly and squirted water onto her sweaty brow. Andie giggled involuntarily, forever amused by Tammy's childlike antics.

Caught off guard by the laughter, Tammy whirled around. Her mouth dropped open as she spotted Andie.

"Andie?" she asked in astonishment. She lowered her sunglasses and gawked, then let out a shriek and bounded across the blacktop, leaping the fence to wrap her in a crushing bear hug.

"I don't believe it. I just don't believe it!" Tammy said as she squeezed her tightly. "I don't know whether to hug you or ring your scrawny neck," she said hoarsely, her voice cracking with sobs. "Jeez-us, Andie, where the hell've you been?"

"That's some way to greet an old friend," Andie replied as she brushed away glad tears. Wrenching from the smothering embrace, she held Tammy at arms' length, teasing her with twinkling eyes, hoping to keep the mood light.

"Who says we're still friends?" Tammy snarled, punching Andie hard in the chest. "You take out of town, never even saying good-bye, never calling to tell me whether you're alive or dead and then you come back, twenty damn years later and expect me to welcome you with open arms? I don't think so," her voice rose an octave with each furious syllable and echoed across the playground, bringing startled glances from the parents arriving to collect their children.

"Tammy, might I remind you what YMCA stands for? Young Men's *Christian* Association. That means watch your language, missy."

Tammy scowled, muttering under her breath, "I've got to dismiss my kids." She began to walk away, striding purposefully toward the gang of boys. "Don't you be going anywhere though, lady," she warned over her shoulder. "You've got a lot of explaining to do."

After the last straggler left, Andie and Tammy climbed to the top of the wooden bleachers and stretched back on their elbows, letting the hot sunshine beat down on them. Tammy sipped her water bottle pensively, biting her tongue, taking time to calm down and measure her words carefully.

"I was really sorry about your mom's passing," she said finally. "I thought for sure you'd come home for the funeral."

"I would have, except I didn't find out until after the fact."

"That's nice."

"It certainly wasn't pleasant."

"So, where the hell've you been?"

Andie met Tammy's penetrating glare unwaveringly, shading her eyes with her forearm and shrugging casually. "Oh, nowhere special. Just here and there."

"Here and there? For twenty years?" Tammy frowned, raising a cynical brow. "Give me a break."

"Tammy, my story's real long and hard to tell," Andie said, dancing skillfully around the issue. "Let's start with you. Why don't you tell me what you've been doing with your life?"

Tammy nodded, conceding to Andie's solemn expression. "Okay, I can go first, if you'd like," she replied amicably. "Let's see, when we last saw one another, I was leaving for UT. I graduated with a degree in secondary education and came back to Pine Prairie. I took a job at the high school as the girls basketball coach and I also teach American History to the junior class delinquents."

"Why Pine Prairie? Of all the places on God's green earth to settle down, why would you pick here?"

"Why not?" Tammy smiled, extending her arms expansively. "Who could ask for anything more than this?"

"So, is that all?"

"What do you mean is that all? Hell, isn't that enough? What'd you expect out of me, a Nobel Prize?"

"Hardly," Andie said with a chuckle. "Believe me, that was the farthest thought from my mind. How about a husband or some kids?"

Tammy shook her head. "Nope, neither. There's no one in this town worth having. I dated a guy for a while when I was in Austin, but I dumped him when I moved back here. We never saw eye to eye on much anyway. Men, for the most part, are a big pain in the butt."

"Don't you ever want to have kids?"

"I have kids, a whole big slew of 'em," Tammy grinned. "My students are my kids, and I get a whole new set every four years, which is a much better deal than most parents get." She stretched her fingers and cracked her knuckles, eyeing Andie with spunky determination. "Okay, chickadee, I've killed enough time telling you about my complacent little life. Let's talk about yours for a while."

Andie cleared her throat, shifting self-consciously on the hard wooden bench. "What do you want to know?"

"Well, for starters, let's talk about the summer you disappeared. You remember that summer, don't you? Me to UT, you to Mississippi State."

"Yeah," Andie sighed. "I remember that summer well. Daddy died, Mama flipped, and life was just never the same."

"And then you left."

"Yes, and then I left."

"Just like that?"

"Just like that."

Tammy pursed her lips in frustration. "Your mother really freaked out after you left, acted really weird. Told us you ran away from home, but I didn't buy it, not for one minute. You weren't the runaway type. Ol' Doris acted so bizarre that I started checking your back yard for shallow graves."

She paused, staring broodingly off into the distance, her thoughts focused intently on a time gone by. "Your mom was bad off, but not nearly as bad off as Cole."

Andie shuddered involuntarily, her heart skipping erratically at the mention of his name. Cole Dewberry, her high school sweetheart, the one who hung the moon. His haunting image leapt into her mind: his handsome face, wavy black hair and soulful gray eyes. She could almost hear his laughter, feel the warmth of his smile. She melted at the thought of him and smiled softly, overcome by an overwhelming sense of longing, her soul crying out to be near him, her arms yearning to hold him tight.

"Cole *really* wigged when he found out you were gone," Tammy's voice tugged at her insistently, pulling her out of her daydream. "He was absolutely beside himself, camping out on your mother's porch, patrolling the neighborhood, even threatened to postpone going off to school so he could look for you. His daddy put a stop to that nonsense though. He loaded Cole up and drove him to Starksville himself, just to make sure he went."

"I'm sorry," Andie said, lowering her eyes, her voice filled with guilt. "I never meant to hurt him, or you."

"Well, despite your good intentions, we were hurt, both of us. Hurt and downright baffled, wondering what we'd done to deserve such shabby treatment." Tammy's voice was gruff with bitterness. "After a few months, I gave up all hope of ever seeing you again, but not Cole. I don't think he gave up hope until you didn't show up for the ten-year reunion." She glanced over, her steely look piercing Andie's soul. "I'm really curious, Andie, so spill. Where've you been?"

"I left here early that morning before the sun even came up," Andie began reluctantly, her voice solemn, her blue eyes clouded and far away. "It was really damp and foggy, and the air was thick with humidity. The air was thick, but not nearly as thick as the silence in our car. I bet Mama and I didn't speak two words all the way to Dallas, not even when we got to DFW and it came time to say goodbye. We never spoke a word. She just took me by the arm and put me on the first flight out of Dallas to David's."

Tammy's eyebrows shot up in surprise. "David's? Really? That's the last place I would've expected you to be, with the way y'all fought and all."

Andie didn't respond. Instead, she heard her brother's voice, floating through her mind like a distant ghost:

"*Let me call my friend Brandon in Atlanta, Andie,*" he had said soberly, his expression pleading, begging her to listen to the voice of reason. "*Let's put an end to this once and for all so you can get on with your life.*"

Andie had stared through him, her eyes blank and lifeless. "*My life? What life would that be, David? I don't have a life, not anymore. My life is gone.*" All that she had treasured had been taken from her, her dreams and expectations shattered.

Andie shook her head, erasing the traumatic memory to go on with her story. "I stayed in Huntsville with David and his wife Charlotte for nearly a year, then moved on to Biloxi where I went to school, got a job, married and started a catering business. Ten years later, I got a divorce, kept the business and stayed in Mississippi while my ex moved to Tennessee with the kids." Andie shrugged nonchalantly, meeting Tammy's probing eyes. "That's pretty much it."

"So that's it in a nutshell. Is that what you're telling me?"

"That's what I'm telling you."

"Bullshit, Andie. There's more to it than that. I want to know what the hell made you go to David's in the first place? What made you throw away your plans for college, not to mention the love of your life, and run to Huntsville, Alabama? It had to be more than the undeniable urge to spend time with your beloved brother."

"You're right. There was more to it."

"No kidding. So, spit it out already! I've spent the last twenty years worrying whether you were alive or dead. I at least deserve to know the truth."

The relentless pit bull in Tammy wouldn't give up until she drew blood. *And she's right*, Andie admitted, wringing her hands nervously. Tammy deserved to hear the whole story, but telling her wouldn't be easy. Another face came to mind: a tiny face with brilliant eyes and rosy cheeks. She had only seen it briefly, but would remember it for the rest of her life.

Andie swallowed, forcing a hard lump from her throat, and squeezed her eyes shut, holding back a river of scalding tears. "Yes, Tammy. There was more to it," she murmured. "Much more."

"Quit stalling, will ya? Nothing can be that bad."

"No, not by today's standards anyway. In today's world, it's something frighteningly commonplace, but twenty years ago it was almost unspeakable."

"You had a debilitating drug habit?'

"No," Andie laughed softly. "Although that might've been easier on me." She hesitated and took a deep breath. "I was pregnant, Tammy. That's why I left."

Tammy sucked in her breath sharply, her muddy-brown eyes as big as saucers. "What did you just say?" she stuttered in disbelief.

"You heard me."

"Pregnant!" Tammy continued to stare in astonishment, slapping her palm to her chest. "Cole?"

Andie nodded solemnly.

"My God! And you didn't tell him?" Tammy's voice rose hysterically. "You were pregnant with Cole Dewberry's baby, and you left town without telling him? Are you crazy?"

Andie set her jaw, determined not to cry. She fixed her gaze on her tightly clenched hands, unwilling to meet Tammy's outraged stare. "It seemed to be the right thing to do at the time, given his baseball scholarship and all," she said softly. "I just wanted Cole to have a good life, to live out all his dreams."

"And you think he could achieve that without you? Don't you know that being with you was part of his dream? You actually believe that, not knowing what happened to you, he could just push all memory of you aside and continue on as if nothing ever happened?"

"I don't know what I believed."

"That's pretty damn obvious," Tammy shot back, her stare piercing Andie like a dagger. "So, where's the baby now? Biloxi, Tennessee or here with you?"

"I don't know."

"You don't know?"

"No. I haven't seen her since the day she was born." Andie looked up, her face ashen, her sorrowful eyes haunted by pain. "I gave her up for adoption."

"Why? Never mind." Tammy held up her hand, halting any further explanation. "I know. It seemed the right thing to do at the time." She took off her cap and scratched her head, perplexed. "Whose idea was that? Or did you come up with it all on your own?"

"It was David's idea."

"Of course it was. Good old David, always the brilliant one. He never gave a damn about anyone but himself." Tammy sighed heavily, sliding a sympathetic arm around Andie's shoulders, her heart twisted by the grief-stricken expression on her face. "I'm so sorry, honey. You've really had a tough time."

"You don't know the half of it," Andie sniffled loudly, wiping her drippy nose on the edge of her sleeve. "I've been an absolute mess since the day the baby came. I left Huntsville right afterward, hating everyone associated with the adoption, especially my mother and David.

"I made it okay in Biloxi. I met my ex-husband, Freddie, shortly after I got there. He was wonderful to me. Freddie LaRue's a kind, decent human being, and he certainly didn't deserve any of the grief he got from me.

"Our marriage got off to a good start. I was happy and Freddie was happy. Then Freddie wanted a family, and things began to change. We had Dana first. My God, she was beautiful, so sunny and happy. She was a wonderful baby, more than anyone could ever ask for, but I just couldn't feel anything for her. I wouldn't even hold her.

"The doctors blamed it on postpartum depression, but I don't know. I don't know how to explain it. It was like I just snapped, like giving birth to Dana burst the dam, bringing it all flooding back. From the moment she was born, I pushed Dana away, longing instead for my firstborn. Every single time I looked at Dana, I ached for Shannon. I know it was wrong to feel that way, but I just couldn't help it."

Andie closed her eyes, resting her head on the steel rail behind her, unhappy tears cascading down her cheeks and drying instantly in the heat of the scorching Texas sun. *Oh God, why didn't I do things differently?* She chastised herself, resisting the urge to beat her head against the guardrail. Regret was a hard thing to deal with and it had taken its toll. Years of remorse had cut a deep path through Andie's heart, leaving her wounded and hollow.

She opened her eyes to view Tammy's incredulous face and felt the need to clarify. "Now, don't get me wrong — I love Dana. I really do. She's a great girl. It's just that at the time I could offer her no affection.

"Our son Jerry was born two years later, and although I felt a little bit more for him than for Dana, even he did nothing to improve my poor mental status. I was deeply depressed and withdrew from everyone, even the husband I adored. After ten years of dealing with it, poor Freddie'd had enough, and he and I divorced."

"You poor kid." Tammy reached over, squeezing Andie's hand consolingly. "It wouldn't be right for me to be mad at you now. All this kinda takes the wind out of my sails. I can't believe you kept it from me all these years. Why didn't you tell me?"

"In the beginning, I didn't tell you because I didn't want Cole to find out. Then, as time went on, I suppose I didn't contact you because I was ashamed."

"Ashamed? Oh Andie, sometimes you are so stupid." Tammy laughed lightly and shook her head, smiling broadly in a show of support. "Okay, so now I know. When are you going to tell Cole? Or are you?"

"I planned to tell him this weekend, assuming he'll be here. That's my real purpose in coming."

"If that's the case, then you should get your chance. He's home. I saw him last night at Joe McCoy's."

"Joe McCoy's? Good lord, is that old honky tonk still around?"

"Sure it is. Hey, it ain't much, but it's all we got."

Cole was in Pine Prairie. Andie's pale face lit up. "How did he look?" she asked shyly, casting a sidelong glance at Tammy from beneath thick lashes.

"How do you think he looked? He looked simply gorgeous. When I saw him, he was strutting his stuff around the pool table and outrunning women, as usual."

"Did you talk to him?"

"Briefly. Shoot, I could barely get near him. He was surrounded by a pack of our matronly female counterparts, desperately seeking some means of escape."

"Isn't he married?"

"There was a Mrs. Dewberry for a while. Some girl he met at Mississippi State." Tammy wrinkled her brow, trying to recall the details. "But they've been divorced for several years now, I think."

Andie's heart swelled hopefully, and she concealed an optimistic smile. Cole was unattached — that was one of the first positive things to happen to her in a long time. Maybe there was a chance. If she still loved Cole, then maybe, just maybe, he might have some affection left for her. Maybe there was room for happiness in her life after all.

Tammy's mouth stretched into a thin smile as she studied Andie's lovesick expression. "I'd get that syrupy look off my face if I were you," she said sternly. "Cole might just harbor a little resentment toward you, I'm afraid. I wouldn't expect him to be ready to kiss and make up, if you know what I mean."

"Thanks for the warning. I'll keep it in mind." Andie shaded her eyes against the blinding sun and squinted at Tammy, waiting patiently for her next question.

"Then I take it you *are* going to the reunion. You want me to pick you up? You damn sure don't want to enter that lions' den alone."

"Pick me up? Don't you have a date?" Andie kidded, laughing loudly at Tammy's irate frown.

"Hell no! Don't you listen? I already told you that there's no one in town to date and from what I saw of our former classmates last night, none of them look worth a damn either, with the exception of Cole."

Tammy glanced at her watch and jumped up from her seat. "C'mon, Shepherd, let's go. I'll make you dinner."

Andie shook her head. "Nah, I think I'll pass. I'd like to be alone for a while. You know, to gather my thoughts and put myself back together." She looked up, meeting Tammy's eyes, their gaze locked in mutual understanding. Finally, Tammy nodded.

"Suit yourself," she said, shrugging with facetious indifference. She began her descent down the bleachers, stopping midway down to glance back over her shoulder. "It is good to have you back, Andie. I have missed you, even if I was pretty pissed off." She flashed a mischievous grin and then continued to the bottom of the stands, calling out obnoxiously, "I'll meet you tonight then, at the gym, eight o'clock. Be there or be square."

Andie watched her saunter away, whistling a jaunty tune as she climbed into her four-wheel drive. *Good old Tammy*, she thought fondly. For all her crustiness, she really had a heart of gold.

"Coming clean with her was much easier than I imagined," Andie realized, sighing with relief. "One down, one to go."

The thought of telling Cole made her sick. Drained and filled with apprehension, Andie rose wearily and headed toward home.

Back at the house, she had a good cry and a stiff drink, successfully locating Jake's secret stash of whiskey. "That was good," she said, lifting the bottle to pour another. She gulped it down smoothly, letting the fiery liquid burn her throat, praying it would drown her sorrows. She debated finishing off the bottle, but decided against it, thinking it would be unwise to show up at the reunion toasted.

"As if the rumors flying around about me aren't bad enough. All I need is for people to think I'm a lush," she muttered and put on a pot of strong coffee before teetering upstairs to take a shower.

Later, dressed in a soft-blue linen sheath and matching flats, she stood in front of her closet door, studying her reflection in the full-length mirror. Remembering Tammy's remark about their matronly female counterparts, she peered more closely, narrowing her eyes as she critically inspected her appearance. She thought she had aged pretty well, but now she wasn't so sure.

*I haven't changed that much*, she mused, pinching the flawless skin on her cheeks, squinting at the faint crow's feet around her eyes. She was five foot eight and despite having given birth to three children, managed to retain her slim, willowy figure. Her skin was smooth and lightly tanned from the rare afternoons she'd managed to slip out of work to walk on the beach, and her blonde hair was trimmed to her shoulders in an attractive style, a definite change from the long ponytail of her teens. *I don't look that old*, she thought. *Nowhere near thirty-eight.* No, she certainly didn't look ancient. She only felt it sometimes.

On the outside, she still looked the same, but inwardly she was much different. *Did it show?* Did her face give away the pain she had endured? Looking at her, one would never suspect her anguish. However, those who knew her best could see a change, no matter how small. The difference was in her eyes. Although still bright blue, they had lost their brilliance and become dull, etched with sadness that would never fade.

Grabbing her purse, Andie descended the stairs, lost in thought. Her lonely heart still hoped to find Doris curled up on the couch with her nose buried in a mystery novel. It was hard being in the house alone. She missed her parents terribly and longed for a comforting touch. It was funny how she thought of them now. She had allowed her thoughts to linger on them longer in the past twenty hours than she had in the past twenty years.

Bleakly, Andie recalled the days following her father's death and her mother's depression and withdrawal. Had it not been for Cole, Andie would have lost her mind. Cole had been her rock, her shoulder to cry on, the one she ran to for comfort. He had consoled her, cradling her tenderly in his arms, kissing her and assuring her that all would again be right.

When Andie discovered she was pregnant later that same summer, Doris was still not herself. She lost control, yelling and screaming, slapping Andie hard across the face and accusing her of things that were not only unfair, but also untrue. Her cruelty in the days before Andie's departure caused a permanent rift between them, something Andie grew to regret as she matured. She let too many years go by without making amends with her mother, and now it was too late. She would never get another chance to say, "I'm sorry." And that's what bothered her most.

Pushing away her grim thoughts, Andie moved to the front door, butterflies fluttering wildly in her stomach. "Wish me luck," she flashed a nervous smile to the family portrait hanging in the entryway. "I'm gonna need it."

She closed the door, walking slowly toward the rental parked in the drive, already regretting her decision not to ride to the dance with Tammy.

# 2

Dwight D. Eisenhower Memorial High School. Andie drove slowly alongside the flat-roofed structure, staring up at the generic concrete walls and double stories of identical rectangular windows. She stopped her car near the front entrance, craning her neck to peer inside, imagining the echo of obnoxious voices drifting down the corridors, intermingled with the metallic slam of lockers and light-hearted laughter. She listened, wide-eyed, to the haunting noises of yesteryear.

*I've got to get out of here*, she thought hysterically. *This trip is becoming more and more like a really bad episode of 'The Twilight Zone'*. She tore her gaze from the building and threw her car into drive, zooming around the corner in the direction of the gymnasium.

She wheeled the little Escort into a parking space at the back of the school and eyed the jammed lot warily, breathing a huge sigh of relief when she spotted Tammy's silver four-wheel drive. *Good, she's here*, she cheered silently. *At least I'll have one friendly face to look for in the crowd.*

She cut the engine and sat in the car, her palms growing sweaty. She clutched the steering wheel, staring apprehensively at the gym. "I can't do this," she said aloud, biting her lip as her stomach churned miserably.

*Yes, you can*, her confident inner voice assured her, pushing her gently, giving her the courage she needed to face the old ghosts. *You can do this, Andrea LaRue.* She drew a deep breath, then got out and strolled purposefully toward the building.

Swinging open the glass double doors, she was hit with memories of game night, the sound of cheering students and the rhythmic thudding of basketballs against the wooden floor. Eisenhower gymnasium — Tammy's favorite oasis. Andie smiled and stepped inside, pausing timidly in the lobby and glancing uneasily around the dimly lit room.

The gym was decorated for the reunion as it had been for so many other dances in the past, with the bleachers pushed in neat stacks against the wall and green and white steamers crisscrossed colorfully across the vaulted ceiling. Vividly hued helium balloons with ribbon tails bobbed festively above cloth-covered tables, and the brightly illuminated stage showcased a live pop band, churning out disco tunes as they played to a packed house of Eisenhower alumni.

*It's a capacity crowd all right*, Andie quickly noted. *Looks like all one hundred and seventy-five members of our illustrious graduating class made it back for the big shindig.* She studied their laughing, smiling faces, trying to recall their names as she scanned the room for Tammy.

"And who have we here?"

She felt a light tap on her shoulder and whirled around to face Cynthia Walley, the senior class secretary, in charge of manning the front door. Cyn drew in a sharp breath and gawked at her, her eyes wide with astonishment.

"Omigod, Andrea Shepherd! What a surprise!" she patted Andie's shoulder enthusiastically, regaining her poise while displaying a wealth of insincere affection. "So good to see you! Didn't expect you here tonight though, honey. I heard you were dead."

"Well, that's certainly a pleasant thing to say." Andie eyed her with mounting irritation. Cynthia Walley had not changed one bit. *She's every bit as annoying now as she was then*, Andie thought, watching her shuffle through paper badges arranged alphabetically on a folding table. She begrudgingly accepted the name tag Cyn held out to her and hurriedly peeled off the paper backing, slapping it to her dress. Ignoring Cyn's string of nosy questions, she made her way into the crowded gym without another word, feeling Cyn's intrigued stare boring into her back.

"That was a wonderful welcome," Andie mumbled under her breath as she sidled through a group gathered near the door. "Of all the people I could see first, Cyn would have to be the one."

Just over the threshold, she encountered an ocean of familiar faces, the names of old classmates coming back to her in a flash, rolling off her tongue as if she had seen them only yesterday. She glided easily through the crowd, exuding much more confidence than she felt, issuing cheerful greetings as she made eye contact with incredulous childhood pals, discovering to her amazement just how many of them remembered that she had dropped off the face of the earth shortly after graduation.

"Andie Shepherd! God Almighty! How the hell are you?"

"Andie! Good lord, girl! Where've you been?"

"Oh my God! Andrea Shepherd! Where did you come from?"

She was surrounded, suffocated by the thick crowd, feeling claustrophobic and violated by their intrusive questions. She began to harbor serious thoughts of fleeing when, much to her relief, she heard someone call out, "Hey, Coach Whitworth!"

Andie did an about-face and spotted Tammy navigating her way through the throng, dressed in a clingy, sparkling short black dress and high heels, her curly locks secured away from her face by a rhinestone headband. Andie blinked in surprise, stunned that beneath her gym clothes and baseball caps, Tammy Whitworth had blossomed into a very attractive woman.

Tammy spied Andie encircled by the pack of prying classmates and quickly elbowed her way through the mob. "Hey, y'all! Coming through!" she announced loudly, issuing a boisterous universal greeting, then rescued Andie, pulling her to one side. "I told you it'd be a lions' den," she hissed gruffly.

"It hasn't been that bad," Andie said with a forced smile, unwilling to admit that she'd been uncomfortable.

"Oh really? Is that why you looked like you were about to throw up back there?"

"A mere figment of your imagination, my dear. I've never felt more at ease," Andie fibbed smoothly and quickly changed the subject. "And look at you, all dressed up like that! You look fabulous!"

"You don't have to sound so amazed, Andrea. I clean up pretty nice when I want to." She flashed a saucy grin, inspecting Andie's appearance approvingly. "Look at you, for God's sake. You don't look much different now than you did the night of our senior prom."

"Liar," Andie scoffed, playfully rolling her eyes.

"Okay, so I'm a liar, but I had to return the compliment. What'd you expect me to say? You look like warmed over dog shit?"

"You are such a class act."

"Aren't I though?" Tammy wrinkled her nose with a smirk and took Andie by the arm, guiding her through the masses while delivering impromptu observations about their classmates.

"Look over there, Andie," she said, pointing toward a GQ-looking young man with slicked-back hair. "You know who that is? That's George Pappas, that little weasly nerd from our chemistry class. I heard he's big time into computers and worth about a gazillion dollars." Tammy chuckled, shaking her head in amusement. "You 'member the time I chased him through the lunchroom, trying to give him a wedgie, and he wet his pants? I wonder what his snotty little socialite wife would think about that? Maybe I'll just go over and remind him of that little incident."

Andie giggled, wearing a cheerful smile, relaxed and greatly entertained. They pressed on with their tour, pausing frequently to chat with old friends and acquaintances.

"Jeez, will you take a look at some of these people?" Tammy whispered loudly. "I can't believe how some of them have let themselves go. And talk about irritating. Thank God most of them have moved on to parts unknown, otherwise *I* might've gone screaming away into the night the way you did," she winked, teasing Andie good-naturedly. "And you know what? The more I think about it, the more I'm convinced that you had the right idea."

"Speaking of, whose bright idea was it to put Cynthia Walley in the lobby?" Andie asked cleverly. "Why would anyone want *Cyn* to be the first person seen at the class reunion?"

"I think it's a form of crowd control. There's no telling how many people tucked their tails and ran as soon as they saw her lurking around the front door."

"I know. That thought crossed my mind the minute I saw her."

Tammy put out her arm suddenly, halting Andie in her path. "Whoa, I need a rest," she declared, reaching down to remove one of her shoes. "These heels are murder. What the hell was I thinking?" She rubbed her sore toes, grimacing and massaging a cramp.

They found an empty spot on one side of the room and paused to people-watch. Tammy rested against a stack of bleachers, kicking off her other shoe, and glanced expectantly around the packed house. Andie joined her, leaning against the cool cinderblock wall, laughing with Tammy and tapping her toes to the disco sounds of Donna Summer.

*So far, so good*, she thought. Things were really going better than she'd expected. She rested her head against the wall, closing her eyes as she listened to the band.

"Now aren't you glad you came?" Tammy asked, tugging in unladylike fashion at her slip.

"Uh-huh," Andie murmured with a smile. "I wouldn't have missed this for the world."

She knew he was there even before she saw him. The tingle down her spine alerted her like radar. Suddenly overcome by déjà vu, Andie lifted her head, spotting him among a sea of people on the dance floor. She instantly recognized the familiar masculinity of him — the trim, athletic build, the handsome face and the dark curly hair. With her heart in her throat, she watched as Cole Dewberry strolled casually across the gym floor, stopping to trade stories with some players from the former school baseball team, shaking hands and flashing an easy smile.

Time had indeed been kind to Cole. He was as attractive as ever, unchanged save a hint of gray shadowing his temple. Andie stared at him, completely spellbound, remembering the boy and loving the man. It was as if no time had passed, as if she'd seen him only yesterday. For Andie, nothing had changed.

Never taking her eyes from his face, she elbowed Tammy hard in the ribs, nodding in his direction. "He's here," she breathed, her cheeks flushed, her voice barely above a whisper.

Feeling her unwavering gaze upon him, Cole turned and caught sight of Andie across the crowded room. His face paled as though he'd seen a ghost. "Dear God," he blinked, his gray eyes growing huge. "I don't believe it."

Distractedly, he excused himself from his ex-teammates and began to walk slowly toward her. He measured his steps as he gathered his wits, his eyes fixed on Andie's face.

"Shit, and now for the moment of truth," Tammy muttered under her breath. "And mind you, Andie. He doesn't look real happy."

With every step, Andie grew increasingly apprehensive, her heart pounding wildly. In the instant it took him to cross the floor, she remembered everything about Cole Dewberry.

She remembered his quick wit, his strong arms and his deep, warm kisses that had weakened her knees and led to many nights of parking in Old Man Honeycutt's pasture. She flushed at the memory of his touch, suppressing the urge to frantically fan her hot face. Instead, she licked her dry lips and managed a weak smile as he reached the spot where she and Tammy waited, planting himself in front of them and greeting them with a wry smile.

"Hello, *Coach Whitworth*!" he hailed Tammy merrily and playfully punched her shoulder. "I heard you were teaching and thank God daily that I don't have kids in this school district."

"Hey, that's your loss," Tammy shot back with a huge grin. "You might find that your kids would benefit greatly from being taught by someone such as myself — a person with both brilliance and a terrific sense of humor."

Cole applauded her quick comeback with a hearty laugh then turned to Andie, holding her with a cool, level stare for what seemed like an eternity before finally speaking in a voice as cold as ice.

"I wish I could say that I'm glad to see you, Andie," he said cynically, taking her aback with his hostility.

"That's not a very nice way to greet an old friend, Cole," Tammy intervened smoothly, giving him a stern frown. "Couldn't you at least think of something more socially acceptable to say?"

"I seem to recall that Andie and I were a little more than friends."

Andie felt herself blush under his gaze, well aware that she had to find some way to acknowledge him. "A bit more, I would say," she said quietly, unable to tear her eyes from his frigid stare. "How are you, Cole? You look wonderful."

"Thank you. I could say the same thing about you, if I were in a more giving mood." His mouth tightened into a stubborn line. "But after twenty years of wondering just what the hell happened to the woman I loved, I've lost all desire to be complimentary toward you or about you."

He shoved his clenched fists deep into the pockets of his tailored pants, regarding her bitterly. "Now, if you had bothered to show up for the ten-year reunion, maybe I could've been more civil, because ten years ago I still gave a damn."

With a final glare of contempt, he turned his back to her, facing Tammy, his smile thin and strained. "Now that I know Andrea is alive and well, my mind is finally at ease. It was great seeing you, Tammy. Now, if you'll excuse me, I'm going to collect some dances from the women who've bothered to remember I exist." He stalked away without looking back.

"I'd say that went well," Andie murmured unhappily as she stared after him, tears welling in her eyes. *How dare he insinuate that I forgot about him?*

Seeing the crushed look on Andie's face, Tammy slid a compassionate arm around her shoulder. "I'm sorry, honey," she said soberly. "I told you he was a tiny bit bitter."

"A tiny bit? My God, he might as well have shot me through the heart."

"He still cares about you," Tammy declared confidently. "I could see it in his eyes. Behind all that ice was that same old lovesick look he always had whenever he looked at you. Trust me, Andie, if he didn't still care, he wouldn't have been so shitty."

"What a classic Hallmark greeting," Andie chuckled lightly as she wiped away her tears, grateful for a moment of humor.

Tammy took her by the arm, pulling her toward a group of women chattering happily around the cash bar. "C'mon," she coaxed soothingly. "What you need right now is some good, old-fashioned, catty gossip."

Andie remained at the reunion as long as she could, making an effort to enjoy herself and block Cole from her mind, but she failed miserably. Every time she turned her head, she saw him and her eyes trailed his every move. He made no further attempt to acknowledge her, nor did he even look her way. It was as if seeing her again had satisfied many years of wonder and now for him it was over.

For Andie, it would never end. Her heart ached for him and she wished desperately that she could do something, anything to make amends.

She glanced down at her watch. "I think I'm gonna call it a night," she said, wearing a wistful expression as she turned toward Tammy. "I've had about as much fun as I can stand for one evening."

Tammy gave her a severe look. "What about the 'coming clean with Cole' portion of your pilgrimage? Is that no longer important?"

Andie laughed skeptically. "Well, *Coach*, unless I climb right up there on that stage and announce it over the loudspeaker, I see no hope in telling Cole Dewberry anything tonight, seeing how he's so receptive toward me and all." She leaned over, kissing Tammy's cheek. "I'll call you tomorrow before I leave for the airport," she said as she turned to leave, casting a playful glance over her shoulder. "Maybe you'll come visit me now that you know where I am."

She skirted the edge of the crowd, making it to the front door without running into Cole or being delayed by any further cross-examination from her classmates. Padding across the lobby, Andie thought she had it made, but fell short at the last moment.

"Leaving so soon?" Cyn piped up, spotting Andie just as she put her hand on the door. "And all alone?"

"Why wouldn't I be? I arrived that way, didn't I?" Andie snapped, scowling crossly at Cyn as she pushed open the heavy glass. She heaved a sigh of relief as she stepped into the warm night air.

"I'm glad that's over," she said, striding hurriedly across the pavement toward her car. "I would rather walk across hot coals than go through that again. And I could easily go another two decades without hearing another word out of Cyn Walley."

It was well after midnight when Andie pulled into her parents' gravel driveway. She trudged wearily up the front steps and unlocked the door, going directly upstairs, determined to get a good night's sleep and get out of town first thing the next morning. She changed into a loose cotton sleepshirt and climbed into bed, squeezing her eyes tightly shut as she tried to block all thought from her mind. Nevertheless, her effort was in vain. Her mind still raced, and she tossed and turned restlessly, thrashing around under the sheets.

"Oh, this is just ridiculous!" she cried out in frustration, throwing back the covers and getting out of bed. She headed back down the steps to the kitchen, and made herself a cup of hot tea before slipping out onto the front porch. "This is better," she said. "Anything's better than being cooped up in that house alone."

It was a great night to be outdoors: slightly cool with a full moon and a light breeze swaying the branches of the tall willow trees alongside the house. With a sigh, Andie kicked off her slippers and settled on the swing, curling her long legs beneath her. Resting her head against the cool metal chains, she closed her eyes, rocking gently in the peaceful night air. She welcomed the silence, hoping that after the nerve-racking events of the evening it would soothe her to sleep.

"I should've known I'd find you here."

Andie jumped as his voice came out of the darkness, and she lifted her head to see Cole climbing the front steps. "You always did like that old swing." He paused, leaning against the porch rail as he offered her a hesitant smile.

Andie eyed him cautiously. "I take it you're in a more giving mood now?" she questioned him curtly, not bothering to disguise the hurt in her voice.

Cole glanced at her sheepishly. "If you're mad, I know I deserve it," he said. "I've come to apologize. My behavior earlier tonight was inexcusable. Never in my wildest dreams did I imagine I could act that way. I've played this out over and over again in my mind and always thought that if I ever saw you again, I'd take you in my arms and kiss you like there was no tomorrow. Instead I insulted you, told you off, and then turned my back on you."

"I can't say I really blame you after I deserted you the way I did," Andie said, motioning him to sit down.

Cole vetoed the chair against the wall, opting instead to join Andie on the swing, settling into the corner opposite her and stretching out his legs. Andie shivered from the nearness of him and yearned to touch him, kiss him and throw herself into his arms with wild abandon, but wisely refrained.

"I'll have you know that I just survived the blistering lecture of a lifetime," Cole informed her with an easy grin. "I thought maybe Tammy's temperament might improve with age, but boy, was I ever wrong."

"I can describe Tammy in many ways," Andie said, "but mellow is not one of them."

"Would you know her if she was any other way? I've been told that she's one hell of a terrific coach. I'm glad she's doing what she always wanted to do."

"How about you?" Andie asked softly. "What have you been doing with your life?"

"Well, let's see, we've already covered your disappearance," he said with a mischievous wink. "So, after that I went on to Mississippi State and played ball for a few years while majoring in engineering. I started dating a little sorority princess during my junior year and made the grave mistake of marrying her after we graduated. We divorced a little over ten years ago. Now I live happily alone just outside of New Orleans."

"New Orleans!" Andie managed to keep a straight face, letting Cole's casual revelation sink in. Cole lived in New Orleans. All these years she had lived in Biloxi, hungering for just a glimpse of his sweet face, and all along he had been only a little over an hour away.

"Why did you divorce?" she asked after recovering from her shock.

"Well to be honest, before Kimberly, I'd never met a completely self-centered, self-absorbed individual. But believe me, she fit the bill. She couldn't stand the fact that I had to work to support the lifestyle to which she had become accustomed. She was extremely putout that I couldn't just stay home and devote my entire existence to catering to her every whim."

Andie laughed at his condescending description of his ex-wife, guessing from his annoyed tone that there was more to the story than he would admit. "Do you have any children?" she asked, adding silently: *Other than our daughter?*

Cole shook his head. "Good lord, no," he answered in mock horror. "A child would've ruined Kimmie's perfect figure." He chuckled good-naturedly. "No, seriously, I would've loved to have a couple of kids, but Kimberly doesn't like children. Another of our many conflicts."

"Irreconcilable differences?"

"More than I can count," he said. He reached over, patting her hand as he studied her appreciatively. "You look wonderful, Andie. I don't think you've changed one bit since the last time I saw you."

"You haven't gotten a really good look at me then, have you?" Andie joked, her eyes sparkling playfully. "I've changed quite a bit actually. If not externally, then certainly internally."

Cole turned toward her, sliding his arm along the swing's back, taking in her wistful expression. There was a certain sadness about her, he decided, emptiness from a source he couldn't begin to pinpoint. What had happened to the bubbly young woman he had loved so deeply? He had to ask. He had to know why she had thrown it all away and disappeared into that sultry August night.

"So, Andie, you want to tell me just a little bit about what you've been doing with your time for the last two decades?" He tried to sound casual.

Terrified and trembling inside, Andie decided not to break the news about the baby immediately, but tell him the other details of her life first. "Well, let's see," she mused, stroking her chin. "I spent a year in Huntsville with David and Charlotte then I relocated to Biloxi, finished school, got my business degree and started a catering business with my husband, Freddie LaRue.

"Two daughters, a son and an ex-husband later, I still live in Biloxi and run the catering business. And that's about it," Andie babbled nervously. When she finished, she drew a deep breath and glanced over at Cole.

Cole listened to her hasty recitation with amusement, his eyes twinkling as he laughed. "That was the fastest description of twenty years I've ever heard in my life."

He leaned forward and gave her a light kiss on the lips, sending an electric charge through her body. Her heart melted as she stared into his eyes, remembering in an instant a baby with eyes the same shade of gray. She quickly dropped her gaze.

Cole reached out, tilting her chin up as he studied her face. "Why did you leave me, Andie?" he asked softly, his chest aching. "I would've done anything for you, bent over backward to keep you here, changed my entire world if you'd asked me to."

"It's hard to explain." Andie looked away, unable to bear the crushed expression on his face. She chewed her lip, her heart pounding deafeningly in her ears, filled with almost crippling anxiety at the thought of telling him the truth.

Cole creased his brow, observing her reaction. Something was definitely bothering her, but he couldn't put a finger on what. *She's so hard to read that I'm not sure if I'll ever get to the bottom of it.*

"So tell me about the kids," he suggested cheerfully, hoping a discussion of something more pleasant might relax her and lead to what was really on her mind.

He couldn't have known his good intentions would backfire. The knot in the pit of Andie's stomach grew as she struggled for words. "My younger children, Dana and Jerry, live with their father in Tennessee," she said, noticing the surprise on Cole's face. "I was having some problems at the time we split, and it was best for them to be with him," she explained.

Cole nodded slowly, accepting her explanation without judgment. "And your oldest child? A daughter, right?" Andie nodded, fidgeting nervously. "Does she live with you?"

With an ashen face, Andie studied her hands, picking at her long, manicured nails, afraid to say aloud what could no longer be left unsaid. She couldn't look at him as she admitted, "I don't know where she is."

"Why not?" Cole leaned closer, sensing that she was finally going to reveal all.

Andie ran a trembling hand through her hair. "I haven't seen her since I let her go, almost twenty years ago."

She looked him in the eye, watching as he absorbed her statement. He appeared puzzled and distracted, then quickly calculated, reeling in surprise as he realized the truth.

"Andie?" he stammered uncertainly. His eyes grew wide as he searched for the right words. "Twenty years ago? Are you saying what

I think you're saying? Are you telling me that we have a child together? Is that what you're telling me?"

"When I left Pine Prairie twenty years ago, I was pregnant. I left to stay with David and Charlotte until after the baby was born. David made me realize that adoption was the best solution for the baby and for me."

She looked over at a stone-faced and silent Cole. "But David was wrong," she said as hot scalding tears began to flow in unchecked rivers down her cheeks. "It wasn't for the best. I haven't been the same since I let her go. I still yearn for her. Not a day goes by that I don't long to see her, to hold her, to touch her face. She was so perfect, so beautiful. And she had your eyes, Cole. She had your eyes."

Andie began to sob openly, her face twisted in anguish, remembering the tiny baby who had been ripped from her arms. Her entire body ached with remorse, and she waited for Cole to take her in his arms and provide the comfort she'd needed for years. She needed to cling to him, to draw strength from his embrace. She reached for him, blinded by tears, but Cole moved away, recoiling from her touch.

He was stunned and livid, shaking with anger, his lips pursed tightly. With a face still glazed in shock, he managed a withering stare. When he finally spoke, his tone was curt and strained.

"How convenient for you and David to count me out when you came up with that solution for getting rid of our child," he blasted her through clenched teeth. "Why didn't you tell me, Andie? Why?"

"Because I loved you and didn't want to ruin your life!"

"Do you have any idea how I mourned when you disappeared?" Cole took her by the shoulders and shook her, his fingers pinching her tender flesh. "Your mother wouldn't tell me anything and Tammy didn't know anything either. I searched and searched for you! When I saw you tonight, I didn't know whether to laugh, cry, dance a jig or just shake the life out of you. I've hated you for leaving me, but I've also hated myself for loving you, in spite of it all. I've loved you with my whole heart for so many years. I couldn't make myself stop." He looked away, overcome with emotion.

Andie saw a glimmer of hope and took the opportunity to jump in. "I love you too, Cole," she said. "I tried to forget you, tried to move on, but I couldn't. I've never loved anyone but you."

Cole regarded her coldly, holding up his hand to stop her stream of words. "Notice I said *loved*," he said, his voice husky with anger and grief. "You've betrayed me in the worst way — much worse than I ever imagined. That child was as much mine as it was yours, and I deserved to know the truth. You know, I thought I could forgive you anything, but I can't forgive you this. I can never forgive you for denying me my only child."

He leapt from the swing and strode furiously across the porch, moving quickly away from her. Andie ran down the steps behind him, clutching his arm desperately.

"Cole! Please! Please don't leave me. Please give me a chance to explain," she begged tearfully.

Cole stopped abruptly in his tracks, turning to give her one last icy stare. "There's nothing left to explain, Andrea. I've heard enough."

He shook her hand off angrily and stormed across the yard to his car. He jumped in and revved the engine, then roared away, throwing gravel in his wake. His car disappeared and Andie was left standing on the lawn in her nightshirt and bare feet, staring forlornly after him.

Her rubbery legs gave way and she crumpled to the ground, weeping as her heart broke completely in two. It was too much to bear. She'd lost so much in her lifetime: her parents, Shannon, Freddie, Dana and Jerry. Cole was her last hope, and now he too was gone, lost forever.

# 3

After spending most of the night crying on the lawn, Andie awoke early, hastily showering and packing her bags. With nothing to keep her in Pine Prairie, she was anxious to be on her way. The trip to Texas had been necessary in the great scheme of things, but it had also been a disaster. Cole's reaction had been worse than she could ever have foreseen.

The only good thing that had come of her visit was her renewed friendship with Tammy. Andie phoned her early to say goodbye and fill her in on the previous night's catastrophe.

"Oh honey, I'm so sorry." Tammy tried to be sympathetic, but she wasn't surprised. *She* had felt betrayed when Andie told her the news. She could only imagine how Cole must have reacted.

"Thanks," Andie muttered, rubbing her throbbing temples, irritated over their topic of conversation, yet glad to have Tammy's shoulder to cry on. "I just wish I had the chance to make Cole understand that if I had to do it over again, things would be so different."

"Hindsight is twenty-twenty, baby," Tammy sighed dismally. "There's nothing you can do about it now. Go home, Andie, and try to put this all behind you. I'll visit you soon, I promise."

Andie returned the telephone to the bedside table and glanced wistfully around her bedroom one last time as she scooped up her bags. Slowly, she descended the staircase, memorizing the house for future reference, uncertain of when, if ever, she would return. She replaced the drop cloths over furniture and opened the creaky old front door, looking back over shoulder and saying farewell.

On the return flight to Biloxi, Andie sadly recounted the depressing events of the past few months. "Every move I make is wrong," she sighed, leaning her forehead against the window, watching as the plane ascended into the clouds, leaving her life in Texas behind.

It was becoming increasingly obvious that saying she was sorry would not fix every mistake. Dana and Cole were just two examples of that failed theory. Cole would probably never forgive her, but with Dana, there was still a small glimmer of hope.

During her last few visits to Tennessee, Andie felt her daughter loosening up, letting down a little of her guard and slowly allowing Andie to get closer. If she played her cards right, maybe she would get another shot at repairing her broken life.

She arrived at her seaside cottage in Biloxi shortly before dusk. Setting her bags on the porch, she unlocked the front door and called out for Chips. Hearing her voice, the smoky gray cat came flying down the hall and she scooped him up, cradling him and rubbing his head as he purred a contented greeting. Emotionally drained and weary, Andie closed the front door and carried Chips into her bedroom.

She stripped off her clothes and pulled on an old T-shirt before curling up on her bed, snuggling deeply under a sunny yellow comforter. Chips settled next to her on the pillow, purring as Andie offered him a dejected smile.

"It's just me and you, Mr. Chips," she told him, stretching her fingers to scratch his ears. "And it'll probably be that way for a long, long time."

After Freddie left, she hadn't wanted another man in her life. She never missed a male presence until now. Seeing Cole again brought it all back, and she yearned for him more than ever.

"Fat chance of ever seeing him again," she cursed at the ceiling. "So much for honesty being the best policy."

All honesty had done for her was make Cole so furious that she doubted she would ever hear from him again. "I wish I had just kept my mouth shut!" she muttered as she rolled onto her side, punching her pillow in frustration.

"Just go to Texas, Andie — spill your guts and clear the air," she mocked her brother's advice, rolling her eyes. "Thank you, David, for another brilliant suggestion." She groaned and flopped onto her stomach, pulling the sheet over her head.

Cole turned onto Interstate 20, dreading the long drive back to New Orleans. However, time might pass more quickly this trip. Andie had given him plenty to think about.

He hadn't been prepared to see her at the reunion. Looking across the gym and spotting her beautiful face had come as a total shock, baring feelings he had repressed long ago. At the sight of her, his heart soared, and he knew in one glance that he was still very much in love with Andie Shepherd.

On the day Andie vanished, he had been inconsolable, unable to fathom what had happened to her. The circumstances of her disappearance had been so bizarre. They had been so happy, and he couldn't figure out what made her leave. He had been much too naïve to suspect a baby.

After months of asking and searching, he had given up. He settled into his new life at Mississippi State and tried to put Andie in his past. He had dated plenty, but none of those enticing Southern co-eds could compare to Andie, at least not in his mind. Over time, his contempt for Andie grew. He hated her for leaving him and hated himself for still wanting her.

He met Kimberly Eishen at a football game during the fall of his junior year. Kimberly was petite with long sandy hair that fell in ringlets around her tiny face. She was the only child of an Oklahoma oilman and heiress to a substantial fortune. She was used to getting exactly what she wanted when she wanted it. She spotted Cole in the crowded student section at Scott Field and decided then and there that he was the one for her. She flirted with him across the bleachers, batting her long eyelashes, determined to make him hers.

He should have known better than to get involved with her. Drawing from his experience with women, Kimberly Eishen was the kind of girl he could barely tolerate. She was beautiful, but she was also spoiled and prone to frequent mood swings. Knowing how she was, he should have dropped her after their first date.

"I should've run while I had the chance," he laughed bitterly, gripping the steering wheel tensely as he shook his curly head.

He should have run, but he didn't. He couldn't. There was something about Kimberly that enchanted him, and after graduation they were married in a lavish ceremony in Tulsa.

They settled in New Orleans where Cole took a job with a petroleum company, and the first several years were relatively sunny. As newlyweds, the sexual component of their relationship made Kimberly's childlike temperament bearable. However, in the years that followed, Cole grew tired of her selfishness and unreasonable demands. She refused to give him children and rejected his wants and needs. They argued most of the time they were together, and after seeing that their marriage would not get better, Cole filed for divorce.

After a bitter parting of the ways, Kimberly returned to Tulsa to be close to her father, and Cole remained in New Orleans, selling the luxurious house Kimberly had insisted upon and moving into a modest one with his black Labrador retriever, Estelle. For the last ten years, it had been just Cole and Estelle, intermingled with a girlfriend or two, none of whom meant much to him. Cole did not intend to marry again.

He thought of Andie often over the years, remembering her with great affection and wondering what had happened to her. He checked in periodically with Tammy, hoping that she had learned something about Andie's whereabouts, but his efforts had been in vain. Tammy hadn't heard from her either. He attended their ten-year class reunion, hoping that Andie would be there. When she didn't show up, Cole became determined to push her out of his mind for good.

But he couldn't forget about Andie altogether. She haunted him, resurfacing in his memory just when he thought she was gone. Several times over that next decade he had attempted unsuccessfully to find her, searching unfortunately for Andrea Shepherd, not Andrea LaRue. Time passed quickly and the announcement for the twenty-year class reunion arrived in the mailbox. He hadn't dared to hope that Andie would be there. But she was.

"Yep," he pounded his fist against the dashboard in disgust, scolding himself within the sanctuary of his car. "I handled that well. What an idiot! You wait half your life for the girl to reappear and the first thing you do is take her to the mat."

The hurt in Andie's eyes made him regret his scathing words. Wanting to make amends, he returned to the spot by the bleachers where he left her, only to find Tammy standing there alone. After enduring a heated dressing-down, Cole left the reunion and headed for the Shepherd house in search of Andie.

Making up with Andie had been wonderful. Her soft kiss made him want to devour her, to pull her tightly in his arms. But he kept his head, and it was a good thing. The bombshell she dropped sent him into a tailspin.

After a fitful night of little sleep, he drove by the Shepherds' house again, hoping to see Andie before she left town. Her rental was gone from the driveway, so Cole retraced his route, traveling down the winding two-lane road to Tammy's house near the center of town.

He found Tammy on her knees in the flowerbed, weeding her geraniums before the intense heat of a June Texas day set in. Seeing his car pull into the drive, Tammy sat back on her heels. She shielded her eyes from the blinding sunlight with her forearm, regarding Cole expectantly as he approached.

"Thought I might see you this morning," she said matter-of-factly.

"I came looking for Andie," Cole replied. "She here?"

"Nope, you missed her." Tammy squinted at her watch. "Her flight left out of DFW about twenty minutes ago." She noted Cole's disappointed expression. "I hear you got some shocking news last night."

"You could say that," Cole said, settling on the front stoop, staring reflectively at his clasped hands. "It was a very enlightening evening."

Tammy leaned forward, patting his leg. "You may feel like she betrayed you, but remember, Andie thought she was doing what was best under the circumstances."

Cole snorted in response. "I just can't believe she deceived me this way," he growled.

Tammy narrowed her eyes, shooting him an annoyed look. "Spare me the martyr act, Romeo," she said. "Since when is this all about you? What about her? You're not the only one who got hurt in this whole deal."

She laid her trowel in the dirt and threw her hands on her hips, berating him harshly. "Have you taken a really good look at her, seen the look in her eyes? Andie may try to act like she's the same person we knew twenty years ago, but she's not. Having that baby changed her whole life. That girl has been through more heartache than we'll ever know."

"Yeah, sure."

"Yeah sure, nothing. She never got over leaving you and always regretted giving the baby up for adoption. She's gone through years of terrible depression pining for her lost child. She sacrificed her marriage and her other two children because of it. So I wouldn't say that Andie hasn't suffered every day for the last two decades."

"It's just like you to take up for her."

"You're damn right. I'll take up for Andie until the day I die," Tammy shot back with a snarl. "Don't think I'm condoning what she did, because I'm not. She was wrong. She should've considered you before giving up the baby. But that's neither here nor there. It's over and done with now, and who are we to judge what she did twenty years ago?"

She weighed Cole's reaction to her words with a critical squint. "Now that you know the truth, you can do with it what you want. You can hate her, forgive her, forget her, whatever. Just don't condemn her, not until you've walked in her shoes."

Cole reflected on Tammy's words as he drove and decided to take her advice. He should have handled the situation with Andie better. He frowned, sorry once again for his hot-tempered outburst. "That's what I get for spouting off without thinking."

He told Andie that he no longer loved her, but it was a lie. He knew that he would always love her. He loved her, but could he forgive her?

It was tough to learn that he had a child. Cole heaved a great sigh, staring at the golden sunset before him, trying to envision what she was like. His heart was heavy, aching for the child he would never see.

What Andie had done to him was inexcusable, definitely one of the dirtiest deeds he'd been dealt. Could he forgive her?

He shrugged, filled with uncertainty. "That remains to be seen," he said and stomped on the gas, shooting down the highway for the last leg of his journey home.

# 4

Monday morning dawned sultry and hot, the epitome of June on the Gulf Coast. Andie awoke with the sun, kicking Chips out of bed and stumbling blindly across the room toward the bathroom. After an invigorating fifteen minutes under the Shower Massage, she emerged refreshed, dressed in a simple cotton shirtdress and sandals, ready for a day at the office.

She found Dell at her computer, pencil clenched tightly in her teeth, toiling over the numbers for the booming business. Andie slipped quietly into the office and leaned against the melon-hued wall, smiling broadly as she watched Dell work.

"Hey, boss." Sensing her presence, Dell acknowledged Andie without looking up.

"Dell, why don't you get some sort of life? It's the crack of dawn, for heaven's sake," Andie said, kidding her assistant as she strolled across the room toward the brewing coffee pot.

Dell glanced up, shooting her a wry look as she removed her wire-rimmed glasses. "You're one to talk. I don't notice you sleeping in."

"And waste this beautiful morning?"

"Exactly," Dell agreed with a grin. "How was the reunion?"

Andie groaned, pouring coffee into her oversized cup. "I could've lived the rest of my life without going to that reunion," she said with a frown.

"That bad, huh?"

"I've had IRS audits that were more pleasant," Andie growled as she walked toward her office.

"Well, cheer up. Freddie called while you were away." Dell leaned back in her chair, watching for Andie's reaction.

Andie paused in her doorway, looking back at Dell with a small smile. "Oh yeah?"

"I told him you'd gone to Texas for your high school reunion and he said for you to call him if you needed to talk."

"Thanks, Dell."

Andie closed herself into the solace of her pale yellow office and settled into the chair behind the pickled-wood desk, stretching her slender arms behind her head as she gazed out the window, thinking of her ex-husband. It wasn't that she didn't miss Freddie. She did. She missed their long heart-to-hearts on pillows at night, the sound of his voice, his deep, hearty laughter. And it wasn't that Freddie wasn't the world's finest, because he was. It *was* that she hadn't been able to give it her all, and that was much less than he deserved.

"If only I could've loved him the way he needed to be loved," she sighed wistfully.

It would be comforting to talk to him. Andie picked up the phone, dialing the number to Freddie's Bistro in Tennessee. It wasn't yet nine, but Freddie was already there, preparing for the lunch crowd.

"Hello, you," he greeted her with the affection of an old friend. Andie could picture his handsome face, lit by a cheerful grin peeking from beneath his thick mustache.

"Hi, Fred. How goes it?" she asked with a soft laugh. She leaned back in her chair and cradled the receiver of the telephone against her shoulder, smiling as she listened to Freddie's happy chatter.

Because she still cared for him, she was glad they could be on such good terms. Freddie's new wife, Julie, had a lot to do with that. Gone was the sullen, frustrated man who left Andie for the hills of Tennessee. Revitalized by a happy marriage, wonderful children and a thriving business, Freddie LaRue was like a new man.

"So, Dell tells me you went to the old twenty-year reunion. How was that?" Freddie's voice was teasing, yet laced with interest and concern.

"It was okay. Seeing Tammy again was fabulous. But," she hesitated, not wanting to hurt his feelings.

"But what?"

"But, I saw Cole and told him about Shannon."

"How'd that go?"

"It didn't go well at all. He's pretty pissed. In fact, I think he hates me now more than ever."

"I'm sorry, honey. I know how much he means to you."

"I'll be okay," Andie lied, pushing her bangs back from her forehead in a dismissive gesture. "That's all in the past, anyway. Today's a new day, and I'm much more concerned about my relationship with Jerry and Dana than I am with Cole Dewberry." The change of subject brought a smile back to her face. "How are the kids?"

"They're good." Andie beamed at the pride in Freddie's voice, happy that, if nothing else, she had at least given him two beautiful children. "Thankfully they're both working this summer and staying out of trouble."

"Working? My God, they're getting old."

"Yes, they are, although the rest of us aren't," Freddie joked lightheartedly. "They're good kids."

"I know, Freddie. You and Julie have done a great job with them." They both knew that Andie could take no credit for how well her children had turned out.

"They miss you, Andie. Come see us soon, huh?"

"Yeah, I plan on it," Andie said, her tone heavy with longing and regret. "Give them my love, okay?"

"You got it, sweetie."

She hung up and pulled out the catering schedule to review upcoming events. She was buried in her bookwork when Dell tapped on her office door.

"Andie," she said, sticking her head in, "Bill's here to see you."

Andie snapped her head up, meeting Dell's dancing eyes with laughter. "Well, by all means, show him in, darlin'," she said, putting on her best southern drawl.

Bill Fairgate had been their best customer since Andie and Freddie first opened their doors for business. At fifty-four, Bill Fairgate had never been an elected official, but held more political clout in Mississippi than anyone in office. He was deeply involved in affairs of state — "in an unofficial capacity, of course" — and was well respected by all, earning himself a reputation as a force to be reckoned with.

Bill was a good-looking man, graying-blond and muscular in spite of his years. He had been married once twenty-five years before and after the young Mrs. Fairgate unexpectedly passed away, leaving him a widower with three children, Bill had opted not to remarry. Instead, he chose just to date and never lacked for female companionship. He had a new girl for every season and threw many lavish parties to celebrate his bachelorhood.

Andie and Freddie LaRue had come into his life when Bill, furious with his usual caterer for a shoddy dinner party, happened upon Crème de la Crème while looking for a new provider for his soirees. He was instantly impressed with Freddie LaRue, who was not only professional but also very charismatic.

At first glance, Bill regarded Andie as a great beauty, but dismissed her business sense, chauvinistically speculating that she was only window dressing. He quickly found out he was mistaken. He had been pleasantly surprised to discover that Andie's brains and business savvy outshone her good looks.

Bill inherited Andie with the divorce and never regretted it. For years, Andie had been instrumental in arranging his galas and had done a fine job of it — so fine, in fact, that he had no qualms at all about leaving his catering in Andie's capable hands when Freddie left Biloxi.

He didn't know the details behind the breakup of the LaRues' marriage, although he suspected that it had something to do with Andie's state of mind. She'd gone through an extended period of melancholy just before the divorce, which hadn't gone unnoticed by Bill.

He found Andie incredibly attractive and wouldn't have hesitated for a second to form some sort of romantic relationship with her if he had not sensed that it would be in vain. He suspected that Andie's heart still belonged to another, and that person was not Freddie LaRue. Since he could not have her heart, Bill settled instead for Andie's friendship and over a span of fourteen years their relationship grew into one of unspoken trust and great affection.

On this particular morning, Bill had some time between appointments and thought that a visit to Andie and Dell would be a very pleasant way to kill time. Dell was a peach, attractive with soft brown hair and big doe-like eyes and a sweet disposition that could even soften the gruff Bill Fairgate. He had adored her since the day Andie brought her into the business.

Nevertheless, Andie was Bill's favorite. To visit her was invariably the highlight of any day. Andie was bubbly and energetic, always full of new ideas, which was exactly what Bill liked about her. After Dell announced his presence, Bill slipped past her into Andie's office, his arms outstretched for a giant bear hug.

"Hi, Pumpkin!" he greeted Andie in a booming voice, kissing her fondly before plopping into the soft leather chair across from her desk.

Andie looked up at him, returning his smile, although not in her usual spirited fashion. She looked as lovely as ever, but Andie didn't seem herself, he noted, giving her a long appraising stare. There was a sadness about her, an unhappy shadow crossing her blue eyes, and Bill decided he would make it his business to find out why.

He turned to Dell, flashing a wide grin. "Sugar, would you be a doll and get me a cup of coffee?" he asked, chuckling at her insulted expression. "I know, I know, that's not very politically correct of me, but darlin', I've never cared much about being politically correct."

Smirking widely and shaking her head, Dell left to get his coffee. Bill accepted the steaming cup she brought back to him then shooed her away with a brush of his hand. "Close the door behind you when you go out, baby doll," he commanded lightly. "I want to talk to your boss in private."

Dell and Andie exchanged a curious glance and Dell exited, shrugging indifferently at Andie and closing the door as she had been instructed.

Intrigued, Andie moved to the edge of her seat and looked at Bill expectantly. "So what brings you out so early this morning?" she asked. "Shouldn't you be sleeping in, recovering from your weekend of wine, women and song?"

"Well, I'd come by here on Saturday to thank you for doing such a fine job, as always, with my little get-together last Friday night," Bill began, sipping his hot black coffee thoughtfully.

Andie had to smile at his reference to his "little get-together." It had been an extravagant banquet for more than a hundred people. There had been nothing little about it, but with Bill, nothing ever was.

"When I saw Dell, she said that you'd gone out of town." He eyed her questioningly. "Did you go see Freddie and the kids?"

Andie shook her head. "Not this time," she answered. "Didn't Dell tell you? I went to Texas for my high school reunion."

"Really? What was it, your tenth?"

Andie rolled her eyes impatiently. "Bill Fairgate, don't sit there and try to pretend you don't know exactly how old I am," she exclaimed in forged exasperation. "You know good and well that it had to have been my *twenty-year* reunion."

Bill chuckled at her irritation. "Can I help it if you look so youthful?" he teased. After earning another withering look, he proceeded. "So was it the trip home that caused that melancholy expression on your face?"

Andie glanced at him in surprise. She leaned back in her chair, her eyes clouded and far away. "Yes, I suppose the trip home did make me a little sad," she said.

"Why? It couldn't be the proverbial mid-life crisis. You look too good to worry about that, Shug. Bet you were the best-looking alumni there," Bill said, flattering her with a hearty laugh. "That had to make you feel good in a room full of heifers."

"Fortunately, most of my classmates turned out pretty good. At least I think they did. I certainly didn't notice any cattle in the crowd."

"So what happened in Texas to make you so blue?"

Persistence was one of Bill's staunchest hallmarks and Andie knew he would not give up. When he wanted facts, he got them. There was no way to evade him. With that in mind, she sighed in defeat. "I saw an old boyfriend and told him a secret I've kept from him all these years. He's pretty furious, and I'll probably never see him again."

Bill was fascinated. He clutched his chest comically and shot Andie a look of mock disbelief. "Surely not, Sweet Cheeks. You could never piss a man off that badly."

"You and I both know that I've pissed quite a few men off quite a few times, present company included."

Bill shot her a broad grin, chuckling robustly. "True enough, but not to the point that one look from those pretty blue eyes wouldn't make any man forgive and forget."

"Not this one."

"You sound pretty sure about that, Ms. LaRue. What makes this one so different from the rest of us?"

"This one was an old flame whose child I gave up for adoption without even letting him know I was pregnant."

"Well, that might do it." Bill lifted an eyebrow, unfazed by her incredible revelation. "And when was this?"

"Just before I turned nineteen."

Andie rose from her chair, walking to the window and looking out over Highway 90 toward the beach, her vacant stare fixed on a passing fishing boat as she recanted her tale. "Cole — that's the old flame, Cole Dewberry — and I were in love, ready to go off to college together. He had a scholarship, and I didn't want to spoil his future. So when I found out I was pregnant, I fled without a word, taking refuge with my brother in Huntsville until after the baby was born. After I gave her up for adoption, I moved to Biloxi, finished school and went to work for J.J. Fremont. That's where I met Freddie." She turned a solemn face to Bill. "And the rest is history."

"You regret your decision to give up this baby?"

"Every day since."

Bill considered the facts, steepling his fingers against his chin and creasing his brow, deep in thought. "You ever try to find this child?"

"I've tried to locate her a few times, through private investigators, but they've turned up nothing." Andie folded her arms across her chest despondently, leaning against the wall, the look on her face reflecting her desolation.

"What information did you have to go on?" Outwardly, Bill appeared cool and collected, but inside he was reeling from her unexpected confession, although it made perfect sense. At last, he had the missing piece of the puzzle. This lost baby was the root of Andie's problems, including her withdrawal from Freddie and her children.

"All I know for sure is that she is a girl, born February tenth and adopted by a family somewhere in Georgia — maybe Atlanta. At least that's where the attorney was that handled the adoption."

"I'm sorry you've had such a hard time, Andie."

"It's not been that bad." She tried to brush him off, acting nonchalant. "It could've been much worse."

"So what do you do now?"

"Now? Now I move on. I've spent enough time screwing up my life. I've come clean with everyone I needed to. Now I can live for me."

"If you say so." Bill got out of his chair, taking her by the shoulders and kissing her cheek. "Gotta go, Sweet Pea, but I'll be in touch," he declared with a mischievous grin, turning to leave. "I've got a new girlfriend with a hankering for a Fourth of July party."

Andie laughed and waved him away, sitting back at her desk, attempting to focus on the mountain of paperwork. But she couldn't concentrate. Her mind kept drifting to Cole and their long-lost child.

The baby girl she had named Shannon would be nineteen now, almost a grown woman and probably finishing her first year of college. How strange it was to have a child that old and not have the slightest idea what kind of person she was or what she looked like.

How different would life be now if she had told Cole about her pregnancy? *Would we still be together? Would we still have Shannon?* Andie became frustrated with impossible questions, questions to which she had no answers.

She had told Cole the truth and it was now a closed chapter in her life. It was time to move on.

# 5

Glittering decorations lit up the dark night skies as Andie drove her red Mustang convertible along the deserted streets of Biloxi, returning from Gulfport after an evening spent catering Bill Fairgate's annual Christmas extravaganza. It didn't seem like Christmas. The long, hot sultry Mississippi summer had flown past, filled with weddings, summer parties and get-togethers, most of which had been Bill's. Andie and Dell had worked night and day, spending nearly every waking hour at Crème de la Crème, enjoying their work but having very little time for anything else. Dell was worn out, but Andie welcomed the busy days. They gave her an excuse not to think about Shannon and Cole.

Tammy had been as good as her promise. She arrived for Thanksgiving, pulling into Andie's driveway in her humongous silver four-wheel drive, vaulting from the driver's seat and surveying her surroundings appreciatively.

"Gee, I can see why you left Texas," she called out, waving to Andie on the front porch and gazing in awe at the sandy shoreline across the highway from the little house. "Man oh man, what a view."

She ambled up the walk, pulling Andie into a big bear hug as she reached the top of the steps. "Told you I'd be down to see ya."

"Did you bring the turkey?" Andie grinned ear to ear, opening the storm door to let Tammy into the house.

"Hell no," Tammy laughed, flopping onto Andie's overstuffed sofa. "You're the cook, babe. Not me."

They'd had a great time during Tammy's four-day visit. Andie showed her around town, taking her to the flashy casinos and by Crème de la Creme, acquainting her with the business and introducing her to Dell. Dell and Tammy clicked, finding each other fascinating and funny, and Dell ended up blowing off her family to spend Thanksgiving Day with Andie and Tammy.

After one of Andie's finest meals, Dell returned to her apartment, leaving Tammy and Andie to spend the evening alone. Andie changed into her favorite cotton PJ's, so old that their former baby blue had faded to almost white and so soft that they barely held their shape. Nevertheless, Andie loved them and staunchly refused to part with them.

She scooped Chips up from the foot of her bed and joined Tammy on the living room sofa. Tammy had changed to plaid flannel sleep pants and a giant gray sweatshirt bearing "Eisenhower Wolves" in bold hunter-green letters. She reclined lazily against the arm of the couch, regarding Andie in interested silence, her eyes shining bright with curiosity.

Enjoying the comfortable quiet, Andie stroked the cat affectionately, her long, slender fingers deep in his thick smoky coat. She glanced up, smiling as she caught Tammy's inquisitive stare. "What?" she asked, narrowing her eyes suspiciously.

Tammy chuckled, throwing her tousled head back in throaty laughter. "You are so paranoid," she said with a grin. "Like you think I'm fixin' to interrogate you or something."

"Aren't you?"

"Well, yeah, but that's beside the point."

"So, cut to the chase, Tamara. What is it you want to know?"

"I just want to know how many days you can go without bringing him up."

"Who?" Andie asked innocently.

"Who? You know who," Tammy scowled unpleasantly. "You've asked me about everyone else we've ever known. Why don't you just come right out and ask me if I've heard from Cole?"

"Because I don't care one way or the other."

"Liar."

"I'm not lying." Andie shifted positions, concentrating intently on scratching Chips' ears. He purred gratefully, moving his furry head in time with the rhythm of her hand. "Cole is old news, past history, water under the bridge. He means absolutely nothing to me anymore."

"How can you say that?" Tammy protested, blinking incredulously. "How can you say that Cole Dewberry, the one who hung the moon, swept you off your feet and, not to mention, fathered your first child, means absolutely nothing to you!"

"I'm over it," Andie shrugged her shoulders indifferently.

"Get outta here! You're over nothing. Neither one of you are. I saw the look on your face at the reunion, and I saw the look on his the morning after. You two belong together."

"Maybe neither of us thinks so anymore." Andie met Tammy's indignant glare evenly, sniffing in haughty denial at her ludicrous suggestion. "The night of the reunion I told all. I bared my soul and left the ball in his court. And I've heard not one word from him and it's been almost six months."

"Maybe you should make the first move," Tammy said. Andie Shepherd didn't fool her. She never had and she never would. *The girl still loves Cole Dewberry, regardless of what she says.*

Andie shook her head stubbornly, dumping Chips unceremoniously onto the floor as she rose from the sofa and paced the length of the room reflectively. "No, Tammy, I've moved on. I've made my peace with the past and closed that chapter of my life. So if you don't mind, I'd rather talk about something else." She turned her back, dismissing all further discussion of Cole.

Tammy frowned, wrinkling her brow in aggravation. "Damn hard-headed woman," she muttered quietly, watching as Andie moved out onto the porch. She rolled off the couch to join her, hoping to offer some comic relief to what had become a solemn moment in their Thanksgiving holiday. Once outside, she grabbed Andie's arm, coercing her into a midnight stroll along the beach, clad only in their pajamas.

They walked barefoot along the sand in silence, Andie sullen and pouty and Tammy surprisingly humble, focusing only on the bright moonlight illuminating their path. "I'm sorry," she said finally, looking over at Andie. "I won't bring him up again."

Andie laughed abruptly. "Now who's lying?" she asked, kicking the sand with her toes.

"Okay, then I won't bring him up on purpose."

"Sure you won't," Andie scoffed, and then softened, offering a smile. "Thanks for always sticking by me and understanding. I really appreciate it."

"Hey, that's what friends are for, right?" Tammy punched Andie's shoulder. "Now if you had just opened up a little earlier, say like twenty years ago…"

"Tammy!"

"Okay, okay. I'll shut up." Tammy held her arms up in surrender. "I was only trying to be helpful."

"Well, just stop it, will you? Sometimes your being helpful is more trouble than it's worth."

"That's gratitude for you," Tammy joked as they crossed the road and headed back to the house, stopping on the sidewalk to rinse the sand from their feet with the garden hose. "One minute you're offering me your eternal thanks, and the next you're telling me to go to hell."

"You are really pushing your luck," Andie told her, climbing the steps to the porch. "Keep this up and you won't be invited back."

"Just try and stop me!" Tammy jeered, stomping up the stairs behind her. "It's too late for threats, Andrea. You can't get away from me this time, girlfriend. I intend to be around often to keep you in line. You can't hide from me. Just don't be forgetting — I know where you live."

Tammy's visit was the highlight of Andie's autumn. The warm, sunny Gulf Coast days flowed unnoticeably into winter, making it nearly impossible to get in the Christmas spirit.

The party at Bill's helped put Andie in the mood. His incredible twenty-room stucco house lit the gray winter skies, alive with thousands of twinkling Christmas lights strung from the high peaks of its mammoth roof. Festive candy canes dangled from the branches of giant Magnolia trees, and dancing reindeer graced the front lawn, hitched to a wooden sleigh filled with brightly wrapped packages.

The party was a lively affair with almost two hundred guests. All of Mississippi's elite turned out, dressed to the nines, to munch on delectable hors d' oeuvres and drink expensive champagne. After setting out platters of smoked meats, fruits and crudités, Andie and Dell lingered behind elaborate trays of delicately iced Christmas cakes and cookies, wearing huge smiles as they watched Bill circle the room with his latest love interest draped possessively on his arm.

She was a stunning redhead half his age, swathed from head to toe in red velvet and white fur, looking more like one of Santa's helpers than the date of an affluent gentleman. Bill was in rare form, working the crowd, greeting each with a jovial smile and hearty laugh, pausing mischievously beneath every clump of mistletoe to present his date with a passionate holiday kiss. With each kiss, she slapped his arm, giggling like an adolescent schoolgirl.

"What a bimbo — absolutely gaudy," Dell huffed, inspecting the girl critically. She rolled her eyes in disgust. "You would think someone as savvy as Bill would get tired of dating no-brainers. What he needs is an intellectual woman. Someone with both smarts and beauty."

"Such as yourself?" Andie teased, smiling brightly at her young business partner.

Dell snickered doubtfully. "Not hardly," she declared. "I'm not Bill's type. I was thinking more about you. You'd be perfect for him."

"You think I'm Bill's type?" Andie asked with suppressed mirth. "Does that mean you think I'm a bimbo?"

"I think you're a bimbo, all right — just not Bill's kind of bimbo," Dell kidded with a grin. "You know what I mean, Andie. He's always been a little sweet on you."

"That's silly, Dell. Bill and me? No way." Andie dismissed the ridiculous suggestion with a wave of her hand, shifting her gaze to the throng of elegant partygoers, scanning their hands for empty champagne glasses in need of refills.

"I don't think it's silly," Dell replied, cutting her eyes to Andie as she lifted an empty tray and headed for the kitchen. "No, my dear, it's not silly at all. You're just stubborn — old and set in your ways."

Andie gave her an exasperated look and discreetly stuck out her tongue. Dell giggled again and shot through the swinging door into the kitchen, her laughter lingering in her wake.

The party was a smashing success, lasting late into the night, leaving a weary yet elated Andie to make her way home in the wee hours of the morning. She accepted Bill's thanks at the door in the form of a warm goodnight kiss.

"Kudos, Pumpkin," he said affectionately, squeezing her hands. "Perfect as always."

"My pleasure," Andie replied, giving him a happy smile. "Merry Christmas, Bill."

"Merry Christmas, honey." Bill walked with her to her car, opening the driver's door for her. "Now, don't you forget what I said earlier. I'd love to have you over."

"I won't forget," she assured him, admiring him in her rearview mirror as she drove away. Dell was right. Bill really was a great guy and, at one time, would have made an ideal mate. But not now. Not since the reunion. She sighed, leaning her head against the car window. *Why can't I just let it go?*

She had no real holiday plans. Both Dell and Bill had invited her to spend Christmas with their families, Bill after a celebratory kiss under the mistletoe, and Dell as they unloaded crystal and silver at Crème de la Crème. Andie declined both offers, feeling awkward about intruding on family celebrations.

She considered spending Christmas with David, Charlotte and their twin girls, Erin and Emily, but after years of quiet, solitary Christmases, Andie wasn't sure that she was ready for a big family get-together.

Then there was Tennessee. Freddie had phoned earlier in the week, gallantly issuing an invitation to spend the holidays in Olen with the children. She was considering his offer. Her last few trips had been very encouraging. Dana had seemed a little less sullen, and Andie began to hope for light at the end of the tunnel. Maybe a holiday together would be the glue to mend the break between them.

Preoccupied, she wheeled her little sports car into the driveway and got out, stretching and yawning as she strolled toward the front door. "I will definitely be sleeping-in in the morning," she told herself wearily. "This late night stuff is starting to get to me." She climbed the steps, pausing at the door to dig out her keys.

"You sure keep late hours, lady."

The melodic voice echoed across the veranda and Andie froze, wide-eyed, her keys clutched tightly in her trembling hand. As reality sank in, she recognized the voice and slowly turned to view Cole Dewberry lounging casually in one of her Adirondack chairs, bundled in a navy barn jacket as he patiently awaited her arrival.

Blinking in astonishment, Andie recovered and proceeded to unlock the door. "You certainly didn't have any trouble finding me this time," she said, turning the key and stepping inside, leaving the door ajar.

Cole followed her in and closed the door. He watched as Andie tossed her keys on the fireplace mantel, following her with smoky eyes as she removed her beaded jacket and draped it over the back of a chair.

She was lovely, standing in the center of the living room in high heels and a little black dress, her fair, silky hair pulled back from her face in a simple twist. Watching her, Cole's heart melted — a feat that was not easy, given Andie's icy stare.

He smiled easily at her irritation, leaning casually against the entry wall. "You weren't too hard to find, considering I knew where to look this time."

Andie sat on the couch, removing her pumps with a graceful sweep of her hand, looking up at him with annoyed curiosity. "What are you doing here, Cole?" she asked, tucking her feet protectively beneath her as she curled into the corner of the sofa, stretching her arm nonchalantly along the cushions behind her. She set her jaw defiantly, determined that her face not reflect the wild pounding of her heart. "Didn't you say enough the last time we met?"

Cole walked toward her, moving with deliberate calmness. "I came to say I'm sorry. I shouldn't have said the things I said that night."

He took the chair opposite her and leaned forward, running his hands through his dark hair as he searched her face. "But you've got to understand, I was floored, shocked, caught completely off guard by that little bombshell you dropped on me. My God, Andie, can you imagine how you would feel in my place? I realize now that I should have been more compassionate. You've been to hell and back and then some. But I can't take back the things I said. I can only say I'm sorry and hope that you'll forgive me."

Andie studied him with thoughtful eyes, her stomach flip-flopping anxiously. She nodded slightly, swinging her legs off the couch to stand before him. "You're forgiven," she acknowledged softly, walking toward the kitchen. "Care for a drink?"

"That'd be great," Cole answered cheerfully, relieved that the tension between them was easing.

Andie removed a blender of pina coladas from the freezer, something she kept whipped together for herself and Dell as a much-deserved treat, usually devoured in the wake of particularly stressful catering gigs. She reached for two glasses, filled them with the frosty white beverage and returned to the living room.

Their fingers brushed as he accepted the glass, and the touch of his hand jarred her. Andie flushed as their eyes met, the burning passion of long ago still smoldering between them.

"Why did you wait until now to come?" she asked, steeling herself against him. "Why did you wait until I had put it all behind me and resolved to move on?"

Cole sipped his drink pensively, observing her over the rim of his glass. "I had to come, Andie," he said finally. "I've spent the last several months trying to forget I ever saw you again, trying to deny the way I feel about you and trying to forget that I knew where you were."

He set his glass on the floor and stood, cupping her face tenderly in his hands. "But I couldn't. I just couldn't do it. I love you, Andie. I always have, and I always will. You're the only woman I've ever wanted."

Andie blinked away joyful tears, struggling to remain realistic in the face of blinding emotion. "Oh Cole, we're not the same people we were twenty years ago," she said, quickly pulling away from him. "Too much has happened. It's too late to pick up where we left off."

"I'm not suggesting that we pick up where we left off. I only want to try again, to start at the beginning with a clean slate and build a relationship that will last forever."

"I don't think that would be wise," Andie said, instinctively protecting herself with her prudent words. Her frail emotional state could not withstand another gut-wrenching blow. She moved to the window and stared out at the dark starlit sky, battling her conflicting feelings.

Cole came up behind her, wrapping her in his strong arms. "I know you're scared, honey," he said, his lips brushing the nape of her neck. "Trust me, I'm scared too. But we've got to give this a go. We owe it to ourselves to give our love a chance."

Andie turned to face him, reaching up to trace the line of his jaw with her finger. Cole stared at her, his smoldering eyes burning deeply into her soul. He pulled her tightly against him and kissed her passionately, making her weak in the knees and filling her with desire. She relaxed in his embrace, returning his fiery kiss. Each touch of his lips sent her soaring, feeling so foreign, yet so familiar.

The straps of her dress slid unnoticeably from her shoulders, enticing the rest of the garment to fall in a soft heap on the living room floor. With an alluring smile, Andie took Cole's hand, pressing it to her lips, and led him into the bedroom, tossing Chips aside as she reclined on the bed. She pulled Cole down with her, her eyes locked on his face, and made love with him as if they had never been apart.

She awoke in his arms, rolling over lazily to kiss his handsome face. Cole lifted a drowsy eyelid, smiling at the sight of her. "Morning," he said, murmuring sleepily as he kissed her soft lips.

Andie rested her head on his chest, listening to the steady rhythm of his heart. "Still willing to give it a chance?" she asked quietly.

Cole lifted a brow, clearly bewildered. "Why would you ask something like that?"

"I just thought in the glaring light of day, you might be having second thoughts over things said in the heat of passion."

"Not a chance, lady," Cole chuckled. "I know what you're trying to do, and you're not going to get rid of me that easily, not after it's taken this long to be in your arms again. Unless of course, you're having second thoughts?"

Andie shook her head firmly. "No, I'm in for the long haul."

"Good, then it's settled." He pushed himself up, propping on the fat down pillows piled behind him. "I love you, Andie, and I'm so glad I swallowed my god-awful pride and came here last night. I'm sorry we had to lose so many years together, and I'm sorry I wasn't there for you when you were carrying our child. But I would've been, Andie, if you had only told me."

Andie caressed his face, running a gentle finger down his cheek. "I know, and I'm sorry for not telling you everything then. I was wrong."

"Listen, it's high time we both stop apologizing and saying things that we'll be sorry for," Cole declared, taking her hand from his face and pressing it to his lips.

"Agreed." Andie rolled onto her back and stared happily at the ceiling. "I never thought I would have this again. You and I, back together after everything. This is so unbelievable. A perfect, fairytale ending to a long, sad story."

"Well, almost perfect, except for one essential element — one small, yet extremely vital piece of the story." Cole reached over and stroked her hair, twirling a lock reflectively around his finger. "I've given this a lot of consideration and hope what I'm about to say won't spoil everything between us."

He hesitated, searching her face intently. "We may have missed her formative years, her senior prom, high school graduation and who knows, maybe even her wedding, but I don't want to miss any more of her life."

Andie slowly turned her head, an eerie chill racing down her spine. "What are you talking about?" she asked, although she already knew.

"I'm talking about our daughter. We have a child out there somewhere, and it's not too late for us to get to know her." He jumped out of bed, pulling on his discarded jeans from the night before, his face eager as he glanced her way. "We've got to find her, Andie," he announced. "I want to see her, touch her, get to know her. I just can't go on like she doesn't exist. I'll do anything, search to the ends of the earth if I have to, but I have to find our daughter."

Andie sat in the middle of the mattress, still staring in disbelief.

"Don't just sit there, Andie." Cole plucked off the blanket, pulling her out of bed and into his warm embrace. "We've got things to do, places to go, people to see. Let's get moving, woman. Today we start our search for Shannon."

# *Part Two*

# *Dana*

# 6

"Can one burn in hell for hating her own mother?"

"Oh, Dana, give it a rest. You don't hate your mother."

"Yes, I do." Dana rolled onto her side, punching her lumpy pillow as she glared impatiently across the cluttered dorm room at her roommate Claudette Dupré. "Okay, so maybe I don't hate her, but I do *dislike* her, some days more than others."

"Like today?"

"Yeah, like today." Frustrated, Dana propped against the wall, bringing her knees to her chest and encircling them with her arms. "If it weren't for Daddy and Julie, I don't know where I'd be. God knows Andie has no more maternal instincts than a stray cat."

"I don't believe that," Claudette replied skeptically, poking her chubby fingers deeper into her box of Cracker Jacks. "If she doesn't care about you, then why does she call so much?"

Dana shrugged. "Who knows? Guilty conscience maybe? Or maybe she's just trying to make up for lost time. Whatever the case, she seems to think that now that I'm in New Orleans and closer to her, we're going to have some magnificent mother-daughter relationship."

She paused, scowling at the idea and rolling her eyes angrily. "Boy, do I have news for her. She is sadly mistaken. That cuddly little love fest is not going to happen, not while I still have breath in my body!"

*Just who did Andie think she was, anyway?* Dana cursed, throwing open her English lit text, so irritated she could hardly read the words. Thinking about Andie made her so crazy she couldn't even concentrate. *Damn her.* Aggravated, she slammed the book closed and tossed it onto her desk, then threw her pencil angrily in the air, bulls-eyeing it into a ceiling tile.

Why did she let Andie get under her skin? *If I were smart, I wouldn't even give her the time of day,* she thought bitterly. She certainly didn't have much respect for her, having spent most of her life wondering what she could do to earn her mother's love.

The only real constant in Dana LaRue's life was her father. In Dana's eyes, Freddie LaRue was the perfect parent: always kind, always gentle, always there, devoting his days to loving and caring for Dana and her younger brother, Jerry.

Far from domesticated and nurturing, Dana's tall, goddess-like mother had been little more than a silent figure wandering in and out of her life. As children, Jerry and Dana frequently went for days without a glimpse of her. Andie spent most of her time arranging dinners and lavish parties for influential clients, typically working late into the night, several days a week. Andie was a workaholic and Dana hated it, resenting her mother for loving Crème de la Crème more than she loved her own children.

Dana couldn't imagine what her father had seen in Andie, although she was certain he loved her a great deal. Why, she didn't know. She simply didn't understand it. He deserved so much better, and she told him so often.

"Daddy, why do you keep putting up with this? When are you going to face the music?" she demanded, staring incredulously up at him with eyes alive with fire, her small hands thrown impatiently on her hips. "What are you waiting for? She'll never change. Why do you want to live your life this way?"

Freddie laughed softly, giving her a tight hug and a kiss on the forehead. "You're awfully grown up for such a little girl," he said, tilting her chin up gently with his index finger. "Be patient with your mother, Dana. She loves you, sweetheart. I promise. She's just having some problems right now."

"What else is new? She's always having problems," Dana growled, crossing her arms tightly against her chest.

*Why do I even try to make him see the light? He'll never listen.* He never had. He only defended Andie, as always. Her father would always see Andie as the shy blond teenager with whom he had fallen in love.

Andie's problems never went away. They only grew. The whole family watched as she went downhill, changing from the stunning, confident creature Freddie married to the poster child for depression Dana remembered too well. As her problems extended from weeks to months and finally to years, poor Freddie grew tired of the sullen, tearful figure slumped on the couch and put an end to their ten-year marriage just after Dana's ninth birthday. Dana watched it all from her hiding place behind the living room sofa.

"I can't do this anymore," Freddie announced emotionlessly. He paced the kitchen floor, glancing helplessly at the weeping woman slumped over the dining table. "I'm leaving, Andie, and I'm taking the children with me."

Andie lifted her head and looked at him with red, swollen eyes. "Leaving? What do you mean? Where are you going?"

"I haven't decided yet."

"What about the business?"

"Dear God, Andie! What about the *business*?" Freddie stared at her. "Is that all that concerns you? I just told you that I'm moving out and taking your children, and all you can ask about is the *business*?" He shook his head. "You can have the stinking business, Andie. That's all that matters to you anyway."

"Of course it's not," Andie stammered. "You know I love you and the children."

"Sure you do."

"I do, Freddie. Really."

"You have a helluva way of showing it." Freddie stopped pacing and stood in front of her, a glimmer of pity in his eyes. "Besides, even if you did, this has gone well beyond love."

He knelt beside her, taking her by the shoulders and forcing her to look him in the face. "You're a mess, Andie — a complete and utter emotional mess. I have to leave, don't you see? I have to leave now, and take Dana and Jerry with me, before you take us all down with you."

"I don't understand."

"And you never will, not as long as you continue down your present path." Freddie straightened wearily, too tired to reason with her. "I see what your state of mind is already doing to Dana. You're sucking the life out of her, Andie. I have to get her out now, before it's too late. I only pray that once we're gone, you'll get help. You're in serious need of counseling."

"How dare you stand there and tell me I'm crazy!" Andie flew out of her chair, sending it crashing to the floor. "I don't have a problem," she screamed at him, pointing a finger sharply into his chest. "You're the one with the problem! You're just not man enough to stick around and work it out."

Freddie closed his eyes and shook his head slowly. "Believe what you want," he said. "It won't change a thing. The children and I are moving out tomorrow."

Freddie moved Jerry and Dana to the rolling green hills of eastern Tennessee, taking all that they owned in cardboard moving boxes packed tightly in a U-haul trailer. They settled in the sleepy little town of Olen, moving into a rustic A-frame at the base of a tall mountain range. Freddie opened a small bistro and quickly took the townspeople by storm with his dynamic personality and outstanding culinary talents. His little restaurant flourished, and Freddie became much happier and more relaxed than Dana had ever seen him.

Jerry loved Olen and their new school, excelling in academics and making new friends. But Dana hated Olen, loathing both their new home and her well-meaning schoolmates. She kept to herself, shunning all attempts at friendship.

Night after night, she lay in bed, staring into the darkness, her heart breaking over the loss of her mother. Even after the years of emotional neglect, Dana still loved her, missing her so much it hurt. Every night she waited for Andie's phone call, the one telling them how much she loved them and missed them. She hoped desperately that her mother would realize how much she needed them and dash to Tennessee.

"Just one call, that's all I want," she pleaded to the darkness. "All you have to do is call, and I'll come running."

But Andie never called or came, leaving Dana even more heartbroken and distraught.

Julie Dempsey saved her. Dana might have grown into a miserable, bitter young woman had it not been for Julie. She frequented the bistro, spending her lunch hours perched on a stool at the wine bar snacking on fresh fruit and iced tea.

Freddie noticed her immediately, initially attracted to her because she reminded him so much of Andie. "She's incredible," he told his cook. He leaned on his elbows at the counter and stared at her, totally entranced. Day after day, he watched her, hedging an introduction from one of the waitresses and slowly getting to know her over friendly noontime chats.

Like Andie, Julie was tall and slender with long blond hair and big blue eyes. As the weeks went by, Freddie was captivated by her bubbly personality and compassionate heart, finding her capable of showing emotion that Andie never could.

His feelings for Julie grew, and soon he began seeing her on a regular basis. Kind and accepting, Jerry bonded with her right away, thriving in her sunny presence. Dana was more cautious, fearful of trusting another woman. She was not anxious to get her feelings crushed again.

Yet, in the two years her father courted Julie, Dana was never disappointed or hurt, and at last they connected, becoming close friends and confidantes, sharing afternoons of shopping and movies, gossiping and girl talk. Dana blossomed under Julie's tender supervision, learning to love and trust again, and evolved into a happy, well-adjusted teenager.

Julie and Freddie married just after Dana's twelfth birthday, and for the first time in her life, Dana felt like she had a real family.

Then it happened. Shortly after Dana turned sixteen, Andie came back into their lives without warning. Dana dashed in from school one afternoon to find Andie sitting with her father and Julie in the living room, laughing and talking comfortably like old friends. Dana gaped in stunned silence at her beautiful mother, watching in disbelief as she rose from the couch and moved across the room for a tender embrace.

"Hello, Dana."

The feel of Andie's soft arms around her, together with the flowery scent of her perfume, triggered all the hurt and resentment she had harbored for years. Every vile emotion she had repressed since leaving Biloxi sprang maliciously to the surface. She wrenched from Andie's hold and pushed her away, then whirled around, looking to her father for an explanation.

Before Freddie could speak, tall and gangly Jerry bounded through the front door, halting mid-step to stare at Andie. "Mom!" he cried out as he rushed into the room.

*He still loves her.* Dana's mouth fell open in disgust. *Stupid kid!* How could he be so blind?

Through narrowed eyes, she watched as he ran to Andie, throwing his arms eagerly around her neck. Andie smiled, kissing his cheek and whispering softly into his ear.

Dana turned away in distaste, offering her father a frigid stare. *How could you do this to me?*

"Kids, your mother wants to talk to you," Freddie said, clearing his throat nervously. He took Julie by the hand and went into the kitchen, leaving Dana with no choice but to listen to Andie.

A beaming Jerry sat on the couch, holding tight to Andie's hand, while Dana kept her distance, taking a chair at the far end of the room. She sat stone-faced, her arms folded tightly across her thin chest. She drummed her fingers impatiently against her upper arms, frowning angrily at Andie and Jerry's overzealous displays of affection. They sat in uneasy silence, the clock on the wall ticking away the minutes as they stared at one another, unsure of what to say.

Finally, Dana spoke up. "So, what is it that you want?" she snapped. "Nobody wants you here. You shouldn't have come!"

Andie seemed to be expecting her attitude and appeared unscathed by her daughter's sharp tongue, which only made Dana madder. "I've come to say I'm sorry. Sorry for everything," she said softly, nervously twisting her rings, her gaze shifting from Dana to Jerry. "The way I treated you was wrong. True, I was hurting, but I was hurting over something that had nothing to do with your father or with you. I know now how very much I love you and how much I need to be a part of your lives. I've come to apologize and beg for your forgiveness."

She sounded so sincere and pitiful. Dana didn't buy it, but Jerry gave in immediately. "I'm happy you're here!" he told her with high-pitched giddiness, giving her a tight hug and bright smile. "And I'm not mad at you, I promise. I'm just so glad to see you again. I love you, Mom."

*What a pushover*, Dana snarled, shooting him a withering look. *How could he forgive her just like that? How could he forget all the years without her, all the months without even a word?*

She studied Andie's face, her stomach knotting with building fury. *How dare you sit there like a martyr, promising us the world with your smile? We loved you and you broke our hearts. Nothing can make up for that — no dazzling grin, no empty promises, no hollow words of love. Nothing.*

"Dana?" As if reading her thoughts, Andie met her icy stare expectantly.

"I have nothing to say to you," Dana said, jumping out of her chair. "Why don't you just go back to Biloxi? We have a mother now. We don't need you anymore."

She stalked from the room without a look back, the slamming door announcing her exit. Trembling with rage, she ran away from the house as fast as she could, the sound of her feet pounding the ground echoing in her ears. She cut through a field of wildflowers and headed in the direction of the neighborhood park.

She found solace on the swings. She linked her fingers through the chains and twisted back and forth, dragging the toes of her white canvas sneakers through the dirt. "How dare she come back after all this time and act like she's done nothing wrong," she fumed aloud. "She doesn't even deserve to see us, much less expect us just to forgive and forget." She twirled round and round in the swing, muttering and cursing under her breath.

Julie found her just before dusk, coming toward her with a dark-blue cardigan draped around her shoulders and a concerned expression on her face. She took the swing next to her, rocking idly back and forth, offering Dana a sympathetic smile. "You okay, honey?" she asked gently.

Dana sighed. "I'm fine, I guess, considering."

"Don't you want to come back to the house and tell Andie good night?"

"Nope." Dana stopped her swing abruptly, looking Julie straight in the eye, her mouth clamped in a tense line. "I have nothing to say to her."

"Dana, I can certainly understand your anger. You have every right in the world to be upset, but you should really cut your mother some slack. She came all this way to make amends. The least you could do is give her a chance."

"She had her chance. She blew it. She doesn't get another one."

Julie sighed, defeated by the stubborn set of Dana's jaw. "Well, sweetie, you're certainly old enough to make your own decision about this, and we'll respect your wishes. We won't push you to make up with your mother."

"That's good, because you'd be wasting your time. I'm not changing my mind."

"Why don't you come on back home? It's getting dark out here and a little cool."

"I'm not stepping one foot back inside that house as long as she's there." Dana pushed off, swinging high into the air. "Just send Jerry back to get me when she's gone."

Not only did Dana refuse to see Andie for the remainder of the weekend, but she also shunned her during her next several visits, making Andie pay for every time she had turned her back on them. Nevertheless, Andie was persistent in her newfound devotion to her children, traveling to Tennessee many times each year and writing and calling often to keep her memory fresh in their minds.

At first Dana resented Andie's perseverance, certain that she would again desert her for something more important. But over time, Andie's actions showed that she was sincere and Dana began to relax, heeding Julie's words of advice and getting to know Andie all over again.

When she allowed the wall of resentment between them to fall, Dana found there were times that she genuinely liked Andrea Shepherd LaRue, although she'd rather die than admit it.

Andie was smart, funny and entertaining, almost always knowing what to do or say to put Dana at ease. They spent long hours talking while hiking through the hills surrounding Olen or in front of a roaring fire in the den of Andie's rented condo. They lunched at The Bistro, joined often by Freddie, who, despite the years they had been apart, still cared for the mother of his children. Joined by Jerry, Andie and Dana often went to the movies or bowling, enjoying the time they all spent together.

Dana was starting to like her, but still didn't trust her. She never let down her guard, knowing in the back of her mind that there would always be another child who Andie wanted more.

Dana knew all about Shannon, her darling big sister out in the world somewhere. Andie had told her and Jerry about the baby she had given up for adoption as soon as she thought they were old enough to understand.

Dana resented Shannon, knowing of her mother's incurable longing for her, and prayed that she had been swallowed alive by a sinkhole.

She just didn't get it. What was it that made her and Jerry so insignificant? After all, they were Andie's flesh and blood too. They had lived with her and were there to give her love and affection, while Shannon had never been there for Andie, nor would she ever be.

Dana spent years tormenting herself with questions about her mother and Shannon, trying desperately to come up with answers, but always failing miserably.

"Why do you think she loves Shannon best? Do you think it's because we look like Daddy?" Dana grilled Jerry after one of Andie's visits, sharing her insecurities with the one person who might understand. "Do you think Shannon looked like Andie?"

"Gee, Dana, how would I know?" Jerry answered, giving her a bored look before turning back to the television set.

"Do you think Andie loved Shannon's father more than she loved Daddy?"

"Don't know."

"You've got to have some opinion about it."

"I don't have to have an opinion because it doesn't matter. Why are we going into this again? We've been through this a thousand times, Dana, and it's pointless. I can't believe you spend so much time dwelling on it."

"And I can't believe it doesn't matter to you! Is there nothing she can do that will make you see her for what she really is?"

"Let it go, Dana," Jerry warned. "Let it go before it eats you alive."

But she couldn't let it go. Dana wouldn't give up until she knew what made Andie LaRue tick, and what she could do to be in her good graces, just like Shannon.

# 7

It was around the time of Dana's high school graduation that she first observed the remarkable change in Andie. During the week she spent with them in Tennessee, Andie was animated, more alive than Dana had ever seen her. Her skin was dewy, her cheeks rosy and her eyes alive with twinkling fire. Dana scrutinized her in open-mouthed amazement, liking the change in her mother, but wondering what on earth could have happened to alter her so dramatically.

"What's the deal with Andie?" she asked, plopping down next to Freddie in a red leather booth near the back of The Bistro. "She looks great. I've never seen her look so great."

"Your mother's in love, Dana," Freddie replied, smiling softly. "I always knew that Andie would look beautiful in love."

"In love? With who?" Dana perked up, her curiosity piqued. *Andie actually showing affection for another human being? That's something I never thought I'd see.*

She looked to her father for an answer, but he turned away. Freddie wouldn't elaborate, and Dana didn't push him, knowing that while his love for Julie was deep and strong, his hurt over Andie was still there, making him wish that he hadn't wasted all those years loving her.

Dana was accepted to Tulane and moved into the dormitory in August, taking with her a fuzzy green stuffed rabbit named Boo-Boo

Bunny and a photo album filled with memories of Tennessee. She shared a microscopic room with Claudette Dupré from Chalmette. Claudette was huge, a hulking figure of a young woman with frizzy, straw-colored hair and a crooked smile. At first Dana was a little afraid of her, not at all sure what kind of person she would be, but eventually Dana discovered that Claudette was okay, sometimes even funny. She and Claudette would never be close, but Dana could live with her, at least for the first semester.

Freddie and Julie were disappointed when Dana chose Tulane, unhappy that she would be so far from home. However, Andie was thrilled, delighted to have her daughter living only a little more than an hour away. She called the dorm room often to chat and remind Dana of how much she'd like to see her. Andie considered the frequent calls an excellent way of bonding. Dana considered them an excellent source of irritation.

"Why don't you give the woman a break?" Claudette probed as Dana slammed down the receiver after one of Andie's calls. "She only wants to talk."

"What do you know about it?" Dana snapped, jerking her head around and staring scornfully at Claudette. "You don't know anything about me or my mother."

"I know she cares enough to call. That says something."

"She's good at playing games," Dana replied cynically. "And she should be — she's been at it for years."

"Do you really believe she's just interested in yanking your chain?"

Dana sighed and flopped onto her lumpy bunk, burying her chin into her pillow as she looked wistfully up at Claudette. "I don't know what to believe where she's concerned. I just know I'm tired of being hurt by her."

Dana was not altogether sure she liked living so close to Andie. True, their relationship was improving, but it had done so slowly, with extended periods of rest between visits. She didn't think she was ready for an every-weekend test of wills.

One late September evening during Dana's first semester, Andie called again, hoping to persuade Dana to come to Biloxi. "Oh come on, Dana," she said kiddingly. "Jerry's been here a thousand times. Why are you being so difficult?"

Dana slumped in her chair, drumming her fingers impatiently on the desktop. She wasn't in the best of moods and had grown weary of Andie's pressure. "I don't get you at all," she sputtered grudgingly into the phone. "The first eighteen years of my life you wanted nothing to do with me, and now suddenly you can't get enough of me. What gives?"

"Dana, don't be this way. I just want to spend some time with you."

"Why, Andie? Why make the effort now?" Dana barked crossly, her voice rising. "What is it you want from me? What, is it absolution? Is it forgiveness? Is it unconditional love for all the years you ignored Jerry and me? For all the years you simply pretended we didn't exist? Is that what you want from me?"

"I just want you to call me Mom again."

"Don't hold your breath."

"You're awfully cynical for someone so young."

"If I am, then you're to blame. Maybe I might've turned out differently if I'd had the loving influence of my mother during my formative years."

"I understand your animosity..."

"You understand nothing."

"I thought we had moved past all this."

"Well, you thought wrong."

"Are you ever going to forgive me?" Andie's sigh floated over the line, heavily laced with remorse.

Hearing the sorrow in her voice, Dana felt a slight twinge of guilt. *I really should be ashamed,* she thought. *I am such a little shit.* Andie really was trying hard to make up for her mistakes, almost bending over backward in her effort, and at every turn, Dana retaliated, throwing up a rigid barrier, snapping her olive branch like a bothersome twig.

Dana summoned all her emotional energy, letting her guilty conscience override her better judgment as she leaned across to study the calendar pinned above her desk. *Nope. Nothing circled in red.* Her weekend was free. "If you really want me to," she said hesitantly, already regretting what she was about to say. "I'll come to Biloxi this weekend."

"You will?" Andie's voice changed as she perked up, becoming bubbly with excitement. "That's terrific! Should I come Friday afternoon and get you?"

"No. I'm not a baby. I can drive." Dana bit her head off, forgetting their momentary truce. *I'll come on my terms, lady — not yours. There's no way I'm getting trapped there.* "I do have a car, you know," she added lightly, trying to soften her curt reply. "It's not much of a car, but it'll get me there."

"I'm so glad you're going to come. It'll be fun, honey. You'll see."

"Yeah," Dana remarked as she hung up the phone. "It'll be loads of fun, a regular barrelful of monkeys." She sighed and laid her head on the desk, beating her forehead against its cool surface. "Good lord! How dumb was that? I can't believe I just gave in to her. Why am I always such a sucker? I only hope I don't live to regret this."

After patting herself on the back for successfully navigating her way through bumper-to-bumper rush hour traffic in New Orleans, Dana steered her trusty Honda toward Biloxi, finally exiting Interstate 10 onto Highway 90 at Pass Christian. She followed the highway distractedly, unable to keep her eyes off the old Southern homes lining the roadway. "So cool," she murmured dreamily.

She passed through Gulfport and entered the more touristy sections of Biloxi. Stopping at a traffic signal, she studied her surroundings with growing interest, swept over by déjà vu as she viewed the once-familiar surroundings of her birthplace. She cranked down her window, letting in the salty air and gazing out at the palm trees and sailboats crowding a roadside marina until the light turned green. She acknowledged the honking horn of the car behind her and pressed on the gas, continuing her unhurried tour through the city.

Ten years had passed since she'd last seen Biloxi, and the changes were amazing. It still looked like her hometown, in a vague sort of way, although some of the quaintness had vanished with the appearance of the grand casinos. Biloxi was still beautiful, but had transformed from a picturesque seaside city into a dazzling tourist town, alive with excitement and the lure of easy money. Whether this was a good thing or not, Dana couldn't quite decide. The mix of elegant Southern architecture and modern progress was surreal.

Following the directions Andie gave her, she found her way to Crème de la Creme, pulling into the parking lot, her mouth stretching into a huge grin. "Well, thank God for small favors," she said. "At least this place hasn't changed."

The business her parents had established was still in the same pink stucco building with its white awning flapping above the entrance and overflowing flowerbeds of fragrant tropical blossoms in shades of purple, yellow and coral gracing the bricked walkway. Dana got out of the car, strolling leisurely toward the stained-glass entrance. She tried to appear calm, but her nerve endings tingled anxiously. She felt a little uncomfortable, having been coaxed into unfamiliar territory. This visit would definitely be different. This time, she was treading on Andie's turf.

"Why did I let her talk me into this?" she muttered under her breath as she neared the entrance. "I should have just followed my instinct and stayed in New Orleans. This could turn out to be one of the stupidest moves I've ever made."

She reached the door, placing her hand gingerly on the handle. *Run, Dana, run!* A little voice from deep within urged her to flee.

"Oh hell, it's too late to turn back now. I've come all this way. I might as well stick around for the consequences," she grumbled, taking a deep breath and pushing open the door.

She was greeted by the scent of fresh eucalyptus and gardenias, intermingled with the lingering aroma of homemade brownies. She slipped through the door and into the reception area, looking up to see a pert young woman seated behind a desk.

"Oh my gosh, you have to be Dana!" the woman squealed enthusiastically, her pretty face lighting with a bright smile. She bolted from behind the desk and took Dana by the arm. "Come on in!"

She chattered happily as she led Dana through the office, oblivious to Dana's wary expression. "I'm Andie's assistant, Dell. We've never met, but I've heard all about you. In fact, I feel as though I already know you. And I have to tell you, you're as pretty as your pictures."

"Gee, thanks," Dana commented dryly, looking past Dell to the open window, wishing she could jump out. *What was I thinking?*" she asked herself again. *Coming here is going to turn out to be a nightmare. I can already tell.*

"Andie will be so glad that you arrived safely. She was so worried about you driving in all that New Orleans traffic."

"I don't know why. I do it all the time."

Dell giggled, patting Dana's shoulder reassuringly. "I know it, honey. She's just being silly. Moms are that way, you know."

She paused in front of a doorway, pushing Dana inside. "Andie, look who's here," she sang out gaily.

Andie leaned over the desk, buried up to her elbows in orders and paperwork. She glanced up and her face brightened.

"Dana! Hi!" she threw down her pencil and quickly crossed the room, giving Dana a light hug. "Welcome back to Biloxi. You made it much earlier than I expected.  I take it you didn't have any trouble getting here?"

"Am I too early?" Dana asked cautiously, eyeing the disarray on Andie's desk. "I don't want to be in the way. I can go bum around town for a while if you're still working."

"My desk always looks this way. I'm just a slob," Andie laughed. "No, I'm done with work for the entire weekend. Most of it can wait until Monday, and what can't, I'm leaving to Dell."

"Sure, just desert me, why don't you?" Dell teased from the corridor, watching them with a smile.

"What do you say we get out of here?" Andie suggested, grabbing her purse. "You and I have places to go and people to see."

"Whatever," Dana said with a nonchalant shrug. "It's your game plan. I'm just along for the ride."

"You're actually going to let me call the shots? That's a first."

"And probably a last, so don't get too used to it."

"Don't worry. I won't! I'm not that stupid," Andie laughed again and put her arm around Dana's waist, guiding her out of the office and down the hall with Dell at their heels. "See ya Monday, Dell," she called over her shoulder, hustling Dana toward their waiting vehicles.

"See ya boss!" Dell called back with a wink. "Y'all behave yourselves, ya hear?"

Andie had moved from the large home she once shared with Freddie into a small cottage with an ocean view. Dana followed her there, driving behind Andie's red Mustang, apprehension and uneasiness knotted tightly in her gut.

"I think I would have rather spent the weekend with Claudette," she mumbled, yanking hard on the steering wheel as Andie took an unexpected turn. "Claudette may have her bad points, but at least she doesn't make me a nervous wreck."

Following Andie's lead, she pulled down a sandy drive, nodding in approval as the pretty little house came into view. "Andie has good taste," she observed, throwing the car into park.

Andie waited next to the Mustang, her arms outstretched in a welcoming gesture. "Here we are," she said, her expression cheerful and her tone bright.

"I like it," Dana said, nodding toward the cottage as she followed Andie down the walkway, hanging back shyly as her mother trotted onto the porch, keys in hand.

"Me too," Andie said, unlocking and pushing open the door. "Come on in and I'll show you around.

Dana lugged her duffel bag up the concrete front steps and stepped into the house, glancing around appreciatively. Andie's house was crisp, clean and feminine, adorned in light florals, white wicker and antique lace. Dana took a very quick inventory of the furnishings, spotting not one item from her childhood. "You got new furniture," she remarked, her tone strained and verging on accusatory.

"Yes, I did." Andie set her straw bag on the dining table and turned toward Dana, her eyes honest and clear. "I made a fresh start, got rid of all reminders of the past."

"Like me and Jerry?" Dana offered Andie a cool stare, overflowing with bitterness.

Andie leaned against the table, her gaze soft and unwavering. "No. Making my way back to you and Jerry was the most important part of my plan for a new life."

Dana remained silent, sizing Andie up with doubtful eyes, unwilling to trust her instinct that her mother was telling the truth. Andie noted her disbelieving expression and decided to tread lightly.

"Hey," she said, quickly changing the subject. "Let's get you settled in."

Dana nodded and hauled her bag down the hall, trailing Andie into the guest room. "Up to now, this room hasn't gotten much use," Andie said, moving aside to let Dana pass. "But I'm hoping that will change."

Dana dropped her bag and looked around, letting out a squeal of delight when she spotted Chips stretched across the bed, basking lazily in the warm sunlight that filtered through the open drapes. She flew across the room, scooping the fuzzy tomcat into her arms and burying her face deeply into his soft gray fur.

"Hello kitty," she whispered tenderly, nuzzling her nose cozily against his. "I've missed you, honey."

From the door, Andie watched their tender reunion through sentimental tears, silently kicking herself again for the years she threw away. How stupid she had been to miss the amazing transformation of the tiny girl she remembered into this wonderful young lady. She slipped quietly into the room, sliding her arm around Dana's shoulder. "I'm glad you're here, Dana," she said, her voice soft and sincere.

Dana lifted her eyes, her chin tucked neatly atop Chips' bushy head and returned Andie's warm smile. "Yeah, me too."

Andie chose not to risk her good fortune. She patted Dana's arm and moved to the door. "I'll leave you two to bond," she said, smiling as she pulled the door closed behind her.

Dana cuddled the cat close to her chest, rocking him slowly, mesmerized by the comforting sound of his deep, throaty purr. Things were beginning to look up. *Maybe this trip will be worth it after all.*

They dined that evening with Bill Fairgate, passing on his offer to eat Italian at La Cucina inside Beau Rivage. They opted instead for somewhere more traditional — Chappy's Seafood in Long Beach, a wonderful restaurant nestled cozily under tall oaks along the coast.

Bill spotted them as soon as they arrived and bolted from a window-side table to greet them. He immediately enveloped Dana in a huge bear hug. "Miss Dana LaRue," he said in a loud, brassy voice, drawing out each syllable of her name with immense southern charm. "I knew who you were the minute I saw you. I haven't seen you since you were a tiny little thing, but I'd know Freddie's daughter anywhere." He flashed a grin and released her, turning to Andie and presenting her with a resounding kiss on the lips.

"Hello, Sweet Cheeks," he said, winking at her mischievously. "You're looking good."

"You don't look too bad yourself, sailor." Andie laughed, returning his kiss with a warm smile.

Bill linked his arm through hers and took Dana's with the other, leading them down the length of the room to their cloth-covered table, happily barking small talk as they went.

Walking beside him, Dana studied Bill's face intently, searching her memory bank, trying to place his handsome features. He said that they had met yet Dana couldn't remember ever having seen him before. However, she found that she liked him instantly and listened to his tall tales and stories with genuine laughter, grinning shyly at his colorful use of language and the nicknames he had for her mother.

After dining on Stuffed Shrimp Pontchartrain, followed by red velvet cake and coffee, Andie excused herself to the ladies room, leaving Bill and Dana alone. Dana sat back and stared out the window, watching as the bright moonlight danced across the waves, sending its silvery fingers deep into the dark waters of the Gulf. She smiled with rare contentment, glad for the second time that day that she had come to Biloxi.

"It's about time you finally decided to make peace with your mama," Bill's gruff voice cut smoothly through her thoughts. "She's a fine woman."

"If you say so," Dana commented dryly, meeting his inquisitive gaze with a cool stare.

Bill suppressed an amused smile, recognizing her inherited stubborn streak. "You're a lot like her, you know."

"That's funny. Most people say I'm like my father."

"You look like Freddie LaRue, all right enough, but you're Andie's daughter through and through."

"I don't know why you say that. We're nothing alike. Ask anybody."

"I don't have to ask anybody, little missy. I can see it with my own eyes."

"And I guess that makes you an authority."

"I am an authority where your mother is concerned. Most people don't know Andie the way I do, present company included," Bill informed her, exuding an air of smug confidence. "And despite what you think, you're very much alike. You're both smart, beautiful, witty, hard-headed and spoiled rotten."

"I hardly think so," Dana replied, lowering her eyes disdainfully, her feathers ruffled as she swirled her spoon in her half-empty cup of coffee. "I haven't exactly lived a life that is conducive to being spoiled, regardless of what you think you know. You may know my mother, but you don't know me at all."

Bill didn't comment, but smiled condescendingly, steepling his fingers against his chin and sizing her up with wise eyes. Dana looked away, angry and unwilling to meet his gaze.

*I am two seconds away from giving him a real piece of my mind,* she thought furiously, bunching her fists beneath the crisp tablecloth.

Andie reappeared, halting Dana's plan of action. "Did y'all miss me?" she asked teasingly, looking from Dana to Bill. Her face was cheerful as she slid into her chair.

"But, of course, Pumpkin," Bill replied, reaching over to cover her hand. "My world is never the same when you're away."

Dana rolled her eyes, annoyed by their syrupy exchange. "Whatever," she muttered sarcastically, stabbing at her leftover cake. Bill and Andie's pet names and sugary affection were sickening. *What exactly is the extent of their relationship?*

Dana spent the rest of the evening observing Bill, taking note of the discreet affectionate glances he threw Andie's way. Andie seemed equally fond of him, although not openly so. Nevertheless, there was an unspoken bond between them. *Is Bill Fairgate the one responsible for bringing Andie back to life?*

*Eek, I wonder if he's going to be my stepfather?* Jolted by the sudden notion, Dana lifted her head, sneaking a wide-eyed peek at her cozy dinner companions. *God forbid! He's old enough to be my grandfather.*

All the same, Bill was a nice-looking man with a dynamic personality and was clearly very wealthy. The cut of his clothes alone screamed "money." And he definitely treated Andie right. A woman could certainly do worse. Even Andie.

They left the restaurant together. Dana walked briskly toward the red Mustang with Bill and Andie strolling behind her, swinging their loosely clasped hands. Andie tossed her the keys, and Dana ran to the car, hoping to avoid any further discussion with Bill.

She did not get her wish. Whistling a jaunty tune, Bill came around to Dana's side of the car and settled her into the passenger's seat, fastening her seatbelt securely and presenting her with a good night kiss on the forehead. "Bye, Bill," she said curtly.

"Good night, Cupcake. Nice to see you again," he laughed softly, unfazed by her frostiness. "Don't be a stranger now, you hear?"

Dana suppressed a snarl, denying her natural inclination to be nasty. Instead, she drew from years of Julie's etiquette lessons and managed a polite nod, watching Bill saunter around the front of the vehicle to tell Andie goodbye.

They embraced warmly and Andie quickly pecked his cheek, then jumped into the car, starting the engine and lowering the convertible top before speeding away with a happy wave. Her face was giddy and her blond hair flew behind her in the breeze. She looked much younger than forty. "So, what did you think of Bill?" she asked, casting an inquisitive look Dana's way.

"I liked him okay," Dana admitted with a shrug. "Although he's real lucky I didn't tell him to go straight to hell."

Andie flinched, cutting her wide eyes to her outspoken daughter. "That's awfully blunt. Did I miss something?"

"No," Dana scowled and stared out the window.

"You know, you *were* a little sullen-acting after dinner. What happened while I was in the bathroom?"

"Nothing."

"Now, don't give me that. You're riding in your mother's car, cussing Bill like a sailor. Something must've happened."

"We had words, okay?"

"Words? What kind of words?"

Dana sighed in exasperation. "Forget about it. It's not worth going into. Let's just say I got the impression that Bill thinks he knows it all."

"What makes you think that?"

"Oh, he just pissed me off."

"How?"

"By saying that I was just like you."

"That pissed you off? Don't you want to be like me?"

"That depends on whether we're talking about the bad, depressed Andie who pushed away her husband and deserted her children, or the good, angelic Andie who loves life and everyone in it."

"I don't deserve that," Andie said. Even though her eyes didn't leave the road, Dana could see the deep hurt she had caused.

"Sorry," she replied sheepishly, sensing that she had crossed the line. She chewed her fingernail, knowing she should keep her mouth shut, but couldn't. It was against her nature. She had to keep it going. "Is he your boyfriend?"

Andie glanced at her, her eyes round with surprise. "Bill? Where did that come from?" she asked, flabbergasted laughter bubbling up in her throat.

"Dad says you're in love. I just wondered if Bill was the one."

"Oh."

"Well? Is he?"

"Dana!"

"An-die!"

"No, Bill is not my boyfriend. There! Does that satisfy you?"

"Sure was a lot of goo-goo-eyed staring going on at that table to just be friends."

"I assure you that there's nothing going on between me and Bill Fairgate. He's a dear friend, that's all."

"So, if not Bill, then who?"

"You're certainly being nosy tonight."

"Hey, you're the one who insisted that I come to Biloxi. I didn't have to, you know."

"I invited you here to have fun, not to interrogate me," Andie replied self-consciously, dancing around the question and earning an irritated stare. "I don't really think my social life is any of your business."

"So much for me being a part of your life."

"Okay, okay." Playing into Dana's guilt trip, Andie yielded with a small laugh, a rosy flush creeping onto her cheeks. "Yes, I have a boyfriend."

"Do I know him?"

"No. He lives in New Orleans."

"Am I going to get to meet him?"

"Is tomorrow soon enough?"

"I suppose," Dana answered with feigned indifference and turned her head to conceal a pleased smile. *So, Andie does have a boyfriend, and she actually cares enough to introduce me to him. That's a change. Things are definitely looking up.*

# 8

Cole arrived on Andie's doorstep early Saturday morning, casually dressed in khaki shorts and a polo shirt, and was dragged across the front threshold by a large black Labrador retriever. Andie sailed across the room to greet him, laughing as he became entangled in Estelle's leash.

"Here, let me help you," she said, grabbing Estelle and smiling up at him. She tiptoed up to kiss him, her eyes twinkling with delight, then motioned Dana to join them. "Dana, come meet Cole Dewberry and his sidekick Estelle."

Dana shook Cole's hand, taking in his good looks from the top of his gray-streaked head down to the white Nike tennis shoes on his feet.

*Now, this is more like it!* she thought with an infatuated smile. *To hell with Bill Fairgate — this man is a looker. No wonder Andie blossomed.*

"Very nice to meet you," she breathed aloud. She batted her thick eyelashes in flirtatious fashion, throwing her cascading locks of curling ebony hair over her shoulders and flashing her dazzling teeth. *My God, he takes my breath away*, she thought, feeling her cheeks grow warm and rosy.

"You too, Dana," Cole acknowledged with an easy smile, his eyes never leaving her face. "You're every bit as pretty as your mother said you were."

Dana giggled vivaciously and playfully slapped his arm. "Oh, don't you believe a word she says," she drawled. "You know she lies." She threw a catty look in Andie's direction, then let go of Cole's hand and flounced out the front door. "Let's go," she called over her shoulder. "I'm ready for a day on the town."

"Whoa! She speaks with a double-edged sword," Cole commented dryly, lifting an intrigued brow as he studied the brunette sliding down the front banister. He reached out to squeeze Andie's hand, noting the dismayed look on her face. "Don't let her get to you, Andie. She's just a kid."

Andie offered a weary smile. "Kid or not, she knows exactly what she's doing." She shifted her gaze to Dana waiting on the lawn, her ebony eyes scrutinizing them curiously. "I know I haven't been the best mother, but why does she always find the need to stab me through the heart?"

"She's just doing it to get attention. You know, showing off for her mom's boyfriend. She'll straighten up."

Andie took Cole's advice and brushed aside her hurt, smiling up at him as she pushed open the screen door and stepped outside. "Well, at least you're off to a good start," she declared with forced brightness, taking his hand as they went down the stairs. "You managed a feat not many can accomplish. You made her smile."

They left Estelle locked in a fierce standoff with Chips and climbed into Cole's white SUV, traveling to Gulfport to catch the boat ride to Ship Island, one of the barrier islands off the Mississippi coast. They enjoyed a day of fun in the sun, picnicking under a shaded pavilion and strolling along the island's beaches.

"I can't believe I'm actually having fun," Dana mumbled begrudgingly as she sat in the sand, letting the crystal-clear gulf water splash over her toes. She had to admit that she was having a ball, seeing a side of Andie she'd never experienced before. The Andie she had known as a child had all but vanished, replaced by a smiling woman with a sense of humor and a delightful laugh. She looked back over her shoulder, gazing thoughtfully at Cole and Andie as they played Frisbee along the shore, grinning half-heartedly as they collided and fell chuckling to the sand.

"What have you done with my mother?" she asked mockingly, whispering softly to herself as she studied the lovely blond hanging on Cole Dewberry's arm. "You're definitely not Andie LaRue."

She spent most of the day discreetly monitoring Andie and Cole, witnessing their many looks of open fondness and mutual admiration. They were obviously deeply in love, each hanging on the words of the other, using every opportunity to touch or hold hands, exchanging chaste kisses and flirtatious winks. To think that she suspected Andie was in love with Bill Fairgate was now laughable. After seeing her with Cole, there was no doubt who had her affection.

*Daddy, forgive me*, Dana thought, feeling a stab as she gazed at Cole with increasing fondness. *I can't help but like him. If anyone had to steal Andie's love, at least it's him. I can forgive her for loving him.*

They returned to the cottage late in the afternoon, catching quick showers to wash away the beach sweat and sandy grime before Cole grilled steaks on the back patio. After a tasty meal backdropped by a brilliantly setting sun, he graciously retired to the study with Estelle to catch forty winks on the hide-a-bed, leaving Andie and Dana some much-needed privacy.

Taking advantage of their time alone, Andie made cappuccino, carrying two steaming mugs from the kitchen to lounge with Dana on the living room floor. They sat Indian style, facing one another on the braided rug, wearing matching at-ease smiles as they sipped their coffee and relived the events of the day.

"So, how do you like Cole?" Andie set her empty cup on the end table and leaned back on her elbows, eyeing Dana happily as she stretched her shapely tanned legs comfortably across the carpet.

"I think he's great," Dana said, her face lighting up. "Great-looking, charming, wonderful personality and a petroleum engineer to boot — wherever did you find him?"

"In Pine Prairie, Texas." Andie giggled at Dana's astonished expression. "Cole and I grew up together," she explained with a grin. "We were an item once upon a long time ago in high school and hooked up again a couple of years ago at our reunion."

Dana's inquisitiveness took over and she began firing questions. "Hooked up again? Are you nuts? What on earth possessed you to let him go in the first place?" she demanded incredulously. "He is just to die for."

"Oh, you know, Dana. Things happen." Andie shrugged, averting her eyes uncomfortably.

*It must have been something pretty damn catastrophic*, Dana reasoned silently, scratching her head in bewilderment as she studied her mother's melancholy expression. *It would take a friggin' nuclear holocaust to tear me away from a man like that.*

*Of course!* It came to her in a flash and her hand froze, locked in position atop her head. High school…twenty-two years ago. That had to be it. The time frame was right. It must've had something to do with the baby.

"Did Cole know about Shannon?" she asked pointedly, involuntarily scooting closer to Andie as she awaited her answer.

Andie shook her head, her eyes dull and fixed on a time gone by. "He didn't then. He does now."

Analyzing the tragic look on Andie's face, Dana suddenly put two and two together, deducing that Cole must be Shannon's father — the very man Andie mooned over while pushing Freddie and her children away. Her infatuation with Cole and the easy contentment she'd developed with Andie quickly vanished.

"Cole's her father, isn't he?" She lashed out at Andie angrily, her face bright red with indignation. "My God! Don't you think you should've told me that before now?"

She scrambled from the carpet, her fists balled tightly by her sides, and stomped around the room, her voice rising with each hysterical syllable. "What did you do, lure me here to play a part? What, were the two of you amusing yourselves with a little game, pretending that I was your long-lost daughter? Was that it, Andie? Was it the torrid tale of two star-crossed lovers reunited, sharing a lovely weekend with their only child?"

Dana glared at her, her dark eyes pools of fury. "I should've known this weekend wasn't about me. It was never about me. It's all about her! It always has been. Shannon's the only one you've ever wanted!"

"Dana, don't be ridiculous!"

"Oh, just go to hell!"

"Hold on, young lady. Watch your language. That's not a very nice thing to say, especially to your mother."

"It's appropriate, given the circumstances."

"I don't think so."

"I don't care what you think!"

Dana stormed from the living room and fled down the hall, hastily snatching up her discarded clothing scattered around the guest room and stuffing them angrily into her duffel bag.

"Where are you going?" Andie stood in the doorway, her face pale and troubled, frowning as Dana slung her bag over her shoulder.

"I'm going back to Tulane," Dana sputtered, regarding her with bitter resentment. "So sorry to end the fun, but I won't be a willing participant in your sick little fantasy."

"Oh Dana, honestly. I don't know where you got such a vivid imagination." Andie let out a defeated sigh, giving up when she recognized the stubborn set of Dana's jaw, a Shepherd trait if there ever was one. Reasoning with her now would be impossible. "I can't let you leave like this, especially not this late at night. Stay here. I won't bother you, I promise. Just stay here tonight and leave in the morning."

Dana glared at her in heated silence, her breathing labored as she weighed her decision. Finally, she dropped the duffel bag onto the floor with a thud and retreated into the bathroom, slamming the door and clicking the lock. She leaned against the wall, her ear cupped to the door, listening as Andie shuffled from the room and quietly shut the door. Only then did she venture from the lavatory, her chest heavy and her eyes filled with tears. She threw herself onto the bed, pulling Chips into her arms for comfort. She lay staring into the darkness, furious with herself for being deceived. *I should have known. Andie doesn't care for me. She never has, and she never will.*

After a frustrated night of tossing and turning, Dana emerged from the bedroom on Sunday morning to find Andie on the front porch, curled up in a wicker chair, sipping hot tea and gazing blankly out at the gulf. Dana studied the dark circles beneath her mother's eyes and was consumed with shame.

*Good lord, what would Daddy and Julie think if they could've heard me last night?* she wondered in embarrassment. She didn't have to ask. She knew what they would think. Freddie would be disappointed and Julie simply mortified, appalled by her insensitive and childish behavior, not to mention her extravagant use of foul language. She would have been severely chastised and made to apologize on the spot.

Lying at Andie's feet, Estelle spied Dana and thumped her tail in greeting. Andie looked over her shoulder, casting a guarded smile in Dana's direction. "Hi," she said hesitantly, cautiously testing the waters before jumping in.

Taking it upon herself to do the right thing, Dana slid into the chair next to Andie, eyeing her apologetically, a humbled expression on her face. "Good morning," she said shyly, accepting the cup of tea Andie offered her.

"Good morning," Andie replied cheerfully, gracious enough to act as if nothing had happened. "Sleep well?"

"Well enough, considering," Dana replied with a shrug and quickly looked away, conscious of Andie's probing gaze. "Where's Cole?" she asked, anxious to change the subject.

"Gone out for doughnuts. It's a ritual. To Cole, Sunday just isn't Sunday without his cream-filled Krispy Kreme."

"Sounds like a good plan to me," Dana stared across the highway to the water, listening to the lonely sound of calling seagulls. "I'm sorry about last night," she said soberly, studying her hands, unable to look Andie in the face. "You know how I am. I can be awfully unreasonable and do have a tendency to lose my mind sometimes."

"Don't worry about it, honey," Andie accepted her apology with a quiet smile, bending down to stroke Estelle's ears. "I'm sure finding out that Cole is Shannon's father did come as a pretty big shock. I guess I should have told you the truth from the beginning, but I sincerely didn't think it would matter.

"We weren't playing games with you or pretending that you were anyone other than who you are. I just wanted you to meet the man I love."

"It's okay," Dana replied with a shrug, and they fell into an easy silence, another fragile truce drawn between them. Andie refilled her teacup and sipped it slowly.

Dana studied her intently, questions welling up inside her. "Did you ever love Daddy?" she asked softly, blinking away salty tears.

Andie snapped her head around, staring at Dana in astonishment. "Of course I did," she said gently, a faraway twinkle replacing the stunned look in her eyes. "At one time Freddie and I were very happy. The loss of that happiness was my fault. Everything that happened in earlier years caught up with me, leaving me with some tough issues and problems to resolve. I went through kind of a mental breakdown and forgot what I had. Basically, I lost my mind and threw away happiness with both hands."

Andie paused as her voice grew shaky, her expression wounded and filled with regret. She swallowed hard, forcing back choking sobs and glanced at Dana with a weak smile. "Cole and I are together now, but we still have a lot of things to work through. I wronged him in ways that aren't easily forgiven. But Cole isn't the only one I've wronged."

She reached out, taking Dana's hands and squeezing them tenderly. "I'm so sorry for the way I was with you, honey, and I'll spend the rest of my life trying to make up for all the years I threw away.

"And you were wrong. Shannon is not the only one I ever wanted. I wanted you, baby, more than you'll ever know." Andie faltered, brushing away streaming tears. "I love you, Dana, and have since the moment you were born. I could never love any daughter more than I love you, and I'm so proud of the young woman you've become. Please give me another chance — another chance to be the mother I should have been."

At last, Andie spoke the words Dana had waited nineteen years to hear. Holding tight to her hand, Dana sobbed openly, overjoyed to finally know the truth. Her mother loved her. *She really loves me, and not just the memory of a lost child.*

She flung her arms around Andie's neck, embracing her tightly, ecstatic tears coursing freely down her cheeks. "I love you too, Mom!" she said, weeping softly into Andie's shoulder. She held on to her, determined never to let her go, feeling the gaping hole in her heart finally begin to mend.

Andie raised her hand and stroked Dana's long dark hair lovingly, happy tears sparkling bright in her deep blue eyes. She'd waited so long for this moment. At last, she'd been forgiven. To have Dana's love again was heaven.

"Hey girls, there's no need for crying!" Cole called out robustly, marching up the walkway with a doughnut box in one hand and a tray of Styrofoam coffee cups in the other. "I hurried with the doughnuts as fast as I could. Gee!"

He joked with them to dry their tears, sensing that he was witnessing the long overdue reconciliation between the love of his life and her estranged daughter. *Thank God*, he thought jubilantly, a happy bounce in his gait as he mounted the front steps and joined in their embrace. Seeing them patch things up was the crowning touch to his reunion with Andie.

Dana left for New Orleans that afternoon, escorted to her car by Andie and Cole. After she had loaded her bags in the trunk, Andie kissed her affectionately, cautioning her for the hundredth time to be careful on the highway.

"I will, Mom," Dana said, rolling her eyes in pseudo-irritation. "Jeez, lighten up, will ya? I told you. I'm not a baby anymore."

"You'll always be a baby to me," Andie replied in her most motherly tone, winking at her playfully.

"Hey, don't start getting all mushy on me. You'll make me regret ever coming here."

"I hope not." Andie put her hand on Dana's shoulder, the look on her face tender and sincere, "Having you here this weekend has been the highlight of the last decade."

"Except for him, I guess," Dana grinned, jerking her head in Cole's direction.

"You just can't let it rest, can you?"

"What can I say? I like to get in the last word."

Cole jotted his home number on the back of his business card and handed it to Dana, chuckling in amusement as he listened to them squabble. "Here, call me. I'll take you out to dinner. Unless, of course, you really like eating that lousy cafeteria food."

Dana accepted the card, smiling up at him with delight. "You got a date," she said, kissing his cheek warmly. "You're all right, Cole Man," she joked as she climbed into the Honda and then as an afterthought, shot him a stern look. "You take good care of my mother, you hear?"

Cole nodded, sliding a protective arm around Andie's shoulders. "I'll do my best, even though I'm sure it'll be a chore. This family seems to have more than its share of difficult women."

"You love it!" Dana yelled out her window as she drove away, answering their farewell with an enthusiastic wave.

She traveled back to Tulane, driven by an overwhelming surge of elation, feeling that she finally knew her mother. After nineteen lonely years, she and Andie were at last on the road to a relationship. They had weathered the worst and survived.

From now on, they would be fine. Dana was sure of it. After all they had been through, she couldn't imagine anything that could possibly come between them again.

# Part Three

# Diane

# 9

Diane sat in a daze, staring out the window with a dreamy expression on her face, watching the striking figure high atop a Palomino mare fly across the pasture, the skirt of her dress hiked up above her knees and her long black hair whipping loosely in the wind. Diane held her breath, watching the horse gallop at break-neck speed toward the high rail fence, then let out a silent cheer as the animal sailed effortlessly across the barrier, rider intact, her arms thrown up in victory.

"She's so wonderful! Why, oh why can't I be just like her?" Still wearing an enchanted smile, Diane exhaled pathetically, envious of the rider's zest for life, and pressed her face against the glass, following the retreating rider with an adoring gaze.

Her grandmother, Beatrice, sat across the room, needlepoint in hand. Hearing Diane's pitiful sigh, she glanced up, offering her an offended stare. "Good heavens!" she exclaimed, her eyebrows knitted tightly by her disapproving frown. "Why on earth would you ever want to be so unrefined?"

"Mother's not unrefined. She's just different — a real free spirit."

"Free spirit? Is that what you call it? Nonsense! Your mother is the most ill-bred, rude, obnoxious woman I've ever met. She belongs right back in the swamp she slithered out of."

Diane pressed her lips together tightly, biting her tongue. She turned her back, squinting out the window into the sunshine as she searched the horizon for her mother. "But she's so beautiful," she mused aloud.

"Beauty is only skin deep, Diane. And why should you care anyway? You're beautiful."

"I'm not beautiful — not like she is. She's breathtaking and exciting. I'm plain — plain and boring with dull brown eyes and awful red hair. I'm doomed. No man will ever want me. Who's even going to look at a woman with red hair?"

"Your red hair is a family trait and something to be proud of," Beatrice reprimanded her sternly. "You look like your father, Diane, and there's certainly no shame in that."

"Looking like Daddy is not going to get me a husband."

"You needn't worry about finding a husband. You don't have to be a beauty. You're a Carson, my dear, and you don't get any better than that." Beatrice dismissed Diane's fears with a smug wave of her hand and then turned her attention back to her embroidery, signaling that the discussion was over.

Diane Rochelle Carson was the crown princess of an affluent family, born into a clan of Southern bluebloods whose lineage dated back to before the Civil War. As the only daughter of Lois LeJeune and Geoffrey Palmer Carson of Eden Glen, Georgia, Diane was part of a dynasty known for its vast wealth and immense influence in Southern politics.

Diane's father, Palmer, was an attorney, as were his father and his grandfather, and headed the Carson Law Firm on East Bay Street in downtown Savannah, one of the most prestigious firms in the Deep South. Diane's earliest memories were of her kind and adoring father: tall and handsome, with a droll sense of humor, contagious laughter and a radiant smile that lit his entire face. Diane was a true Daddy's girl and Palmer idolized her, indulging her every whim. She was never left wanting or wondering. From the day she was born, Palmer granted her every desire.

Diane was crazy about her father, but her mother absolutely fascinated her, leaving her in a constant state of awe. Lois LeJeune Carson was an exotic beauty of French descent with pale creamy skin, shimmering ebony hair, feisty cat-green eyes and a fiery personality. She was vivacious and hot-tempered with a mind of her own and was unwilling to bow to anyone, a trait that most well-bred, soft-spoken ladies of Georgia found offensive. Diane found it irresistible.

Diane thought of her parents' love affair as a fairy tale — a real-life fairy tale come true, complete with happy ending. At first glance, her parents didn't seem to match at all. They were so incredibly different, from two very different worlds. But after watching them together, seeing their undying affection and how well they complemented one another, anyone could see that they were a match made in heaven. Anyone, that is, but her grandmother.

"How did Mother ever end up here?" Diane asked curiously, still at the window, perking up suddenly as Lois reappeared, zooming across the field in the direction of the stables.

"I often ask myself the very same question," Beatrice sniffed disdainfully, glancing up from her needlework with a lofty roll of her eyes. "To this day, I'll never know what your father was thinking."

"Oh, Grandmother, please tell me again how Mother and Daddy met!" Diane pleaded excitedly, tearing her eyes from the window. She swiveled on the piano bench and sat on her knees, her shiny patent leather shoes tucked neatly beneath the hem of her frilly white dress. Eager for entertainment, she beseeched her grandmother with big brown eyes, only to be shot down by Beatrice's reproachful stare.

"Diane Carson, I'll do no such thing! That is my least favorite subject and something I definitely do not care to discuss. Now, turn right back around and practice those scales. You sound awful." Beatrice threw down her canvas in frustration and pushed out of her chair. "I'm going to look for Tressa," she announced haughtily. "I don't know why I pay that girl to be your nanny. She's obviously not doing her job. Every time I turn around good, one of you is under my feet!"

Beatrice stalked out of the parlor in a huff and retreated down the hall, leaving Diane sitting at the baby grand, dejected, with a long face and a chest heavy with disappointment. "I don't know what the big deal is," she mumbled unhappily. "All I wanted to hear was one lousy little story. But then again, why would I even bother to ask her?"

Quizzing Grandmother always proved fruitless. Beg though she might, Beatrice would never divulge even the tiniest bit of information about her parents' romance. Diane sighed, leaning her elbows against the ivories and cupping her chin in her hands.

Her Aunt Daisy breezed in from the kitchen, finding her moping alone. She stopped in the center of the parlor, throwing her hands onto her ample hips. "What's the matter with you?" she asked, raising an inquisitive brow. "You look like you just lost your best friend."

"I just wanted to hear about how Daddy charmed Mother away from New Orleans, and Grandmother refused to tell me."

"That worn out old story? Please, Diane, you've heard that story a hundred times. In fact, I think you could recite it to me, backwards and forwards," Daisy said, watching as Diane's bottom lip protruded in a pronounced pout. Giggling, she crossed the room and took a seat, giving her niece a conspiratorial smirk as she patted the cushion next to her. "Okay, okay, if you insist. Come here, Sugar, and let Auntie Daze tell you all about it."

Diane joined her on the sofa and Daisy threw an arm around her shoulders, leaning her chestnut head against her niece's, whispering softly as if she was sharing the most guarded of secrets.

"Once upon a time, your daddy, Geoffrey Palmer Carson, was Eden Glen's most eligible bachelor and legendary womanizer of three counties. The summer following his graduation from law school, Mama and Daddy sent him away to New Orleans, with high hopes that he'd sow his wild oats and develop into the respectable citizen they expected him to be."

Daisy laughed mockingly, flashing Diane a sly smile. "Which only goes to show how well they really knew him," she added cynically. "Anyone with any sense at all knows that boy has a mind all his own! He wasn't going to settle down until he got good and darn ready…"

Accompanied by his best buddy Tommy O'Grady, Palmer set out on his expedition with great expectations of wine, women and song and descended upon the Crescent City, determined to take it by storm. Immediately upon their arrival, he and Tommy embarked on a three-month celebration, carousing from party to party with beautiful women on each arm, filling their nights with dancing, romancing and fine French cuisine. Palmer was having the time of his life and was in no great hurry to return to Georgia, feeling that he could never tire of the endless round of cotillions and soirées.

"This is the life, Thomas, my friend," he said, grinning expansively as they entered another festive ballroom for yet another ball held in their honor. "Why would I go back home when I could stay here and do this? They don't really need me there. I could spend the rest of my days here, eating and drinking, entertained by a new lovely lady each night. What more out of life could a man desire?"

Tommy laughed appreciatively as Palmer glanced around the crowded room, eyeing his choices. "Which shall it be tonight, Tommy boy? A blonde or a redhead?"

"I was thinking brunette," Tommy replied distractedly, his eyes fixed on the overflowing dance floor. Palmer followed the direction of Tommy's admiring stare, peering through an ocean of humanity, catching sight of the one woman who would make him eat his words.

She was a tall, raven-haired beauty in a dress of crimson red, with a brilliant smile and fiery eyes the color of jade. She was outgoing and spirited, unquestionably the life of the party, and as the sound of her bright laughter rang in his ears, Palmer was overcome by an incredible sensation of warmth.

"Now that's the kind of girl to take home to Mother," he murmured, smiling broadly, never taking his eyes from her face.

"Not *your* mother," Tommy replied skeptically. "Do you know how appalled Beatrice Carson would be if you, her only son, showed up with that less-than-genteel young woman?"

"To hell with Mother."

"Oh sure. You can spout that now — you're seven hundred miles away. But just take that lovely little dove back to Savannah and see what happens. Then you won't be so brave."

In his heart, Palmer knew Tommy was right. Beatrice would never approve. This girl would never fit the mold she had in mind for the next Carson bride. Nevertheless, in spite of all good sense, she completely captivated him and he smiled, enchanted as he watched her, taking in her bewitching loveliness while mentally trying to devise a plan to meet her. It would be much easier thought than done.

A sea of eager admirers surrounded the breathtaking brunette, and she took turns dancing with each of them, batting her eyelashes flirtatiously as she looked deeply into their eyes, flashing her radiant smile as she listened attentively to their ego-inflated stories. Entranced though he was, there was no way Palmer could penetrate the barrier of young suitors encircling the object of his newfound affection. There were just too many of them. Instead, he did the next best thing. He went to her father.

Palmer asked around until he found him, lounging casually near the punch bowl, his hands full of crudités. As it turned out, Lois LeJeune's regal father, Robert, was much easier to get an audience with than his lovely daughter, and Palmer approached him with an easy smile. "Mr. LeJeune, I would be honored if you would allow me to introduce myself," he began proudly, summoning all the pretentious breeding Beatrice had instilled in him. "I'm Palmer Carson from Savannah."

Robert's eyes flashed with recognition, and he shook Palmer's outstretched hand enthusiastically. "Mr. Carson of Savannah, I believe this party is for you," he joked with a hearty chuckle. "How are you enjoying our fair city?"

"I'm enjoying myself immensely. New Orleans is beautiful, and the cuisine is second to none."

"And the ladies? Surely you've danced with some of our charming young ladies?"

"Ah, yes. I've met several young ladies and I agree: they are charming. However, none of them are quite as enchanting as your daughter."

Robert raised a quizzical brow, following Palmer's lingering stare. *Of course, Lois,* Robert sighed to himself, shaking his head in wonder. *Why can't that girl go anywhere without attracting so much attention? If only she were more like her sister.*

Now she had another man interested in her, and a very influential man at that. Robert scrutinized the young man before him, weighing his intentions. After seeing that Palmer had only the greatest respect and admiration for his daughter, he smiled amiably.

In unison, he and Palmer glanced toward the dance floor where Lois waltzed with one of her numerous dance partners, her vibrant skirts of red whipping wildly about her ankles as she twirled around the floor. "My Lois is indeed bewitching," Robert said, sizing Palmer up with a sweep of his wise hazel eyes. "Perhaps you would like to meet her?"

"Nothing would delight me more, sir."

"Perhaps over dinner at our house tomorrow evening?"

"I gladly accept your kind invitation." Palmer shook Robert's hand warmly, feeling not one ounce of guilt over using his name and social position to finagle an introduction to the lovely Lois. He was willing to do anything just to meet her.

Robert LeJeune was a widower with two beautiful daughters, Nicole and Lois. Nicole at nineteen was a docile young woman, obedient and trustworthy, the perfect Southern lady. Robert's chest swelled with pride every time he looked at her. Dear Nicole was the apple of his eye and would easily make a wonderful wife for any suitable admirer.

Then there was Lois. Robert sighed and shook his graying head sadly. *Mon dieu, that girl was a handful!* Although a great beauty,

Robert's younger daughter was far from meek and mild. Lois was a feisty eighteen-year-old, always looking for something exciting to keep her entertained. And for Robert, her wild ways were a source of constant worry.

"You'd better marry her off soon," advised Father Rousseau, the parish priest, giving Robert a stern frown. "Have her wed before she makes a fatal mistake that could cost her reputation and yours."

Lois had countless young beaus, none of which Robert considered to be suitable enough to marry his baby. "Nothing but bums and clowns," he ranted to Nicole. "Why can't she attract someone respectable? A doctor, a lawyer, a senator's son? Does she actually enjoy hanging around with those hoodlums?"

"Oh Papa, they're hardly hoodlums," Nicole laughed brightly, resting an affectionate hand on his forearm. "They're only young men, still in search of themselves and what life has to offer. Give them time. Someone will prove himself worthy." Her eyes twinkled teasingly as she beguiled him with her smile, and Robert relaxed, giving up his tirade, for that day anyway.

Despite Nicole's encouraging words, none of Lois' current suitors showed any promise whatsoever. He had begun to give up hope, thinking that maybe he would have to marry her off to the next somewhat suitable man.

Then suddenly appeared Palmer Carson, like a ray of welcome sunshine on the cloudiest of days. More than suitable, the man was considered quite a catch. *And he is interested in Lois.* Robert smiled. Palmer Carson was the answer to his prayers.

He informed Lois and Nicole of their dinner plans the next morning over a breakfast of croissants, tea and heavily-creamed chicory coffee. "Palmer Carson of Savannah is coming for dinner tonight," he announced casually, refilling his cup and glancing across the table to his daughters, discreetly gauging their reactions.

Nicole, the good child, beamed dutifully at him, gracefully accepting his statement without question or protest. However, Lois glared over the rim of her coffee cup, raising an eyebrow, her green eyes narrowing suspiciously. "Who is that?" she asked snidely.

"Oh," Robert answered innocently, "just a man."

"Really? You make him sound like a shrine."

"Oh, Papa, I know who he is," Nicole spoke up, gushing her admiration breathlessly. "I met him at the cotillion last night. He was quite charming."

"If he was so charming, why didn't I notice him?" Lois asked, lowering her cup, regarding her sister skeptically.

"I don't know how you missed him, Lois. He *was* the guest of honor."

"So? That doesn't make him wonderful." Lois smirked at her, shrugging indifferently, then turned to Robert, her mouth shaping into a pout. "Do I really have to be here? I'd really rather do anything other than hang around here for another long dinner with another dull man."

"If you've never even seen the man, how do you know he's dull?" Robert asked her, carefully suppressing an amused smile.

"I just have the feeling that you're matchmaking, and your taste in men for me is dreadful."

"Why do you think I'm bringing him here for you?" Robert asked teasingly, his eyes sparkling with mirth. "I could be bringing him here for Nicole."

"You never bring them here for Nicole. You like all her boyfriends."

"I'm not matchmaking, Lois." Robert laid his napkin on the linen tablecloth, fibbing smoothly as he rose from his place at the head of the table. "And yes, mon amour, you do have to be here."

Therefore, it was in a state of great exasperation that Lois LeJeune caught her first glimpse of Palmer Carson. At half-past six, she heard the summoning peal of the front bell and scurried down the upstairs hallway, concealing herself on the landing of the grand staircase as she watched Peter, the valet, welcome him into the front hall.

"Goodness!" She eyed him in astonished appreciation, gripping the banister tightly and leaning forward, sticking her head through the slats in the railing to get a better look. Palmer Carson was a tall man, probably twenty-four or twenty-five years of age, with thick hair the exact color of her roan pony. He had a handsome face, an inviting smile and, in spite of her opposition to her father's matchmaking, Lois LeJeune found herself genuinely attracted to him.

"Mr. Carson, welcome!" Robert hurried out of the study, hailing Palmer enthusiastically.

Hearing her father's voice, Lois straightened quickly, smoothing the skirt of her sage-green gown with her suddenly moist palms as she prepared to descend. "I can't believe Papa finally brought one home actually worth meeting," she mumbled incredulously, unexpectedly nervous at the thought of coming face to face with him.

Nicole glided gracefully down the staircase, humming a cheerful tune, catching sight of Lois out of the corner of her eye. She stopped, breaking off her tune mid-song. "What are you doing, Lois?" she asked, her voice lively with tinkling laughter. "I thought you would already be downstairs. Don't you want to meet our guest?"

"You bet I do," Lois said, scrambling eagerly from her hiding place.

"He's awfully handsome, don't you think?" Nicole murmured, casting an approving gaze down the carpeted stairs.

"Don't get your hopes up, dear Nikki," Lois scowled, hooking her arm firmly through her sister's. "Just remember, Papa brought him here to meet me, not you."

They went into the parlor together, with rosy cheeks and uncharacteristically shy demeanors. Robert rushed to them, his face brightening the moment they entered the room. "Ah, here they are!" he declared enthusiastically. "Come, girls. Meet our guest."

"Miss LeJeune." Coming forward to greet them, Palmer bowed slightly and flashed a dazzling smile, kissing Nicole's hand before turning to Lois. "And Miss LeJeune."

With a wildly thumping heart, Lois lifted her eyes, completely spellbound as she met Palmer's intense gaze. He lifted her hand to his lips, looking deeply into her eyes, and Lois felt the smoldering passion of love at first sight surge through her like a bolt of lightning.

Robert watched them with a pleased smile. He had finally achieved his goal. It had been years in the making, but in the end, had only taken one short moment. His baby girl was finally in love. In the brief instant it took his lips to brush her hand, Lois was lost forever to Palmer Carson.

After a summer courtship of Lake Pontchartrain picnics, French Quarter strolls and long candlelit dinners, Lois married Palmer, climbing from her bedroom window to elope with him, married by Father Rousseau under a starlit sky with Tommy and Nicole standing by as witnesses.

"Boy, is Bea going to be pissed," Tommy remarked, throwing his head back with laughter as Palmer slid a gold wedding band onto Lois' finger.

"She'll get over it," Palmer replied, casting a mischievous look over the top of Lois' veil.

"You can say that now," Tommy shot back boisterously, his eyes dancing with glee. "But you'll be singing a different tune this time next week."

Palmer displayed a sly grin, then beamed at his new wife, amazed at his incredible good fortune. He didn't care what Beatrice thought. Lois was perfect.

"Was Grandmother mad?" Diane looked over at Daisy with an amazed expression, her eyes round with fascination and delight.

Daisy burst into loud giggles. "Oh Lordy, yes!" she said, her head bobbing up and down as she laughed. "I'll never forget the day Palmer brought Lois home. What a day that was! I'd never seen such an uproar! Mother was simply livid, ranting and raving that she'd been deceived. It took years for the pandemonium to die down."

Daisy squelched her laughter, wiping the tears from her eyes. "But your Aunt Cecilia and I were happy for Palmer, and for us. We could see right away what a great girl Lois was. Gosh, she was fun! We did love Lois, although we certainly didn't envy the fight she had ahead with Mother..."

On the train to Savannah, Palmer told his new bride all about his family. "My father, Charles Cameron Carson, is a gentle old guy, several years older than my mother, Beatrice. You'll like Father, Lois, and he'll like you. He's a sweetheart, " Palmer told her, his eyes bright, brimming with happiness every time he looked at his beautiful wife. "However, Mother's another story. Ol' Bea can be a bit stuffy when she sets her mind to it — which is most of the time." He patted Lois' leg reassuringly, noting her apprehensive, wide-eyed stare. "Just ignore her, Shug. It'll be in your best interest.

*This should be a treat,* he chuckled softly to himself. *I can't wait to see Lois and Mother together.*

The newlyweds moved into Carson House, the three-story, white Georgian mansion on the sprawling family estate sixty miles outside Savannah, settling in a private suite of rooms on the third floor. Palmer assumed his role as partner in the law firm and Lois assumed her role as Mrs. Palmer Carson, genteel lady of the manor. And she hated it.

Loving Lois as he did, Palmer understood her feelings and did what he could to ease her adjustment to life with his family. He spent as much time with her as possible, slipping away from the office early on Friday afternoons, taking her on weekend trips into Savannah or to

Atlanta. Catering to her wild, carefree side, he presented Lois with Sadie, a palomino mare, giving her some freedom to get out of the house and come and go as she pleased.

Palmer's younger sisters, Daisy and Cecilia, lived just down a winding dirt road, on separate estates with their husbands. Lois doted on her soft-spoken sisters-in-law, and Daze and Cee found Lois' outrageous ways refreshing. "You are such a welcome change from the boring debutantes we're used to," Cee told her with a grin.

"I'll say!" Daisy agreed, clutching Lois' arm with glee. "Will you teach me to spit, Lois? And chew tobacco and cuss like a man? I really think it would be fun. Will you teach me? Please, please say you will."

"If you really want me to," Lois replied doubtfully, answering her request with an indifferent shrug. *Chew tobacco, indeed! These girls must really think I'm backward*, she thought with amusement. *If that's the case, I think I'll give them a run for their money.*

She set about the task of proving her worth, confiscating packets of tobacco from the stable hands, giving them to Daisy and Cee, watching with humor as they chomped and spit, laughing outrageously when they turned a putrid shade of green. She taught them to ride bareback through the thick pine trees bordering the family estate, wearing pants stolen from their brother's closet. And she schooled Daisy in the fine art of cursing like a sailor, grinning as she tried to find ways to insert her new vocabulary into daily conversation. Beatrice was appalled.

"You'll pay for this one day," she told Lois angrily, pointing a finger in her face.

Lois met her gaze evenly, her green eyes dancing with delight. "Sure," she laughed, smirking defiantly. "We'll see."

"You're not making friends with Mother, Lois," Palmer teased her later in the sanctity of their bedroom, chuckling as she revealed her latest antics with Daisy and Cee. "You could at least try to be nice."

Lois arched a brow, looking at him skeptically. "Not until she does," she said staunchly. "I'll not have her thinking I'm weak."

"Anyone who has spent five minutes with you knows you're not weak."

"Well, nevertheless, I'm certainly not going to give her anything to run with."

Defying Beatrice's wishes, the three young women continued to see one another and became fast friends, sharing long afternoons of devilish fun, spending the sultry days of summer riding horses through the thick forests and wading up to their waists in the fishing holes dotting the flat pastureland surrounding their family home.

"Mother would just die if she saw us!" Daisy hooted with glee as she stripped off her white dotted-swiss dress and flung it onto a tree branch. She grabbed Cee, pulling her screaming all the way down the dock, and threw her in, cackling uproariously and jumping in behind her. Coming up for air, Daisy bunched her slip tight against her waist, giggling as she tromped with Cee through the murky water.

Lois looked on from the bank, shielding her eyes with her forearm, laughing at their childlike antics. *Now, I've corrupted them,* she thought with an evil grin.

"Aren't you coming in, Lois?" Cee called out, ducking her head under and squirting water from her mouth like a fountain.

"Not a chance," Lois smirked, sinking to the ground, finding a cozy spot on the grass and smoothing her skirt over her knees. "And let ol' Bea get wind of it? Not a chance. I'm already in enough trouble over the chewing tobacco."

Despite Beatrice, Lois' early days in Eden Glen were relatively happy and stress free. She played with Daisy and Cecilia and stayed out of Beatrice's way. However, her happy-go-lucky days were short-lived. Shortly after her second wedding anniversary, Lois found out she was pregnant. Numbly, she left the gynecologist, her face white and her eyes huge as she walked directly down the street to Palmer's office.

"I'm going to have a baby," she announced, closing his office door and leaning against it, so frightened she thought her heart would pound out of her chest.

Palmer dropped his pen and left his chair, crossing the room in one flying leap, lifting Lois effortlessly by the waist and spinning around with her in a circle. "A baby, Lo! That's great!" His face was transformed, lit by a jubilant grin.

"Stop it, Palmer. You're making me sick," Lois offered him a weak smile as he set her on the edge of his desk, kneeling before her, cupping his hands over her knee. She looked down at him, her head swimming, her stomach queasy and her face turning green. "I'm scared, Palmer. I don't know anything about babies."

"It'll be fine, Lois. No one knows anything about babies until they have them. You're brilliant, my darling. You'll figure it out." Palmer stood, embracing her with all his might and kissing the top of her head. "Don't worry about anything. Mother will help you."

As Palmer had predicted in the beginning, Lois was crazy about her father-in-law, Charles. The two were very close and remained great friends until the day Charles died. Lois was heartbroken. She had grown to love Charles dearly and hated that he passed away, leaving her to deal with Beatrice alone.

Beatrice Carson was a tall, thin woman with the same reddish-brown hair shared by her son and daughters. Her eyes were chocolate brown, her complexion smooth and creamy, and Lois decided that Beatrice would have been a very attractive woman if she had only smiled, even once. When she first arrived at Carson House, Lois was terribly young and easily intimidated by her, feeling as though she would never be accepted. Things didn't get much better with time.

"You're being silly, Lo," Palmer reassured her smoothly as he ran his hand down the length of her silky black hair. "Mother loves you like her own daughter."

"Then she doesn't think much of Daisy or Cecilia either, does she?"

"Lois, come on, honey."

"Don't 'Lois, come on, honey' me." Lois pulled from his embrace, her eyes flashing defiantly. "Your mother hates me, and she's going to have a fit when she finds out about this baby!"

"Nonsense. She'll be thrilled."

"Yeah, we'll see."

As it turned out, Lois was right, as was evident the night she and Palmer broke the news that Beatrice would soon be a grandmother.

"This will never do!" Beatrice objected, her voice shrill, growing cold as she turned her steely eyes upon Lois. "I will never allow her to raise my grandchildren. She cannot take care of a baby. Dear lord, just look what she's done to your sisters. She has them acting like fools, neglecting their husbands, gallivanting through the countryside in their underwear and splashing around in fish ponds like idiots. And they're grown women! Can you imagine what she'll do to innocent children?"

"Mother, how Cecilia and Daisy choose to act has nothing to do with Lois," Palmer said wearily, cutting his eyes apologetically to his wife.

"I beg to differ." Beatrice directed a reproachful stare his way, chilling him to the bone. "My daughters never acted this way before you brought her here. I will not stand by and see my grandchildren brought up as little heathens."

"I hardly see how you can stop us, if that's how we choose to raise them."

Beatrice stood, gripping the table firmly, her fiery gaze melting him in his seat. "Just watch me," she hissed, pure acid lacing her voice. With a final withering glare, she whirled around, holding her head high, her posture confident and ramrod-straight as she left the room.

Squaring his shoulders, Palmer stared after her, his expression grim. He glanced at Lois and forced a reassuring smile. "She's all talk, Shug. She won't interfere with our children. I won't let her."

Lois obliged him with a thin smile, wishing she could believe him. Beatrice was a tyrant and not easily stopped. She moved her hand across her lap, resting it against the slight swell of her abdomen, feeling a cloud of impending doom settling upon her. No matter how vehemently Palmer reassured her, she couldn't shake the feeling that they had a long eighteen years ahead of them.

Just before Geoff's birth, Palmer became heavily involved in a murder trial, forcing him to spend long hours in Savannah, sometimes working late into the night. "I wish you were home more," Lois complained, propping her swollen ankles up on his lap. "I'm so lonely here at night with only your mother for company."

"I know, honey," Palmer said, tenderly massaging her legs. "But if I don't give this case my full attention, my client will hang and I'll never be able to live with myself."

One important case followed another, and another, until soon Palmer was rarely home at all. Taking advantage of the situation, Beatrice acquired the upper hand, using every opportunity to rule a tired and very pregnant Lois with an iron fist, deviously seeking a way to take control of her grandchildren as soon as they arrived, determined that they be raised in a fashion suitable of their aristocratic lineage.

Plagued by difficult births, first with Geoff, then three years later with Diane, Lois was weak. Beatrice encouraged her to rest, convincing her that she didn't have the strength to tend to children.

"I know you want me to die, but I'm not going to," Lois sputtered loudly from her hospital bed, earning surprised stares and double-takes from the nursing staff. "I'm going to live, Beatrice — just to spite you."

"Now, Lois. Don't be a goose," Beatrice's melodic tone gushed sugar. "Of course, you're not going to die, but you have been through quite an ordeal. You just follow doctor's orders, rest and get your strength back. I'll take care of the rest."

Too drained to use good judgment, Lois made the fatal mistake of letting down her guard, and Beatrice moved in for the kill, installing a nanny in the nursery while Lois wasn't looking. And there Tressa stayed, becoming a permanent fixture, with Beatrice nixing any chance of an overthrow.

"You'll not be taking charge of my children," Lois informed her the day she was released to bed rest at Carson House, glaring defiantly at her mother-in-law from her sick bed. "As soon as I recover, that nanny is gone."

Standing in the entryway, Beatrice flashed an acidic smile, a self-satisfied glint illuminating her icy brown eyes. "You will do no such thing, my dear. Tressa stays." She moved with catlike grace into the room, standing over Lois, her smile widening to a malicious grin. "You aren't so high and mighty now, are you, with Palmer busy at work and Daisy and Cecilia in Europe. I knew under that white-trash demeanor you weren't anything but spineless and weak. You can't even get out of bed. It's taken me years to get to this point, but I finally have you where I want you. Now, I'm in control."

That evening, Palmer strolled in from work, finding Lois propped up in bed, her brow creased in perturbed concentration. "Hey Lo," he said jovially, bending down to give her a kiss. "What's the matter, honey? You look fit to be tied."

"I think your mother's poisoning me. That's why I'm not getting any better."

"What?" Palmer stared incredulously, curbing his urge to chuckle when he saw the serious look on her face.

"Any other woman with a three-month-old baby would be out running marathons by now."

"Hardly," Palmer grinned, removing his jacket and taking a seat on the edge of the bed. "So, you think Beatrice is trying to poison you."

"She is. Why else would she give Daisy and Cecilia the money to go on a European vacation? She plans to get rid of me while they're gone."

Palmer couldn't help it. He had to laugh, earning an irritated glare from his agitated wife. "Oh Lois, you're being ridiculous!" he said, catching his breath, wiping amused tears from his eyes.

"Laugh if you want to, but I will not eat one more bite of anything that woman makes for me."

"If that's the case, then I highly suggest you learn to cook. If not, you won't have to worry about my mother poisoning you. You'll simply starve to death," he leaned across, kissing her tightly pursed lips, his eyes twinkling merrily. "Look, honey. Daisy and Cee had that tour planned long before you ever came along. They only postponed it when Father got sick. And as far as your not getting well goes," he took her affectionately by the shoulders, his expression tender and concerned, "you've had a very hard time with both babies and it will take some time for you to fully mend."

"Now you sound like your mother. The two of you obviously don't know me very well."

"Lois, darling, I know you inside and out. You are by far the strongest woman I've ever known. But even you can't outwit Mother Nature. You will have to heal in a timely manner, just like the rest of us."

*I may not be able to outwit Mother Nature, but I will outwit Mother Carson,* Lois thought determinedly. *It will just take a little time, but in the end, I will come out on top.*

That's what Diane remembered most about her childhood. At a very young age, she had figured out that Lois was her mother, but couldn't recall her being around much during those early years. Thinking back to the face that appeared most above her crib, she remembered not her dark-haired mother's but the mocha-hued face of Tressa, the young girl Beatrice hand-picked to take care of her. Diane had to give her credit. Beatrice knew a good nanny when she saw one. Tressa did an excellent job and was very attentive, showing the Carson children great love and affection. In theory, Diane should not have wanted for anything, but in reality, she did. In reality, she wanted her mother.

Although she and Geoff were sheltered as much as possible from her influence, Diane knew that Lois loved them. She knew from Lois' nightly visits to the nursery. Every night her mother slipped in, tiptoeing silently to bend over their beds, relying on the light of the moon to gaze lovingly into their angelic slumbering faces, kissing Diane and Geoff tenderly on the forehead before sneaking out again. "Je t'aime, bébé," she would whisper softly in Diane's ear, smoothing her hair back from her face, her touch gentle and soothing. "Pretty soon, I promise, we shall have our way."

Lois bided her time, playing Beatrice's game as she slowly regained her strength and gumption, discreetly fighting her mother-in-law's ironclad reign by seeing her children on the sly. Tressa never told, and Geoff and Diane were thrilled. Over the years, Diane watched Lois gain ground and cheered her on, knowing in her heart that eventually Lois would win.

Sure enough, as Lois grew older, so did Beatrice, finally having a massive heart attack and becoming too weak to fight her feisty daughter-in-law. Lois hired a nurse and banished Beatrice to the east wing of the house, vowing to never see her again, but not before she helped settle her in.

Arriving in her new suite of rooms, Beatrice sat wordlessly in her wheelchair, appearing broken and feeble, watching as the nurse folded and put away her things. Pausing in the doorway and seeing the pitiful look upon her face, Lois almost felt sorry for her. *Maybe I've been too hasty,* she thought, staring guiltily at the elderly woman. *Maybe I should have just let her be.*

Beatrice sensed her presence and cast a wickedly keen glance her way. It was then that Lois realized nothing had changed. Despite her weakened appearance, Beatrice was still Beatrice and deserved anything she got.

Lois strolled nonchalantly into the room dressed to the nines in a scarlet taffeta gown and stood over her mother-in-law, placing a hand on each armrest and smiling smugly into her pinched, wrinkled face. "You aren't so high and mighty now, are you?" she remarked lightly, throwing Beatrice's own words back at her. "You've lived long enough to finally get a taste of your own medicine. It's taken me years to get to this point, but I finally have you where I want you. I'm finally in control, and I have to admit, it feels good."

"If I had to be bested," Beatrice shocked her by speaking, her voice gravelly and weak, her sharp eyes never leaving Lois' face. "At least it was by you. You're a strong woman, Lois, and a perfect match for my son."

Lois straightened, taken aback, careful to keep her surprise to herself. "Well," she said, her tone bright and confident. "That's a lovely sentiment, Bea, but unfortunately, it is much too little and very much too late."

Beatrice flinched as if Lois had slapped her, her steadfast glare exuding absolute hatred. Lois smiled complacently, smoothing her skirt, and then gracefully exited the room, feeling Beatrice's piercing eyes like twin daggers in her back.

So in the end, Lois won, putting Beatrice in her place, and assumed her rightful place as lady of the manor by the time Geoff and Diane returned from their first year at their respective finishing schools. With Beatrice out of the way, Diane and Lois grew closer, spending all of

Diane's school breaks together, traveling to New Orleans to visit Grandfather Robert and Aunt Nicole or venturing to New York for a shopping spree. They toured Europe, staying in posh hotels, vacationing in the Alps, cruising around Greece, flying to Paris for fittings with top designers. Diane was thrilled with the wonderful sights and expensive clothing, but was more thrilled to finally spend unlimited time with her mother.

"This summer has been so much fun and I'm really going to miss you. You don't have to go away to school if you don't want to, Diane," Lois told her as she watched her pack. "Miss Colleen's was Bea's idea, not mine. This is your last year. You could stay home, go to public school, be a normal kid, if you'd like."

"That's okay, Mother. I'll go ahead and go. I really don't mind Miss Colleen's," Diane replied, her light-hearted smile sincere. She actually liked it there, finding Miss Colleen's School for Young Women welcome relief after so many years of Lois' and Beatrice's tumultuous game of tug-of-war.

"You want to be there?"

"I have friends there, Mother, and it's good experience for me."

Lois slapped her palm to her forehead, shaking her head sadly. "Good Lord, Diane. I'm too late. Beatrice brainwashed you. No telling how many years it will take me to deprogram you."

"Do you always have to be so melodramatic?"

"I'm not being melodramatic. We're talking about Beatrice, Diane. Her touch can be deadly."

"Oh Mother, honestly." Diane slammed the lid of her trunk shut, offering her an irritated stare. "I will miss you — I really will, but I can't wait to get away from you for a little while. I love you, but sometimes you drive me crazy."

# 10

Diane graduated from Stephens College at twenty-two with a degree in liberal arts and no husband, fiancé or steady boyfriend, a detail that bothered her tremendously. Grandmother Beatrice had long since passed away, but her nagging voice lingered in Diane's mind, ringing out clearly an instilled old-school belief: "*An unattached young woman of your age, Diane, is destined to be a spinster.*"

Diane was perplexed by her lack of attachment. In her four years at Stephens, she had socialized with students from other colleges and had many first dates, several second dates, but nothing more permanent or lasting. She returned to her family home in Eden Glen with no hope of a husband and forlornly expressed her dismay to Lois as she unpacked her trunk in her large, airy bedroom on the second floor of Carson House.

"I did my best, Mother. I really did. I joined a sorority and attended every social event possible. You remember my roommate, Catherine Magill? She had a date nearly every night and just about as many proposals of marriage. I just don't understand what I did wrong."

Lois recovered from her surprise and issued a hearty laugh. "Diane, please!" she said, dismissing her daughter's concerns with a flippant wave of her hand. "I think it's admirable that you didn't get engaged to the first schmuck who asked you. It just goes to show you that you don't need a man to be happy."

Diane sighed heavily, giving her mother an irritated scowl. "Don't you listen at all? I didn't get engaged to the first schmuck who asked me, because *no one asked me*." She snatched a starched shirt from her suitcase, snapping it angrily before shoving it onto a hanger and stuffing it into her overflowing closet.

"And who says I'm happy?" she retorted, whirling around to face Lois with her hands on her hips. "I'm not happy, not yet anyway. I don't ask for much out of life. All I want is a comfortable home, a husband who loves me and a house full of kids."

Lois rolled her eyes, clearly aggravated by what she considered Diane's lack of ambition. "For heaven's sake, Diane, there's more to life than being married and having children."

"How would you know? You married Daddy when you were eighteen."

"Only because Palmer was exceptional. Believe you me, missy, I would have never considered settling down with any of those clowns who courted me in New Orleans. If Palmer hadn't come along and swept me off my feet, I would have been quite content to take care of myself forever."

"You can say that now," Diane said, frowning in exasperation. "You weren't old enough then to know any better."

Lois slid from her seat at the foot of the canopy bed and took Diane gently by the shoulders, clucking her tongue affectionately. "Chère, there's a mate for you out there somewhere. Just be patient. Your time will come. Don't be rushing it along. Live a little. Enjoy your freedom."

Diane went about her days in a mundane fashion, filling her empty hours with volunteer work at local hospitals and charity fundraisers for various community organizations. Much to her dismay, her social life was almost nonexistent. The population of Eden Glen hadn't produced any more favorable suitors for her than it had when she was growing up, and her exposure to the cream of the crop of Savannah was minimal. Her shy, introverted personality didn't do anything to help her cause. Despite the fact that she was extraordinarily pretty, the men Diane encountered seemed to prefer her more gregarious female counterparts.

Lois looked on in frustration as Diane struggled to find her place in the great scheme of things, wishing fervently that her only daughter had inherited just one ounce of her own flirtatious disposition.

"For God's sake, Diane, speak up," Lois fussed, standing next to her during the Christmas dance at the country club, elbowing Diane sharply in the ribs as yet another potential admirer walked away. "What on earth makes you so shy, girlie? You'll never hold a man's attention if he can't even hear what you're saying."

"Mother, please." Diane flushed bright red as Lois' words echoed through the crowded ballroom, causing elegantly coifed heads to turn in their direction. "Lower your voice; you're embarrassing me."

"Well, you should be embarrassed. Spark up, for heaven's sake! For a girl who only wants to get married and have babies, you sure let a lot of fine men just slip right through your fingers."

"Maybe I just haven't seen anyone worth my attention."

"You know what your problem is?"

"No, but I'm fairly confident that you're going to tell me."

"Your problem is that you're boring."

"Thanks a lot, Mother."

"No, I don't mean that in a bad sort of way. I mean that you're generic, standoffish, appear cool and aloof. That puts a man off. You gotta smile at 'em, Diane — laugh, dance, joke, tell them what they want to hear. That's what I did."

"Isn't that flirtatious behavior what attracted all those clowns in New Orleans?"

"Listen here, missy. I may've had to put up with a few losers, but look where it got me. That very same flirtatious behavior is what landed your father."

"That might have worked for you, Mother, but it's not going to work for me. I don't have the personality for it."

"You're bland, like tapioca."

"Some men like tapioca."

"I'd love to see the one who does," Lois huffed, walking away, shaking her head. "What on earth am I going to do with that girl?"

Diane met Jay Forest the following spring at her brother Geoff's wedding to Patricia Langford, one of Virginia's elite. Geoff met Patricia while in law school, and they became engaged shortly after graduation, postponing the wedding until Geoff had taken the bar exam and established himself in the family practice.

The wedding was held in Patricia's hometown, a quaint little city in Loudoun County, just outside of Washington, D.C., in northern Virginia. Diane traveled to the wedding with her parents, riding in the back seat of the Mercedes wedged between her aunts Daisy and Cecilia.

Cecilia had lost her husband of thirty years the previous summer when Prentice passed away unexpectedly after a severe bout of pneumonia. Diane had been sad for her. "Auntie Cee must be very lost and lonely without Uncle Prentice," she mused aloud, looking to her mother for confirmation.

"Ordinarily, I might agree with you," Lois replied with a shrug. "But don't feel sorry for Cecilia because Prentice is gone. I think she loathed him for years. His death may very well have been the key that opened her cage. I doubt very seriously that she feels anything, except a profound sense of freedom."

"Mother! You ought to be ashamed."

"Why, missy? There's no shame in the truth."

"If Auntie Cee despised Uncle Prentice so much, why didn't she just get divorced?"

"And disgrace the Carson family with something as scandalous as a divorce?" Lois raised an eyebrow in mock indignation. "Beatrice would never stand for it."

"Mother, Grandmother has been dead close to seven years now."

"She may be dead, but trust me, old Bea is not resting in peace. I'm certain she's still wandering the earth in shackles, rattling her chains, waiting for an opportune moment to make her presence known."

Aunt Daisy remained married to Daniel, her husband of twenty-nine years. However, today she was traveling alone. Daniel had been detained in Savannah with unfinished business, but would be flying into Dulles International Airport the following day to join them for the wedding. Unlike Cecilia and Prentice, Auntie Daze and Uncle Daniel appeared to be happy, as did her own parents. With Daisy snoozing soundly against her shoulder, Diane peeked into the front seat, smiling softly as she observed Lois and Palmer.

Lois was snuggled very close to him, chattering animatedly and smiling as she nudged him with her shoulder, reaching up to stroke his graying hair softly with her well-manicured hand. Diane beamed happily, knowing how in love her parents were. As far as they were concerned, there was no one else in the world.

"Still as much in love as they were the day he brought her home to Carson House twenty-seven years ago," Auntie Cee whispered in Diane's ear, taking note of Diane's enraptured gaze. "Theirs is the kind of love to strive for, Diane dearie — the kind of love that endures for all time."

"I'm trying, Auntie Cee. I'm trying, but it's a lot easier said than done," Diane smiled wistfully, turning her head. She stared out the car window, taking in the breathtaking rolling green mountains of Virginia's scenic highways, intermingled with soft pink cherry blossoms and pristine white dogwoods. "It really is beautiful here," she murmured. "It's amazing that Geoff managed such an impressive setting for his wedding." *At least he's having a wedding*, she thought, letting out a heavy sigh.

"You know, Diane, sometimes the right man comes along when you least expect it." Cecilia spoke up, breaking into her thoughts.

Diane glanced back at her. "Like Uncle Prentice?" she asked, raising a teasing brow.

"Hell no. Certainly not like Prentice. I'm still waiting for mine."

"Auntie Cee, you ought to be ashamed," Diane scolded, giving her a stern look. "How can you say such a thing about Uncle Prentice? I swear, you're becoming more and more like Mother every day."

"And is that such a bad thing?" Lois asked, turning in her seat, eyeing Diane with ill humor.

"I guess that all depends on how you look at it." Diane dropped the subject and turned away, keeping her attention focused on the view outside her car window until finally they arrived at a charming little bed and breakfast where they would spend the next five days.

Diane first caught sight of Jay Forest four days later at the wedding reception. Elegant in her lavender bridesmaid gown and upswept hair, she stood with the noisy congregation gathered at the punch bowl, half-heartedly mingling and engaging in idle chit-chat until she could gracefully exit.

*I simply loathe crowds, especially crowds like this,* she thought miserably, feeling the uncomfortable throb of an impending headache starting at her temple as she offered her grandiose cousin Oscar a winning smile. *These have to be the most pretentious people on the face of the earth. I would much rather be back at the bed and breakfast, spending a quiet evening with a good book. I hope Geoff appreciates my great sacrifice.*

She caught a glimpse of a passing relative and grabbed Auntie Cee's arm. "Wasn't that your cousin Morton?" she asked curiously, nodding toward his balding head.

Cecilia looked around, tiptoeing to see over the crowd, her flower-covered hat teetering precariously atop her highly-teased gray hair. "Yes, Diane," she answered, craning her neck, her brow creased in concentration as she studied the retreating figure. "I believe it was."

"I thought he was in prison."

"He was. He must've gotten out on parole."

"Obviously. I wonder if Geoff knows he's here? He'd have a fit if he knew the black sheep of the family crashed his wedding."

"Why don't we tell him then?" Cee cackled devilishly, nudging Diane in the side.

Diane rewarded her humor with a consenting smile, but chided her just the same. "Auntie Cee. Behave now. I wouldn't do that to Patricia."

"Seriously, Diane, I don't think Morty would crash. He has a little more class than that — a little more, but not much. I think your mother invited him."

Diane nodded, her lip curling in exasperation. "Of course she would," she said. *It would be just like her to do something like that. Sometimes Mother displays no sense whatsoever.*

"Speak of the devil," Diane murmured as Lois happened by in a swirl of periwinkle blue organza. Diane caught her arm, pulling her aside. "Mother!" she hissed incredulously. "Did you invite Morton Carson to Geoff's wedding?"

"Yes, missy. I did. What of it?" Lois eyed her daughter defensively. A spasm of irritation crossed her face as she firmly stood her ground while balancing two plates overflowing with Swedish meatballs and spring rolls.

"I cannot believe you did that."

"Why not? It would be rude not to invite your father's cousin."

"You know how Geoff would feel about having a convicted felon at his wedding reception."

"What Geoff doesn't know won't hurt him. As caught up as he is in the festivities, I doubt he even notices. Besides, I hardly think of someone paroled for tax evasion as armed and dangerous," Lois scolded her, her eyes flashing angrily. "Honestly, Diane, get over it. Sometimes you're a bigger snob than your brother." She and Diane locked eyes, glaring at one another in a feisty battle of wills until Diane dropped her gaze and looked away, sorry that she confronted her.

Satisfied with her victory, Lois offered a thin smile, her expression taut and stormy. "Now, if you'll excuse me, I'll take your father his plate before it gets any colder." She marched away, her full skirt rustling briskly against her ankles.

"Oh, now you've made her mad," Cecilia fretted, wringing her hands and biting her lip as she watched Lois push through the crowd.

"If I hadn't made her mad about that, it would've been something else. Lately, in her eyes, I can't do anything right." Diane shook her head in disgust, patting Cecilia's arm reassuringly before making her way back to the punch bowl. "I might as well have another drink. It's going to be a long night."

She lingered by the punch bowl, refilling her champagne punch, overcome suddenly by an eerie tingling along her spine, getting the distinct feeling she was being watched. She turned her head, keeping her eyes carefully veiled, expecting to meet Lois' piercing stare. Instead, what she found was quite extraordinary.

She spotted him across the room, leaning casually against the rose-covered banister of the grand staircase. He was tall — well over six feet—with the build of an athlete and the smile of a Greek god. His thick hair was as golden as summer rays of sunlight, and his eye-pleasing presence filled the entire room, radiating an aura that held Diane's fascination. As she studied him, their eyes met and Diane flushed, quickly averting her gaze. She turned her attention to Patricia's boring cousin Francis, suppressing a yawn as she politely pretended to listen to his mindless babbling.

Diane encountered the handsome stranger again, this time outside in the Langford rose garden. Tired of the constant chatter and noise, she inched toward the exit and retreated outside, rubbing her temples, hoping desperately for five minutes of peace and quiet. "I simply cannot listen to one more word out of Francis' mouth," she mumbled wearily, stepping out into the courtyard, closing the French doors behind her.

She leaned against the doors and sighed heavily with relief, then moved toward a wicker settee she spotted nestled in a semi-circle of fragrant rose bushes. She settled back gratefully against the inviting cushions, inhaling the perfume drifting from the coral-colored blossoms surrounding her hiding place. She closed her eyes, reveling her moment of silence.

"I think you have the best seat in the house."

A deep male voice invaded her domain. She had been discovered. With a reluctant moan, she opened her eyes, ready to engage in more polite conversation with a total stranger. Her breath caught in her throat as she turned to the person standing next to her. It was the handsome blond man from the foyer.

"Hello," she exhaled, struggling to maintain her composure as she stared into his engaging olive-green eyes, taking in the beauty of him all over again in one sweeping glance.

"Out for some fresh air?" he asked. She nodded breathlessly and he alluded to the empty spot next to her. "May I join you?"

"Of course," she said, sliding over. "I just needed a few minutes away from all the commotion."

He grinned in agreement. "I take it you don't care for these society weddings any more than I do."

"I'm used to them. I've been raised on them."

"Well, so have I, but it doesn't mean I have to like them," he scoffed. "If I weren't so fond of Patricia, I wouldn't have come at all." He flashed a dazzling smile, leaning his head toward hers. "So how about you and I blow out of here?"

Diane blinked in surprise, the shy child in her taken aback by his forwardness. *Daddy would just have a fit*, she thought incredulously, well aware that Palmer Carson would throttle this mystery man for even suggesting his daughter leave a family wedding with a perfect stranger. It just wasn't proper.

"I can't just leave," she stammered, flustered, offering the first excuse she could think of. "The reception isn't anywhere close to being over."

"Oh come on, what would you really miss?" he asked, his eyes dancing naughtily. "A little cake cutting, a boring toast, some drinking of champagne. And you don't have to worry about fighting to catch the bouquet. I'll happily rid you of any need to compete to be the next one married." He leaned closer, sliding a casual arm around her slender shoulders. "Let's just cut out of here, find a cozy spot where we can be alone and have our own party."

Diane felt his warm breath on her ear as he nibbled her lobe and she drew her breath in sharply, shocked by such a seductive proposition from a complete stranger. *Just who does he think he is?* she fumed. She was Diane Carson, a proper Southern lady, not some loose woman or streetwalker he could just pick up with some alluring words. She elbowed him angrily in the side, shrugging his arm from her shoulder, glaring into his dumbfounded face with livid eyes.

"I'd take you up on that tempting offer, but I think my brother might be a bit offended," she said huffily. "After all, this is his wedding."

The Greek god appeared astonished, but instead of backing off as Diane had hoped, he chuckled, throwing his head back with hearty laughter. "So you're little Diane," he said, taking a second look at her through eyes twinkling with good humor. "Geoff's baby sister. I've heard all about you."

Diane narrowed her eyes, regarding him suspiciously. Being a friend of her arrogant brother certainly didn't endear him to her, and he wasn't doing or saying anything on his own to fall into her good graces. "And just who are you?" she demanded, crossing her arms defiantly.

"I'm sorry, how rude of me," he said, extending his hand. "I'm Jay Forest, a distant cousin of your new sister-in-law, Patricia."

"How do you know my brother?"

"I went to law school with Geoff. In fact," Jay grinned proudly, "I'm the one responsible for introducing Geoffrey to his new bride."

"Why? What did she do to you?"

"You are a spirited little thing," Jay said, raking Diane up and down appreciatively. "You certainly don't look like a mealy-mouthed spinster to me."

"Who said I was?"

"Your darling brother, just two days ago, in fact," Jay patted her arm, smiling broadly at Diane's insulted glare. "Tone down, little sister. I just said that you didn't fit his description. To the contrary, I think you're quite attractive. And feisty. I like that in a woman."

"I don't care what you like," Diane responded hotly, leaping from the bench and stalking up the cobblestone walk toward the house. "I've had enough peace and quiet for one evening. Now if you'll excuse me, I think I'll just go back inside."

Jay appeared at her side, a huge smile on his face and amusement leaping mischievously in his eyes. "Allow me to escort you, Miss Carson," he said, suppressing his laughter as he hooked his muscular arm through hers.

Diane snatched her arm away, shooting him a loathing look. "No, thank you," she said through clenched teeth. "I can make it just fine on my own." She flounced away, ignoring the entertained chuckle that followed her up the walk.

"I'm sure you can," Jay said under his breath, continuing to stare after her admiringly, unscathed, even at the rarity of being shot down by such a stunning woman. He never thought it would happen. He'd finally found a woman stimulating enough to spend time with. Diane Carson might just be one challenge he would have to take.

For as much as he irritated her, Diane could not keep her eyes off Jay Forest, watching him for the remainder of the reception, following his every move from beneath a veil of thick russet lashes. He was impossibly abrasive, yet undeniably appealing. Everything about him called out to her, urging her to talk to him, to be by his side. Nevertheless, she stubbornly refused her inner longing, holding her ground from her spot next to the bride's table, smiling and talking to her new sister-in-law instead of satisfying her own infatuation.

As Geoff and Patricia left for their Bermuda honeymoon, Diane stood beside her parents on the steps of the Langford mansion, watching jealously through a rain of rice and birdseed as the incredible Jay Forest linked arms with two of Patricia's bridesmaids and made his way toward a waiting limousine.

*I could just kick myself,* she thought, frowning unhappily. She'd done it again. Once again, she had a chance with a magnificent man, and once again, she had blown it, pushing him away with her staunchly reserved demeanor instead of being receptive, or even just being nice.

Usually, it didn't bother her, but this time, it was different. This time she sincerely cared about the impression she left, and she had the distinct feeling that the impression she had left with Jay Forest was not favorable.

Diane returned to Georgia the following morning with Lois, Palmer and Auntie Cee, staring glumly out the window of the Mercedes, thinking of Jay Forest, furious with herself for letting him get away.

"Diane, what did you think of Patricia's cousin?" Lois' brisk voice cut through her dismal fog, startling her, and Diane glanced over her shoulder into her mother's inquiring face, filled with embarrassed warmth over having her thoughts read.

"Jay? I found him unpleasant and highly irritating," she replied, sniffing indignantly, turning her head so Lois couldn't see the rosy flush creeping onto her cheeks.

Lois raised an eyebrow, watching her daughter's uncharacteristic reaction knowingly. "Oh, did you now?" she said, pressing her lips together, checking the pleased grin that threatened to stretch across her face. Diane wasn't fooling her. She knew Diane as well as she knew the back of her own hand, and, highly irritating or not, Diane had a definite crush on Jay Forest. Lois could see it in the depths of her velvety-brown eyes. It was there — the all-too-familiar look of a girl in love.

"Well, I hate to hear that, missy," she added, merry laughter tinkling in her voice as she struggled in vain to take on a more scolding tone. "You'll have to get over that, Diane. He's family now, and I'm sure you'll be seeing him again."

"Oh joy," Diane rolled her eyes in exasperation for Lois' benefit, even though she could barely conceal her elated smile. "I can hardly wait."

Back in Eden Glen, Diane settled into a routine, going about day-to-day life, working part time at the local chapter of the Red Cross and spending the rest of her time with Lois and her aunts. She thought of Jay Forest almost daily, the memory of how much he annoyed her erased by the memory of how incredibly handsome he was, and how very irresistible.

*How will I ever get over meeting a man like him?* She rested her chin in her hands, sighing forlornly, lost in a miserable daydream of love thrown away.

"What's wrong with you, Diane dear?" Auntie Cee asked, gazing worriedly at Diane as she lay slumped in the chaise lounge on Lois' screened-in back porch, staring dejectedly out at the sparkling pond on the east side of the house. "Are you sick?"

*Lovesick, maybe*, Lois thought wryly, lowering her well-worn copy of *Gone with the Wind* and looking over at her sullen daughter. "Nothing's wrong with her, Cee," she said. "She's just decided to spend the rest of her days growing old on the back porch here with us."

"Nonsense," Daisy spoke up from her chair in the corner, dropping her needlepoint to her ample lap, eyeing her only niece sternly. "You're much too young to wile away your time with us, Diane. You need to get out, be with people your own age and meet the man of your dreams."

*I've already met the man of my dreams*, Diane thought crossly, folding her arms against her chest and turning her back to them. *And by now, he probably doesn't even remember that I exist.*

Patricia and Geoff returned from their honeymoon and moved into Carson House, taking a suite of rooms down the hall from Diane's on the second floor. Patricia was a lovely girl, bubbly and cheerful, and

Diane welcomed her company, finding that her presence helped tremendously in breaking up the monotony that had become her life.

Patricia got Diane out of the house, insisting that she accompany her shopping and sightseeing in nearby Savannah. "I have to see everything there is to see, so I can tell my Mama all about it," Patricia drawled, dragging Diane toward the waiting BMW, her wedding gift from Geoff. "I need a good history lesson, Diane. What good is it to live in the *real* South if you don't know anything at all about it?"

During their frequent outings, Diane discreetly interrogated Patricia about her captivating cousin, gathering bits and pieces of information about him as often as she could, careful never to rouse Patricia's suspicions with her numerous prying questions.

"What about your cousin Jay? Why isn't he married?" she asked, keeping her tone nonchalant, studying her fingernails as they strolled through Forsyth Park.

"Jay? I don't think he'll ever get married," Patricia replied, pretending she didn't see the intrigued light in Diane's eyes. "He's too picky."

"Really."

"Yes, really. He's gone through more women in the last year than I've gone through pantyhose."

"That many?"

"Yep. It'll take a downright miracle to get that boy to the altar. Like I said, he's too picky. He'll settle for nothing less than a gorgeous woman with a brain, a great personality and a sense of humor to boot."

*Well, that counts me out,* Diane thought, forcing a bright smile as she faced Patricia. "Well then, it appears he's destined to stay a bachelor. And it's his own fault too. No one can possibly live up to his expectations."

Jay Forest resurfaced when Diane least expected it, showing up in Savannah just three months after Geoff and Patricia's wedding. Geoff returned home from the law office, joining the rest of the family in the formal dining room for the evening meal. He kissed Patricia affectionately then took the high-backed chair next to her, casually sipping iced tea and engaging in pleasant dinner conversation.

"I forgot to tell you, Patricia," he said, smiling at his pretty bride. "Your cousin Jay's in town. Breezed into the office today, out of the blue, throwing around so much charm that my secretary will never be the same."

Diane stopped mid-bite, staring open-mouthed at her brother, her extraordinary reaction to Geoff's announcement going unnoticed as he and Patricia continued their exchange of words.

"Really?" Patricia grinned with delight. "What's he doing here?"

"He says he's here looking for a job."

"What happened to the firm in D.C.?"

Geoff shook his head, peering skeptically over the rim of his crystal iced tea glass. "I haven't a clue. I thought he would love the prestige of the firm in Washington, but apparently I was wrong. Something has suddenly made him want to move south."

Diane choked, dropping her fork, sending it clattering onto her salad plate, earning startled looks from everyone at the table as she clutched her throat with her hand. "Here?" she sputtered, grabbing her water glass, gawking wide-eyed at Geoff. "Surely you're not thinking of hiring him?"

Palmer and Geoff exchanged a puzzled glance, looking from Diane's flushed cheeks to Lois' knowing smile. "Geoff and I are seriously considering it, darling," Palmer replied, creasing his brow in concern. "Is that a problem?"

"Not for me, Daddy," Diane lied, keeping her tone nonchalant. "But don't you think your clients might find him offensive?"

"Jay? Offensive?" Geoff threw back his ruddy head in laughter. "You've got to be joking, Diane. Having him on board could only be an asset. The guy oozes charm. We'll be rich."

"How long will he be in town? When will I get to see him?" Patricia interrupted, tugging eagerly at Geoff's arm.

"Soon." Geoff looked down at his watch. "In fact, I expect him any time now. He said he'd be out after dinner."

Diane nearly jumped out of her skin, panic-stricken, and hurriedly pushed back her chair, tossing her linen napkin onto her untouched plate. "Excuse me, please," she said, lowering her eyes and rushing from the room, her quickly vanishing figure followed by four sets of dumbfounded eyes.

"What's her problem?" Geoff asked, watching his sister bolt up the front staircase, taking the steps two at a time in her hurry to escape to her room. "What gives, Mother?" He stared down the table, starting a chain reaction of heads pivoting in Lois' direction.

Lois carefully guarded her perception of Diane's abrupt departure, smiling innocently in the face of their inquiring stares. "I don't know,

Geoff. You know how odd your sister is sometimes. Maybe she's just not feeling well," she answered, settling casually back in her chair.

"She did look a little peaked," Patricia added, glancing toward the stairwell with concern.

"Yes, but not that peaked," Geoff noted, eyeing his mother. "This doesn't, per chance, have anything to do with Jay Forest, does it?"

"What are you asking me for, son?" Lois asked, her eyes dancing with mirth. "You're the one who knows everything. Figure it out for yourself."

Jay arrived at seven-thirty, wheeling up in a late model Jaguar, springing from the car with great excitement and enthusiasm. Keeping her face carefully hidden in the folds of the delicate lace drapes, Diane watched from an upstairs window as he sauntered toward the veranda, viewing his good looks with a scornful eye. His confident demeanor brought to mind his overbearing arrogance, and Diane dropped the curtain, huffing loudly and flouncing away from the window just as Jay rang the bell.

"Hello, Patty." His warm voice floated up the stairwell as Patricia squealed down the hallway and threw herself into his waiting arms. Diane paused, listening to his voice, captivated by its rich sound. She leaned over the banister, craning her neck for a glimpse of him.

"Married life must agree with you, cousin," Jay told Patricia with a broad smile as they made their way arm in arm down the corridor. "You're just glowing."

"Hello, Jay." Palmer came from the library, extending his hand warmly. Geoff and Lois closely followed, offering cheerful greetings to their guest. One family member was obviously missing and Jay looked around expectantly.

"Where's your sister, Geoffrey?" he asked with a grin. "I was rather looking forward to seeing her again."

"She's upstairs, laying down," Geoff informed him as they passed through the arched doorway of the richly paneled room. "She was fine until she heard you were coming. Apparently the thought of seeing you again has made her sick." He slapped Jay heartily on the back, chuckling loudly as if he had just told the world's finest joke.

"Some day, Geoff," Diane scowled, balling up her fists, muttering under her breath as she stomped down the thickly carpeted corridor to her suite at the end. She entered the room, leaving the door slightly ajar, and flopped face-first across her bed.

Throughout the long evening, she listened to the jovial voices drifting from downstairs, becoming familiar with Jay Forest's deep laughter and melodic voice, smiling in spite of herself each time she heard it. Midway through the evening, Lois stuck her head in the door. Diane lay bundled under scalloped sheets, chin in her hands, head cocked to the side, straining to hear the conversation from the library.

"You look pretty silly sitting up here all by yourself," Lois said, padding across the room and sitting on the edge of the bed. "Aren't you coming down?"

Diane lifted her eyebrows, looking up at Lois with disdainful eyes. "Oh, I don't think so. Not as long as *he's* here."

Lois laughed at Diane's expression. "He's not really that bad, Diane. In fact, I rather like him," she said, reaching out to brush a wild strand of red hair from Diane's forehead. "Absolutely breathtaking young man — almost bewitching. Throws off plenty of natural sex appeal."

"Mother, stop, please. That kind of talk from you is disgusting," Diane protested, shooting Lois a mortified look. "You can think what you want, but I don't want to hear anything else about him."

"I don't know why your mind is so dead set against him."

"Didn't I just say I didn't want to talk about him?" Throwing back the covers, Diane sat up, glaring impatiently at her mother. "You're entitled to your opinion, and I'm entitled to mine. I only pray that Daddy has the good sense not to hire him so I don't have to see him all the time."

Jay settled into his new position at the Carson Law Firm the following month, moving into a comfortable three-bedroom townhouse in Savannah and becoming a regular visitor to Carson House. Patricia was positively thrilled at the prospect of seeing her favorite cousin so frequently, but Diane found his incessant visits almost intolerable. It was impossible to spend every afternoon and evening shut in her bedroom, so she learned to put up with him, sometimes even managing to exchange a civil word or two.

After a month of constant calling, Lois began to suspect that Jay's visits weren't exclusively for the benefit of seeing Patricia. By Thanksgiving, she was sure of it. She took inventory of the way Jay watched Diane when he thought no one was looking, the soft expression that filled his eyes at the sound of Diane's voice, and the joyful smile that swept over his face the moment she entered the room.

"I don't care what Diane says," she muttered, watching through the parlor door as they tried to avoid each other. "There's attraction between the two of them, and it's up to me to make sure that she doesn't bungle it."

The Saturday before Christmas, Jay arrived for his nightly social call, stepping from his car and surveying the bright strands of Christmas lights gracing the grand house before him, nodding in pleased appreciation as he bounded up the steps onto the wide veranda.

Knowing he would come, Lois waited for him, wrapped in a warm wool shawl. She patted the rocker next to hers as he approached. "Hello, Jay," she called out. "Pull up a chair and let's chat for a minute, just you and I."

Jay regarded Lois inquisitively then took the chair she indicated, lacing his fingers behind his head and stretching his long legs out comfortably in front of him. "What's on your mind, Mrs. Carson?" he asked, flashing a smile oozing with charm.

Lois rolled her eyes. "For God's sake, boy," she snapped, making a face. "I've told you a thousand times. Don't call me Mrs. Carson. Mrs. Carson was my mother-in-law and someone with whom I'd rather not be confused. Just call me Lois."

"Yes, ma'am." Jay rocked slowly back and forth, waiting patiently for her to proceed. The chill of night air began to settle in and he cupped his hands around his mouth, blowing breath and rubbing them together in an effort to keep them warm.

His edginess amused Lois but she concealed her smile, giving him a long look, her fingers steepled as she leaned them against her chin. "Seems to me that you sure spend a lot of time around here," she said.

"Yes ma'am."

"Sixty miles, one way, almost every night."

"Yes ma'am."

"Any particular reason why?"

"I like to come out here. After being away at college so long, it's nice to be able to see so much of Patricia."

"Oh, so you come all the way out here to see Patricia."

"Patricia and I have always been very close," Jay scrambled to explain, shifting uncomfortably.

"Like kissing cousins, huh boy?"

"No ma'am, it's nothing quite so incestuous, I assure you," Jay chuckled, struck by her unusual sense of humor. "I like to visit Patty, but I come out to see Geoff too."

"Uh-huh. I can certainly understand why. My son is so *relaxed* and easy to be with."

"Aw, Geoff is a little abrasive, but I'm used to it. We've been friends for years."

"That's all good and fine, but I would think that a handsome, single young man like you would much rather be out on the town, looking for a lady friend."

"I keep my eyes open."

"Well, I don't doubt that you're truly fond of Patricia. She's a lovely girl, although, I'll never quite understand just what you see in my son." Lois leaned forward in her chair, gazing superiorly into his face. "However, I've got a pretty good idea about your real intentions here."

"Really? And what would they be?" Jay asked, amused. "I can't believe you'd think I have an ulterior motive."

"Don't play games with me. You and I both are too smart for that." Lois studied him smugly. Jay looked away, clearing his throat, suddenly self-conscious. Lois grinned, choking back laughter, enjoying her little game of cat and mouse. She relaxed in her chair. "You think you're pretty smart," she declared lightly. "But you'll never be smarter than me. I figured you out a long time ago."

"Is that right? How so?"

"I figured out that all the time you spend around here has something to do with Diane. Am I right?"

"Diane!" Jay shot upright in his chair, an embarrassed flush spreading to the roots of his blond hair. "Lois! How could you possibly think..." he stammered, trying to deny it, but couldn't — not under Lois' probing stare. "Okay, okay," he conceded sheepishly. "You win. Have I really been that transparent?"

"Only to a trained eye, such as mine. I'll warn you, Jay," Lois said, nodding toward the front door. "Every time you cross over that threshold, you enter a lion's den. Diane isn't just real receptive toward your presence."

"So I've noticed."

"You need an ally, and I mean someone other than meek little Patricia. You, sir, need me on your side."

Jay smiled broadly, admiring Lois' straightforwardness, and nodded in agreement, sliding to the edge of his seat. "Duly noted," he kidded solemnly. "And just what do I have to do to get you on my side, Lois?"

"I don't ask for much. Just be straight with me. Tell me what your intentions are with Diane." Her intense eyes raked over him, boring into his very soul. "She's my only daughter, and I won't have you playing her for a fool."

"I would never do that. I have only the best of intentions, Lois, I swear. I'd like to marry her, or even just date her for a while if she'd let me." He paused, a hang-dog expression on his face as he studied his hands. "But I don't see that happening. It's pretty discouraging when she won't even give me the time of day."

"You barely know the girl. What makes you so sure you want to spend the rest of your life with her?"

"I've been around enough to know that she's the one for me," he glanced up, meeting her eyes, his voice ringing sincere. "I've never met anyone like her. I really can't explain it, Lois. It's the weirdest thing I've ever experienced. I only know I've loved her from the first moment she shot me down."

"Shot you down?" Lois laughed, brightening with delight. "After all my nagging and lecturing, I am glad to know that she learned something!" She rocked back and forth, her gaze shifting from Jay's anxious eyes to the fertile green pastureland before them.

"I tend to mistrust people's motives," she said softly. "Whether they be money or position-oriented or such nonsense as that. However, love at first sight I understand completely. You have my blessing and my support." She stopped rocking. "I like you, Jay Forest. You bring out the best in her."

"That's pretty obvious."

"You'd never know it now, but Diane has always been painfully shy. Your influence on her can't be anything but positive. Her intense dislike of you has brought out the only spunk in her I've ever seen."

"Thanks. That's encouraging."

"Don't worry. Diane doesn't dislike you as much as she wants the rest of us to believe."

"You could've fooled me."

"She's crazy about you, son — she just doesn't know it yet. She doesn't have much experience in the romance department. The truth is, Diane wouldn't know love if it snuck up behind her and bit her on the ass."

Jay flinched, casting an amazed look in her direction. "Are you always so blunt?"

"Most of the time, so get used to it. I'm rarely, if ever, commended for my lady-like manners or my social skills."

"So, do you have a plan?"

"Do you have to ask?"

"I figured you'd given this some thought."

"You bet I have. With Diane, strategy is something you can't afford to be without. The way I see it, if we leave things as they are now, we'll all be dead and buried before Diane ever comes around."

"So what's my first move?"

"Number one, Jay: you can't just go running in there, professing your undying love for her. That'll just scare her off. You have to move in subtly, trick her, make her think it was all her idea."

"I have no idea what you're talking about."

"Just leave it to me, son. We'll bring her around. Now go on inside and throw around some of that irresistible charm."

Jay sprang from the rocker, pausing to kiss Lois' cheek. "Thanks Lois," he said with a playful grin. "If we pull this off, I'll owe you one."

"If we pull this off, you'll owe me more than that," Lois informed him sternly, hiding her amused smile. "I'm getting old and I'm ready for some grandchildren, so get to work."

Jay bolted through the front door, almost colliding with Diane at the foot of the staircase. Having thrown her off balance, he took her by the shoulders, steadying her as she blushed, staring into the depths of his green eyes, struggling to fix an annoyed look on her infatuated face.

"Why are you here again?" she asked impatiently, ignoring the searing warmth that spread through her body at his touch. She threw his hands off her shoulders. "Don't you have a home?"

"Hello Sis," Jay responded casually, flashing a mocking grin. "I see you're as pleasant as always."

Diane pursed her lips, scowling, her eyes narrowed with contempt, while inwardly, her heart was singing, soaring at the sight of him.

"Jay, is that you?" Geoff stuck his head out from the front parlor. "Good, we've been waiting for you. How about a game of poker, you, me, Patricia and Father?"

"Sounds good to me," Jay replied, smiling down at Diane's bitter sneer. "How about Sis here?"

"I have no intention of playing poker with you," Diane retorted quickly, traipsing ahead of him into the parlor, her head proudly in the air. "I'm working on a jigsaw puzzle with Auntie Cee."

Sensing that something was going on inside the house, Lois moved in from the veranda and breezed easily into the parlor, surveying the family gathering before her with a dismayed shake of her head.

Jay, Geoff, Patricia and Palmer were gathered around the mahogany game table, engrossed in a game of cards, and Diane was across the room, her head bent over the giant jigsaw puzzle she worked with Cecilia.

*My God, this will never do,* Lois grumbled silently, regarding Jay with irritation. *Never leave a man to do a woman's job.*

She crossed the room casually, walking up beside Jay's chair and nudging him in the shoulder. "Move out, Jay," she said in a bossy voice. "I'm taking your place. I'm in the mood for a little poker."

Geoff, Patricia and Palmer stared at her, shooting identical looks of disbelief. "What are you talking about, Mother?" Geoff asked incredulously. "You've never played poker in your life. You probably don't even know how to play."

"I beg your pardon, mister," Lois said brusquely. "I happen to be very good at poker. When I was a girl in New Orleans, I played all the time. Only then, it was strip poker. Now get up, Jay, and give me your chair."

As Jay gave up his seat at the table, Lois shrugged the cashmere cardigan from her shoulders and tossed it across the room, hitting Diane in the back. "Diane, be a good hostess and take Jay out for a while. Go for a drive. Show him the Christmas lights. I hear the Hendersons down the street have a real beautiful display."

Lois ignored the pained look on Diane's face, shooing her and Jay out the door with an impatient wave of her hand, then turned her attention back to the trio gathered around the game table, meeting three pairs of suspicious eyes.

"Mother, have you gone mad?" Geoff demanded, throwing his playing cards face down on the table and folding his arms across his broad chest. "Why in God's name would you send Jay out with Diane? We were always taught to be kind to our guests. What were you thinking? Diane will claw his eyes out. She hates his guts."

"I know what I'm doing, Geoffrey," Lois replied, rifling through Jay's discarded hand of cards to hide her sly smile.

"What are you up to, Lois?" Palmer asked, his eyes dancing mirthfully behind his reading glasses.

"Carrying on a fine family tradition started by my dear father — I'm matchmaking," Lois said, giving Palmer a nostalgic smile, disregarding the choking response from Geoff's side of the table.

"Good God, Mother! Matchmaking? Please."

She turned her gaze toward Geoff, giving him a wry smile. "And you, Geoffrey, aren't you a newlywed? Don't you and Patricia have anything better to do than hang around down here with us?"

"Surely you're not trying to send me to my room?"

Ignoring her son's frown, Lois dropped her cards, sliding around the table to take Palmer's arm. "I'm really not in the mood to play poker after all," she said with a chuckle.

She pulled Palmer from his chair and guided him toward the back porch, laughing at his sourpuss scowl. "What's wrong with you?" she asked, her eyes dancing merrily with amusement. "Don't you like my matchmaking?"

"I was just thinking. What does Jay Forest want with our daughter?" Palmer asked suspiciously, overprotectiveness blanketing his face like a shroud.

Lois settled him onto the floral divan and poured him a much-needed brandy, handing it to him as she sat down. "No more than you wanted when you sauntered into my daddy's house in New Orleans," she replied with a saucy smirk.

Palmer shot her an exasperated look, draining his brandy in one swift gulp. "That's not funny, Lois," he said dryly. "Diane's just a baby."

"Diane's a grown woman and it's high time she had a little romance in her life," Lois said. "Besides, I thought you liked Jay."

"I do. Just not for Diane. She deserves a prince."

"Who says he's not?"

"He's not a prince. He's a slick-tongued womanizer!"

"Much like you were?"

"I was a prince."

"He's fine for Diane, Palmer. Have you even seen the way he looks at her?"

"How could I miss it? I've wanted to wring his neck."

"Jay's had his fair share of women, I'll be the first to admit. However, I think Diane may just be the one to settle him down. Look at you, Palmer. It only took one woman to tame you forever." Noting Palmer's distressed expression, Lois smiled gently, covering his hand with her own, feeling compassion for his reluctance to share his baby with another man. "She's not going to stay a little girl forever, Palmer — safe and secure, sleeping under your roof. You've got to cut your apron strings, man. Let her go."

"I find it very hard to consider Diane an adult, Lois. She'll always be my little girl," he said adamantly, his eyes growing misty. "And I'll never be ready to let her go."

Outside Carson House, Jay settled Diane into the passenger's seat of his car, then slid in on his side, starting the purring engine and heading down the lane in the direction of the Henderson estate. He held his tongue, not daring to take his eyes from the road. The atmosphere inside his Jaguar was hostile, thick with resentment. Hardly the mood he'd hoped for. *Jeez, Lois. I hope you know what you're doing*, he thought, cutting his eyes to his grim and wordless passenger.

Diane stared out the window, silent and sullen, not knowing what to say, furious with Lois for putting her in this position. She was very aware of Jay in the seat next to her and shifted her eyes cautiously, catching a glimpse of his incredibly handsome profile. She inhaled deeply. He smelled wonderful, manly and clean, his scent a mix of soap and a hint of expensive aftershave.

*Stop it, Diane*, she scolded herself harshly, resisting the urge to fall all over him. *Remember, keep your distance. He's nothing but trouble.* She could lecture herself until the cows came home, but her resolve was growing thin. Given their close quarters, how would she ever maintain control?

They passed the brightly lit Henderson estate and came to the river bridge, strung with hundreds of white lights, reflecting like twinkling stars against the dark water below. Jay pulled the car onto the shoulder of the road and looked over at Diane. "It's a nice night out, Sis," he said. "Let's get out and walk for a while."

Diane shrugged agreeably, climbing out of the car to join him on the bridge. It was a pleasant evening, especially for so late in December, crisp and cool, without a cloud in the sky, a fact reflected by the silvery rays of the moon lighting their path. They leaned against the railing, looking back on the festively decorated manor in the distance, an uncomfortable silence lingering between them.

"I'm sorry that Lois forced you into this," Diane spoke first, looking down at her hands, nervously picking at her fingernails. "I know there are many other things you'd rather be doing."

"I wouldn't say that," Jay chuckled lightly, not bothering to conceal the sparkle in his eyes. "Despite what you think of me, Diane, I happen to like you. Quite a bit, actually. I think this is the first chance I've had to be alone with you since the wedding."

He turned to her, grinning devilishly. "And I think we should take up where we left off at the reception. What was it I was saying to you just before you decided to walk away in a huff?"

He wrinkled his brow in mock concentration, drumming his fingers against his chin, shooting her a sidelong glance as he snapped them in delight. "Oh now, I remember. I was asking you a question."

"Don't even go there, Jay," Diane warned, glaring at him through narrowed eyes, grateful that the evening shadows hid the rosy glow of her cheeks.

"Now, Sis. You know I have to ask again, especially since you've had time to think it over."

"Jay..."

He inched closer, sliding a muscular arm around her shoulders and leaning his blond head into hers. "How about you and I cut out of here, find a cozy spot and have a party of our own?" He batted his eyes innocently, smiling into her annoyed face.

"Don't you ever give up?"

"Not until I get a straight answer out of you. You've never given me a definite yes or no."

"I think you know the answer."

"Do I?"

Diane pushed him away with a sharp nudge. "Oh, go away," she said irritably. "I hate you."

Jay laughed, shaking his head in amusement. "No you don't. In fact, I think you love me. Truly, madly, deeply."

"You flatter yourself."

"Maybe, but I don't hear you denying it."

"Why should I lend credence to the delusional ravings of a fool?"

"Such inbred snottiness, Diane. Just one of the many things I love about you."

"Will you please shut up?" she snapped, turning away from him, hugging her arms to her chest as she stared into the rippling water running swiftly under the bridge beneath her. "I don't want to be in love with someone like you," she admitted quietly, in a voice so soft that Jay had to strain to hear her words.

"What, devilishly handsome, witty and vulgarly wealthy?"

"And cocky, arrogant, conceited and full of himself," Diane jerked around, meeting his lingering gaze, suddenly ashamed of herself for being so tough on him. "Not that those aren't all fine qualities, if you're looking for that sort of thing," she added quickly, reassuring him with a light touch of her hand. "No offense, Jay, but I always wanted to marry someone more like my father."

"And you don't think that old Palmer is cocky, arrogant and full of himself?" Jay asked incredulously, his eyes wide with cynical disbelief. "Come on, Diane. It's a well-known fact that the Carson men have been offensively full of themselves for generations. Your brother Geoff is one of the most pompous men I've ever known, but I love him anyway."

"Now, if that isn't the pot calling the kettle black."

"Well, I fit right in, don't I?" He grinned expansively, leaning back on his elbows, lounging against the rail of the bridge. "See, you can marry me. I'm more like your father than you thought."

"Don't be ridiculous, Jay. I can't marry you. I don't even like you."

"A minor obstacle," he replied, winking playfully as he linked his arm through hers, pulling her alongside him down the length of the bridge. "You don't have to like me now. Just give it a little time, Sis. I'll grow on you."

He took her hand and they strolled in silence, admiring the brilliant Christmas scenery, their minds drifting off in other directions. The excitement over the impending holiday was falling short, giving way to their fledgling romance. Jay kept his eyes on the road ahead, grinning ear to ear, immensely pleased with himself. *Lois will be so proud of me*, he thought, his chest swelling with good cheer. *I'm this close to winning her over.*

Uncertain of exactly what had just transpired, Diane remained close-mouthed, regarding Jay through new eyes, smiling thoughtfully. *He's a no-good womanizing idiot, but God help me, I'm just nuts about him, stupid though I am for allowing myself to feel this way. I have no other choice. I have to give him a shot.*

# 11

Their first official outing took place two days before Christmas when Jay enticed Diane into the city to meet him for lunch and an afternoon of last-minute holiday shopping. "Let's go to dinner, then take a ghost tour," Jay suggested at the end of the day, chuckling inwardly at her appalled expression. "A group is meeting over at Reynolds Square, right after dark."

"No, thank you," Diane answered disdainfully. "I'd rather not, if you don't mind. Being out with you is scary enough."

"Oh well, it was worth a shot," he replied and continued cheerfully down the sidewalk beside her, his arms loaded with packages, heading toward the parking garage where Diane had left her car. He glanced at her, wearing a lopsided grin. "So, am I growing on you yet?"

Diane looked up, taking in his eager face, her heart leaping with joy. "A little," she shrugged, keeping her expression purposefully blasé. "But don't go getting excited and push your luck. You're doing okay, but you're still not doing that great."

However, Jay did grow on her, more than she'd ever care to admit. Throughout the holidays and into the spring, their relationship flourished, moving from light conversation during his nightly visits to somewhat open affection. For sanity purposes alone, they were determined to keep their budding romance hidden from the rest of the family. Everyone, that is, except Lois. There was simply no way to keep anything from her.

"Going out with Jay again?" Lois inquired slyly, sneaking into Diane's room as she dressed, taking a seat on the ancient cedar chest at the foot of the bed.

Diane whirled around, attired only in her slip, a floral silk dress clutched to her chest. "Oh. Yes," she admitted casually, her cheeks flaming, biting her lip to hold back any words that might reveal the gushing affection she now held for Jay. "He invited me to dinner, at The Pink House no less, and who am I to turn down a free meal?"

Lois lifted a brow, clamping her lips closed tightly, careful not to spoil anything by speaking too soon. "Finding him a little more bearable, I take it?" she commented casually, pretending not to care, using the hem of her blouse to polish a spot on Diane's brass footboard.

"Somewhat," Diane tried to remain equally aloof, but simply couldn't do it. Overcome by schoolgirl giddiness, she tossed the dress aside and rushed forward, her face radiant, excitedly clutching her mother's knee. "Oh, Mother! I can't stand it. I have to tell you. I was so wrong about him! Jay is simply wonderful! These past few months, I've seen a whole new side of him and I think — and this may be a bit premature — but I think he may be the one."

"The one? Really? That obnoxious philanderer?"

"I know what I said about him, and for the most part, it was true. But I think he's really changed. I don't think he's even seen another woman since he started dating me."

"Well, God forbid, Diane! I should certainly hope not." Lois feigned horror, but inwardly, her heart was singing. *I think it's really going to happen this time,* she thought deliriously. *God love you, Jay Forest. I think you just might be able to pull this off.*

"Do you think I'm foolish to feel this way?" Diane asked sheepishly, sitting back on her heels.

"Well," Lois paused, cautiously weighing her answer. "I've seen you make stupider choices," she admitted coolly, her reserved expression giving no clue to her glee.

The doorbell echoed through the house, followed by the sound of Jay's hearty laugh, and Diane scrambled from the floor, throwing her dress over her head, combing frantically through her tousled hair with her fingers. She stepped into her shoes and grabbed her purse off the dresser, dashing to the door, glancing back at Lois eagerly. "Do I look okay?" she asked, pausing in the doorway, her eyes leaping in anticipation.

"Do you really think he'll notice?" Lois asked cleverly, the corners of her mouth twitching with hidden laughter.

"I certainly hope so," Diane batted her eyelashes and tossed her head flirtatiously, her long chestnut curls cascading over her shoulders as she flashed Lois an effervescent smile. "I bought this dress just for him."

*Oh yeah*, Lois thought in jubilant satisfaction, watching her skip from the room. *She's gone.* She trailed Diane down the hall, pausing at the top of the stairs to view her descent.

Jay met her at the bottom, his face transformed when she came into sight. He took her by the hand and leaned forward, whispering an affectionate greeting meant only for her. Diane giggled and gazed up at him, her face aglow, giving his hand a fond squeeze as they strolled toward the front entrance. She glanced back at Lois, offering her a happy smile.

"Good night, Mother," she sang out in a cheerful voice, winking playfully as she stepped out onto the porch.

"Hey! Where are they going?" Geoff appeared out of nowhere, yanking aside the parlor drape to stare after them, his brow creased in exasperation.

"Out," Lois replied, reclining gracefully on the sofa, wearing a self-satisfied grin, enormously pleased with the way things were proceeding.

"Again?" Geoff let go of the curtain, dropping to the piano bench with a muffled thud, his expression puzzled. "You know," he mused aloud, looking to Lois for confirmation. "For two people who can't stand the sight of one another, they sure seem to spend a lot of time together. What do you think that's all about?"

"Oh, Geoff," Lois rolled her eyes, sighing so heavily the gust of breath ruffled her bangs. She shot him an annoyed look, shaking her head impatiently. "Get a clue."

Coming back from the city, Jay pulled his car to the side of the road, just outside the exterior walls of the estate. "Why are we stopping here?" Diane asked, glancing at him in bewilderment.

"I thought I'd walk you to the door," Jay replied, hopping from the car and sauntering ahead of her to unlatch the gate.

"From way out here? It's a good quarter-mile to the house." Diane unlocked her door and got out, joining him on the cobbled drive, her cotton sweater draped loosely about her shoulders.

Jay flashed a comical grin, his white teeth gleaming in the dim light of the moon. "The way I see it, by stopping out here, there is no way that Geoff could have possibly seen my headlights. Therefore, we are much less likely to encounter his beady little eyes peering at us from behind the curtains."

"Are you saying my brother's nosy?"

"No. I'm saying your brother's a pretentious, meddling fool who needs to learn to mind his own business."

"That's what I meant," Diane laughed, accepting his outstretched hand. They strolled on through the darkness, swinging hands, shielded from moonlight by a thick canopy of Spanish moss and mimosa. Diane looked up, eyeing the shadowy trees, listening to night sounds and smiling in contentment. "Hmm," she sighed. "I just love this time of year."

"I just love that it's not humid yet," Jay commented dryly. "But that's not far behind. Can you believe it's almost Easter?"

Diane shook her head. "No, I can't. Sure seems like it got here in a hurry this year."

"You know what they say — time flies when you're having fun."

"Are you having fun?" Diane asked pointedly, feeling unusually brave, then ducked her head shyly, almost afraid to hear his answer.

Jay gave a start of surprise, unaccustomed to her being so straightforward. "Sure," he responded casually, offering a nonchalant gesture. "I'm having a great time, although it's been pretty sedate."

"Is that a bad thing?"

"Bad? Not necessarily. Let's just say that time spent with you is much different from my usual brand of tawdry pleasure."

Diane stiffened, turning away in an offended pout. "I'm sorry I'm so boring," she sputtered in an icy tone, jutting her chin out defensively.

Jay's mouth stretched into an animated smile. Shaking his head at her rigid posture, he reached out, placing a warm hand on her cold shoulder. She cringed at his touch and tried to move away, but he stopped her, pulling her tightly against him, hypnotizing her with his vivid green stare.

"Did I say you were boring?" he asked, his eyes twinkling with mirth. "I swear, I've never seen anyone so prone to taking the defensive."

He bent down, kissing her fully on the lips, then held her limp body in his arms, smiling warmly into her flushed face. "I do not find you boring, Diane," he whispered, his voice husky with emotion. "In fact, I've never met a more exciting woman in my entire life. The truth is, I love you — and I know that you feel the same way about me."

Diane gaped at him, her brown eyes like saucers, gulping furiously as she tried to come up with an appropriate response. "I don't know what to say," she stammered, her cheeks bright red, her lips still warm and tingling from his kiss.

"Then *please* don't say anything," Jay advised sharply, releasing her from his embrace. "I know you. If I give you ten seconds to think about it, you'll just deny it, and I'll be right back where I started."

He took her hand and they walked on, each wondering what to say next. They topped the hill above the main estate and Carson House came into view, its soft lighting and white columns rising above the fog beginning to drift in from the river. Diane breathed a sigh of relief, grateful to be given a way out of an uncomfortable discussion. "Race you!" she yelled, sprinting ahead of him, breaking into loud giggles as he caught the end of her skirt and slowed her pace.

"Cheater!" she taunted him, strolling next to him as they climbed the front steps. She paused beside one of the Corinthian columns, resting against it, her features bright with good humor as she gazed up at Jay.

"I'm a lawyer, Diane," Jay reminded her laughingly, leaning in, positioning his palm just above her head, his face mere inches from her own. "What did you expect? We attorneys all lie and cheat to win, haven't you heard?"

He grinned cynically, focusing his impassioned gaze on her mouth, intent on delivering another long goodnight kiss when a flutter of the living room drape caught his eye. "Damn! I knew he was psychic!"

"Who?" Diane giggled, amused by the perturbed look on his face.

"Geoff! Who else? The guy would rather die than give me a break," Jay jerked his head toward the window, offering his friend an unfriendly gesture. From inside, they could hear Geoff's entertained chuckle and Jay had to smile, despite his frustration.

"I better get going," he said, brushing his lips against Diane's cheek. "Any privacy we might have had is gone."

"That's my family for you. Someone always has to be right in the middle of everything," she tiptoed up, giving Jay a quick embrace, the muscular firmness of his chest giving her chills. "Good night," she breathed, her voice unsteady and wavering with desire.

"Good night, Sis," Jay winked at her and trotted down the steps, hands in his pockets, ready for a healthy trek back to his car.

"Hey," she called out, halting his retreat. "I hope you're not mad at me, you know, about earlier."

"Nope," Jay turned, his eyes twin crescents of mirth. "I'm not mad at you, nor have I given up on you. I'm certain you'll come around, sooner or later," he flashed a classic smile and sauntered away, pausing to give her one final gaze over his shoulder. "For the time being, do us both a favor and forget I said anything at all."

But she couldn't forget. It was all she could think about as she watched him walk away. "He loves me," she murmured, light-headed, her heart swelling with joy. "Now what do I do?"

On her way into the house, Diane had to own up, if only to herself. She had fought against it, but in the end her resolve had been crushed. She had fallen head over heels in love. All her life, she had waited to fall in love and now she had — with Jay, the very least likely person. "Darn him for growing on me," she laughed softly, padding toward the stairs. She passed Geoff on the way up, oblivious to his smug stare, and drifted blissfully to her bedroom, lost in wonder and rapturous delight.

They became engaged on Easter Sunday when Jay presented her ring with a little help from the Easter Bunny who waited in the pasture next to the Baptist church, holding out a brightly colored basket for Diane.

"Who did you pay off to get an Easter basket?" he demanded, peeking over her shoulder to view her chocolate bunny and painted eggs.

"I didn't have to pay anyone off," Diane informed him superiorly. "I earned it. All good little girls get visits from the Easter Bunny."

"Well, are you going to share?"

"Have you been good?"

"Well, ya know," Jay shrugged, grinning mischievously. "I could've been better."

Diane giggled, her eyes dancing playfully. "Then I don't think you deserve to partake in my Easter goodies."

"Oh really? What if I just dip my hand in and take some anyway?"

"You'll have to catch me first!" Diane took off running, kicking off her new pumps as she dashed toward a shady grove of tall pines and blooming azaleas. She slid under the tallest tree, dropping gracefully to the grass, clutching the basket tightly as Jay skidded to a stop in front of her.

"Candy hoarder!" he teased, trying to snatch the basket from her iron grip.

"Okay, okay," Diane bargained, lifting the basket out of his reach, batting her lashes innocently. "I'll share, but it'll cost ya."

Jay lowered his arms, narrowing his eyes suspiciously. "How much?" he asked, loosening his tie and removing his summer jacket.

"Depends on what you want."

"How much for the bunny?"

"The bunny's not for sale."

"That's hardly fair. The bunny's the best part."

"My basket. My bunny."

"Okay, fine. How much for an egg?"

Diane glanced down into the basket, taking a quick inventory of its contents. "I'll sell you an egg for a kiss."

Jay's eyebrows shot up in feigned surprise. "That's all? One kiss?"

"Well, it's got to be a good kiss."

"A good kiss should be worth a least two eggs."

"Do you want an egg or not?"

"I guess so," Jay leaned down, kissing her warmly, running his hands up the arms of her pastel suit, resting them on her shoulders. Diane closed her eyes, reveling in his touch, electricity surging through her as their lips met. She relaxed against him, caught up in the moment, forgetting all else, including the basketful of goodies.

"Got it!" Jay bellowed, laughing loudly, holding the chocolate Easter bunny high in the air.

"Hey!" Diane protested, her eyes flying open in surprise. "Play fair! I thought you were a grown-up."

"Where did you get that idea? Never once have I pretended to be mature," he studied her face with amusement, flashing her a charming smile, and gave in, presenting the bunny as a peace offering. "Here, spoiled sport. Take this and give me my egg."

Diane snatched the bunny from his hand, tucking it securely beneath her arm, then held out the basket. "Pick," she beamed.

"You sure?"

"Yes."

Jay reached in, picking out the solitary egg of metallic gold, its shiny enamel gleaming in the morning sun. "This is a good one," he declared, holding it up for her to see.

"Not the gold one!" Diane objected loudly. "The gold one is special!"

"Now who's not playing fair? You put no stipulations on which egg I could have when you haggled for that kiss. The golden egg is mine, fair and square."

"Fine," Diane huffed, throwing her back against the tree trunk, her arms folded tightly across her chest in a pronounced pout.

"Yum, yum. I wonder what's inside. You know, the gold egg's always got the best stuff in it," Jay chuckled devilishly, crawling over the grass to sit beside her, and ripped open the egg with relish, delighting in the pained look on her face. Diane rolled her eyes and looked away, exasperated, still putout with him for grabbing the best egg.

"Hey, will ya look at this? Jeez, Diane — this is better than Cracker Jacks!"

At Jay's outburst, she spun around, just in time to see him pluck a glittering circle of gold from the half shell in his palm, holding it high in the air, bright rays of sunlight reflecting blindingly off its brilliance. Astonished, Diane gawked, speechless, her eyes darting from the sparkling diamond to Jay's immensely pleased face.

"Looks like you should've let me keep the rabbit," he teased, studying the bauble in his hand. "How much do you think this is worth?"

Diane shook her head slowly, clearly bewildered.

Jay slid the ring onto his pinkie, twirling it before her face. "It's awfully pretty, but it looks kind of silly on me, don't you agree?"

"It does look a bit ridiculous," Diane swallowed hard, stammering her response.

"I'll tell you what. Let's make a deal. I'll trade you this ring — on one condition."

"You want the bunny?"

"The bunny? Hell no, this ring is worth the bunny and all the eggs, at least. I want the whole kit and caboodle, sister. Hand it over."

Diane willingly pushed the basket toward him and held out her palm. "Okay, done," she said eagerly. "Gimme."

Jay took her outstretched hand, lifting it to his lips, kissing her open palm as he gazed deeply into her eyes. "I'll let you keep it all, if you'll marry me."

"I don't know what to say," Diane breathed, unable to drop her eyes, her cheeks flaming with warmth. "This is all so sudden."

"Sudden? Hardly. You had to know this was coming, Diane." He let go of her hand and pulled her into his arms, his embrace passionate and firm. "I've wanted this since the first time I saw you, standing by the punch bowl at your brother's wedding reception, so naïve and beautiful in that incredible lavender dress. I couldn't take my eyes off you. I watched you sneak out those French doors and followed you to the rose garden, determined to take you home with me. I thought it would be a piece of cake, but what did I know? You showed me. You shot me down, boring a hole right through me with those fiery brown eyes, knocking me on my butt and putting me right back in my place.

"I tried to go back to D.C. and forget you, but I couldn't. It was too late. I was already hooked. So you see, Sis — this isn't sudden. Not at all." He caressed her hand, sliding the ring onto her finger. "I've loved you since the first moment I laid eyes on you. Say you'll marry me, Diane. I mean it. You'll always be the only girl for me."

Diane tore her eyes from the brilliant band, gazing up at him with misty eyes, brushing away a tear with the back of her hand. "Sometimes you say the sweetest things," she whispered, smiling at him.

"It's always some kind of stall tactic with you, isn't it, Sis?" Jay asked mockingly, lowering his head and shaking it sadly. He lifted his eyes, giving her a direct look. "I won't be quite so sweet if you don't hurry up and give me an answer."

Diane laughed, tracing his clenched jaw tenderly with her finger. "Of course, I'll marry you, Jay. How could I not? I've waited for you my entire life." She kissed him, her lips lingering on his cheek, and then rested her head on his shoulder, closing her eyes, hearing the chimes of the church belfry tolling in the distance.

"Oh good lord!" her eyes flew open and she tore from Jay's embrace, leaping from the grass. "We've got to go. We're late for Easter dinner."

"Well, that will never do, will it? All things considered, it might be in our best interest to stay in your family's good graces." Jay grabbed the Easter basket and jumped up, smiling playfully as he handed it to Diane. "Don't forget your candy."

"Thanks," Diane accepted the basket, returning his smile. "I love you," she said softly.

"I love you too, Sis," he reclaimed her hand, squeezing it tightly. "You've made me very happy."

They strolled ecstatically toward the church parking lot, swinging their hands, lost blissfully in their own thoughts. "I hope you talked this over with Daddy," Diane spoke up, breaking the easy silence between them. "You know how he hates surprises."

Jay glanced at her, wearing a quizzical grin, his brows lifted with entertained speculation. "If that's the case, then this should prove to be a very interesting afternoon."

They pulled up in front of Carson House, leaving the car in the circle drive. Diane rushed up the steps ahead of Jay, bursting through the door and into the dining room where the family gathered for traditional holiday ham. Jay strolled in behind her, pausing in the entryway, leaning against the wall with his hands tucked casually into the pockets of his tailored trousers.

"Well, well, well," Geoff looked up, throwing them a look of extreme irritation. "So glad the two of you could join us." He glanced at his watch and stared pointedly at Diane, silently scolding her for being so lax in social graces.

Diane ignored him and held out her hand excitedly, darting around the table to flash the five-carat diamond in Lois' face. "Look, Mother, look!" she squealed, her face glowing with happiness.

Beaming with pleasure, Lois threw her linen napkin onto the lace tablecloth, taking Diane's hand to admire her ring. "It's just beautiful, Diane," she said, giving her a gentle squeeze. "Absolutely stunning." She looked past Diane and offered Jay an exuberant smile, her twinkling eyes conveying congratulations.

Geoff scrambled to his feet, lunging across the table, curiosity getting the better of him. "What is it?" he demanded, craning his neck to get a better look.

"Jay's asked me to marry him," Diane glanced back over her shoulder, assuming a posture of superiority, daring her brother to utter one derogatory word.

"Oh good lord!" Geoff flopped back in his chair in defeat, staring incredulously across the room to Jay. "Have you been drinking?" he asked, his jaw hanging open in shock.

"As a matter of fact, yes," Jay replied, joking with him nonchalantly. "Celebratory champagne, to be exact."

"And on Easter Sunday. How very uncouth," Geoff shook his head, rubbing his temples in despair, regarding Jay in horrified disbelief. "I don't believe this!" he fumed, slapping his hand on the table. "You could have anyone you wanted. Anyone! Out of all the women in the world, why on earth would you pick her?"

Jay shrugged, offering him a lopsided grin. "I don't know, Geoff. I kind of like her, and I thought it was the only way I could get into the family."

"If you wanted in that badly, I would have made you an honorary member. You don't have to marry my sister."

"Now you tell me," Jay slapped his palm to his forehead, finding it hard to keep from laughing. "It's a little too late for that now. I've already asked her and being the honorable kind of guy I am, I just can't go back on promises that way. It's not good for business." He winked at Diane and came forward, throwing an arm around her shoulder, embracing her tightly and kissing her cheek.

"I'm glad you find this so funny," Geoff replied with a cross frown, his brow creased in exasperation. "What's not good for business is the messy divorce I'll have to handle when you wake up on your honeymoon and find her sleeping next to you."

"Geoffrey, that's enough," Palmer came around the table to offer his best wishes. "You made a good choice, son," he told Jay in a hearty voice, pinching Diane's cheek affectionately. "You don't get any better than my Diane."

He yanked Jay aside, giving him a warning glower. "Be very sure before you do this," he cautioned in a low voice, his stern eyes speaking volumes. "You do realize that marriage is forever, don't you? I do not condone divorce, nor will I stand for any running around on your part. I'll not have you disgracing my daughter in any way, shape or form."

"I am very aware of the consequences of my actions," Jay replied solemnly, meeting Palmer's unyielding stare with confident eyes. "I love Diane, and plan to spend the rest of my life making her happy."

"Good answer!" Palmer slapped a firm hand against Jay's back in a congratulatory gesture, offering him an enthusiastic smile. "Those are very pretty words," he said lightly, steering Jay back to the table. "Let's hope you can back them up."

After dinner, Lois beckoned Jay outside, linking arms with him as they strolled across the long veranda. "You've made me a pretty happy woman, Jay Forest," she revealed with a fond glance. "And believe you me, that's not an easy thing to do."

"I'm glad, Lois," Jay patted her arm with a smile. "I want nothing more than to make you happy."

"You are so full of shit."

Jay chuckled, offering her an offended look. "I'm hurt, Lois. How could you think that about me? Next to Diane, you're the only woman I aim to please."

"And you'll please me even more when you produce some grandchildren," she informed him, eyeing him authoritatively. "I want a little girl first, I think. One just like Diane."

Jay laughed, looking over at her with twinkling eyes. "You got a deal, Lois," he said, guiding her back toward the front entrance. "I'll see what I can do."

"You take care of Diane, Jay. You hear?" she shook her finger at his nose, her face completely serious. "I took your side and defended you to Palmer. Don't you dare make me eat my words."

Jay and Diane married the following Christmas in a candlelit ceremony at the Eden Glen Baptist Church. Diane spent the months leading up to the big event in jubilant anticipation, finally seeing her goal of wife and mother looming before her, a bright light at the end of a very long tunnel. Palmer went all out for the wedding, sparing no expense. "After all, you only get married once and nothing is too good for my little girl," he advised the wedding coordinator, giving him free rein. Diane and Lois spent countless hours poring over plans and guest lists, selecting just the right dress, flowers and six-tier wedding cake.

"I'm exhausted!" Elated to at last be home from yet another shopping excursion to Atlanta, Diane collapsed into a chair, dropping her shopping bags around her in a heap, lolling her head to the side to stare wearily at her mother.

Lois stood in the entryway, sporting a perturbed expression, eyeing Diane warily as she reached up to remove her hat, letting her dark tresses tumble from the constraint of her barrette. "You might as well not get worn out now," she told Diane, waltzing into the study. "We've still got a million things to do."

"I thought that's what the wedding coordinator was for."

"Don't complain to me, missy. You were the one who wanted this huge extravaganza, not I."

"Daddy wanted it too."

Lois offered her a thin smile. "I don't see your father around, toting you from place to place to gather your trousseau. Nope, missy. I'm all you've got, so you better straighten up or you'll be doing this all on your own."

Just as Diane and Lois were on the verge of killing one another, the big day finally arrived. People flocked to Eden Glen from all directions, converging on Carson House like a mob scene. Diane avoided the crowd, dressing nervously upstairs in her bedroom, surrounded by close friends, her voice strained and her palms sweaty as she fretted over every little detail. Catherine Magill, her roommate from Stephens, flew in from Jacksonville to serve as maid of honor and spent the morning helping her primp.

"Oh, Diane! Your dress is divine!" Catherine exclaimed, pushing through the circle of sorority sisters to finger the yards of Irish lace and silk adorning Diane's dress. "What a lovely, lovely gown. Here, let me do that." She took the pearl-encrusted headpiece from Diane's hands, climbing up on a footstool to attach it. "Louis Durand?" she inquired, her mouth full of bobby pins.

"No. A Danielle Laurent, from Paris."

"An original. How heavenly! Your mother's?"

"No. The dress is mine," Diane corrected her with a huffy sigh, searching the room until she found Lois in the mirror's reflection. "You know, Mother, that's really pitiful," she declared in a chiding tone. "Any decent Southern woman would have a wedding gown to pass on to her daughter. It's so sad that we have no family heirloom like that to pass down from generation to generation."

"Good Lord, Diane! How dare you imply that I'm a decent Southern woman," Lois sputtered, hands on her hips and her high-heeled feet spread wide. She shook off her sister Nicole's calming hand, rolling her eyes extravagantly. "You're the only woman I know who can stand in a ten-thousand dollar designer wedding dress and complain that you're not wearing someone else's old hand-me-down."

"Oh Mother, it's not that," Diane replied, impatiently tossing her head, sending bobby pins flying across the room, thwarting Catherine's valiant attempt to secure her headpiece. "It's just a break in tradition, that's all."

"Well, what do you want me to do — go dig Beatrice's dress out of moth balls so you can wear a family heirloom?"

"Of course not. Don't be ridiculous."

A light tap sounded at the door, interrupting their squabble. "From the sound of all the bitching, I would say that I've successfully located my mother and sister," Geoff said, sticking his head in, smirking devilishly as he scanned the room.

"What do you want?" Diane snapped suspiciously, spying his face in the mirror. "And why are you here? You're supposed to be at the church with Jay."

"Jay's with Patricia. It's all under control," he flashed a winning smile at the bridesmaids, his mouth dropping open as he took in the lovely bride with upswept hair standing in the center of the room. "I would've never believed it in a million years," he said, eyeing his sister with astonished delight. "My, my, Diane. I'm shocked. I never thought I'd see the day that I would find you beautiful."

He stepped inside and closed the door, striding quickly to her side, his eyes lit in rare appreciation. "Today is that day, little sister. You're simply stunning. Jay's a lucky man."

"Are you sick or drunk?" Diane rolled her head to the side, this time careful not to disturb the anchoring of the veil, and softly kissed his cheek, her unusual show of affection surprising them both. "Thanks, Geoff," she said with a smile, her eyes twinkling mirthfully. "I know just how hard that was for you to say, and I do appreciate it."

"Must be the champagne," he shot back with a grin. "We've been sampling, you know."

"I can only imagine. I suppose Jay has a flask stashed for the ceremony."

"Not today," Geoff replied, retreating to the door, getting in a jab on his way out. "The groom is not drinking. I wouldn't let him. I want him to be stone-cold sober when he takes his vows so he can't plead unsound mind when he wakes up in the morning and realizes what he's done."

Forgetting the veil and the cathedral-length train behind her, Diane whirled around, grabbed a vase from the nightstand and threw it at him, narrowly missing his head as he scampered out the door. His hearty chuckle echoed back at her as he ran down the hall, yelling out facetiously for the absent groom-to-be, "Jay! Run for your life, man. It's not too late to get away!"

"Diane," Lois began, her tone angry as she wagged her finger in the direction of the bride.

Nicole caught her arm, bringing her blistering lecture to a halt. "Come, Lois," she urged gently, pulling her out of the room. "Let's give the girls some space to finish getting ready."

She led her sister down the hall, positioning her at the top of the stairs, taking a seat next to her. They waited together, shoulder to shoulder — two sisters dazzling in similar styles of chiffon, one in vibrant rose, the other in a flattering shade of soft yellow. Noting the irritation on her face, Nicole stroked Lois' shoulder soothingly. "You shouldn't get so annoyed with her, Lois."

"I know, but she can be so infuriating sometimes. Having a rip-roaring snorting fit and throwing things across the room at her brother like that — and on her wedding day, no less! My mother-in-law is rolling over in her grave."

"Since when do you care what you're mother-in-law thinks?"

"I don't. It just seemed appropriate to point out."

"It wasn't that bad, Lois. Besides, Geoff deserved it, slinking around the room that way. He was just looking for trouble."

"He always is."

"Don't be so hard on Diane. She's just nervous. Like you said, it is her wedding day. I'm sure she didn't mean to snap at you."

"To the contrary. I'm sure she did," Lois glanced at her sister, frowning at her sudden giggle. "What are you laughing at?"

"At you," Nicole declared, wiping giddy tears from her eyes, "finally getting a taste of your own medicine."

"What's that supposed to mean?"

"Now, don't go getting all swelled up at me, Lois. It's just that Diane reminds me so much of you when you were younger — so proud and quick-tempered."

"I've never thought of her as being like me. Diane's too prissy."

"No, chère, I have to disagree. Diane is very much like you, especially today."

"Trust me, Nikki. She's not. It's only the wedding. She usually doesn't act this way, at least not to this extreme. Nevertheless, if it weren't the wedding, it would be something else. Diane's always putout over something," Lois grinned wryly. "What is it about weddings that brings out the worst in people?"

"I don't know, but weddings seem to affect even the most level-headed badly, and they're supposed to be happy occasions."

"I don't understand it. I'm just glad that Palmer and I had the good sense to elope."

"Me too," Nicole declared with a snicker, shooting Lois a sidelong look. "I would have hated to see you on a day like today."

"I would've been much cooler-headed than Diane, I can promise you that," Lois said, encircling her knees with her arms, propping up her chin as she gazed thoughtfully at her sister. "Why do you suppose you never married, Nikki?" she asked softly.

Nicole smiled pensively, caught off guard by Lois' question. "I don't know. I guess I never found the right man," she glanced at Lois, her eyes dancing merrily. "Besides, how could I possibly top the one you married?"

"Oh please! Don't give me that. Palmer is a jewel, but I'm sure there are many out there just like him."

"No, not really," Nicole rested her head against the banister, a faraway look shadowing her face. "I suppose there were one or two, many years ago, that I might have considered marrying, but I didn't. Somehow I couldn't stand the thought of leaving Papa all alone in that big old house."

"You gave up the best years of your life to take care of Papa?" Lois stared at her, blinking incredulously. "I can't believe he let you do that."

"Papa didn't *let* me do anything, Lois," Nicole enlightened her in a chiding tone, her eyes bright with indignation. "I stayed with Papa because I wanted to. How dare you peer down your nose at me like I'm some sort of pathetic old maid? Like it or not, we all can't be you. Don't you dare act like you feel sorry for me. I'll have you know that I've been quite content with my life."

"Nicole, I never meant..." Lois trailed off, frustrated at being misunderstood.

Hearing the guilt in her sister's voice, Nicole reached over and covered Lois' hand with her own. "It's okay," she said gently. "Someone had to look after Papa, particularly during those later years. And now that Papa's gone, who knows? I'm still quite young — relatively speaking, of course. There still might be a Prince Charming out there, waiting especially for me."

"I'm sure there is, Nikki," Lois grinned, relieved to be forgiven, standing abruptly and yanking Nicole to her feet. "And who knows? He may be here already, at the church, waiting with the rest of that mob for our tardy bride." She pivoted abruptly, barking down the hall, "Diane! Get a move on or you'll be late for your own wedding!"

They stood arm in arm, watching as Diane came out of the bedroom, a vision of loveliness in silk and lace, her long train looped carefully over her outstretched arm, trailed by Catherine and the other bridesmaids, giggling excitedly and fussing over her veil.

"What a beautiful bride," Lois marveled, instantly forgetting her dismay, her chest swelling with pride at the sight of her breathtaking daughter.

Nicole leaned her head on Lois' shoulder, her eyes growing misty. "Thanks, Lo," she murmured, smiling at her through joyful tears.

Lois glanced at her, raising a curious brow. "Whatever for?"

"Just for being you. You're the greatest."

At seven o'clock, Diane floated down the aisle in yards of flowing white silk, supported by the strong arm of her father, preceded by six of her sorority sisters and one very green-faced sister-in-law. Patricia Langford Carson was expecting her first child and was miserable, battling morning sickness on a daily basis. Peering through folds of tulle, Diane glimpsed her queasy face worriedly. "Are you going to make it, Patricia?" she hissed, taking a moment to check on her as she took her place next to Jay.

"I'll be fine," Patricia assured her, nodding weakly to her handsome cousin as he leaned forward, showing his concern. "You two just do your thing and quit fretting over me. I promise I won't throw up until it's over."

"You heard the woman, Diane," Jay said, exhibiting a witty grin, squeezing Diane's hand affectionately as he guided her to the altar. "Quit your stalling and let's tie the knot."

The rest of the ceremony went off without a hitch, witnessed by several hundred of the South's elite. The elaborate reception that followed was featured the next morning in all the major society pages, filled with images of a glowing and blissful Diane, holding tight to Jay's arm, feeding him wedding cake and admiring the diamond band he had placed on her finger. Diane looked back on the newspaper clippings with exhilaration, admiring the stunning couple in the pictures, feeling as though she was living in a dream.

"Here's to a perfect day, a perfect bride and groom and a perfect life to come," she echoed the sentiments of Catherine Magill's toast, smiling in elation. It really was a dream come true.

After their Caribbean honeymoon, Diane and Jay moved out of Carson House, relocating down the lane to a red brick house next door to Auntie Cee. Jay went back to work and Diane settled in, filling her days unpacking gifts and writing thank-you notes. Mundane though it seemed, she was content, exuberant, in fact — ecstatically happy and crazy in love, and much to Lois' delight, wanted to start a family immediately.

"Let's have a baby, Jay," she whispered, lying in his arms, nuzzling against his neck and kissing him softly.

Jay examined her eager face, his eyes twinkling mischievously. "You Carsons crack me up," he chuckled light-heartedly. "You can't stand it if Geoff has something you don't, can you?"

Diane frowned, shooting him an irritated look. "Carson? I'm a Forest now, remember?"

"Yes, I seem to vaguely remember some sort of ceremony in which we willingly participated," Jay teased her with a grin. "However, no matter how you sign your name, my dear, you will remain a Carson, through and through, until the day you die. Not that you can help it. It's genetic, Sis. There's just no way around it."

"Whatever," Diane waved her hand in a dismissive gesture, poking him firmly in the chest. "Think whatever you want, smart aleck. My desire to have a child has nothing whatsoever to do with Geoff. I've always wanted a baby — much more than I ever wanted a husband, really."

"Thanks. That's comforting."

"Oh, you know what I mean." She rolled onto her stomach, encircling her arms flirtatiously around his neck and pulling his face even with hers, her eyes pleading. "Please, honey. Please? Just one little bitty baby? It won't be that much trouble, and I promise to take really good care of it."

"A puppy would be easier."

"Don't be cute."

"You don't think a puppy would be easier than a baby? I do. In fact, I've been thinking of getting a dog. I've had my eye on this great-looking golden retriever."

"Why do you try so hard to aggravate me?"

"Because I'm such a sucker for that fiery little flash you get in your eye," he laughed, studying her annoyed expression and pointing at her. "See! There it is! Man, honey. You look like you're ready to deck me."

"I am ready to deck you," Diane growled through clenched teeth. "I can't believe you're being so obstinate. You'd think I was asking for the Taj Mahal!"

"I'm sure you will before it's all said and done," Jay chuckled again, unfazed by her withering stare. "Didn't anyone tell you that our marriage is still in the honeymoon phase? We've been married barely six months. We're supposed to be all gushy and lovey-dovey, and here you are, already nagging like a fishwife."

Diane squirmed out of his arms, throwing up her hands in disgusted resignation. "Will you stop! I would appreciate it if you would be serious for one minute. I really want to talk about this."

"Okay. I'm serious. Shoot."

"I'm not asking for that much, Jay. All I want is one teeny tiny little baby."

"Oh, don't beg, Diane. It's so beneath you." Jay couldn't help but kid her, earning the full brunt of her annoyance. Her mouth tightened into a stubborn line and she turned her back to him, folding her arms angrily across her chest.

"Okay, I went too far. I'm sorry." Curbing his playful laughter, Jay touched her bare shoulder, trailing his lips along her neck. "If you really feel that strongly about it, I guess I can accommodate you with one tiny baby."

Diane glanced at him skeptically. "What about the golden retriever?"

"We can have both," he suggested cleverly, wrapping his arms tightly around her waist.

"Are you sure?"

"Sure, I'm sure, but believe me, it's not without motive. From what I understand, there's a certain technique to be mastered in order to conceive a child and I, for one, definitely won't mind the practice. In fact," he nibbled at her ear, giving her goose bumps and sending chills down her spine, "I suggest we get started now. You know what they say — practice makes perfect."

Practice they did, but not for long. Diane became pregnant in August, shortly before Patricia gave birth to Geoffrey Palmer Carson III.

"I told you I was good," Jay announced proudly over Sunday dinner, terrorizing Geoff and winking comically at Diane. "I got it right on the very first try. How long did it take you, Geoff? Five or six months?"

Diane giggled and Geoff became flustered, huffing and clearing his throat. "I hardly think that's any of your business," he said, puffing up like an old toad.

Jay laughed, clinking his water glass to Diane's. "That's what I thought."

Diane was ecstatic, loving every sensation associated with her pregnancy. She reveled in her fatigue, delighted as the hormone surges gave her swollen tender breasts and crippling morning sickness. Every evening, she and Jay cuddled in the hammock strung between two tall oaks in their back yard, patting the tiny swell of her abdomen tenderly while discussing names for their unborn child. They couldn't have been more thrilled.

"Which one do you like?" she asked Jay, showing him the catalog of baby furniture. "The maple or the cherry?"

Jay grinned cheerfully, his eyes never leaving her face. "I like you," he said, plucking the magazine from her hands and enfolding her in a tight embrace. He wrapped his arms around her waist, resting his hand on her stomach. "I can't wait," he whispered, tenderly kissing her ear. "I can't wait to see you all chubby, with swollen ankles, waddling like a duck with an ice-cream cone in each hand."

"Ugh!" Diane glanced back at him, wearing a frown. "You make it sound so wonderful."

"It is wonderful," he replied, smoothing a swirl of chestnut curls back from her face. "You're wonderful, Sis — you and our baby. God truly smiled on me the day he brought you into my life. You're the best thing that's ever happened to me."

Their elation was short-lived when Diane miscarried during her fourteenth week. She was devastated, sobbing brokenheartedly in Jay's arms all the way home from the hospital, listening to his consoling whispers as he tenderly stroked her hair. "It's okay, honey. It's okay."

"It's all my fault," Diane sniffled, laying her head against Jay's chest.

"Don't be absurd, honey. This is not your fault."

"It *is* my fault! I brought it all on by jumping the gun, buying baby clothes and fixing up the nursery. If I had just remained patient, none of this would've happened. I jinxed it."

"Don't be stupid," Jay comforted her, tilting her chin up and tenderly caressing her cheek. "I'm telling you — it just wasn't meant to be. We'll just have to try again, sweetheart, which doesn't bother me one bit. I like trying."

"You would think of it that way," Diane gave him a grateful smile, taking the Kleenex he offered and blowing her nose. "Did I ever tell you that I love you?" she asked.

"A few times, here and there, but not nearly often enough," he replied with a teasing chuckle, pulling her closer. "Words are wonderful, but actions are better, and I can think of many ways in which you can get your point across."

They tried again, with much success. Less than a year later, Diane was pregnant. Under the care of the best obstetrician money could buy, she nursed her health, taking it easy and relaxing at home in bed or lounging on the back porch at Carson House, allowing Lois to coddle her and make much over her delicate condition.

This time everything was going be fine. Diane was convinced.

Again, Diane miscarried, never making it to the twelfth week of her second pregnancy. "I don't understand," she sobbed to Jay, burying her face in her hands as she sank onto the edge of their brass bed. "I didn't do anything wrong. I took good care of myself. I didn't try to guess the sex or pick out a name. I didn't even look at baby furniture this time. Why does this keep happening to me?"

"It's not your fault, sweetheart," Jay said, taking her grief-stricken body into his arms. "We'll just keep trying. The third time will be a charm, honey. I promise."

Right after Geoff and Patricia's third wedding anniversary in early June, both Patricia and Diane became with child, finding out about their pregnancies within days of one another. Diane was cautiously optimistic, determined not to get her hopes up as she and Patricia glowed happily together, spending their days with Lois, Daisy and Auntie Cee, piecing together tiny quilts in shades of mint green and daffodil yellow.

Eight weeks passed, then twelve, and finally, at sixteen weeks, Diane began to relax. *This child will make it*, she thought joyfully. *This child will be our firstborn.*

Thanksgiving approached and the weather turned cooler, bringing with it brilliantly changing foliage on the ancient trees surrounding Carson House. Diane, bundled warmly in an old white sweater of Lois', sat on the front veranda with Jay, cuddled deeply in the crook of his arm. Looking off in the distance, she smiled affectionately as she watched Lois and Palmer stroll arm in arm toward the stable on their way to saddle Sadie and Jasper for a Sunday morning ride.

"Your folks are amazing," Jay said, his eyes following the direction of Diane's stare. "Do you suppose we'll still be that much in love after thirty years?"

"I don't see why not," Diane leaned her head back against his chest, tilting up her face to gaze adoringly into his eyes. "I anticipate what I feel for you only growing stronger as time goes on."

Jay bent down to kiss her, their lips scarcely touching before they heard Lois' anguished wail coming from the stable. Quickly brushing

Diane aside, Jay vaulted from the veranda, running like a mad man toward the barn with Diane at his heels, forgetting her condition as she ran to her mother. They found Lois kneeling beside Palmer's fallen body, holding his limp hand and pleading for him to open his eyes, his body lifeless on the hard stable floor. Jay dove beside them, feeling Palmer's throat frantically for signs of a pulse.

"Diane, run to the house and call an ambulance!" he directed brusquely as he began performing CPR. Diane dashed out the door, sprinting as fast as her ballet-slippered feet would carry her, her chest aching from exertion and fear. She met Geoff on the front steps, shrieking hysterically as she ran past him. "Go to the stable, Geoff. Hurry! It's Daddy."

She heard the thud of his shoes as he clamored down the stairs, and she flung open the front door, her pulse roaring deafeningly in her ears. She bolted to the phone, her hand trembling and clammy as she lifted the receiver.

"Please, please send someone quickly," she begged the emergency operator. "It's my father. Please, it's my father." She slammed down the phone, frantic sobs catching in her throat as she collapsed against the banister, clutching it weakly and allowing the tears to come. "No," she wept, throwing back her head with an anguished plea. "Please God, no! Don't take my daddy." She sank to her knees, covering her face with her hands, wailing in agony as the noise of sirens drew near, finally becoming loud enough to drown out the sounds of her grief.

The funeral of Geoffrey Palmer Carson Sr. was on a Saturday, five days before Thanksgiving. In the days before the funeral, Diane stayed at Carson House with Lois, hoping her presence would alleviate some of the anguish she felt over the loss of her beloved Palmer. The first few days were terrible. Lois was a pitiful sight, so proud and silent, wandering absently from room to room, hiding her enormous grief.

"Mother, you know, it's okay to cry," Diane told her gently, sitting next to her on the bed, hoping she would open up.

Lois didn't utter a word. She just sat staring blankly into space, her face ashen, twisting a lace handkerchief round and round her finger until Diane thought her heart would break. "Mother, please say something," she pleaded, her voice cracking. "Yell, scream, curse! I don't care, only please, please just talk to me. I miss him too."

Lois looked at her, her eyes filling with tears. She drew Diane into her arms, stroking her long chestnut hair, her shoulders shaking as violent sobs wracked her body. They clung to each other — mother and daughter — sobbing brokenheartedly, grieving for the man who meant so much to them both.

By the end of the week, Diane was numb, having cried an ocean of tears since that dreadful morning in the stable. "I can't believe this is happening," she whispered hoarsely to Jay on the way to the cemetery, sheltered in the crook of his arm in the back of the limousine, her shaky voice threatening to dissolve into devastated sobs. "I just keep waiting to wake up from this hellish nightmare, but no matter how hard I try it just won't go away."

Losing her father was the worst thing Diane had ever experienced. Her pain was indescribable. She mourned him with every ounce of her being, wondering how she could cope without her father's doting smile and tender embrace, without hearing his deep, velvety voice and loving words of encouragement. Carson House seemed so empty, void of happiness and affection. Home would never be the same without him. A gaping hole had been torn through its foundation, leaving it cracked and unsteady, and above all, devastatingly grim.

The final blow — the final insult to injury — was the searing pain that ripped through Diane's abdomen as she stood between Lois and Jay at the cemetery, coupled with the terrifying warmth of blood gushing down her legs. Grimacing, she gripped Jay's arm, her knuckles white, a low moan escaping through her tightly clamped teeth. She met Geoff's worried stare, all color draining from her face as she was hit by another sudden wave of excruciating pain. Pallbearers dressed all in black, solemnly lowering her father's casket into the ground was the last sight she beheld before, wordlessly, Diane crumpled into an unconscious heap beside her father's grave.

She awoke in the hospital with Jay by her side, his face pale and drawn. She didn't have to ask. She knew immediately by the deep sadness etched in his eyes. She had lost the baby, their last chance for a child of their own. She ran her hand weakly across her stomach, confirming their loss, and looked up at Jay, clasping his outstretched hand, choking back bitter sobs as sorrow washed over her like a wave.

"Diane, honey, it's okay," Jay whispered, blinking back tears as he stroked her hair. "We'll try again. We'll get the best doctors and go every route there is to go. We'll find some way to have our baby. I promise."

"No." Diane raised her head, staring wearily into his haggard face. "Never again, Jay. I can't go through this every year. My heart just can't take it."

She lay back against the pillows and stared at the ceiling, anesthetized by grief, hot tears streaming down her face. *My entire life, I've never wanted for a thing*, she thought dismally, feeling the dark cloud of depression descending upon her. *I've had all that privilege could buy, but now, when I need it most, no amount of money can help me. All the money in the world can't buy me the ability to carry a child.*

First her father, and now this. It was almost too much to bear. She rolled onto her side, facing the wall, her heart twisted in anguish and shock, allowing her tumultuous thoughts to ramble. *Daddy always said that life has a funny way of playing tricks on you*, she recalled ironically. To want a baby so desperately and not be able to have one was life's cruelest trick of all.

She gave in to her despair, allowing the tears to come, burying her face in her pillow, weeping brokenheartedly until at last she drifted into an exhausted stupor.

The next year was tough for Diane, spent floundering in a deep pool of melancholy. The miscarriage, coupled with the heart attack that killed her father, had come so unexpectedly, like thieves in the night, robbing her of all emotion. Outwardly, Diane was a zombie. Inside, she was tortured, mourning Palmer and her unborn babies, and adamantly refused any further discussion regarding a child. She gave away the baby clothes she had so lovingly chosen and closed off the nursery, resolving never to darken its door again. There would be no baby, not for Jay and her, and she would just have to learn to live with it.

Jay threw himself into his work, and she passed her days with Lois and Patricia, reading novels and playing half-heartedly with two-year old Palmer, Geoff's revered firstborn. She pretended she was fine, acting as if nothing had ever happened, as if a baby were the farthest thing from her mind. But inside, she could never forget, and her heart ached desperately for a child of her own.

The one bright spot in her year came in March with the birth of Geoff and Patricia's second son, Cameron. Holding him at the hospital, Diane bonded instantly with the beautiful baby boy, losing herself in his bright eyes, falling deeply in love. Patricia allowed Diane as much time with Cameron as she wanted, hoping it would ease some of her haunting pain.

"Oh Geoff, look at her. It's just so unfair," Patricia said forlornly, observing Diane out on the front lawn rolling in the grass with baby Cameron. She dropped the curtain and turned to Geoff with a sad sigh. "I wish there was more I could do. I feel so helpless and guilty because our baby lived and hers didn't."

For six months, Jay watched Diane, his heart torn in two by her ashen face and the dark shadows around her lifeless eyes. He searched desperately for a solution to his wife's deep sadness, longing to see her spunk, to see the fire blazing in her brown eyes and to hear her bubbly laughter echo through their home. Never had he felt so powerless and worthless.

"Look at her," he said, gazing out the kitchen window, his face etched with grief, studying Diane as she sat listlessly on the porch swing, her hair limp and skin colorless, pushing herself back and forth apathetically. "I'd give anything to see her smile."

"I know." Patricia came up behind him and placed a soft hand on his shoulder, her voice gentle and soothing. "I miss that too."

"I can't stand this. I've got to do something, but I don't know what to do, Patty. I just don't know what to do." His voice cracked and he ran a troubled hand through his hair, staring out the window, his face perplexed. "Should I put her in therapy?"

"She doesn't need therapy, Jay. She needs a baby."

"What a novel idea," he snarled in frustration. "Any ideas where I might come up with one?"

"You don't have to be ugly."

"I'm sorry, Patricia." Jay reached for her hand, giving it an apologetic squeeze. "I didn't mean to bite your head off. The truth is, I thought we'd give it a year or so, then try one more time, but Diane won't even discuss it. She is dead set against another pregnancy."

"I can't say that I blame her. She's been through enough." Patricia studied him quietly, her expression thoughtful. "Have you considered adoption?"

"I have, but Diane won't go for it. She says she's through with the baby business, that it no longer matters to her."

"She's lying."

"Of course she's lying. I've never seen a woman with stronger maternal instincts. Lying or not, I won't push her. No matter how I feel about it, she's my wife and I won't go against her wishes."

Over the weeks that followed, Jay watched Diane's relationship with Cameron, seeing the smile he yearned for, noting how her face transformed every time she held the chubby baby in her arms. Watching them together, he knew what he had to do. *By God, if going behind her back is the only way to solve this, then that's what I'll have to do.*

He approached her in late October, joining her in the backyard hammock to watch the sun set in the dusky evening sky. He reclined next to her, pulling her into his arms and resting her head on his chest, running his fingers through her long chestnut hair. "Sis, you remember Brandon McClure?"

"Your classmate in Atlanta?"

"That's the one. I talked to him today."

"And what did Brandon want?"

"Well, actually I called him," Jay felt her probing stare but couldn't bring himself to look at her. "In fact, we've been talking for a while now, almost four months."

"Really? And are you going to share the reason you brought this up or just continue to leave me guessing?"

"You see, Diane," Jay hesitated, nervously clearing his throat. "Brandon specializes in adoption."

"And?"

Jay felt her body tighten, becoming tense and rigid in his arms. *Oh God, I hope I'm doing the right thing,* he thought anxiously. *This will either be the solution or the end of it all.*

He swallowed dryly, mentally squaring his shoulders. "*And* he has this client, a young pregnant woman in Alabama who wants to give up her baby."

Diane wrestled from his embrace, her eyes flashing wildly. "And this concerns us because?"

"Because, for the last four months, I've had Brandon searching for a child to adopt."

"How dare you go behind my back this way!" she lashed out bitterly. "I'm done with babies."

"Diane," he held fast to her shoulders, his eyes pleading. "Don't do this. Adoption is our answer. I know you still want a baby."

"But I want a child of our own, one created by us, one I carried and gave birth to," Diane choked, breaking into strangled sobs.

Jay held her tightly, tenderly lifting her chin, searching her face. "Honey, it will be no different, I promise you," he assured her gently, his soothing voice tugging at her heart. "I've seen you with Cameron and know how much you can love. Once you hold that baby in your arms, it will be yours, and you will love it no differently than if it were of your own flesh and bone."

"You're wrong." Diane pulled away and rolled from the hammock, her shoulders bowed in grief. "I could never love someone else's baby."

"I guess we'll find out in February. I told Brandon today to go ahead with the paperwork, that we wanted the baby."

"Well, you can just call him back *tonight* and tell him to forget it, because I don't want it," Diane screamed, spitting out her words with contempt, then whirled around and stalked off toward the house. "I don't want someone else's baby! If I can't have my own child, I just won't have one at all!"

She slammed the back door, shaking the house to its rafters, and ran down the hall, salty rivers streaming down her face. She locked herself in the bedroom, ignoring Jay's repeated request to be allowed inside. She threw herself on the bed, sobbing hysterically, her heart breaking, feeling betrayed, her chest aching with hurt and uncertainty.

She tossed and turned all through the night, carefully weighing the decision so heavy on her mind. *I so desperately want a baby, but can I really love the child of another woman?*

It terrified her, knowing that she could never carry a baby to term and that adoption was her only choice for motherhood. *What if it doesn't work out? What if I go through with it and feel nothing whatsoever for this child? I could never forgive myself.*

She finally slept, dreaming of sweet baby faces and heart-melting coos, waking with an answer for Jay. She found him in the guest room sleeping in his clothes and knelt on the bed beside him, gently touching his face.

"Call Brandon McClure," she said softly, smiling as Jay opened his sleepy eyes. "Tell him we want the baby."

They anticipated the birth of their baby on pins and needles, suffering through the impossibly long holiday season, feeling as though each day spent waiting was a thousand hours long. Diane cautiously reopened the nursery, flooded with heart-wrenching memories of her unborn children, putting on a brave face as she prepared for the child to come. "Please let everything go as planned," she prayed. "I can't bear another disappointment."

The call came in February, shortly before Valentine's Day, interrupting a romantic candlelit dinner at The Pink House. As Jay grabbed the buzzing pager at his waist, he and Diane locked eyes, exchanging an apprehensive yet overjoyed stare. Jay bolted from the table, rushing to the telephone to call Brandon McClure. He returned, animated and flushed, a jaunty smile illuminating his face. "Let's pay the check and get out of here," he said, his voice quivering with excitement as he attempted to maintain his composure. "We're going to Atlanta."

Diane fell in love the moment she saw her, the cherubic baby girl with downy blond hair and rosy pink cheeks. As the nurse placed her in Diane's waiting arms, she gazed down into the tiny girl's sweet face, marveling at the tight grip around the finger the baby clutched in her fist, and kissed the top of her head. Jay stood next to them, his eyes filling with jubilant tears, watching the perfect union of mother and child in ecstatic wonder, aware that their most fervent wish had finally been granted. At long last, Jay and Diane had a child of their own.

They brought Zoanne Annette Carson-Forest home the following day, arriving at Carson House to a parlor overflowing with family and overjoyed friends. Lois met them at the door, stealing Zoanne from Diane's arms, cuddling the baby to her chest.

"Welcome home, baby girl," she whispered, lifting the fluffy pink blanket with her fingertips and kissing her new granddaughter tenderly on the forehead. "It's about time you got here. We've been waiting for you for years."

At last Diane learned the true meaning of unconditional love. She found it in her baby girl. Zoë's blond-haired, bright-eyed beauty lit Diane's world like the most brilliant rays of sunshine, filling her days with unimaginable joy, her happy coos and toothless smiles melting Diane's heart into a shapeless puddle of euphoric goo.

Watching her blossom from a tiny infant into a sunny little girl, Diane admitted that Jay had been right. From the first moment she'd held Zoë in her arms, it was no different. She could have loved no child more. At last, Diane was truly happy. With Zoë, her life was complete.

# *Part Four*

# *Zoë*

# 12

Young Palmer Carson leaned sullenly against one of the Corinthian columns adorning the front of Carson House, wearing a suit much too expensive for the average twelve-year old, his hands shoved in his pockets and a disgusted look on his handsome face as he watched the chaotic scene unfolding before him. His father and his Uncle Jay were dressed in their Sunday best, busily rearranging furniture on the veranda, aided by his mother Patricia, dressed to the nines in aquamarine, and his Aunt Diane, lovely in floral pink with a wide-brimmed straw hat topping her auburn tresses. His brother Cameron was annoying, as always, running helter-skelter down the length of the porch, his tie loosened and askew, trailed laughingly by a petite blond in sky-blue taffeta. Palmer narrowed his eyes in contempt at the sight of her, staunchly resisting the overwhelming urge to stick out his foot and trip her as she flew past.

"Does Zoë really have to be in the picture?" he inquired caustically, casting an irritated look at his grandmother.

"Of course she's going to be in the picture," Lois snapped, cradling a tissue-wrapped spray of red roses in her arms, its decorative ribbons matching exactly the golden hue of her dress. "Everyone is. I want a full family portrait to commemorate my sixty-fifth birthday."

"But she sticks out like a sore thumb!"

"Only because she's so much prettier than you are," Jay interjected with a proud grin, reaching over to playfully pinch Zoë's cheek.

"No — only because she's not a real Carson," Palmer retorted, his eyes flashing with indignation.

"Geoffrey Palmer Carson!" Lois bellowed across the veranda, scaring the poor photographer half out of his wits. "Don't you dare start that again! She's every bit as much a Carson as you are."

Palmer let his extreme distaste for his nine-year-old cousin override his good judgment, foolishly defying Lois by continuing to air his views. "She is not. She's not even a blood relative. She doesn't deserve to be in a family portrait. She's just some poor orphan Aunt Diane took in out of the goodness of her heart. She probably dug her out of a dumpster."

"I beg your pardon!" Diane sputtered, her face flushed with anger. She spun around, confronting her brother Geoff, slapping his arm furiously for laughing. "Why do you let him go on like this? Why don't you say something to stop him instead of just egging him on?"

"I would," Geoff said, checking his entertained chuckle as he looked over her shoulder, "but Mother is just about to get it all under control."

Lois threw down her congratulatory spray of roses and stalked across the porch, grabbing Palmer by the ear and yanking it soundly. "I've had just about enough of your mouth, young man," she informed him testily. "You make her cry before we take this picture, and I'm skinning you alive!"

"But Grandmother, I didn't say anything that wasn't true!"

"You should get your facts straight before you go shooting off that big mouth of yours," Lois said, releasing his ear after one final pull. "In spite of what you'd like to believe, your cousin wasn't dumped unwanted anywhere. Jay and Diane searched high and low for her and waited a very long time."

"And paid perfectly good money for her too, I might add," Geoff threw in for good measure, earning a sharp elbow to the ribs from his wife.

Lois ignored him, going on with her lecture. "I don't know what has gotten into you, Palmer. I can't believe Geoff is raising you to be such a snob."

"I don't know why not," Diane cut in cynically. "It's only appropriate, Mother — like father, like son. Thank God Cameron takes after Patricia."

Ten-year-old Cameron climbed up on the porch rail beside his cousin Zoë, taking her hand protectively, disheartened by her long face. "Don't listen to Palm, Zoë. He's nothing but a pig, and you know it."

"I heard that," Palmer joined them, reclining on his elbows against the rail, shooting his brother a superior look.

"Yeah, I know. I meant for you to." Cameron dropped Zoë's hand and got in his face, his fists tightly clenched and his eyes leaping menacingly. "You say one more word about Zoë, and I'm decking you."

"Let's take this damn picture and get it over with!" Lois shouted in exasperation, signaling the photographer. She swept her roses off the floor with a grand flourish, clutching them tightly in her arms, then turned to issue a word of warning to her family. "Everybody here better smile and look like you're having the time of your life, or I'm killing every last one of you!"

"One, two, three," the photographer counted and snapped the photo, his flash blinding them, freezing for all time the dazzling smiles of the Carson clan, their angelic faces never betraying the ferocious brawl that had just ensued.

Zoanne Carson-Forest had the perfect childhood. As the only child of Diane and Jay, she grew up in the lap of luxury, never wanting for anything, basking radiantly in the love of all those around her. She never knew an unhappy moment and truly had it all: a father who adored her, a mother who catered to her every whim and a grandmother who thought she was the greatest. For Zoë, life couldn't have been any better.

She had always known she was adopted. The fact that she was of different lineage was hardly a secret. The Carsons couldn't have disguised it if they had tried. Although her coloring was similar to Jay's, one could tell she hadn't sprung from his loins. There were too many generations of red-haired, brown-eyed Carsons to produce someone so purely blond. Despite the fact that she was not their biological child, Zoë never doubted her parents' love for her. Their devotion was a constant in her life, always there — reassuring, encouraging and supporting her.

She grew up in a red brick house surrounded by arching live oaks and bright azaleas, next door to her Great-Auntie Cee and just down a winding lane from her grandmother Lois. She spent her nights at home with her parents, but spent most of her days at Carson House, inheriting

Diane's childhood bedroom with pink-champagne-colored walls, a serene place where she hid all her treasures. She frequently stayed weekends with Lois while her parents were away, sleeping in a white wrought-iron canopy bed under sheets trimmed with the finest lace and a quilt of pale yellow, mint green and rose, pieced together by her great-grandmother, Adrienne LeJeune.

Zoë's two cousins, Palmer and Cameron, also lived at Carson House, sharing most of the second floor with her Uncle Geoff and Aunt Patricia. The brothers were alike in appearance, sharing the same characteristic Carson coloring, but thankfully had personalities as different as night and day.

Geoffrey Palmer Carson III, also known as Palmer, was tall and lanky, highly intelligent and as pompous as his name. He was the oldest and had long ago established himself as the celebrated heir-apparent to the Carson throne. Palmer had little use for Zoë, regarding her fair-haired beauty and sunny personality with jealous disdain. He taunted the rest of the family for making such a big deal over his adopted cousin and greatly resented having to share the limelight with her. He considered her to be well beneath him in stature and rarely missed an opportunity to get in a jab at her.

Charles Cameron, the younger son, was everything his brother was not. Fondly referred to as Cam, Cameron was older than Zoë by eleven months, with dark reddish-brown hair that sprouted from his head in a helmet of unruly curls. He was a fireball, having inherited Lois' intense jade-green eyes and impassioned disposition, and displayed boundless energy, much more than any member of the Carson family had shown for generations.

Palmer found his brother almost as offensive as Zoë. "Zoanne is adopted, and Cameron is a product of the recessive gene pool," he explained to anyone who asked, "probably the result of mixing bad blood into the family centuries ago."

Zoë and Cameron were inseparable, sharing a mutual adoration for one another and a mutual dislike of Palmer the third. They spent every waking hour together, attending the local grade school, spending their summers in cutoff shorts and T-shirts, wading in the muddy waters of the ponds surrounding Carson House or fishing with cane poles off the edge of the wooden boat dock. Sharing their innermost thoughts, secrets and dreams, Cameron and Zoë traveled the countryside together, dashing on horseback across the green pastures of the family estate, graduating in their teens to racing along the twisting back roads in Cameron's black Porsche 911, the top down, wind whipping through their hair, radio blaring as they sang at the top of their lungs.

Lois loved her three grandchildren equally, but received the most pleasure from Zoë and Cam. In Cameron, she'd found a kindred spirit. In Zoë, she saw herself. She indulged their carefree spirits and nurtured their resistance to traditional family ways, taking them under her protective wing, determined to make them into better-rounded people than Beatrice had made Geoff and Diane.

Consequently, Lois objected the loudest when Diane and Jay elected to send Zoë to boarding school at the tender age of fifteen, making their announcement over Sunday dinner. "Zoë's leaving next month for Miss Colleen's," Diane mentioned offhandedly, helping herself to another serving of fresh black-eyed peas.

"What on earth for!" Lois exploded, her fiery eyes snapping angrily. "We have fine schools right here in Eden Glen."

"We think it's time she gained a little refinement."

"Refinement? My God, Diane — you've already got her taking every piano lesson and dance class offered in Chatham County. Just how much refinement does one fifteen-year-old need? She's plenty refined. There's no need to send her off to that place."

"You didn't have any problem sending me off to that place."

"If you recall, it was not I who sent you off to Miss Colleen's. It was Beatrice — and you hated every minute of it."

"I did not! I liked Miss Colleen's."

"You did not. You used to call me nearly every night, crying."

"I *never* called you crying."

Lois pursed her lips, contemplating thoughtfully. "No," she conceded cheerfully, "you're right. You never did. That must've been Geoff."

Geoff gawked at her, sputtering in protest, keenly aware of Palmer's reproachful stare. "I *never* cried."

Diane's mouth fell open and she lit into him, spitting like a hellcat. "Yes, you did, you big titty baby, all the time!"

"You're delusional."

Lois cleared her throat, tapping her water glass with her knife. "Excuse me, *children*," she eyed Geoff and Diane disapprovingly, "but could we please get back to the matter at hand?"

"By all means." Geoff immediately gave his consent, still glaring at Diane.

"I see no need in shipping Zoë off," Lois reiterated, frowning sternly at Diane. "You may have liked it there, but *you* were different, Diane. You belonged there. Zoë has way too much personality to be reined in with all those mealy-mouthed little debutantes."

"Mother, please," Diane sighed, rolling her eyes indignantly. "If *you'll* recall, Zoë is our child, and we'll send her to any school we'd like."

"Don't I have any say in this?" Zoë spoke up, peering up at them with a long face as she twirled her fork apathetically in her mashed potatoes and gravy.

"Not this time, honey — because you'll only side with her," Diane said, jerking her thumb at Lois before flashing Zoë a reassuring smile. "Daddy and I know what's best for you, sweetheart. You'll love Miss Colleen's. You'll see."

"For once, I have to side with Grandmother." Palmer chose precisely that moment to express his unsolicited opinion, leaning back in his straight-backed chair, his fingers steepled arrogantly against his chin. "I think it would be a great waste of funds to send Zoë to Miss Colleen's. She's just not cut out to be one of the upper crust, not being a *real* Carson and all."

"Oh God, don't start that again," Geoff shook his head in disgust, giving his son a weary stare. "You're just going to set her off."

"Palmer," Lois jerked her head in his direction, a haughty gleam in her eye.

"See," Geoff nodded self-righteously, "I told you."

"Young man," Lois cleared her throat and spoke louder, getting his attention. "There's not one drop of *Carson* blood flowing through my veins," she reminded him frigidly, "and I am far from being white trash, I assure you."

Palmer turned bright red, scowling unpleasantly at being bested. Zoë glanced over at him, batting her eyelashes, a sugary smirk spreading over her face at his humiliation.

"Excuse me, please!" Palmer grumbled, glaring at his cousin. "I've suddenly lost my appetite." He threw back his chair in a huff and stomped from the room.

"Me too." Cameron pushed away from the table and followed Palmer into the hall, reaching out powerful hands to grab him by the lapels, jerking him to an abrupt halt. "I've had about enough of your attitude, brother dear," Cameron said, issuing a scorching look, his fiery green eyes burning holes right through his brother. "If I've warned you once, I've warned you a thousand times. One more word out of you — you smug, pompous, son-of-a-bitch — and I'm taking you to the mat," he promised in an intimidating tone, his face mere inches from Palmer's.

Palmer wrestled his jacket from Cameron's grip and smoothed down the collar, glaring at him, an intense frown on his bright red face. "I'd like to see you try," he retorted gallantly, his chin squared in defiance.

"Don't tempt me."

"I *know* there's not about to be a fist fight in my front entry," Lois' voice interrupted them from the dining room.

"Take it outside, boys." Geoff backed her up, sticking his head into the corridor.

"After you," Cam said to Palmer, gesturing grandly toward the door.

"Meet you out there," Palmer answered, swallowing hard, his eyes darting nervously as he looked for a way out.

"Sure you will," Cameron laughed and walked away, still chuckling. "What a wimp."

He collected Zoë from the dining room and they slipped out the back door, heading in the direction of their favorite fishing hole. "I can't believe they're sending me away like this," she sighed glumly, plopping down on the dock, dangling her fishing pole into the murky water of the pond. She kicked her legs back and forth, her woeful eyes downcast and her bottom lip stuck out in a fretful pout.

"I know," Cameron agreed, throwing his arm chummily around her shoulders. "What'd you do to piss them off?"

"Nothing bad enough to deserve this."

Cameron laughed. "It's not the end of the world."

"It might as well be!"

"Nothing is ever as bad as you think."

Zoë gave him a dirty look. "You can say that, Cam. You don't have to leave home and live with total strangers who you have absolutely nothing whatsoever in common with! You get to stay here."

"Yeah, I get to stay here — *with* Palmer. Some consolation prize."

"I'd take Palmer any day over the kind of girls Lois says are at Miss Colleen's."

"Mealy-mouth little debutantes?"

"Exactly."

"You'll fit right in." Cameron cackled devilishly, and Zoë punched hard him in the arm.

"Jerk," she snarled, sticking her lip out further as she stared unhappily into the water, struggling to hold back angry tears.

Seeing that she was about to crumble, Cameron yanked her blond ponytail playfully. "You're not going to be that far away, Zoë. I'll come visit, every day if I have to."

Zoë raised her eyes, a hopeful expression lighting her face. "Promise?"

"Cross my heart," he said. "I'd never leave you there to rot alone."

Despite the opposition, Diane enrolled Zoë in her alma mater, Miss Colleen's School for Young Ladies, fifty miles from home. After spending the last month of her fifteenth summer shrouded in dread, Zoë was pleasantly surprised when Miss Colleen's didn't turn out to be too bad at all. The old girls' school was actually quite pretty with Victorian architecture, tall trees and immaculate gardens bursting with bright blossoms of red, lavender and pink. The campus was littered with girls of all ages, attired in mini-skirts and denim shorts, chattering animatedly on roller skates or gathered around blaring radios, comparing notes on the latest super group. While taking in the scenery, Jay shot Diane a questioning look.

"Mealy-mouthed little debutantes?" he remarked inquiringly, his mouth stretching into an amused grin.

Diane nodded and laughed, linking her arm through his as they continued down the path. "Apparently things have changed since Mother was last here," she said, her eyes sparkling with delight. "I almost wish she was along for the ride so she would quit acting so sullen."

"She's going to act sullen, no matter what," Jay chuckled good-naturedly. "I don't think it's where we're sending Zoë that bothers Lois. I think it's that we're sending her, period."

"Oh, she'll cheer up after she sees how happy Zoë is here."

"I hope you're right."

"About her cheering up or about Zoë being happy here?"

"Both."

They settled Zoë into her room, a generic cracker box on the second floor of McKenzie Hall, helping her unpack and make her bed. As the afternoon drew to a close, Diane and Jay reluctantly said farewell, each kissing Zoë and giving her a tight embrace. "You're going to love it here," Diane assured her for the thousandth time, her brown eyes filling with tears.

Zoë pushed her toward the door with a giggle, handing Diane her purse as she shooed them out the door. "Get out of here before you start crying," she grinned, giving them a flirty little wave. "I'm supposed to be the one crying, not you. Now, go home. I'll be fine."

She watched from the window as they exited the building, an overly bright smile on her face as she gave them another convincing wave goodbye. As their car pulled away from the curb, she plopped dismally on the edge of her bunk, staring forlornly around the room, taking in the boring beige walls and generic white furnishings and sighed heavily, already missing her family.

"I'm going to be absolutely miserable," she whimpered, flopping backward on the bed. As she contemplated her wretched existence, the door flew open with a bang and she sat up with a start.

A dark-haired girl dashed quickly over the threshold, balancing a suitcase precariously in each hand and a cosmetic bag slung haphazardly over one shoulder. She blew into the room like a breath of fresh air, flashing Zoë a vivacious smile as she dropped the bags in a heap on the drab tile floor. "Hey, Roomie," she said, extending her hand for a hearty handshake. "Leigh Streete, damn glad to meet you."

Zoë returned Leigh's enthusiastic smile, surveying her new roommate with great interest as she removed the felt beret topping her shining locks and tossed it with carefree abandon onto the dressing table across the room.

Leigh Streete was a little thing, hardly bigger than a minute, with straight ebony hair cut bluntly at her chin in a style reminiscent of Scout Finch. Dressed smartly in navy walking shorts and a crisp white blouse, she was attractive with an apple-blossom complexion, high cheekbones and almond-shaped eyes in the most fascinating shade of deep violet. She spoke with a sultry Southern drawl, in a voice bigger than she was, and possessed a throaty laugh, contagious even in Zoë's depressed state of mind.

Leigh was from Atlanta and had been sent to Miss Colleen's in a last-ditch effort by her parents to contain her spirited personality. "My mother thinks I'm out of control," Leigh revealed dramatically, collapsing on the bunk opposite Zoë's. "But I'm not out of control. I just want a life, you know what I'm saying?"

Over the course of the first semester, Zoë and Leigh became fast friends and confidantes, gossiping instead of studying, spending nights in their tiny room bundled in cozy pajamas, eating popcorn while discussing their friends and families.

Leigh knew of the Savannah Carsons. "Who doesn't?" she asked with an unaffected shrug, lounging flat on her back on the carpet between their bunks. "I met your cousin Palmer once at a country club cotillion in Atlanta," she informed Zoë with a scornful laugh. "My God, what a snob. How did you fare so well? You don't act like a snob."

"Sure I do," Zoë answered kiddingly, rolling onto her stomach and fluffing her pillow beneath her chin.

"No, you don't. I've seen many snobs in my short lifetime, and you're definitely not one of them."

"We're not all like that. My grandmother Lois would skin me alive if I ever acted like I was better than anyone else. Besides, I'm adopted."

"No!" Leigh's eyes grew wide with surprise. "Really?"

"Promise."

"Uh-uh!" Leigh squealed and scrambled off the floor, joining Zoë on the bed, giddy with excitement. "That is *so* cool. I always wanted to be adopted."

"Why?"

"So I could declare, once and for all, that I'm not genetically linked to Tom and Carol Streete. At least then I'd have a good excuse for why they're so stupid, and I'm not."

Zoë laughed. "I guess that's as good a reason as any."

Leigh moved closer, her expression solemn. "Doesn't it feel weird?"

"Knowing I'm adopted? Not at all. I've certainly never been treated any differently."

"Don't you want to look for them? Your real parents, I mean?"

"Jay and Diane are my real parents."

"You know what I mean. Your birth parents — don't you want to find them?"

"Not really. I never really thought about it."

"But I think it would be so awesome to at least find your birth mother," Leigh persisted, chewing her lip in concentration, her eyes lighting with a sudden idea. "Let's do it, Zoë!" she said, grabbing Zoë's shoulders. "I could help you. What if she's somebody famous, you know, like a ballet dancer or a Hollywood star?"

"I seriously doubt that."

"But you'd never know for sure, now would you?" Leigh frowned at Zoë's lack of enthusiasm and released her, shaking her head in disapproval. "I can't believe you aren't the slightest bit curious. Don't you want to at least know what she looks like?"

Zoë shrugged and flipped onto her back, staring up at the ceiling apathetically. "Maybe," she answered, sounding as nonchalant as she felt. Before Leigh's zealous interrogation, she'd never given it a thought. "I'm just not consumed by any real, burning desire to find her," she replied honestly. Being adopted was not something she dwelled upon, and the thought of having another mother rarely entered her mind. Diane was the only mother she'd ever known.

On weekends, the students at Miss Colleen's were free to come and go as they pleased, and every Friday Zoë journeyed back to Eden Glen, leaving the dormitory in a long sleek car with her father or her Uncle Geoff. Leigh rarely went home to Atlanta. Zoë couldn't decide if it was because she didn't want to go or her parents didn't want her to come. The closer she and Leigh became, the more distressed Zoë grew over leaving Leigh all alone at Miss Colleen's, feeling like a traitor, deserting her to spend time in the company of her loving family.

"Why don't you come home with me this weekend?" she suggested at Halloween, peeking over her history book at Leigh. "We could go trick or treating."

"What, and give up a weekend here in the lap of luxury?" Leigh remarked cynically, indicating their tiny dorm room with a sweeping gesture.

"It might be good for you."

"C'mon, Zoë. Your family doesn't want me there."

"Sure they do. My grandmother always says the more the merrier."

"Your grandmother has never had to put up with someone as obnoxious as me."

"Yes, she has. We have Palmer, remember?"

"Oh yeah, I forgot about him." Leigh grinned, tapping her chin indecisively, almost committing, then shook her head. "Nah, I think I'll pass this weekend. I've got stuff to do."

"What stuff?"

"Just stuff," Leigh offered a thin smile, her jaw set stubbornly.

"There's no stuff you have to do that couldn't wait until Monday."

"Drop it, Zoë, okay?" Leigh snapped, frowning humorlessly. "I'm not going home with you this weekend and that's final. End of discussion."

Zoë didn't argue. She had already learned that there was no arguing with Leigh. Instead, she spent the winter twisting Leigh's arm, nipping at her, continuing well after Christmas break until finally Leigh gave in and agreed to spend the weekend in Eden Glen. "I had to do something to get you off my back," she growled to Zoë as she threw her bag into the trunk of Jay's car. "If you had begged me to come home with you one more time, I would've screamed."

Jay chatted happily with the two girls on the hour drive to Eden Glen, laughing at Zoë's anecdotes and getting to know Leigh. "I hope you two are hungry," he said as they pulled through the gates of the estate. "Your mother's made a real special dinner."

"Mother cooked?" Zoë raised a curious brow. "That's a first."

"Surely not a first," Jay corrected her, his eyes crinkling merrily. "Maybe a second, but certainly not a first."

"We're eating at home? What's the occasion?"

"Geoff took Patricia and the boys up to Massachusetts to check out Palmer's school."

"What fun. I'm sure Cam was thrilled."

"I'm sure he was," Jay agreed drolly, cutting his eyes to Zoë. "Anyway, your mother thought that she'd make dinner at the house for a change and invite Lois down later."

As they drove past the main house, Leigh pressed her face to the window, blinking in awe. "That's my grandmother's house," Zoë whispered, leaning over Leigh's shoulder, her voice tinged with pride.

"So I gathered," Leigh commented, her gaze lingering on the breathtaking mansion as they continued down the lane. "It's gorgeous. When was it built?"

"Mid-1800s," Jay answered. "Right before the Civil War. Ask Lois about it after dinner. She'll give you a complete history lesson."

"I'll bet," Leigh murmured, looking ahead down the road, focusing her gaze on the pair of houses coming up on the right.

"The stucco one belonged to my great aunt Cecilia," Zoë explained, pointing at the first house. "She passed away a few years ago."

"I'm sorry."

"Yeah, me too. She was a grand old lady — she and my aunt Daisy both. Aunt Daisy's been gone since I was a little girl," Zoë reflected pensively, sadness hanging on her words. She perked up suddenly as the next house came into view, pointing it out excitedly to Leigh. "And this is our house, and look! There's my mom!"

Jay wheeled into the driveway and Zoë jumped out before he stopped the car, dashing pell-mell toward the attractive redhead standing on the lawn. Leigh grinned self-consciously as they embraced, then exited the car, meeting Jay at the trunk to retrieve her bag.

"I've got it," he told her with an easy smile. "Go say hi to Diane."

"I'm so happy to finally meet you!" Diane said, pulling Leigh into a warm bear hug and kissing her cheek. "I've been begging Zoë for months to bring you out here. I'm so glad you could finally come."

"Thanks for having me," Leigh murmured softly, her demeanor uncharacteristically pristine. Zoë covered her mouth with her hands, her eyes dancing as she tried not to laugh.

Diane suspected nothing and slid an arm around her waist, guiding her into the house. "You're welcome honey, any time."

Within minutes of arriving in Eden Glen, Leigh felt at ease, finding that the infamous Carsons didn't intimidate her in the least. *So much for my two-headed Martian theory,* she thought comically, walking with Diane into the all-American red brick home. *So far, they're the most normal family I've ever seen — darn near Ward and June Cleaver.*

She watched Zoë with her parents as they unloaded the car, observing their relationship in jealous wonder, her chest burning with envy as she emitted a wistful sigh. *I'd give anything to have parents like that,* she thought sadly. Her own parents were a joke.

Leigh instantly fell in love with Jay and Diane, amazed at how quick they were to treat her as one of their own. As soon as she crossed the threshold, Diane latched on to her, presenting her with a huge purple teddy bear and a plate of homemade chocolate chip cookies, then gave her a grand tour of the house and exquisitely landscaped grounds before showing her to her own lavender-hued bedroom across the hall from Zoë's.

"Your parents are nice people," Leigh said as she settled in, hoisting her suitcase up onto the quilt-covered bed and flipping open the locks, preparing to unload her clothes.

"I told you they were pretty decent," Zoë said with a grin, taking a stack of T-shirts from Leigh's bag, moving them to an empty bureau drawer.

"This is a great room," Leigh gazed around, taking in the frilly bedclothes, crisp draperies and wide-open view from two picture windows. "It looks like it came right out of a magazine or something."

"Yep. This room has always been one of my favorites. It used to be yellow."

"I bet that was nice. Why'd they change it?"

"Because I told them your favorite color is purple."

"They changed the color of this room, just for me?" Leigh marveled, beaming happily, her pretty face brightening in awe. "Why?"

"They wanted you to feel welcome," Zoë replied lightly, giving her a fond hug. "I told you they'd love having you here." She stretched her arms above her head, stifling a yawn. "I think I'm going to go grab a shower," she told Leigh, padding casually to the door. "Just make yourself at home. I'll come get you when it's time for dinner."

She closed the door behind her, leaving Leigh sitting on the edge of the bed, her violet eyes round with astonishment. "So, this is what real families are like," she whispered, a trail of frustrated tears trickling down her cheeks. "I've gotten more love from Zoë's parents in one day than I've gotten from my own in a lifetime. And they're total strangers."

She sniffed loudly, wiping her streaked face on her sleeve, retreating into the bathroom to splash cold water on her face. She stared at her sad reflection, biting her lip, determined not to cry. "Cheer up, spoiled sport," she scolded the girl in the mirror, forcing a bright smile. "You've got nothing to cry about, kid. Right now, you're in heaven."

She changed her clothes, trading in her worn jeans for a nice cotton sheath. "I think I'm really going to like these people," she mused aloud, watching from the window as Jay and Diane crossed the lawn, arms linked cozily, their faces aglow with good cheer. "I just hope I can make them like me."

Jay and Diane did like Leigh, immensely, bonding with her over dinner. Leigh basked in their affection, overwhelmed and appreciative of their genuine fondness. She joined in on the dinner conversation, telling funny stories about herself, but chose not to elaborate on her home life, finding it painful to discuss, especially in such happy surroundings.

Lois got more out of her than anyone, joining them after the evening meal for chocolate cake and coffee. She headed straight for Leigh the moment she entered the room, thrusting her hand out enthusiastically. "I'm Lois," she said, giving Leigh a no-nonsense smile. "Not Mrs. Carson, not Zoë's grandmother — just Lois."

Leigh took her hand, studying the grand madame of the Carson clan with great interest. "Hello, Lois," she murmured politely. "I'm Leigh Streete."

"Well, Leigh Streete, we're glad to have you here," Lois said jovially, motioning her to sit, choosing one of Diane's newly-acquired wingbacks upon which to prop her own feet. "Zoë tells me that you're from Atlanta."

"Yes, ma'am."

"Atlanta's a pretty place — not nearly as beautiful as Savannah, but pretty just the same." Lois accepted the cup of heavily creamed coffee Diane held out to her. "Tell me about your family," she requested, regarding Leigh thoughtfully, quickly picking up on her reluctance.

Leigh lowered her eyes and fidgeted uncomfortably, unwilling to look Lois in the eye. "What would you like to know?" she asked softly.

"Names and occupations are always a good place to start," Lois urged, anxious to learn what the girl had to hide.

"Their names are Tom and Carol, and they live in a high-rise penthouse in downtown Atlanta," Leigh began hesitantly, her face flushed with shame. "And their occupations? Well, my father was in banking and my mother was an actress, although I don't really know what it is they do these days, except socialize. To be truthful, they've never really had to do much. They're both trust-fund brats and, except for a fleeting moment or two over the past decade, are basically pretty worthless."

Diane flinched, staring in astonishment, unused to such outspoken hostility from a fifteen-year-old child. Zoë felt her eyes misting over with sympathetic tears and stretched her hand over the couch cushions, resting it consolingly on Leigh's arm.

*I knew her folks weren't in the running for parents of the year, but I had no idea they were this pathetic,* she thought, risking a glance at her mother, meeting her appalled gaze.

Leigh cut her eyes to Zoë and Diane, noting their shock, then looked at Lois, their eyes locking in mutual understanding. Lois gave a slight nod, and stood abruptly, depositing her coffee cup on the end table with a bang.

"Hey, you know what?" she said loudly, her odd facial expression sending Zoë and Diane a silent warning. "I left my reading glasses up at the house, and I sure don't want to walk up there all alone in the dark to get them. Be a doll, Leigh, and walk with me."

"Sure," Leigh agreed eagerly, relieved to find a way out of the awkward discussion. She trailed Lois out the door, scampering quickly to keep up with her brisk pace, and bounded down the front steps behind her.

Zoë glanced skeptically at her mother, nodding toward her grandmother's retreating figure. "Since when does she wear reading glasses?" she asked suspiciously.

Diane smiled broadly, a wise twinkle in her eye. "She doesn't," she replied lightly, her voice laced with knowing laughter. "She's just being Lois."

Lois and Leigh strolled side by side down the lane toward Carson House, Leigh's flat shoes making scuffing noises along the pavement. Leigh stared blankly into the darkness, her heart heavy as she thought about her parents.

Lois considered her forlorn expression. *I know I should leave the girl alone, since it's really none of my business anyway.* She debated with her nagging conscience, but couldn't leave well enough alone, choosing instead to stick with her customary way of doing things, plunging headfirst into the middle of Leigh's personal life. *Well,* she rationalized, *the child needs someone to talk to. Besides, I see absolutely no sense in letting sleeping dogs lie.*

"So, you want to tell me about them?" she asked aloud, staring ahead impassively, giving Leigh a way out if she really wanted it.

"No," Leigh responded curtly, glancing at Lois, her eyes shining with unshed tears, "but I will."

She shuffled along, anxiously twisting her fingers, her voice trembling as she spoke. "We're not very close, my parents and I. In fact, I've never felt very comfortable with them at all. How do you live comfortably in the shadow of the great Carol Collins-Streete?

"My mother was at the height of her career when she got pregnant, and I guess having me was the end of her world. She always said her career really ended the day I was conceived. And my father hasn't been any better about it. He simply chooses to pretend that I don't exist.

"They've always acted like I was in the way, underfoot, stealing their freedom, keeping them from their parties and impromptu trips abroad," she paused, her voice cracking as she brushed away bitter tears. "I don't think they really wanted me, and I know they don't love me. The truth is, they consider me more of an inconvenience than a cherished child, which is why I ended up at Miss Colleen's in the first place."

Lois nodded sympathetically, her mouth set in a tense line, her heart going out to the wistful girl before her. "If it's any consolation," she muttered encouragingly, "her career was over long before she had you. Carol Collins never was really much of an actress."

She grinned, touching Leigh's shoulder gently in a show of support. "There are always going to be people like that, Leigh — cold, unfeeling, selfish people who care about nothing but themselves. Those kind of people can make you feel pretty worthless if you let them." She stopped in the middle of the road, giving Leigh a somber look. "What's important to remember is you can't let people like that get to you. They're the ones with the problem, missy — not you."

"Thanks," Leigh whispered gratefully, her sad expression replaced by an inquisitive smile. "How'd you get so wise?"

"Experience," Lois enlightened her with a cackle. "I had a mother-in-law very similar to your parents."

"No!" Leigh scoffed, issuing a doubtful laugh. "There's no way anyone in this family could be like that."

"Oh yes, trust me. There are a few still with us today. My son and grandson are two prime examples. Nevertheless, neither can hold a candle to the almighty Beatrice. She was the antichrist."

They reached Carson House, and Lois insisted upon taking Leigh through, showing her each showcase-perfect room, giving a complete account of present and former occupants, along with a lively anecdote of its history. They ended their tour on the veranda, taking adjacent wicker seats, relaxing in comfortable silence as they listened to the haunting sounds of frogs and crickets echoing distantly through the thick night air.

"Did you grow up around here?" Leigh asked curiously.

"Lord no, girl!" Lois laughed, her expression pleasingly nostalgic. "South Louisiana."

"Really? You don't sound like it."

"I've been away a long time," Lois replied matter-of-factly. "I married Zoë's grandfather and moved here when I was eighteen."

"Any regrets?"

"Heavens no! Best move I ever made. I would've gone to the far ends of the earth to be with him. Palmer Carson was one of a kind."

"Sounds like you really loved him."

"Oh, I did — still do. He was something else: handsome, smooth — absolutely larger than life. I was so very much in love with that man. I don't think I'll ever get over losing him."

"Is that why you never remarried?"

"I suppose, although I had plenty of opportunities. I wasn't always a silver-haired old woman," Lois revealed with a mischievous grin, mirthful crinkles springing up around her green eyes. She eyed Leigh's coal-black locks thoughtfully. "My hair used to be about the color of yours, and honey, I was quite a dish."

Leigh laughed merrily. "I'm sure you were. I bet you were quite a handful in your day."

"In my day?" Lois raised a questioning brow. "I'll have you know, missy, I'm still quite a handful!" she chuckled, amused by her own cleverness. "Anyway," she rocked, deep in thought, "they came in droves after Palmer died — widowers, divorcees, never-been-weds — tap-dancing and showing their wares, all vying for my hand. However, I politely refused them all. None of them would do. I'd already had the best. Anyone else would seem second-rate. There is just no replacing a man like Palmer."

"He sounds wonderful. I wish I could've known him."

"I wish you could've too. He's been gone a while now. He died the year before Zoë was born," Lois answered softly, perking up with a happy thought. "We still have a piece of him here, though. My grandson Cameron is darn near the spitting image of him."

She slapped her hands briskly on the arms of her chair and rose, flashing Leigh a sunny smile. "I guess we had better get back to the house before Diane sends out the bloodhounds."

Leigh jumped out of her seat and joined Lois on the stairs, falling in step with her as they hurried down the road. "Thanks for cheering me up, Lois," she said appreciatively, "and for making me feel so welcome."

Lois looked over at her, a bright smile on her face. "My pleasure, Leigh Streete. You're a pretty easy girl to like." They walked on in pleased silence, happy with their newly formed friendship.

As they neared Diane and Jay's, Leigh suddenly remembered, grabbing Lois' arm. "We forgot your reading glasses!"

"That's okay, honey," Lois chuckled, her eyes twinkling. "I didn't really need them anyway."

It was during Leigh's second visit to Eden Glen that she first met Cameron. The warm late-spring afternoon found Zoë and Leigh lounging on the porch at Jay and Diane's, with Zoë stretched across a lounge chair deeply engrossed in *To Kill A Mockingbird* and Leigh perched on the porch rail deeply engrossed in the Top 40 tunes blaring from the radio beside her. Leigh leaned back, hugging her knees, rolling her head to the side to offer Zoë an exasperated stare.

"Would you give it a rest?" she groaned, nodding toward the well-worn book clutched tightly in Zoë's hands. "Put down that god-awful book and let's go do something fun."

"Just a sec," Zoë said without looking up from the yellowed, dog-eared pages. "I'm almost to the next chapter."

"I don't know why you want to waste all your spare time reading anyway. Jeez, don't you get enough of that at school?" Leigh turned away with a sigh, rolling her eyes, catching sight of a magnificent black stallion charging across the pasture, sailing effortlessly over the high rail fence surrounding the Forests' property. The red-haired rider whooped wildly as the horse skidded to a stop at the end of the long drive and patted the horse's neck with affectionate congratulations.

"Oh my God!" Leigh stammered. "What a fine looking stud — and the horse ain't so bad either." She was transfixed, unable to tear her eyes away, stretching her arm behind her, frantically patting Zoë's calf to get her attention. "Zoë, who's that guy?" she asked breathlessly. "He's hot!"

Zoë looked up, smiling warmly as she observed her tall, athletic cousin on horseback, making his way down the road. "Oh, that's Cam," she said casually, taking note of Leigh's open mouth, lifting her book back over her face to hide her amusement.

"Your cousin, Cameron? You mean, *Palmer's* brother?" Leigh continued to gawk at the attractive boy atop the mighty steed, an admiring twinkle dancing in her violet eyes. "There's no way they're related," she declared skeptically. "He's adopted too, right?"

"No," Zoë laughed.

"You think he's got a girlfriend?"

"I think he has several."

"What a shame," Leigh let out a disappointed sigh. "Although, that is one club I wouldn't mind joining."

Cameron reached the front steps, pulling in on the reins to halt Shadow and vaulted from the saddle, flashing a grin. "You escaped from the girls prison, I see," he remarked wryly as he plopped down on the top step. He eyed Zoë mischievously and stretched his legs lazily out in front of him.

"Paroled," Zoë responded, glancing up from her book, "for good behavior."

"How'd you swing that?"

"Sold cigarettes to the guards."

Cameron chuckled appreciatively, turning his gaze on Leigh. "Who's your friend?"

Leigh stared at Zoë, clearing her throat impatiently as she waited for an introduction.

"She's my cellmate. Cam, meet Leigh Streete."

Cameron leaned forward, extending a friendly hand to a rosy-cheeked Leigh. "Welcome to the House of Carson," he said mysteriously. "I hope you won't be subjected to too many offenses while you're here."

"Nothing I can't handle," Leigh assured him. "I already live with Zoë. It can't get much worse than that."

"Then obviously, you haven't met my brother. He's living proof that things can always get worse."

"I know your brother," Leigh informed him dryly. "And I'm not impressed."

"Neither are we," Cameron laughed. "See, we already have something in common."

*I wish there was more,* Leigh thought adoringly, following his every motion with infatuated eyes. *Like an address, last name, children...*

"Why would you spend your weekend here, anyway? Don't you have anything better to do than this?" He plucked the book from Zoë's hands, tossing it onto the end of her chaise lounge, and pulled her to her feet, coaxing Leigh from the porch rail with the promise of something more exciting. "Get changed, girls," he said. "We're going to town!"

They spent the evening driving to Macon, catching a movie and a pizza afterward. Zoë and Leigh shared the passenger's seat of the Porsche, holding on for dear life as Cameron zipped along the twisting country roads, squealing with delight as he tossed them around the car, using his finest race car driver technique. Downshifting suddenly as he flew into the drive, he screeched to a stop in front of Zoë's house, coming face to face with a grim-faced Uncle Jay.

"You're very lucky it's me standing here, young man, and not your father," Jay scolded him harshly as Leigh and Zoë piled out of the car. "The driving skills I just witnessed would lose you a car."

"Oh, Uncle Jay, lighten up," Cameron leaned out the window, flashing a witty smile. "Come on. Let's go for a spin — I'll even let you drive."

Jay suppressed a grin, trying very hard to remain stern, shaking his head regretfully. "Not tonight, Cameron," he said, turning to go back inside. "Although, I'd really love to."

"What's stopping you, Daddy?" Zoë asked, a teasing sparkle in her eyes.

"Your mother. She'd have my head." Jay bent down and kissed her cheek, ruffling her hair affectionately. "Not too much longer, huh? We've got an early morning tomorrow." With a final glower to Cameron, he went into the house, winking playfully at Leigh as he closed the screen.

Zoë paused on the steps with Leigh at her heels, looking back at Cameron to say farewell. "You behave yourself this week, you hear?"

"I hear you, hot sexy mama!" Cameron laughed, turning over the engine, gunning it as he prepared to speed away. "See ya next weekend, Leigh?"

"Oh yeah," Leigh said under her breath, nodding enthusiastically as he zoomed away, dust flying in his wake, clearly marking his path. "Oh yeah," she repeated to Zoë as they headed off to bed. "I'll be here with bells on. Wild horses couldn't keep me away."

After that, Zoë never had to twist Leigh's arm to get her to Eden Glen. The mere thought of seeing Cameron was enticement enough. Her affection was further fueled when Cameron began driving up to see them, becoming a frequent visitor to Miss Colleen's and a heart throb to all on campus. Leigh was falling — and falling hard. Always vulnerable to rejection, she was careful to shield her sentiments from him, unable to stand the thought of his not returning her devotion. She stayed in the background, watching Cameron make the rounds, taking out a new girl each week, wishing desperately that he would choose her.

"He's just ducky, Zoë," she glowed, lying back on her bunk at Miss Colleen's, staring at Zoë's latest picture of him as she held it above her head. "So ruggedly handsome and so very divine. Don't you think?"

"He's my cousin, Leigh," Zoë reminded her, looking up from her desk with a roll of her eyes.

"Not technically."

"No, not technically — but enough that it feels incestuous to think about him in any other way."

"Do you think he'll be coming up this week?"

"I don't know." Zoë flipped open her textbook with an exasperated sigh. "Why don't you call him up and ask him yourself?"

"No! Then he'll think I'm interested in him."

"Aren't you?"

"Yes, but I don't want him to think so."

"I wish you *would* let him think so. Maybe then he'd quit dating all those long-legged glamour girls, and you'd quit cussing him and them for making you miserable."

"Yeah, whatever," Leigh grumbled unhappily, clutching the photo of Cameron to her chest. She gazed across the room to the mirror, her brow furrowed as she inspected her reflection. "What on earth could he possibly see in them that he doesn't see in me?" she asked fretfully, rearranging her hair with her hands.

"Would you quit being stupid?" Zoë swiveled in her chair, her mouth crimped in annoyance. "Call him, Leigh. You're his friend. He won't think anything about it."

"You call him." Leigh propped the photograph on the bedside table, kissing her forefingers and placing them on his lips. "I'm going to sleep."

"Good!" Zoë applauded, earning a withering stare. "At least now you'll shut up about him." She buried her head in her notes, studying for her exam, feeling Leigh's eyes piercing the back of her head.

"Aren't you going to call him?" Leigh piped up after several silent minutes, peeking out from beneath her sheet, her violet eyes pleading and pitiful.

Zoë reached over and grabbed the pillow from her bed, throwing it and hitting Leigh in the head. "Go to sleep!" she exclaimed, turning her back, ignoring Leigh's beseeching whimper. "I'll call him in the morning," she relented, smiling to herself as she heard the delighted giggle from the other side of the room.

For Cameron, one of the best things about Miss Colleen's School for Young Women was that it was so close to Eden Glen, making it easy for him to slip away frequently during the week to see his cousin. That was the best thing about it. The second best thing about it was the girls. He quickly discovered that the girls at Miss Colleen's were very different from the ones at his high school in Eden Glen.

"I like dating the girls here," he told Zoë and Leigh while visiting one afternoon, lounging with them in the sun on a blanket along the banks of a clearwater stream that ran just outside the grounds.

"What's so great about them?" Leigh inquired, stabbing the ice in her soft drink viciously with her straw.

"I don't know," Cameron admitted with a shrug, fingering the foil mouth on his bag of chips thoughtfully. "I just like the way they are. They look good, smell good, carry on a decent conversation. They're smart and not easily impressed, not like those goofy girls in Eden Glen. It makes me crazy just being around them. I walk into a room and they just fall at my feet. I'm sure it's because of the money."

"Oh, I'm sure that's what it is," Leigh interjected, peeking behind his back to Zoë with wide disbelieving eyes, the look on her face conveying a silent message: *How can anyone be so naïve?*

"He's got a little touch of snobbery in him, just like the rest of your family," Leigh remarked to Zoë after Cameron dropped them off at their dorm.

"And here I thought Cam was perfect," Zoë teased, playing on Leigh's undying affection for him. "Does it make you like him less?"

"Hell no! You know better than that," Leigh retorted, lifting her collage of Cameron photos off the night stand. "I just consider it a delightful addition to his other appealing qualities."

"You," Zoë said, shaking her head sadly as she reached into the fridge for a Coke, "are *really* pathetic."

Of the appealing qualities Leigh mentioned, Zoë was particularly proud of the way that Cameron had struggled to become his own man, staunchly determined to be anything but a spoiled little rich boy. Despite pressure from his parents, he rejected the idea of private school, attending Eden Glen High instead, hanging out with the local kids and playing as many sports as he could get away with.

"I'm not going to any private school, including Saint Andrews Academy," he insisted, tossing the application back at Geoff, his eyes flashing defiantly. "That's where you sent Palmer and look what happened to him."

"And public school is working so well for you," Geoff barked, scowling in irritation. "You've already been expelled once because of that little stunt last year with the principal's daughter. I can't wait to see what's next."

Cameron butted heads constantly with Geoff and Patricia, especially over anything pertaining to his upbringing and station in life, and had the great advantage of being steadfastly backed by Lois. On his own, he resolved not to go to law school, tenaciously resisting the constant prodding from Geoff to go Ivy League, opting instead to apply to Auburn University.

"I don't want to be a lawyer," he declared stubbornly over Sunday dinner, tossing his fork onto his plate. "Everybody is this family is a lawyer. We could do with a little variety."

"And just what do you think you're going to do with your life?" Geoff asked him, his words clipped, draining his wineglass as he fought to keep his temper.

"Get a degree in journalism."

"Journalism! And what will you do with a degree in that?"

"Write," Cameron snarled, his jaw set obstinately.

"Cameron, please," his mother pleaded, beseeching him with a gentle smile. "Your father is only trying to talk to you."

"For as much good as it will do," Palmer commented dryly, sawing at his filet, an entertained smirk on his face.

"I'll get a job as a reporter," Cameron said. "I'll write for a newspaper or be the next Ernest Hemingway."

"Oh, that's prestigious," Palmer retorted.

Cameron turned to him, fixing him with a level stare. "There are things in life that count more than prestige."

Palmer inspected him arrogantly, arching his brow. "Really? Name them."

"How about self-respect? Ambition? Following a dream?"

"Wonderful!" Geoff exploded, pounding his fist on the table, the veins in his neck standing out in livid ridges. "Please don't get a job that pays real money. Please, Cameron. Please allow me to spend the rest of my life supporting you while you're out chasing some ridiculous dream!"

"Geoffrey, calm down before you have a stroke," Lois interrupted, lowering her glass of iced tea. "As usual, you're blowing everything way out of proportion."

"My dreams aren't ridiculous, and you're not going to be supporting me," Cameron informed him coolly, his unwavering stare purposely frigid. "The day I leave this house, I'll no longer be your responsibility." He excused himself and left the table, stalking from the room without a look back, his shoulders squared with unyielding determination.

"Geoff, go after him. You can't let him leave this way," Patricia cried out, her eyes filling with anxious tears.

"Oh Patricia! For God's sake," Geoff snapped, reaching for a fresh bottle of wine. "He's not going anywhere — not today anyway. He's still in high school."

Lois left them in the dining room discussing Cameron's doomed future and went outside, seeking the prodigal grandson in question. She found him on the dock, laying flat on his back, sunglasses on, staring up at a cloudless sky.

"Hey Lois." He lifted his head as she approached, offering her an impish grin.

"Hey yourself," she said, lowering her body to the pier, dangling her legs in the cool water. "What're you doing out here?"

"Getting away from in there," he muttered, nodding his head in the direction of the house. "I hate it when Palmer's home on break. That's when the nagging skyrockets to an all-time high."

"That's because he eggs it on, the snotty little shit," Lois commented wryly, her mouth twisting into a sardonic smile. "Well, you don't have to put up with it much longer. He leaves tonight."

"Thank God." Cameron sat up, regarding her solemnly. "Not that I think that's going to be the end of it. Dad's on a roll."

"Don't worry about your father. I'll find a way to deal with him," Lois promised, her eyes gleaming devilishly. "Besides, I wouldn't listen to him anyway. What does he know?" She got to her feet, shading her face from the sun. "It's hot out here. I'm going inside. I just came out here to check on you — and to tell you something."

"What's that?" Cameron asked, gazing up at her fondly.

"Keep up the good work, baby," Lois smiled broadly, patting his cheek with undying affection. "You're the smartest kid I know."

The years went by and Cameron continued to plot his future, hell-bent on doing things his way, venturing to Miss Colleen's one spring evening just weeks before high school graduation with more on his mind than his standing date with a stunning coed. After a chaste kiss goodnight, he left his date and sprinted across campus toward McKenzie Hall, home of Leigh and Zoë. He found Zoë in the front parlor, sprawled on the floor, studying for one of her last exams. He crossed the room in long strides, kicking the soles of her bare feet lightly with his tennis shoe.

"Don't you ever date?" he asked, flashing a teasing grin as she rolled onto her elbows, beaming at him with dancing gray eyes.

"Like I would tell you if I did," she responded kiddingly. "You'd just chase them all away with a baseball bat."

"I know you've been going out."

"So what if I have? I'm eighteen years old, plenty old enough to be seen in the company of boys," she teased him, laughing as he sauntered over to the ultra-feminine couch against the wall and plopped comfortably onto the cushions, wisely refraining from propping his feet up on the glass-topped coffee table. "So what brings you to Miss Colleen's this evening, Cam — other than the fair Ellen MacLeod?"

"Nothing special," he shrugged. "Just checking up on my favorite cousin."

"Sure you are," she eyed him knowingly. "I'm certain that I'm the only attraction that ever brings you to our fine campus."

"Now Zoë. You know you're the only woman I'll ever love."

"Oh, give me a break."

"It's true," he laughed, glancing around the empty room. "Where's Miss Leigh tonight?"

"Upstairs, cramming for her biology final. You want me to call her down?"

"Nah," Cameron answered quickly, shaking his curly head. "If Leigh's taken the initiative to stick her head in a book, far be it from me to lead her astray," he chuckled. "Besides, I came to see you. I come bearing good news."

"What?"

"I got my acceptance letter this afternoon."

"From Auburn? Oh Cam, that's great!" Zoë squealed with delight, leaping from the Oriental rug, and dashed across the room, diving onto the couch to give him a giant bear hug. "I'm so proud of you."

"Thanks. I'm pretty proud myself."

"How did Uncle Geoff take the news? I know he had his heart set on you going to one of the usual family educational institutions."

"Forget it, Zoë. There'll be no Princeton, Harvard or Cornell in this guy's future," Cameron scoffed, an edge of impatience creeping into his voice. "If I went up there, I'd just get caught in the shuffle, destined to be classified as one of *them*. I can't go anywhere without being associated with our famous family, and I'm sick of it. I can think of so many things I'd rather be than a Savannah Carson, and I hate the way everybody expects me to be just like them. I've really had it. I may even change my name."

Zoë giggled at his incensed ranting, filling the quiet room with her laughter. Cameron made a face at her, none too amused with her reaction to his heartfelt speech. "What about you, Zoey-anne?" he asked snidely. "Are you going to have a life of your own or just let them press you into their nasty mold?"

"What do you think, Cam?" she asked, suppressing a grin and lifting her long hair high atop her head, batting her eyelashes coyly. "Am I cut out to be lady of the manor?"

"Somehow, I just don't see you as Madame President of the Junior League," Cameron remarked dryly. "Besides, I've got a better proposition for you. Come to Auburn with me — and bring Leigh. It would be a hoot."

"I don't know, Cam. Mother has her heart set on me going to Stephens, and Leigh will go where I go, just because."

"Conformist!"

"I'm not a conformist. I'm just undecided."

"Jeez, Zoë! Don't be such a sell-out. Do something original for once in your life!"

"I'll have you know that I'm very original," she said huffily and jumped off the couch, heading purposefully for the door. "So original that, unlike the other women in your life, I'm going to tell you to go straight to hell — and then I'm going up to bed."

"Zoë, don't be a butthead."

"Why not? You are."

"Why? Because I'm asking you to create your own destiny?"

"No," Zoë whirled around, "because you're asking me to follow you in yours."

"Should I take that as a no?"

Zoë paused in the entryway, glancing back at him with a smile. "Take it as an 'I'll think about it and let you know tomorrow,' " she answered, her smile broadening to a mischievous grin as she spun around and flounced up the stairs.

Upstairs, Zoë casually mentioned Cameron's suggestion to Leigh. Naturally Leigh was all for it.

"You turn him down and I'm killing you!" she shrieked, hugging her purple teddy bear to her chest with glee. "I can think of nothing I'd rather do than go off to college with Cam. It would be so perfect," she chattered excitedly, leaping from her bunk and pacing the length of the room. "I'm a journalism major — he's a journalism major. I'm fun to be with — he's fun to be with. I'm beautiful — well, you get the general idea. It's fate, Zoë. I'm telling you. Why, we're just destined to be together!" She giggled, looking up at Zoë, fluttering her eyelashes flirtatiously as she danced around the room. "Can we live with him?"

"Over my dead body," Zoë countered, yanking back the covers and jumping into bed. "There's no way I can put up with both of you under the same roof. Your inflated egos would drive me right over the edge."

Leigh dashed across the room, tuning out Zoë's fiery opposition, and dove into bed, her adrenaline still sky high as she snapped off the light. "Me and Cam, living blissfully together in Auburn, Alabama," she sighed, flopping ecstatically back on her pillow. "Life just doesn't get any better than that."

"Oh God," Zoë muttered, pulling her blanket over her head. "It's going to be a long four years."

# 13

After a summer of horseback riding, shopping and leisurely weeks at the beach, the thrilling threesome moved to Auburn University, settling into a three-bedroom apartment off Magnolia Street.

"So this is what you chose over Stephens," Diane murmured in disappointment as she gazed around the crowded apartment. "Quaint."

"Oh Diane, hush!" Lois said impatiently, reaching out to pinch Zoë's cheek. "I think it's wonderful, chère. Just perfect." She turned to Cameron, slumped in a ragged recliner, waiting in moody silence for the family to depart. "And you, mister," she said, pointing a finger in his direction. "You had better take good care of your cousin since you are the one responsible for dragging her here."

"I plan on it, Lois," Cameron responded with a thin smile, cutting his eyes cleverly. "And if you're really nice, I might even look out for Leigh."

"You better not let anything happen to either one of them, Cameron," Geoff spoke up sternly. "You'll rue the day it does." He paused beside his son's chair, reaching out to finger the gold hoop hanging from his left ear. "By the way," he said, his tone disapproving, "nice earring."

Leigh sat on a barstool, swinging her legs, watching the scene unfolding before her with contained amusement. "It's times like these that I truly appreciate having a family that doesn't give a damn," she declared lightly. "You don't see Tom and Carol hanging around here, jumping all over me."

Diane whirled around, staring at her pointedly. "I wouldn't be so smug, if I were you, young lady," she smirked, wagging a finger at Leigh. "You *do* have a family that gives a damn — I just haven't gotten to you yet."

"You'd think I'd moved you to the ghetto," Cameron growled to Zoë, leaning against the door after the Carsons' retreat, a sullen frown marring his face. "Why do they always have to blow everything out of proportion?"

"Because they don't know how to do anything on a small scale. It's always got to be some big production." Zoë came over, laying a consoling hand on his shoulder. "Don't worry about them, Cam. It's not their life now. It's ours. And it's going to be great."

They started classes in late August, with Cameron and Leigh enrolled in journalism and Zoë in human sciences. Zoë and Leigh went the sorority route, going through rush, while Cameron enjoyed life as a fraternity brother, rarely showing his face around their apartment before the first light of day.

Zoë adored Auburn and campus life, glad to be away from the confinement of Miss Colleen's. Auburn was a beautiful little college town — a picturesque setting with rolling green hills and friendly people. Zoë fell in love with the university, finding it a striking contrast of breathtaking historical architecture and state-of-the-art technology, with an incredible athletics program second to none. She made some of her finest memories at home football games, lining the side of South Donahue Drive for the Tiger Walk, cheering the players on as they headed for Jordan Hare Stadium, and during after-game festivities at Toomer's Corner, gathering with thousands of Auburn fans to roll the trees with toilet paper, celebrating victory late into the night.

"I can't imagine what college life would be like anywhere else," she exclaimed to Leigh, grinning ear to ear as they made their way home in the wee hours of the morning after one such post-game celebration. "I think we've found the best in the world right here!"

She spent most of her time out of class at the sorority house, the Strutting Duck or Fink's Grill, socializing and collecting new admirers. She dated quite a bit, but not enough to become serious. Cameron effectively prevented that from happening, his watchful eye cramping her style at every turn.

"What does that guy want with you, Zoë?" he scowled, fending off yet another advance while they were playing pool at Fink's, his threatening glower running off a nice freshman from Zoë's English comp class.

"Oh Cam, give me a break," Zoë rolled her eyes, leaning on her pool cue. "He's harmless. His father is a minister in Charleston."

"That doesn't mean anything," Cameron argued, bending over the table to take his next shot. "I'm sure the same theory that applies to the preacher's daughter also applies to his son."

Zoë also began volunteering at a free clinic in the neighboring town of Opelika, spending her free afternoons and weekend mornings assisting with patient files. She enjoyed her work and carried tales of the clinic back to Eden Glen, entertaining Lois with colorful anecdotes and annoying Palmer with what he considered her lack of social ambition.

"A complete waste of time," Palmer declared over Thanksgiving dinner, accepting the heaping plate of steaming turkey and cornbread dressing Tressa slid in front of him. "I can understand your going off to college to obtain some sort of degree, but why do you bother to take it so seriously? You should reap the benefits your position in life holds, graduate with honors and settle down with someone appropriate. That's what my mother did."

"And she's been paying for it ever since," Diane remarked, sending Palmer an irritated glare. "After almost thirty years with your father, I think she's more than paid her debt to society."

"Patricia hasn't fared all that badly," Geoff chuckled, glancing at his wife affectionately. "Have you, darling?"

"I'm certain that's a matter of opinion," Jay chuckled, winking teasingly at his cousin Patricia, noting her entertained look. "I'm sure there are days when dear Patty would like to slap me for even mentioning that I had a cousin, much less fixing you up on that first date."

"Probably more days than she'll ever admit," Diane jabbed, smirking obnoxiously at Geoff.

"I thought we were talking about Zoë," Palmer interjected, looking annoyed.

"You were talking about Zoë," Lois spoke up, pointing her knife in his direction, her eyes narrowed in aggravation. "The rest of us were ignoring you and trying to enjoy our meal."

"Ah, the traditional Carson family Thanksgiving." Cameron cut his eyes to Leigh, snarling unpleasantly. "Every year, it gets better and better. In case I forget all the pleasure days like today bring, please remind me to spend Christmas at the nearest refugee camp."

Zoë met Eli Feinstein during her second year at Auburn, literally running into him at a frat house Christmas party as she exited the coveted upstairs bathroom and swerved to miss a stray beer bottle catapulted carelessly down the overpopulated hallway. She ran smack into Eli's firm chest, glancing up at him with a startled expression as she wobbled unsteadily. "Sorry," she murmured, feeling oddly uncomfortable at his reverent stare.

"No problem," he said, steadying her with a strong hand, smiling admiringly as he gazed into her gray eyes. He continued to watch her as she threaded her way down the corridor, and Zoë flushed hotly, acutely aware of his dark eyes drilling holes in her back as she descended the stairs in search of Leigh.

Later she noticed him again, catching sight of him across the throng of drunken college students as he leaned against the fireplace mantel, a pack of infatuated females gathered around him. She nudged Leigh, nodding her head casually in his direction. "Leigh, who's that guy?"

Leigh craned her neck, standing on her tiptoes, discreetly trying to follow Zoë's purposefully indifferent gaze. "Who? Derek Freeland from economics?" she asked, wrinkling her brow questioningly as she studied the vast number of men in the room.

Zoë sighed in perturbed exasperation. "No, Leigh, you bimbo — I know who Derek is," she snapped. "I mean the other guy, the one with real curly brown hair, next to the fireplace, surrounded by all the girls."

Leigh shifted her eyes, finding the man in question. "I don't know," she said, intrigued both by the unknown male and by Zoë's interest in him. "But I can find out."

Leigh skirted the room on a fact-finding mission, returning a little while later with a grin on her face and the information she sought, scooting up to Zoë's side, revealing her findings in a hushed tone. "His name's Eli Feinstein," she said with a proud smile, glancing at Zoë with mischievously twinkling violet eyes. "He's from Long Island, New York, is a second-year business admin major and the heir to a food distribution conglomerate." She watched as Zoë peeked in Eli's direction, catching his eye, flushing bright red as she hastily turned her head. "Why do you ask, Zoë? You like him?"

Zoë appeared flustered, stammering indignantly, denying any attraction. "Like him? I don't even know him, Leigh. Can't a girl even ask a simple question without getting the third degree?"

Zoë peered at him again, this time protected by the thick veil of her dark lashes, observing him discreetly, ready to avert her eyes if he turned her way. "He seems awfully full of himself, don't you think?" she asked, deliberate coolness hanging on her casual words.

Leigh laughed, throwing a chummy arm around Zoë's shoulders as she guided her toward a frosty keg of beer in the center of the room. "Sure he does, Zoey-anne," she said knowingly. "So, I'm sure that you wouldn't like to get to know him better." She chuckled again, catching Zoë's insulted look, speculating in entertained silence. *Why do I get the feeling that this won't be the last I hear of Eli Feinstein?*

Eli did his own research, quickly discovering the identity of the gorgeous blonde from the Christmas party, and phoned the apartment shortly after Christmas break. Cameron intercepted the call, covering the mouthpiece of the receiver with his palm as he looked inquiringly at Zoë, who sat on a bean bag in the living room reviewing notes.

"Some guy's on the phone for you. Says his name's Eli." He gawked in amazement as Zoë dropped her notes and scrambled from the carpet, her elated voice echoing down the hallway as she called over her shoulder. "I'll take it in my room!"

Cameron hung up the phone, shrugging his shoulders in bewilderment as he turned to face a grinning Leigh. "What's her problem?" he asked incredulously, nodding in the direction of Zoë's room.

"Nothing, really. Just a little touch of infatuation, that's all."

"Over this Eli guy?"

"Yes, I believe he would be the one," Leigh said lightly, observing as Cameron's face took on the familiar look of overprotectiveness.

"Who is he?"

"A boy." Leigh toyed with him, choking back laughter at his irritation.

"Be more specific." Cameron pulled a barstool up next to her, frowning sternly at her evasiveness.

"Eli Feinstein: tall, great looking, charming," Leigh counted Eli's many appealing attributes on her fingers, naming them off with deliberate slowness to catch Cameron's attention, "and probably has as much — if not more — money than you do."

"How'd Zoë meet him?"

"I don't think they've been properly introduced yet, if that's what you mean. They just spotted one another at the Delt Christmas party."

"And where was I?"

"Gee, Cam, I don't know. Must not have been your night to stand guard. Lighten up already and let the girl have a date every once in a while. I'm sure her chastity belt is still securely in place."

Cameron scowled unpleasantly as Leigh slid from her barstool, pinching his cheek playfully. "Look on the bright side, Cam," she said, picking up her books and making her way down the hallway toward her own room, her overstuffed backpack dangling heavily from her shoulder. "If Zoë takes Eli off the market, that'll just leave more women for you."

Leigh too had her fair share of admirers. Her unusual beauty and vivacious personality attracted men like flies. She had a different guy each weekend to wine and dine her, flattering her and catering to her every whim. Leigh enjoyed them all, but found them sadly lacking when compared to Cameron Carson.

For six years she'd loved Cameron, and for six years it had done no good. Aside from good company and great friendship, he had virtually no use for her.

"I might as well just throw in the towel," she told Zoë dismally as they cruised Auburn, honking occasionally at the passing vehicles of friends. "I could slink through his bedroom wearing nothing but a seductive smile and all Cam would say is, 'Hey Leigh, what's the deal with our next World History paper?' It's a crying shame, Zoë — a damn crying shame."

"I don't know why you get yourself all worked up in such a tizzy," Zoë chuckled, steering her little sports car onto Donahue to cruise the stadium. "Cam's not that big a prize."

Leigh stared, her eyes large with indignation. "Bite your tongue!" she sputtered. "Cam's the ultimate prize. But I'll never let him know that."

Zoë smiled, looking away so Leigh couldn't see the laughter in her eyes. "Give up the ship, Leigh," she kidded abrasively. "If you're never going to tell him how you feel, you're just wasting your time, pining away for a man who will never be yours."

*This is getting ridiculous,* she added to herself. *I've never met two more stubborn people.*

Everyone has an ideal, and for Cameron, it was Leigh. Leigh Streete, his cousin's best friend: beautiful, petite Leigh with her great smile, glossy black hair and brilliant violet eyes. Cameron had been in love with her from the first moment he saw her perched on the railing of his Aunt Diane's porch clad in jean shorts and sleeveless white shirt, dangling her shapely tanned legs over the side. He was instantly awestruck, never again finding another woman to equal Leigh in his eyes or his heart.

It wasn't just beauty that drew Cameron to her. To him, beautiful women were a dime a dozen, and he had grown accustomed to them falling all over him, vying for his attention. Leigh was different. It was her feisty spirit, do-or-die independence and the uncanny impression she gave of flat-out not giving a damn about him — or anything else for that matter — that made him crazy for her. And now, with Leigh living under the same roof, Cameron was going insane.

They had lived together for two years — he, Zoë and Leigh — in the cramped little three-bedroom apartment off Magnolia Street. He saw Leigh daily, padding into the kitchen in the morning to retrieve a cup of coffee, wearing only a long-sleeved man's dress shirt, or dashing down the hall clad in a tightly-wrapped towel, rushing from their lone bathroom to her bedroom to get dressed for class.

The perfume from her soft skin lingered with him, so familiar that it became part of his senses. He was entranced, but he could never seem to get a moment alone with her. She and Zoë ran night and day, from class to dates to social functions and parties, and the brief glimpses Cameron caught of Leigh in the mornings were as lucky as he got.

Finally, fate worked for him and he did get lucky, returning from a date with Susie Ellerman, homecoming queen and sorority girl extraordinaire, to find Leigh at home alone. She was a vision of loveliness, curled up in the corner of the old tattered sofa, wearing pink-and-gray-checked flannel pajamas and eating popcorn from a huge ceramic bowl, her head lowered as she studied the textbook in her lap. Cameron paused in the doorway, eyeing her in secret admiration until she realized he was there, looking up from her notes to meet his intense gaze.

"Hey Cam," she said, removing her reading glasses, smiling that smile he loved, while his heart melted.

"Leigh," he acknowledged her casually and crossed the room, tossing his keys onto the bar. He joined her on the couch, raising an inquiring brow. "Home on a Saturday night?" he asked mockingly. "How come? You sick?"

Leigh chuckled, laying her book and glasses on the end table. "No, I'm not, but my date was," she said, winking and flashing him a smile. "We went by a party at Ricky Morgan's, and he decided to drink sloe gin. Boy, does that ever make a red pukey mess!"

She laughed good-naturedly, sliding her arm leisurely along the back of the sofa. "Zoë's out with Eli Feinstein, crown prince of Feinstein Foods, so I decided to make the most of the peace and quiet and catch up on some French, with the futile hope that I might actually make a better grade on the next exam than you do." She glanced at him with vivaciously dancing eyes. "How about you? How was your date with Susie Q, the prom queen?"

Cameron sighed, shrugging indifferently. "It was okay, I guess. Just another night of mindless chatter. Sometimes Susie's so flaky, it's a wonder she can put enough words together to form a complete sentence."

"Well, it's your own fault. You've dated the same kind of girl as long as I've known you: outstandingly gorgeous, without a brain cell to call her own. Talk about being stuck in a rut! Don't you ever get tired of dating bimbos and beauty queens?" Leigh asked with a wicked smile, rumpling his hair playfully. "You're a smart guy. Why don't you try dating someone a little more intellectually stimulating?"

"That's easier said than done. I don't know that many."

"On a college campus this size? Please."

"Really, Leigh. I swear it's the truth. I can only think of two girls who are intellectually stimulating — Zoë and you. And you know how that goes. Zoë is my cousin and you are…" he trailed off, a red flush rising in his cheeks, suddenly aware of Leigh's wide and very interested violet eyes.

"And I'm what? What, Cam?" Leigh leaned forward, holding her breath, her heart pounding erratically as she urged him to continue.

"And — and you wouldn't be interested," Cameron finished his sentence abruptly and bolted from the room, mortified over spilling the beans. "'Night, Leigh."

Leigh threw up her hands in aggravation, watching him race down the hall. "For God's sake, Carson! What'll I have to do, draw a picture for you?" she mumbled under her breath, so frustrated she wanted to scream. "You've got to be kidding! Me? Not interested? Please. Where have you been for the last six years?"

Her expression changed, evolving from protective cynicism to overwhelmed bliss as she suddenly became aware of what had just taken place. *Dear God! Cam feels the same way I do.*

For months and months, she'd lived under the same roof with him, enduring all of the other women in his life, tortured, consumed by love and lust. She lay awake in her bed night after night, thinking of him just down the hall, longing to be with him, to touch him, to kiss him. Now, after years of adoring him from afar and keeping her feelings carefully concealed, the time had finally arrived to come clean. She took a deep breath. "Well," she sighed, "it's now or never."

Without another moment's hesitation, she sprang from the couch, flinging her popcorn bowl aside, and padded hurriedly across the threadbare carpet toward Cameron's room, pausing uncertainly outside his door.

"Wait a minute," she gulped, her breath ragged, her heart pounding spastically. "Let's think about this for a second. What if I'm wrong? What if I misread his signals or his remark meant absolutely nothing at all?"

She paced in front of his closed door, wringing her hands anxiously. "If I go into that room and he shoots me down, I'll never get over it. Maybe I'll just go back to the living room and pretend none of this ever happened." She stopped, slapping her palm against her forehead. "What am I saying? I can't just piss away the chance of a lifetime. Of course I'm going into that room!"

She pushed the door open, flying across the bedroom, and bounced onto the bed beside him, propping atop his fluffy down pillow, inches from his incredibly handsome face. "Now, Cam," she drawled, fluttering her eyelashes flirtatiously. "Who says I'm not interested?"

Caught off guard, Cameron stared at her, reeling in astonishment, too stunned to even act poised. "Leigh! Are you insane? What the hell are you doing?"

"Insane? Maybe, yes. I don't know," she giggled, light-headed and giddy, gazing deeply into his vivid green eyes, a hot flush spreading across her face. "I just know that if I don't say this now, I'll never say it."

"Say what?" Cameron asked guardedly, leaning back on his elbows, his bare chest rising above the sheet.

"I'm crazy about you — absolutely bonkers, head over heels in love!" She flung her arms around his neck, kissing him hard on the mouth, and jumped into his lap, curling tightly against him, lifting her eyes to view the bewildered look on his face.

"You're crazy, all right — but not about me," he mumbled, wiping away her kiss, a roguish smile spreading over his face. "Now quit yanking my chain and get out." He dumped her unceremoniously onto the floor.

Leigh scrambled up, hands on her hips, her voice rising with indignation. "I come in here, baring my soul, and all you have to say is get out?"

"What the hell do you expect me to say?"

"You're not making this very easy, Cam," she scolded, towering over him, her eyes alive with fire. "Why don't you believe me? Despite what you're thinking, this is not some kind of game. I love you, damn it! Okay?"

Cameron peered up at her, blinking incredulously, his mouth hanging open in disbelief. "You're serious."

"Well, duh," Leigh rolled her eyes, shaking her head in aggravation. "Jeez, Cameron! For someone who is supposed to be so savvy about women, you sure are stupid."

"Why didn't you say something?"

"I did — just now."

"I mean before now."

"When, in between frat parties and dates with the homecoming queen? I haven't seen you alone more than five minutes in the last two years! Besides, how could you not have known? I've been nuts about you since I met you. I've followed you around like a puppy, drooling over your every move, running to Eden Glen every weekend to be near you. It couldn't have been that hard to figure out."

"And that was supposed to be my big clue? Yeah, you were in Eden Glen every weekend, but I thought you were there for Zoë. Besides that, you haven't exactly been Miss Mary Sunshine, sweetheart. I don't care what you say. You've never acted all goo-goo-eyed and slobber-faced. The last few times I've been around you, you've been all frigid and caustic, a regular little snow queen."

"That should've been a sign."

Cameron eyed her skeptically. "Well, excuse me, honey!" he scoffed. "I didn't know I was supposed to interpret sarcastic and aloof as signs of true love."

Leigh smirked, shrugging indifferently. "So I'm a bitch. What can I say?"

"And here's another thing," Cameron sputtered, wagging a self-righteous finger. "What about all those guys you keep dangling on a string? Huh, Leigh? What about them?"

"What do you expect me to do? Sit on my hands and wait until you finally work your way through every woman in a hundred-mile radius? I had to have some constructive way to bide my time." Leigh grinned, sitting on the edge of the bed, fingering the blanket wrapped tightly around his waist. "Why are we fighting about this anyway? Either you feel the same way I do or you don't."

Cameron looked away, flustered like a schoolboy with his first crush, answering her question without saying a word. "I just don't want to screw anything up between us," he said softly, not risking the slightest glance in her direction.

"As if my little speech hasn't done that already." Leigh took his face in her hands, forcing him to look her in the eye. "All I know is I love you, Cameron Carson — with all my heart, and if I've screwed everything up by saying so, I'll move out tomorrow."

"If you move out, I'm going with you," Cameron said solemnly, pulling her into his arms, encircling her tightly, his eyes dark and smoldering as he stared into her face. "You're not moving out. You're going to stay right here and be just as sarcastic and aloof as you want to be. Because if that's your way of saying 'I love you,' I'll take it any way I can get it." He buried his face in her hair, his warm breath tickling her ear. "I love you, Leigh."

She tilted her face toward his, accepting his passionate kiss, his lips tasting just as she had always dreamed. Exhilarated, Leigh relaxed in his arms, without reservation or fear of rejection, feeling for the first time in her life that she had finally come home.

Zoë paused outside the front door of the apartment, leaning against the brick wall, and put a firm hand on Eli Feinstein's chest, regarding him with amused gray eyes and an unyielding smile. "No, Eli," she smiled, answering his late-night request. "You may not come in."

"But Zoë," Eli said, his East Coast accent as prominent as the pleading expression on his face. "The night is young."

"The night is *not* young." Zoë glanced at her watch, holding her wrist up into the beams of bright moonlight flooding the balcony. "It's one o'clock in the morning."

"I just want to talk."

"We've already had coffee, and talked, and now it's time for you to go," she tapped a playful finger on his tense jaw, smiling up at him flirtatiously. "Now, you know how Cam is, Eli. I don't know how they do things in your part of the country, but down here, your venturing into my house at this time of night would be reason enough for my cousin to kick your butt."

"Is he ever going to like me?"

"He likes you well enough — he just doesn't trust you." She lowered his wandering hand, her mouth crimped in annoyance. "And probably with good reason."

"But Zoë, you have to know that I'm just crazy about you."

"Go home, Eli."

Eli sighed heavily with disappointment. "Five minutes?"

"*No* minutes."

Reluctantly, Eli gave in, kissing her upturned lips. "Good night, Zoë," he said regretfully, turning on his heel in frustration. "I'll call you tomorrow."

"Good night, Eli," Zoë sang out, calling down the stairs after him, wearing a devious grin as she watched him saunter across the parking lot, his posture defeated as he climbed into his gold Jaguar. Giggling softly, she unlocked the front door.

The living room was empty and oddly silent, even for the late hour. Usually one of them — either Cameron or Leigh — would still be up, lounging on the couch, watching some drivel on television. Noting the popcorn spilled haphazardly across the couch cushions, Zoë laid her purse on the end of the kitchen counter and proceeded curiously down the soundless hallway.

"Leigh?" She peeked into Leigh's room, finding no sign of her. Her unmade bed was empty. "That's weird." She passed her own room before reaching Cameron's and stuck her head inside, the sight before her drawing a startled gasp.

She reeled in surprise, her eyes round and gaping. Cameron lay sprawled on his back, sound asleep, rumpled blanket at his waist. Leigh was next to him, her dark head resting peacefully on his bare chest, sheet under her chin, her bosom rising and falling in blissful slumber.

Zoë backed out of the room, a huge grin spreading over her face. "Finally," she said, closing the door quietly behind her. "It's about time. I wonder which one was the first to cave."

Over the course of her college career, Zoë discovered that she truly liked Eli. He was fun — in a spoiled-little-rich-boy sort of way. He was frivolous and devilishly witty, with a careless disregard for money and his fellow man. He considered himself to be above most, but treated Zoë like a queen, finding her to be incredibly beautiful and intellectually challenging. She was unlike any woman he had ever known and seemed unaffected — and unimpressed — with his vast wealth and social standing.

They began their relationship slowly, seeing one another on an occasional basis while Eli continued to sample other women from his stable of admirers, and Zoë continued to have the time of her life, both with sorority activities and her rewarding work at the free clinic. They met often at collegiate social functions. In the beginning, Zoë ignored Eli if he had another date, whereas Eli stared longingly at Zoë, regardless of whether he had another woman with him or not. They played cat and mouse for more than a year until finally, during their junior year at Auburn, Eli decided that Zoë was the only woman for him and resolved to make her his wife.

Over Christmas break, Zoë took Eli home to Eden Glen to meet the family, driving him over the winding roads behind the wheel of his Jag, skidding to a halt in front of Carson House and honking the horn. The entire family greeted them on the veranda, embracing them as Zoë made proper introductions.

Diane regarded Eli with delight. "I think he's just charming," she whispered to Jay, her eyes sparkling with motherly fascination.

Jay regarded him with fatherly suspicion, wondering exactly what Eli's intentions were with his little girl. "I don't think he's charming," he retorted in Diane's ear. "He's pretentious and full of himself. Acts more like God's gift than an ordinary man. He's worse than Palmer."

"Then he fits right in, doesn't he?" Diane laughed at Jay's annoyed expression, yanking a lock of his blond hair teasingly. "I seem to remember another man who acted just like that."

"I was never like that."

"Oh yes," Diane giggled, linking her arm through his. "You were exactly like that and look how good you turned out."

Zoë earned nothing but praise from Geoff and Palmer. Geoff appeared beside himself, and Palmer was jumping with joy, fawning exaggeratedly over Eli, practically swooning at the thought of possibly having a Feinstein in the family.

"And here I've underestimated you all these years." He drew Zoë aside, sliding an unusually friendly arm around her shoulder, beaming with immense pleasure. "I've called you uncouth, said you lacked ambition and class, and now, my dear cousin, you've outsmarted even me. With Eli Feinstein, you're going to marry better than any of us."

"Oh please!" Zoë frowned, rolling her eyes in irritation, and angrily pushed him away. "Get a life." She stalked away to join Eli and the rest of the family in the front parlor, and Palmer followed her, nipping at her heels, determined to become Eli's bosom buddy before the weekend was over.

"Your family seems ready to welcome me in with open arms," Eli remarked later as they strolled along the veranda, enjoying the peacefulness of the starlit night.

"I wouldn't take them too seriously if I were you," Zoë advised him with a smile. "Most of them are pretty shallow, and what pleases them one minute may not apply to the next."

Before she and Eli left on Sunday, Zoë managed to get a moment alone with Lois, finding her hidden away from the Feinstein frenzy, lounging gracefully on the wicker divan on the back porch, reading *Wuthering Heights*.

"You've been pretty quiet this weekend," Zoë said, taking a seat at the end of the divan, tickling Lois' foot lightly with the tip of her fingernail.

Lois looked up, her wrinkled face bright with amusement. "I couldn't get a word in edgewise. I've never seen such a circus."

"So, what do you think of him?"

"The Feinstein boy?" Lois asked. Zoë nodded, grinning at her façade of absent-mindedness. "He's all right, I guess. How long have you been seeing him?"

"Off and on for the last couple of years. Do you like him?"

"I haven't decided yet. More importantly, do you like him?"

Zoë answered with a casual shrug. "I like him well enough, although not nearly as much as Palmer does," she declared, sharing a wicked giggle with Lois.

"Well, he's certainly handsome enough, in a dark and brooding sort of way, of course, and he does have a remarkable pedigree."

"That's encouraging. You sound like you're talking about a dog."

"Going by pedigree is a pretty good way to pick a mate, Zoë. That's how the Carsons usually do it."

"You've never thought like a Carson, Lois — and you never will. Why are you hem-hawing around? What do you really think of Eli?"

"Are you going to force me to be honest?"

"Since when do you have to be forced?"

"Kind of sissified for a man, don't you think?"

"Oh, Lois."

"You asked what I thought, Zoë. You didn't say I had to be nice about it," Lois said, then noted the disappointed look on her granddaughter's face. "Sometimes I'm just too opinionated for my own good," she added semi-apologetically. "I'll just keep my mouth shut and say this: If you like him, well, that's all that counts." She patted Zoë's knee fondly, her eyes crinkling with the pleasure of her company. "I just thought you'd end up with someone more like Cameron, you know, more like..."

"A rebel with a cause?"

"Something like that."

"I leave the rebellious types to Leigh. She's woman enough to handle them — at least I think she is."

"How are my darlings?"

"Fighting, bickering, calling each other names. You know, all the classic signs of true love."

"Got her hands full with my boy, doesn't she?"

"Does she ever."

Lois took Zoë's hands, clasping them affectionately as she offered a tender smile. "All I've ever wanted for you and Cameron is happiness. I think Cameron has found that in Leigh. I want you to be just as happy, Zoë. And if Eli Feinstein is the one who does it for you, then so be it."

Zoë bent her head toward Lois, her gray eyes twinkling confidently. "Don't worry about me, Lois. I'll always be happy — if not with Eli, then just with myself. Who says you need a man to make you happy?"

Lois cackled with joy, throwing her arms around Zoë in delight. "That's my girl!" she declared. "You are truly my granddaughter."

The thrilling threesome returned to Auburn for their final year in August. Cameron and Leigh made it through the summer and were still blissfully happy, so much so that they nearly made Zoë sick. "I think I liked it better when you hated each other," she told them, glancing up from her studies just in time to see them kiss, their limbs entangled in a torrid embrace.

"When was that?" Leigh asked, coming up for air, her face rosy with passion. "I don't seem to recall any feelings of animosity."

"There weren't any — it was just wishful thinking on my part," Zoë scowled, putting her face back into her book. "Sometimes you two are just gross."

"One day, Zoey-bear," Leigh promised. "One day, you'll feel this way about someone and I'm gonna make you eat your words."

"I'd like to see you try," Zoë laughed, looking over at her with a grin. "I don't think there will ever come a day when a man could make me act the way you do."

After Christmas break, Zoë put feelers out, searching for a clinic that would hire her full time. She put in long days at the Opelika clinic, hoping that the powers that be would change their minds about offering her a job.

"It's not that we don't want you, Zoë," Mrs. Kirkpatrick, the office manager, assured her with a gentle smile. "We simply don't have the funding to hire you. You know that, dear."

Zoë joined Eli for an Italian dinner at Provino's, plopping dejectedly into the chair he graciously pulled out for her, leaning her elbows on the table and cradling her chin in her hands, staring up at Eli with a huge pair of puppy dog eyes. "I swear, I'll never find a job," she said, heaving a sigh of resignation.

Eli rolled his eyes. "If you'd quit being so stubborn, I could ensure that you would never have to work another day in your life," he said.

Zoë frowned at him, hardly in the mood for another one of his arrogant lectures. "The vast wealth left by my own great-grandfather is enough to ensure that I will never have to work another day in my life," she reminded him curtly, the indignant fire in her eyes putting him back in his place. "I don't work because I have to, Eli. I work because I enjoy what I do. It's as simple as that."

She sat back in her chair, depositing her silverware on the table as she unrolled her linen napkin, spreading it daintily across her lap before looking up at him expectantly. "I suppose you'll be moving back home after graduation?" She abruptly changed the subject, grabbing her iced tea glass and sipping from it slowly, her eyes glued to him, intently curious.

"Only if you'll go with me."

"Not a chance. Your mother would gut me."

"How can you say that? My mother's crazy about you, Zoë."

"Your mother *tolerates* me, Eli, and then only as a casual acquaintance. She'd never stand for me becoming a family member."

"If you won't go back East with me, then I'll just stay here," Eli said, stroking his chin thoughtfully as he considered her sullen expression. "Say you'll marry me, Zoë. We don't have to live in the Northeast. My father is opening a division of Feinstein Foods in Atlanta and I'll be heading it." He stretched out his hand to take hers, squeezing it tenderly as he gazed into her eyes. "See how much I care for you, darling? I'm even staying in the South for you."

Zoë snatched her hand away, impatient with his sentimental drivel. "God, Eli, don't stay in the South for me," she snapped. "I'm not ready for marriage. Not to you or anyone else for that matter."

"But I am staying," Eli declared smugly, opening his menu to ponder the dinner options. "Sooner or later, you'll change your mind about marrying me. I'm certain of it." He noted the spasm of irritation that crossed her pretty face and smiled gently at her. "I'm not asking for much, Zoë. I only want for us to be as happy as Cameron and Leigh."

"Be careful what you wish for," Zoë told him pointedly, pushing away her untouched appetizer. "Things are not always what they seem."

Regardless of what Eli thought, Cameron and Leigh's relationship wasn't free of conflict, and despite appearances, Cameron did not live locked in Leigh's embrace. During his four years at Auburn University, he had pursued his writing career with a vengeance, fine-tuning his journalistic skills for the rapidly approaching future. Aside from his studies, he logged long hours at *The Auburn Plainsman,* the student-run campus newspaper, and took a weekend editing job at *The Opelika-Auburn News.*

"I have absolutely no intention of ever going back to Eden Glen," he told Zoë during one of their heart-to-hearts, his face etched with fierce determination. "I will never go back to be one of them. I'm going to get a job some place far away from their nasty clutches."

Hell-bent on living up to his statement, he scoured the towns surrounding the university, applying at local newspaper offices, proudly displaying a portfolio packed with his collegiate journalism efforts. His perseverance paid off, and he landed a job at *The Ledger-Enquirer* in nearby Columbus, Georgia, starting as a staff reporter immediately upon graduation. He returned to the apartment in Auburn, excited and ready to share the news with Leigh, only to find that she had a little news of her own.

Leigh had done her share of job-hunting, her career path being vastly different from Cameron's. Over spring break, she took an unexpected trip to New York City with her parents, their invitation coming totally without warning. "Go figure," she marveled cynically to Zoë as she packed her suitcase. "They wait until I'm twenty-two years old to finally take an interest in me."

While in Manhattan, Leigh pounded the pavement, using her good name to pull a few strings, and with her mother's help secured a job with a top fashion magazine. She would begin at the bottom rung, of course, as a gopher on the publishing ladder of success, but Leigh was thrilled nonetheless, certain that Cameron would be more than happy to move to New York City with her.

She was wrong. Cameron was not at all pleased with her decision. "Why New York?" he questioned irritably.

"Why not?"

"I just don't see the fascination in it."

"But, Cam, this is *Fashion Monthly* — a real shot at the big time."

"It's not that great a shot, Leigh."

"I can't believe that you of all people would be so insensitive," she said passionately. "Can't you see how important this is to me?"

"Oh c'mon, Leigh," Cameron barked, throwing up his hands in frustration. "I'll buy you your own magazine, if that's what you want."

"Oh, you will, huh?" Leigh exclaimed bitterly, turning a pair of livid violet eyes on him. "You won't use your family's money to further your own career, but you'll use it to further mine? What, Cam, you can make it on your own, but I can't?"

"That's not what I'm saying."

"Then what are you saying?"

"I just don't see the need in you racing off to New York," Cameron responded indignantly, pacing the living room, his strides long and angry.

"Too bad. I've taken the job."

Cameron exhaled in aggravation. "This is not going well at all," he muttered under his breath and shook his head, approaching her, his face sincere as he took her gently by the shoulders. "I don't want you to leave, Leigh. That's all I'm trying to say. I love you. I want to marry you and settle down, even have a few kids. What do you say?" He flashed his most winning smile, his jade-green eyes highly persuasive.

Leigh stared into his face, every emotion she felt showing in her overwhelmed expression. "Why can't we do that in New York?" she asked meekly, wincing as he began to explode.

"I don't want New York, Leigh! I want here, where we were raised, where our families are. I want our kids to know their grandparents and grow up in an environment that is congenial and safe."

"That's good for you, Cameron — but not for me." Leigh let out a regretful sigh, wishing he could understand. "I love you, Cam, and I love the South — this is my home. But I want more. I could never be content spending the rest of my life in small-town Georgia, giving up everything I could have had to write the local gossip column. I just can't. Maybe I've got too much of my mother in me. Who knows? I only know that I want the big time — and this job offer could be my ticket. I'm going to New York."

Cameron's facial expression changed from indignation to impassive arrogance. He backed away from her, his smile icy and mocking. "Okay fine, Leigh. Have it your way. Throw away love with both hands. I don't care. I'm not going to stop you."

He paused by the bar, scooping up his keys, and grabbed his jacket off the chair. "Good luck with your little endeavor," he tossed over his shoulder. "I hope it turns out to be all you want it to be. But don't call me when you change your mind. You've made your decision. We're through."

He stomped out the door, slamming it furiously without a look back. Leigh stared after him, her expression twisted in sadness. *Good lord, what have I done?* she wondered, covering her face with her hands. Cameron was gone — and he wouldn't be back.

The weeks leading up to graduation were tense. Cameron spent most of his nights crashed on the floor of the frat house, refusing to come back to the apartment while Leigh was there, unwilling to witness the boxes of her things piling up in the living room corner. Leigh sulked around the apartment, missing Cameron but too proud to ask him to come back, preferring instead to languish in her misery.

Deeply disturbed by the whole situation, Zoë observed them with mounting frustration, incapable of comprehending how two people who loved one another so much could be so aggravatingly stubborn. She couldn't believe that they were wasting their last days together in anger, but could do nothing to prompt either to make the first move.

They didn't even bother to put on a show for the family, keeping their distance while the Carsons were in town for graduation. Diane and Jay viewed their split through sad eyes, sorry to lose the chance at having Leigh as an official family member. Geoff and Patricia didn't care enough about the situation to voice their opinions, but Lois let hers be known, loud and clear.

"What's the problem here?" she demanded of Zoë, gesturing disapprovingly at the yards of space between Cameron and Leigh during the obligatory post-graduation photo session. "And don't feed me that line of garbage about there being nothing wrong. I'm not blind or stupid. Any fool can see the hostility between the two of them."

"Cameron broke up with Leigh because she decided to go to New York." Zoë put it as simply as possible, hoping to avoid any further explanation.

"Is that what the problem is? Of all the pigheaded..." Lois began, an edge of impatience creeping into her voice. "Cameron acts like a rebel and claims to be so different, but I'll tell you what. He's just as arrogant and hard-headed as the rest of the men in this family."

She marched over to him, yanking him by the necktie, pulling his face even with hers. "Let me tell you one thing, mister," she barked, her words clipped. "You let that girl go, and you'll live to regret it."

Cameron clenched his jaw, his face hot and pinched with resentment. "I didn't let her go, Lois. The choice was hers, and she made it. There's nothing more I can do."

"There's nothing more I can do," Lois mocked him, her face hard with anger. "Cameron Carson, you are by far the stupidest man I've ever met. You'll be sorry, young man. I promise you that." She spun on her heel and marched away, shaking her silver head in fury.

"Don't let Grandmother get you down," Palmer said, throwing a chummy arm around his brother's shoulder, his face shining with pompous delight, overjoyed at Cameron's predicament. "You're right about this, Cameron. If Leigh really loved you, she'd stay here. A woman's place is beside her man."

Cameron let out an aggravated growl and raised his fist, punching Palmer solidly in the nose. He stomped away, muttering under his breath, shooting Leigh a bitter look as he sailed past.

Zoë came over, touching Leigh's arm consolingly. "Don't worry about it, Leigh. He'll get over it."

"And me," Leigh added softly, looking at Zoë with solemn eyes. "Yeah, I know, Zoë. That's what I'm afraid of."

A truce was nowhere in sight the day Leigh left town. Early that morning, Zoë went into Cameron's room, flipping on the light. "Cam, wake up. It's time for Leigh to leave for the airport."

"Good. Tell her I said bon voyage."

Zoë grabbed a pillow off the floor and threw it at his head. "Cameron Carson, get your sullen ass out of that bed and get dressed. You're taking her to the airport."

Cameron sat up, glaring at her, his expression stony. "Let her mother drive her since she's suddenly so important to her."

Zoë scowled at him, her mouth tightening into a stubborn line. "We're leaving in twenty minutes. If you're not up, dressed and ready to walk out that door, there will be hell to pay. Trust me."

It was a long drive to Atlanta. Cameron gripped the steering wheel in steely silence, refusing to utter one word or even look in Leigh's direction. Leigh was understandably upset, slumped in the passenger's seat, staring out the window, her bottom lip quivering as she fought back unhappy tears. From the back, Zoë tried to liven things up, leaning between the seats, filling their ears with amusing tidbits of trivia. She knocked herself out to be entertaining and clever, only to have her efforts fall on deaf ears. Neither Leigh nor Cameron was listening.

In the parking garage, Cameron took Leigh's bags, walking ahead of them into the airport, his posture proud and ramrod straight. As he dropped her suitcases in front of the ticket counter and stomped away, Leigh glanced at Zoë, her expression grim and full of unspoken regret. "I guess that's his way of saying goodbye," she said, trying unsuccessfully to be humorous, the gloomy tone of her voice indicating her true sentiments.

She checked in and got her ticket, then walked slowly with Zoë to the gate. Cameron joined them at the last minute, appearing from parts unknown, his hands stuffed in the pockets of his jeans. All too soon Leigh's flight was called and she stood, gripping the handle of her carry-on bag.

"Bye, Zoey-bear," she said, her eyes swimming with unshed tears. She hugged Zoë's neck tightly, her body trembling with grief. "I'll miss you so much. I don't even remember what it's like to be without you."

She started to walk away, but stopped suddenly in her tracks, dropping her bag, and ran back to Cameron, flinging her arms around his neck. "I'm sorry, Cameron. I can't leave without saying goodbye." She kissed him hard on the mouth, tears streaming in hot rivers down her cheeks. "I love you." She pulled from his arms and hurried away, not daring to look back, missing the lovesick expression on Cameron's dismal face.

Zoë and Cameron stood soberly, watching Leigh disappear down the enclosed corridor toward the waiting jet. She turned once, looking longingly over her shoulder at Cameron, her eyes filled with sorrow, and then waving slightly, she rounded the corner, stepping gingerly through the open doorway of the aircraft. Zoë lifted her hand, patting Cameron's shoulder consolingly.

Cameron sighed, his heart heavy. "Well, we're right back where we started, Zoë. It's me and you again, two brave souls against the world."

"Go after her, Cam," Zoë pleaded, hoping for a last-minute reconciliation.

"Shut up, Zoë." Cameron turned and walked away, his shoulders slumped in misery.

She hurried after him, determined to make him listen. "It's not too late. Go with her. Don't let it end like this."

"I'm not. She is." Cameron bristled and stood erect, his shoulders squared proudly. "She's letting it end by not staying here with me."

"What's caused you to be so selfish? How could you, in good conscience, ask Leigh to give up this opportunity?"

"Are you saying that you think her career is more important than mine?"

"No, that's not what I'm saying, and you know it. I'm just saying that a job like she's been offered isn't easy to come by. It would be much easier for you to find a newspaper job there."

"I don't see you running to Atlanta with Eli."

"Apples and oranges, Cameron." Zoë grabbed his arm, spinning him around. "I don't love Eli, but you do love Leigh. I just hate to see you throw it all away."

"Too late."

"Don't be this way, Cam."

"What way am I being? I'm not being any way."

"You're turning your back on her just because she wants to pursue her dream."

"She turned her back on me," Cameron roared, stopping in the middle of the concourse, his eyes flashing angrily. "She's gone, Zoë. She left you, she left me, she left us. It's over."

He pulled away, marching toward the escalator. "Let's go home, Zoë," he said. "It's time to get on with our lives." He strode purposefully toward the exit, and Zoë sprinted to keep up with him, loving him but thinking him a fool, wondering what Cameron would do now that he had lost the love of his life.

# *Part Five*
## *Andie, Diane, Zoë and Dana*

# 14

The change in Andie LaRue was phenomenal. There was a light in her eyes, an ever-present smile on her lips and a radiant glow on her face. Bill Fairgate viewed this change with wonder and begrudging jealousy. He suspected that love had something to do with it, and that made him fussy. He wished that he had been the one to bring about such a transformation.

"It's a right fetching day out there today," he said as he sauntered into the kitchen at Crème de la Crème, finding Andie manning the range top, busily preparing for a wedding shower. "Why aren't you playing hooky?"

"A caterer's work is never done." Andie flashed a bright smile over her shoulder. "Dell has the afternoon off, so I'm a one-woman show." She giggled cheerfully, humming to herself as she cracked eggs into a mixing bowl, her face and apron splattered with flour and colored icing.

"Pumpkin, what's up with you these days?" Bill questioned teasingly, leaning on the counter as he watched her work. "You're positively glowing."

Andie glanced at him in surprise, her rubber spatula poised in mid-air. "Glowing? Hmm. Funny, I thought that term only applied to pregnant women and schoolgirl crushes."

"True. It does," Bill raised an intrigued brow. "So, which is it?"

"Well, I'm definitely not pregnant!" she laughed. "I'm way too old to start that again."

"And the crush?"

"Well," Andie avoided his gaze, her cheeks rosy as she scurried to slide her unbaked creation into the oven, "maybe."

"And here I thought it was your renewed relationship with Dana that was making you so chipper," Bill chuckled, his eyes following her with great interest. "You've been holding out on me, Andie. Who's the lucky guy?"

"No one you know."

"Now Cupcake, I know everybody."

"You don't know him."

"Try me."

"Okay, smart guy. We'll see," Andie grinned and closed the oven door, pivoting slowly as she wiped her hands on her smock. "His name's Cole Dewberry."

"Oh, so it is the schoolgirl crush," Bill barked, applauding mockingly. "Or better yet — the high school sweetheart. How long's he been back in the picture?"

"For a while now," Andie said, filling the sink with soapy water. "He showed up on my doorstep last Christmas."

"I usually credit myself with being pretty observant. I can't believe I haven't noticed him hanging around here."

"That's because he doesn't, not a whole lot anyway. He lives in New Orleans and comes over on weekends."

"When do I get to meet him?" Bill demanded, drumming his fingers impatiently. "Or do you plan to hide him from me forever? You can introduce us. I won't embarrass you, Sugar. I promise."

"Sure you won't," Andie winked at him, padding across the floor to kiss his cheek. "Come by any Saturday. I'd love to introduce you."

Bill met Cole by chance, stopping by Crème de la Crème one afternoon to pass some time with Andie and Dell. He breezed through the front door, tossing a bouquet of daisies to Dell. "Here, doll," he sang out as he sailed through the room. "I brought you a small token of my undying admiration and everlasting esteem." He acknowledged Dell's giggle with a nod and grin. "She around?"

"She's in, but you'd better knock first!" Dell warned, laughing at his determined gait as he trudged toward Andie's office.

"Why? She entertaining men in her boudoir?" he laughed, waltzing in the office door, stopping short when he saw the handsome stranger sitting on the edge of Andie's desk.

"Oh! You are entertaining men in here!" Bill exclaimed, studying the dark-haired man attired in khakis and blue denim narrating an animated tale, his face close to Andie's, their expressions agleam in mutual adoration. "It's definitely not Saturday," he barked jovially, striding forward purposefully with an extended hand. "But you have to be the infamous Mr. Dewberry."

"Bill! Hi," Andie jumped to her feet, sending her chair sailing toward the wall. "Come and meet Cole." She turned to Cole with a delighted grin. "Honey, this is Bill Fairgate, one of my dearest friends."

Cole slid from the desk, grasping Bill's outstretched hand with an easy smile. "Cole Dewberry."

"Pleased to meet you, Dewberry," Bill responded curtly, sizing Cole up with a slow, appraising gaze, his eyes flashing an unspoken challenge.

Andie didn't seem to notice. "I think this calls for a celebration," she declared enthusiastically.

"I agree, Cupcake," Bill said, his eyes never leaving Cole's face. "Break out some champagne, Andie. I'm buying."

"If you're buying, I'll break out the best," she giggled and scurried from the room in search of a bottle of Dom Perignon, leaving the two men staring at each other, locked in a silent showdown.

"That little girl means the world to me," Bill spoke first, shooting Cole a menacing look.

"She means a lot to me too," Cole replied, evaluating Bill calmly.

"Well, that's all good and fine, but let me tell you one thing, partner," Bill took a step forward, "you break her heart, and I'll kick your ass." His voice was intimidating and his frosty glare backed up his threat.

"What makes you so sure I'm out to hurt her?" Cole asked coolly. He relaxed against the desk, inspecting Bill with an unruffled stare.

"You did it once. You'll do it again."

"If that's the way you see it, you're wrong. I'm not out to hurt her. Andie and I have worked past our problems, and we're doing fine."

"You're damn lucky to be given a second chance," Bill retorted, peering down his nose, backing down a little as the sound of Andie's high heels echoed outside the door. He lowered his voice, flashing Cole an ominous grin. "Just remember, Dewberry. If you mess up with her, I'll be the one around to pick up the pieces."

"I'll keep that in mind."

"Are you boys playing nice?" Andie bebopped into the room with a bottle in one hand and glasses in the other. She smiled happily at their suddenly angelic faces.

"Of course we are, Jelly Bean," Bill assured her smoothly as he took the glasses from her hand. "We're near about best buddies."

He joined them for a glass of champagne and then departed, pausing to kiss Andie on his way out. "Why don't you meet us for dinner?" she suggested.

"Can't, Pumpkin. I've got a date. Maybe some other time." He stroked her shoulder affectionately and turned to go, offering Cole a final glower. "See ya, Dewberry."

He exited the room, halting briefly outside Andie's office, a confident smirk on his face. "I think I'll just bide my time," he chuckled under his breath, holding his head high as he strolled down the hall. "They may be together now, but it'll never last."


The engagement ring came at Christmas, a large heart-shaped diamond set on a platinum band, sparkling brilliantly on Andie's left ring finger as she held it up for Bill to see. "Looky what Santa brought me," she beamed, her face illuminated with happiness.

Bill took her hand, lifting it eye-level, appraising the ring with practiced skill. "Well, that's a right-pretty little bauble, Cupcake. Let's just hope it doesn't represent an empty promise."

Andie's face fell, her feelings crushed. "What do you mean?" she asked, her blue eyes disappointed and sad.

"You know what I mean, sweetie. I just don't think the two of you will ever make it to the altar."

"I do!" Dell interjected, giddy with glee. "Have you seen them together?"

Bill turned to her, his gaze cool. "Did I ask for your opinion?" he inquired frigidly, gesturing impatiently toward the office door. "Get out of here, Dell. Go find me some bourbon."

"You're a little abrasive this afternoon," Andie pointed out, regarding him sternly.

"I'm only abrasive when the situation warrants it. Trust me, darlin'. Right now, it's more than appropriate."

"You ought to be ashamed. I've never once given you a hard time over any of your girlfriends." She shot him an aggravated look as she got out of her chair and walked toward the office door. "Now, if you're done offering ominous predictions, I'm going to work. I have a party to cater."

As usual, Bill wasn't easily put off. "You're really going to marry Dewberry?" he persisted skeptically, following her to the kitchen, blocking the doorway with his large frame.

Andie laughed at his sour expression, leaning down to remove a cookie sheet of pastries from the oven. "Yes, Bill. I'm going to marry him." She crossed the room, ducking under his arm to exit the building, carrying the tray of desserts toward a waiting delivery truck. Bill trailed her, shaking his head and objecting loudly.

"You're really going to marry that man after he broke your heart?"

"He didn't break my heart," Andie responded as she proceeded back inside. "I broke his, remember?"

Bill shrugged indifferently, undaunted. "A moot point," he declared, catching her hands as she glided past him, his expression sincere. "I'm not trying to burst your bubble, Pumpkin. I just don't want to see you hurt."

Andie's face softened, touched by his concern. She stopped, placing a hand on his shoulder. "I'm not going to get hurt, Bill. I love him."

Bill nodded, satisfied. The look on her face told him what he needed to know. "Just as long as I know you're doing the right thing," he conceded, leaning down to kiss her cheek. "I want you to be happy, Cupcake."

"Thank you, Bill." Andie squeezed his hand and walked away, darting out the exit and leaping into the truck, passing the plate of cream puffs to Dell as she started the engine.

"Damn it, she really loves him," Bill muttered, looking on as they drove away. He gave them a friendly wave goodbye, then trudged slowly to his car, cursing under his breath. "Nothing I can do or say will ever change that. Damn the luck."

It took several months, but the final confirmation he awaited finally arrived in late spring, and he sought Andie out the same afternoon, bearing the exciting news, having spent the better part of two years doing some private research of his own. He had wanted to tell her thousands of times but reluctantly bit his tongue, withholding his information until he knew for sure. It was only when Andie announced her upcoming nuptials that Bill decided the time was finally right.

*Well damn*, he thought, tapping his fingers impatiently on the steering wheel. *I wanted to make this a wedding present, something to give her during our honeymoon. I hate like hell having to give it to her like this, but it's my own fault. That's what I get for dragging my feet — letting the woman I care for most become the only one who got away.*

He wheeled his sleek black Lexus sedan into the parking lot next to Crème de la Crème, empty except for Andie's red Mustang. "Good. She's alone. That might be best, under the circumstances."

He parked his car and strolled casually into the building, passing through the tastefully decorated reception area. He hesitated outside Andie's office. *This is it,* he thought with a tickled smile, rapping smartly on the door before sticking his head inside. "Hi, sexy," he said, grinning wickedly as his booming voice echoed through the room.

"Hello, sailor." Andie glanced up from her desk, welcoming him with a warm smile. "Buy you a drink?"

"You're on. How 'bout a glass of choice Chardonnay?"

"I bet I can swing that. We're bound to have a bottle of wine around here somewhere." She floated to the kitchen, her effervescent laughter lingering in her wake, and returned with two wine glasses. She handed one to Bill and took her seat behind the desk, sipping her wine as she regarded him affectionately.

"Where's Dell this fine spring afternoon?" Bill relaxed in his chair, crossing his legs casually as he studied her pretty face. *Ah, Andie,* he thought, *a true breath of fresh air. How sad that I let her slip through my fingers without even so much as a fight. Damn the luck.*

"Dell's out romancing a prospective client. Mrs. Billie Jo O'Banion over in Ocean Springs. You've heard of her?"

"Fine woman, Miss Billie Jo. Throws one hell of a party, I seem to recall."

"That's what I understand, which is exactly why I sent Dell out to wine and dine her."

"And where is the very fine Mr. Dewberry?"

"In New Orleans until Friday. He does have a job, you know." Andie giggled at the sullen expression on Bill's face, watching as he drained his wine and set the empty glass down on the desk with a bang. "That's a pretty sour face you're sporting, Mr. Fairgate. When are you going to break down and start liking Cole?"

"I never said I didn't like the man, Andie. I like him well enough. I like anybody who makes you so happy." Smiling mischievously, he vaulted onto the edge of her desk, dangling his muscular leg loosely over the edge. "In fact, Cupcake, I like him so much that I've got a little engagement present for you."

"Are you giving us a party?" Andie asked teasingly. "That would be just lovely, but who would cater? I'd never stand for you using the competition, and I hardly think it would be fair if I had to work my own party."

"You know, a party wouldn't be a half bad idea, but this is something entirely different." He was dying to tell her, but paced himself, letting the suspense build. "Honey, after I got over my hard feelings, I decided that I'm sincerely glad you worked things out with Dewberry. I couldn't stand for you to spend the rest of your life miserable." He reached out, stroking her cheek softly. "But, I don't believe he does it all for you, Pumpkin. You may have Cole Dewberry back in your life, but I think there's still a big piece of your heart missing — somewhere out there in the unknown."

He paused, covering her hand, squeezing it tightly with curbed excitement. "Don't ask me how I did this, because I can't tell you," he said, his voice solemn and low. "Let's just say I called in some big favors and pulled a few strings."

"My," Andie giggled, her eyes dancing playfully. "Whatever could it be? You make it sound so clandestine. I'm excited."

"Clandestine? Maybe. Illegal as hell? Probably. Nevertheless, I did it."

"Spill it, Bill. You're making me nuts."

"I found your daughter."

Andie's amused expression froze, a cold chill running down the length of her spine. She stared at him, squinting uncertainly, unsure that she had heard him correctly. "Found her?" She played dumb, struggling to get a grip on her emotions. "I didn't realize she was lost."

"I'm not talking about Dana, Andie."

"Then which daughter *would* you be talking about?"

"It's always cat and mouse with you, isn't it, Pumpkin? I think you know exactly which daughter I'm talking about. Do I have to spell it out for you?"

"Spell away."

"Damn. You take the fun out of everything. Okay then, I'll spell it out for you. Your firstborn, Andie. *That* daughter. I located the child you gave up twenty-three years ago."

She reeled, clutching the desk, an odd ringing in her ears. She gaped at him, her heart pounding erratically, her mouth almost too dry to speak. "Are you sure?" she whispered.

"Positive," Bill assured her with a firm nod of his head. "I never do anything half-ass, Andie. You should know that by now. I wouldn't have told you if I hadn't been one-hundred-percent, tee-totally certain that it was her."

"Who is she?"

"She's got quite an impressive pedigree, that kid of yours. Adopted by James and Diane *Carson*-Forest of *the* Savannah Carsons. You've heard of them, I'm sure."

Andie nodded, dumbfounded, her head spinning.

"I dealt with her grandfather Palmer many times before he passed away, and I've had quite a few encounters with her uncle, Geoffrey. They're a very wealthy and imposing family, as you can well imagine, and you can rest assured that your little girl has been raised in the lap of luxury with a silver spoon tucked neatly in her pretty little mouth."

"Where is she?" Andie asked, sinking limply into her chair, her eyes glazed in shock. "Where is Shannon?"

"Not Shannon, honey," Bill reminded her gently. "Her name's Zoanne, Zoanne Annette Carson-Forest. But she goes by Zoë."

"Zoë," Andie murmured, looking away with a melancholy smile. "Such a different name than the one I chose for her." *To me, she'll always be Shannon.*

It would be difficult to refer to the baby girl as anything else. It was even harder to comprehend that she was no longer a baby. The child who became Zoanne Carson-Forest was now twenty-three — a full-grown woman with a mind of her own.

Andie glanced back at Bill, her brow creased inquisitively as she ran a trembling hand through her hair. "She lives in Savannah?"

Bill shook his head. "No — Columbus, Georgia. Works as a patient advocate in a free clinic."

"She comes from a family like that and she works?"

Bill chuckled and patted her hand. "From what I understand, Zoë Forest's quite a little pistol: fiery, independent, full of her own ideas. Can't imagine where that came from."

"How do I get in touch with her?"

"That's the tricky part. I'd avoid riding up to the Carsons' front door if I were you. I don't exactly think you'd be welcomed with open arms. From what my sources tell me, the best way to contact her would be through her cousin, Cameron Carson. He's a reporter for *The Ledger-Enquirer* there in Columbus. But, I'll warn you, honey. This Cameron Carson may be your cross to bear. They say he's awfully protective of her. Just be aware."

Andie leaned forward, placing a gentle hand on Bill's arm. "Thank you," she said softly, her eyes brimming with ecstatic tears. "I don't know how you did this — or why — but I can never thank you enough."

Bill tweaked her cheek, winking light-heartedly as he slid from her desk. "You've always been good to me, Andie. This is my way of repaying you for years of great friendship and unconditional kindness. Let me know if I can do anything else."

He walked to the door, filled with an odd sense of elation at Andie's joy. *I'm glad I got to be the one to tell her,* he decided cheerfully as he turned the handle to go out, *even if I didn't get to marry her first. It was worth it, if only to see her so happy.*

"Bill?" Andie called out, catching him just as he stepped into the hall.

"Yes, Sweet Cheeks?" he turned, looking back at her.

"Have you seen her?"

Bill nodded, smiling broadly, exhibiting perfect white teeth. "Yeah, I have. Only in pictures, but she's a real knockout. Just like her mother."

Andie was numb, staring blankly into space, too stunned to move, even after hearing the sound of Bill's Lexus driving away. *My God, my God*, she thought deliriously, her hands tightly gripping the arms of her chair. *This can't be real.*

Her baby, hers and Cole's. After all this time, and she knew exactly where to find her. *Cole will be beside himself.*

For three long years they had searched for Shannon, leaving no stone unturned, using every available tool, from researching court documents and the Internet to hiring private investigators and taking out newspaper ads all over the country — all of which proved fruitless. Every paper trail they followed ended abruptly, every tip they received turned up nothing. Any trace of their daughter had been carefully hidden by some unknown, unseen enemy. It was as if Shannon had fallen off the face of the earth. After numerous false leads and disappointments, they had almost given up. And now, Bill had found her.

Andie wasn't certain how he pulled it off. Knowing all she and Cole had been through, she had a sneaking suspicion that his tactics had not been completely aboveboard or legal, but she didn't care. How he did it was not important. What was important was that Bill had given her the most wonderful gift he could have given anyone. He had given her Shannon.

She couldn't wait another minute. She grabbed the telephone, her fingers shaking as she dialed the number to Cole's office in New Orleans. "Hello, Sandy," she said as his secretary answered, forcing her voice to remain steady as she struggled to maintain her composure. "Is Cole around?"

"Oh, I'm sorry, Ms. LaRue. He's not," Sandy sang out cheerfully, unaware that her simple words shattered Andie's heart. "He was called out to a rig in the Gulf earlier today, and he'll be out of pocket for the next few days. Do you want to leave a message for him?"

"No, Sandy. No message." Disappointedly, Andie hung up the phone and slumped in her chair, drumming her fingertips on the desktop as she contemplated her next move.

Cole would be out in the middle of the Gulf of Mexico for the next two or three days, maybe more, and she was standing on her head, anxious to find her way to Zoanne Carson-Forest. "I'll never make it two or three days. I'll go crazy." She threw her hands up in frustration. There was no way she could wait. "I'll just have to pay a visit to Cameron Carson without Cole."

Propelled into action, she reached again for the phone, cradling the receiver against her shoulder as she dialed Dell's mobile. Dell answered, her voice crackling and hollow, surrounded by the sounds of her blaring car radio. "Hey boss, I was just about to call you. I got the O'Banion account," she said proudly, turning down the stereo so she wouldn't have to yell.

"That's great, Dell, really great. I knew you could do it." Andie checked her impatience, forcing enthusiasm into her voice. "Hey, the reason I'm calling is I'm going to be leaving town for a few days."

"Off to New Orleans?" Dell kidded. "Can't stay away from him, can you?"

"No, somewhere else," Andie replied evasively. "I should be back before Cole returns to Biloxi. If he checks in, just tell him I'm away on business."

"Andie? Is everything okay?"

"Everything's wonderful. I promise. I'll tell you all about it when I get back. Just hold down the fort for me, okay?"

"Sure, boss. Whatever you say."

"Thanks, Dell," Andie hurriedly replaced the receiver and bolted from her desk, hastily snatching her purse and keys off the credenza. She raced through the office and out the front door, jumping into her Mustang convertible. She sped away, hell-bent on getting home to pack for her impromptu trip to Georgia.

The ring of the telephone pierced through the darkness, rousing Dana from a deep sleep. She rolled over, eyeing the clock sleepily. "It's almost two a.m.," she noted in irritation. "Who on earth would be calling at such an ungodly hour?"

"Dana, get the freakin' phone," Claudette growled from her bunk, her voice muffled by the pillow she clutched over her head.

Dana dove from her mattress and fumbled blindly through the rummage scattered over the floor, finally locating the phone buried beneath a pile of discarded clothing, answering breathlessly on the fourth ring. "Hello?"

"Dana? It's Mom." Dana instantly recognized Andie's voice crackling over the line, obviously coming from a car phone.

"What's up? Is everything okay?" She jolted upright, unnerved by the late-night call, sure that something had to be terribly wrong. *Andie wouldn't be calling in the wee hours of the morning just for the hell of it.*

"Yes, everything's wonderful!" Andie sounded elated, almost giddy. "I've got great news."

Dana sighed with relief. "You and Cole finally broke down and tied the knot?"

"No, better!"

"What could be better than that?"

"Are you sitting down?"

"It's the middle of the night. What do you think?"

"Sorry. Stupid question," Andie rambled excitedly. "Honey, you'll never guess what! Bill Fairgate found Shannon!"

Dana fell back against the headboard, feeling like she'd been kicked in the teeth. *Shannon!* she thought in disgust, fighting back steadily rising bile. *Good lord, is that why she's calling me in the middle of the night?* She ignored her better reasoning, falling prey to old nagging doubts. *And I was worried that something was wrong, that she might be calling because she needed me,* she raged bitterly. *I should have known better. I should've known she didn't need me.*

Of course, all the excitement was about Shannon. Anything of importance to Andie always was. She's never gotten this excited over anything concerning her real children. Over the two years Dana had been at Tulane, she and Andie had grown closer, sharing long weekends, learning to love and trust one another again. Dana spent most of her spring and summer breaks with Andie, joined frequently by her brother Jerry, who was now a pre-med major at Vanderbilt. She had accepted and cared deeply for Cole, thrilled to have him as a stepfather-to-be. She had honestly begun to think that the worst was behind them.

And now, the very person who had caused all their pain from the beginning had come back to haunt them.

"Dana, are you there?" Andie spoke up hesitantly, hearing only static, already regretting her hasty decision to tell Dana. *Why didn't I just keep my mouth shut?* she scolded herself harshly. *This could have waited, at least until morning.*

"I'm here." Dana swallowed her pride, putting her best face forward for the sake of their sometimes-fragile relationship. "I'm happy for you, Mom," she spoke with grave deliberation, wishing she really meant the words passing through her tightly pursed lips.

"You should be happy for you too, honey. We've found your sister."

"I don't want another sibling." Dana struggled to keep the hostility out of her voice. "Having Jerry is enough, trust me."

"I'm going to Georgia to try to meet her. I'm just leaving Biloxi, and I don't want to go alone. Will you go with me?"

Dana sucked in her breath, her stomach churning. *I can't believe my ears,* she thought incredulously, feeling ill. *First, to be subjected to her overwhelming excitement about finding The Hated One, then to be asked to go along for the ride to welcome her home.* It was almost more than she could take. Scowling unpleasantly into the blackness of the room, she slowly counted to ten.

"Mom, I can't," she finally answered, carefully toning down the shrillness in her voice. "I've got class. Besides, I don't want to meet her. I've been through too much with you to meet her now. What about Cole? I thought he'd go with you. After all, he's her father."

"Cole's out in the Gulf, and I can't reach him."

"Then wait until he gets back."

"I can't wait, Dana. I've waited twenty-three years already."

"Then a few more days shouldn't be that difficult." Dana gritted her teeth, using every ounce of determination she had not to lose her temper.

"I can't believe you'd refuse to go with me. I've never asked you for anything, Dana, but I'm asking now. I don't want to go alone."

"And I can't believe you expect me to go!" Dana gave up all hope of remaining in control. "I don't want to meet her, okay? My life was pretty unpleasant because of her — or should I thank you for that?"

Dana's sudden fury took Andie by surprise. In light of the pleasantness of the past few years, she had hoped they had resolved their differences regarding her years of emotional neglect. But apparently, they had not. "I understand," she replied humbly. "It was callous of me to ask. I'm sorry."

Dana sighed heavily, guilt washing over her like a wave. *She wants to include you in the excitement, dummy. She called to confide in you, and for moral support, and you act like a brat. Way to go, Dana.* She shook her head in frustration. *Just rain on her parade, why don't you?*

"It's okay, Mom," she said aloud. "I'm glad you called and that you felt like this was something you could share with me. I'm truly happy for you, I really am. I only wish I could feel more excited about Shannon."

"Maybe some day, Dana, maybe some day," Andie said softly. She recognized Dana's courageous attempt at compromise and yearned to be with her so that she could wrap her tightly in a reassuring embrace.

*Don't be so insecure, honey. I love you every bit as much as her.* Andie longed to say the words, but refrained, keeping them inside, saving them for another time. *Some day all wounds will be healed and we will be past this, better people for having endured it all.* "I'll call you when I get back, okay?" she said instead, praying for a peaceful end to their conversation.

"Whatever." The bitterness and disappointment in Dana's voice cut Andie's heart like a sharp knife. Saying goodbye, she clicked off her phone, regretful tears springing into her eyes as she drove down the lonely dark highway, heading toward the greatest of unknowns.

Dana replaced the receiver and lay back against her pillow, grateful
for the veil of blackness that hid her face. She hugged her arms tightly
to her chest and swallowed hard, choking back brokenhearted sobs,
letting hot tears of disappointment slide silently from the corners of her
eyes. Her mother was gone again, her love stolen once more by her
older sister Shannon. Dana hated Andie for breaking her heart and
crushing her self-confidence. But more than Andie, she hated Shannon,
as always, for being her mother's favorite, and for reappearing to make
her miserable.

"LaRue, are you crying?" Claudette's gruff voice reached out to her
through the darkness, her tone laced with a slight edge of compassion.

Dana sniffed loudly, wiping her eyes with the corner of her sheet.
"Hell no, I'm not crying," she denied irritably. "There's nothing that
woman can say that means enough to make me cry." She flopped over
onto her stomach, punching her pillow with her clenched fist, and
pulled her blanket over her head.


Cameron returned to the offices of the *Ledger-Enquirer,* making his
way toward his cubicle after covering a warehouse fire downtown. He
sauntered through the newsroom, whistling obnoxiously, winking at his
favorite feature writer, Kelly Clinesdale, as he passed by her desk.

Kelly popped her head up, watching every move he made, sticking
her tongue out at him playfully. "Right here, big boy," she drawled,
batting her eyelashes flirtatiously.

"Later, babe," Cameron kidded, flashing her a lopsided grin. Kelly
Clinesdale was a peroxide-blonde bombshell with a brain and a body to
die for, and he had grown quite attached to her since taking his job at
the newspaper. He dated her often, even spending an occasional night
or two at her two-bedroom duplex when the opportunity presented
itself. Kelly was divine, a perfect ten to most men, but in Cameron's
eyes, she didn't hold a candle to Leigh Streete.

"Eleven months," Cameron sighed, his brow creased in frustration
as he continued down the corridor toward his office. Eleven long,
lonely months since Leigh left for New York City, and they had barely
communicated, other than a simple "hello, how are ya?" caught by
chance via a telephone call at Zoë's. God, how he missed her. He
missed her laugh, her dry wit, her sultry voice in his ear. He missed
waking up with her shapely legs wrapped around his and looking into
the depths of her violet eyes every morning as he raised his drowsy

eyelids. He missed the enticing smell of her perfume that still filled his senses, he missed...

"Hey, Cam!" Eric Webster, the assistant city editor, bellowed across the newsroom, interrupting Cameron's thoughts. He rolled his chair into view, craning his neck, surveying Cameron with mischievous eyes. "There's some lady waiting for you at your desk."

"Oh yeah? What about?" Cameron kept moving, pushing back thoughts of Leigh as he tossed an intrigued look over his shoulder.

Eric shrugged nonchalantly and wheeled back to his computer, his head down as he pecked away on the keyboard. "Don't know, she wouldn't say," he said with a gruff chuckle. "She only said that it was important, and she could only talk to you."

"Sounds promising." Cameron grinned, coming to halt in front of his cubicle. He rounded the corner to find a very attractive woman — tall, blonde and slender, probably in her early forties. He studied her curiously, taking in her flawless complexion and incredibly blue eyes, finding her undeniably beautiful. He was certain he had never seen her before, yet felt that there was something oddly familiar about her, although he could not quite put his finger on precisely what. As he neared her chair, she glanced up and Cameron nodded a quick greeting, offering her his hand.

"Hi, I'm Cameron Carson. You were looking for me?"

"Hello Mr. Carson, I'm Andrea LaRue." Andie stood, taking Cameron's hand, shaking it firmly while assessing him with the practiced eye of a shrewd businesswoman. The young man before her was darling, the picture of great looks and confidence. He carried himself well, exuding self-assuredness of someone twice his age.

*Of course, that's what a little good breeding and a big bank account can do for you*, Andie thought wryly, having no way of knowing that she was dealing with the rebel of the Carson clan.

With a polite gesture, Cameron invited her to sit, then relaxed in the old leather chair behind his well-worn desk, looking across at her expectantly. "What can I do for you, Ms. LaRue?"

"Please call me Andie," she insisted, smiling at him nervously. She glanced around the cluttered cubicle, spotting among his paraphernalia a framed photograph of Cameron Carson with two girls, one brunette and one blonde. Resisting the urge to fly out of her chair to get a closer look, she squinted at the picture, wishing she could see it more clearly, wondering which one, if either of them, was Zoanne.

"Okay, what can I do for you, *Andie?*" Cameron smiled back at her patiently, yet firmly, steepling his long fingers against his chin as he regarded her with open curiosity.

Bill had forewarned her that there would be no beating around the bush with this guy and, as always, Bill had been right. Cameron's probing eyes conveyed a stern message, indicating that she should either state her business or stop wasting his time.

Andie decided to come right to the point and licked her dry lips, meeting his inquiring gaze evenly. "I'm here from Biloxi to discuss a personal matter with you, Mr. Carson," she said, watching his face take on a look of fascinated bewilderment.

"Really? Well, by all means, don't keep me waiting, Andie. What business?" He reached forward and picked up a pen, flipping it from tip to end as he studied her anxious expression.

"Actually, my business has more to do with your cousin, Zoanne Forest, than with you."

Cameron's eyebrows shot up in surprise. "Zoë? What about Zoë?"

Andie's heart pounded furiously and she wiped her perspiring palms down the length of her tailored suit. *God, I sincerely hope I'm doing the right thing,* she thought. It had certainly seemed the right thing to do when she left Biloxi, speeding recklessly along Interstate 10 toward the Alabama state line. It had seemed even more so as she crossed over the Chattahoochee River into Georgia. But now as she sat uncomfortably in a straight-backed chair in Cameron Carson's small, paper-littered cubicle, she wasn't so sure. She felt his intense green eyes upon her, sizing her up, and felt obligated to give him an answer. *I opened the door and got his undivided attention — there's no turning back now.*

"This is really hard for me to say," she faltered, averting her eyes and twisting the hem of her jacket. She cleared her throat, suddenly wishing she had waited for Cole to accompany her. *Here goes nothing*, she thought timidly, taking a deep breath. "I'm Zoanne's mother, Mr. Carson. I gave birth to your cousin twenty-three years ago in February."

Cameron's mouth fell open, and the pen dropped from his hand, making a clattering sound as it bounced across the desk. He gawked at her, suddenly sick to his stomach. *That's it!* he realized as he stared incredulously into the pretty face before him. *That's what's so familiar about Andrea LaRue.* There was no denying it. The woman sitting across the desk from him was simply an older version of Zoë. Andie

LaRue had the same blond hair, the same slender build, even the same facial structure. The resemblance was staggering.

Cameron recovered from the shock and snapped his mouth shut, scrutinizing Andie with an icy jade stare. "What exactly do you want with Zoë, Ms. LaRue?" he asked coolly, pretending her unexpected revelation made no difference whatsoever.

His friendly, easygoing manner was gone, replaced by a chilly, much more reserved demeanor, and Andie recognized that she'd struck a nerve, finding that once again Bill Fairgate's words rang true. Cameron was clearly very protective of his cousin. *I just hope I haven't blown my chances with him by being so foolishly forthright.*

"I want to meet her," she said. *There's no sense in mincing words now.* Andie lifted her chin to give an air of confidence she certainly didn't feel. *Cameron Carson already regards me as the enemy. I might as well go for it.*

"And what does that have to do with me?"

"I was hoping that you'd help me."

Cameron's eyes widened, and he shook his head adamantly, the expression on his handsome face one of mocking skepticism. "And break my Aunt Diane's heart?" he jumped to his feet, slapping his hand angrily against the hard desktop, leaning in toward her, speaking in a fiery, menacing tone. "Lady, are you crazy? I don't know you from Adam, and you just barge in here, expecting me to help you break up my family with something like this! What'd you want me to do, take you home for a family dinner?"

"I understand that you're upset."

"You're damn right, I'm upset. What the hell would possess you to come here? You have no right to expect anything from us."

"But Zoanne's my child. I only want to get to know her."

"Zoë's *not* your child, not anymore," Cameron reminded her curtly, his eyes flashing lividly. "And that was your choice, Ms. LaRue. You gave her up long ago. Zoë's my aunt's child, my aunt's and my uncle's."

"I don't want to come between them," Andie said softly, appealing to him with deep blue eyes. "I was only a child myself when she was born. I had no choice but to give her up. I only wanted her to have a better life than I could offer at the time. But that doesn't mean that I didn't love her. I never stopped loving her, just as I never stopped hoping that one day I might meet her and have the chance to tell her how I feel."

"That's all very touching," Cameron said in a brisk, business-like voice, pulling his chair up behind him as he sat back down, arrogantly impassive to her heart-wrenching plea. "But it doesn't change a thing. You have no rights with Zoë. You relinquished them long ago. Leave her alone, Ms. LaRue. If you love Zoë, let her be."

"I don't know if I can." Andie could tell by looking at him that her honesty didn't win her any brownie points, but she pressed on, throwing all caution to the wind. "So I take it you won't tell her about meeting me?"

"Not a chance." A spasm of irritation crossed Cameron's face, and he set his jaw stubbornly, challenging her with his steely stare.

Andie sighed, her chest heavy with disappointment. Feeling defeated, she rose reluctantly from her seat. *I've hit a brick wall*, she decided, picking up her handbag from the floor. *Time to cut my losses and go.*

It was pointless to continue pressing Cameron, given the icy barrier he had thrown up against her. *And he's supposed to be the easy one of the Carson clan*, she thought wryly. *I can't wait to meet the rest of them.*

"I thank you kindly for your time, Mr. Carson," she said politely, handing him one of her business cards. "I'll be in town until tomorrow afternoon. This is the number to the hotel where I'll be staying. The other is my home address and telephone number — just in case you change your mind." She offered Cameron a smile so like Zoë's it was eerie, and then she was gone.

Cameron slumped in his chair, stunned, not moving a muscle for quite some time after Andrea LaRue left. He still couldn't believe it. All his life, he had listened to his mother speculate about her, his Aunt Diane fret over her, and now she was here — the dreaded birth mother, in the flesh, in his office, asking him to help her meet Zoë. "Why me, Lord?" he groaned, raising his eyes to the ceiling in a plea for mercy. "Am I really that easy a mark?"

*What would Zoë say?* He ran his hand through his hair, wincing as the throb of an impending headache stabbed sharply at his temple. "God, I don't want to tell Zoë about this," he muttered aloud, massaging his pounding head with his fingertips. It sickened him to imagine breaking the incredible news to her, but at the same time, he knew he had no choice. "I've never kept anything from her before, and I'm sure as hell not about to start now."

He glanced quickly at his watch. It was four-thirty, almost time for Zoë to be home from the clinic. He would have to tell her over the phone. He couldn't face her with this. He couldn't bear to witness her expression when she heard, regardless of her reaction. He stared at the telephone, putting it off for as long as he could, then dialed Zoë's number, listening to her phone ring, praying that she wouldn't be home so he could postpone his duty.

As luck would have it, Zoë picked up on the third ring, sounding slightly out of breath from her brisk trot up the stairs to her third floor apartment. "Hello?"

"Zoë?" he said, feeling a wave of acid welling up in his belly. *God*, he thought, panicking. *I don't want to do this*.

"Cam! What are you doing calling me? I thought for sure that you'd be out with Kelly Clydesdale."

"It's *Clines*dale, Zoë, and you know it," he said testily, not missing the undertones of humor in his cousin's chipper voice.

"Whatever," Zoë replied, laughing at his insulted tone. "So, since you're not out with her, how about dinner with me? I'll even cook."

"Not tonight."

"Well, fine, be that way, you old stick-in-the-mud. I didn't want to eat with you anyway."

"Zo, we need to talk."

"What's up? You sound like someone died or something."

"Zoë, I had the most interesting visitor stop by my office today," Cameron hesitated, dragging it out as long as he could before he opened the proverbial Pandora's box, acutely aware of the butterflies turning nauseating somersaults in his gut.

"Oh yeah? Who?"

"A woman from Mississippi named Andrea LaRue."

"And?"

"And," Cameron closed his eyes tightly, gritting his teeth as he casually tossed out the truth. "She claims to be your mother."

The color drained from Zoë's face, and she drew in a sharp breath, overcome by a strange sensation of disembodiment as she sank weakly to the kitchen floor. *My mother*, she thought deliriously. *My God. After all these years, this was the last thing I expected to happen.*

"Zoë? Zoë!" She heard Cameron shouting, snapping his fingers loudly on the other end of the line and slapping the butt of the telephone against the heel of his hand in an effort to get her attention. *I wish you were here, Cam,* she thought. *I need you to give me a big hug and tell me everything will be okay.*

"Cam, stop snapping your fingers! I'm here." Zoë regained her composure, trying not to sound as small and afraid as she felt. "Gee, Cam. You certainly know how to surprise a girl."

"Well, believe it or not, the element of surprise was not exactly what I was after."

"What does she want?"

"She wants to meet you."

"Meet me?" Zoë echoed him doubtfully, drawing her knees into her chest in a protective gesture. "What did you tell her? Never mind that. What am I going to tell my mother?"

"You don't have to tell her anything, Zoë. You're a consenting adult now. It's no longer Aunt Diane's decision to make. It's yours."

"She's still my mother."

"Yeah, well, in a roundabout kind of way, so's the other one."

"Not as far as I'm concerned," Zoë snapped, holding her head in her hands. "I just don't know what to say. Thanks a lot, Cameron."

"Hey, don't shoot the messenger. Would you have preferred that I keep this from you? It would've been a helluva lot easier on me."

"No. You know I don't want you keeping secrets from me. But, Cam, my God, I don't know what to do. What do you think I should do?"

"Nothing doin', Cuz. You can't make me answer that. I'm not exactly objective about this."

"You're not exactly being very helpful either."

"How can you expect me to be helpful in this situation? Telling you to go meet her is like handing you over to the enemy."

"That's a little extreme, don't you think?"

"Not really," Cameron said, and then sat in uncomfortable silence, wishing that he had just kept his mouth shut. But it was too late to have regrets. He betrayed his family and let the skeleton out of the closet, and now he would have to live with the consequences of what he had done.

Zoë hung up, cradling the phone against her chest, pressing her palm into her forehead as she held her pounding head. *This is absolutely unbelievable.* "My birth mother," she murmured, shaking her head numbly.

Although she had denied it to Cameron, in the back of her mind she couldn't help but feel a little exhilarated and curious about the woman who had given her life. *What is she like? Is she nice or mean? Short or tall? Do I look like her?* She had a thousand questions and no one to give her the answers.

She had to talk to someone, but not just anyone would do. Obviously, she couldn't call home about it. *One mention of the old birth mother within the sacred walls of Carson House and all hell would break loose.* Other than Cameron, there was only one person with whom she could discuss this. She hastily dialed Leigh's number in New York.

"Zoë, I was just thinking of you," Leigh said laughingly, glad to hear from her best friend. "I just got off the phone with Eli Feinstein. He's in Manhattan and called me for the thousandth time this week, begging for the inside track on how to make you his lovely bride."

"How very nice," Zoë replied distractedly. She was still stunned, and anxious to tell Leigh about Andrea LaRue.

"What's the deal, Zoë?" Leigh asked suspiciously. "That response wasn't nearly caustic enough, especially given the fact that I just mentioned marriage to Eli. What's up?"

"Leigh, I've got something to tell you."

"Is it good, bad or ugly?"

"That depends."

"On what?"

"Which side of the fence you're sitting on."

"Ooh," Leigh giggled. "It sounds delightfully dark and dirty. Do tell!"

"You're not going to believe it."

"Try me. I'll pretend I'm gullible."

"Guess who showed up in Cam's office out of the blue, wanting to meet me?"

"Okay, I give up, who?"

"My biological mother."

"No!" Leigh gasped, choking and sputtering with excitement, letting out an ear-splitting shriek that made Zoë wince. "Get outta here! Where'd she come from, and how'd she know to contact Cam?"

"What am I, psychic? How should I know where she came from?"

"You're a little testy."

"Sorry, but the whole deal makes me nervous. What do you think, Leigh? Should I meet her?"

"That's a stupid question. You know what I'm going to say. I've been pushing for this since we were at Miss Colleen's. Of course I think you should meet her. Don't you want to?"

"Kind of, although more out of curiosity than anything."

"Then meet her. You owe her that much anyway."

"Owe her? How do you figure? I don't owe her. She gave me up, remember? I don't owe her a thing."

"Yeah, you do," Leigh said gently, her voice unusually solemn. "You owe her for giving you life. She didn't abort you, and she's to be commended for that much anyway. And she was indirectly responsible for what you have now. She did the right thing by you, whatever the reason, by putting you up for adoption. She gave you up so that you could have a better life."

"Yeah, whatever."

"Whatever, nothing. I'd kill or die to have what you have, Zoë. I'd love to have your parents. That lady gave you the world by giving you to Jay and Diane. Hell, I only wish that Tom and Carol had been ballsy enough to give me away, instead of keeping me around and pretending that they really gave a damn about me."

"Which brings us to the biggest dilemma. How do I tell my folks? If I did choose to meet her — and I'm not saying I will — how on earth would I go about breaking that kind of news?"

"Jeez, that's a tough one," Leigh said, pausing thoughtfully. "Maybe I'm not the best one to consult about this, Zoë. You know how I am — I'm a fly-by-the-seat-of-my-pants, can't-see-the-forest-for-the-trees kind of gal. I'm not real good at planning things around other people's feelings. Why don't you ask Lois? She's a wise old bird, and one thing's for certain — she'll definitely tell you what she thinks about it."

"Sure. I'll ask Lois. She'll know what to do."

Zoë still sounded uncertain, but Leigh didn't badger her, electing instead to change the subject. "So, how's Cam? Still dating that bubble-headed bleach-blond from the newspaper? What do you call her, Zoë?"

"Kelly Clydesdale?"

"Yeah, Kelly Clydesdale, that's the one." Leigh attempted a half-hearted chuckle, unaware that the heart she wore on her sleeve was highly evident in the melancholy sound of her voice.

"I think he still sees her occasionally," Zoë responded lightly, quickly noticing the undercurrent of yearning in Leigh's feigned indifference. "I do just happen to know that he's not with her tonight."

"Well, isn't that just a pity? How unfortunate for them both. I don't know how they'll make it through the night."

"You are so hard-headed."

"I'm hard-headed? Please! You're a fine one to talk, Ms. Zoey-Anne Carson-Forest. You are the very definition of the pot calling the kettle black!" Leigh retorted, enjoying a laugh with her friend before falling into preoccupied silence. "So what do you think you'll do?"

"More than likely have a stiff drink and cry on Lois' shoulder."

"In that order?"

"It would probably be helpful."

Immediately after Zoë signed off, Leigh clicked the line, phoning Cameron at the newspaper. "Cameron Carson, what's the matter with you, you big lump-headed, insensitive idiot!" she snapped in exasperation when he came on the line. "You should be shot! You don't break news like that over the telephone."

"Hello Leigh." Despite the nastiness in her tone, Cameron had to smile, thrilled to hear her voice, even if it was through the hard plastic receiver of his office telephone. "I take it you've spoken with Zoë."

"You're damn right I've spoken with her. Carson, I thought you were supposed to be well bred. At least that's the impression you try to give everyone else. How could you do something so thoughtless and stupid?"

"I had to tell her, Leigh."

"I know you had to tell her, but you could've come up with a better way of doing it."

"Okay, Miss Expert Know-it-all, how would you have handled it?" Cameron mocked her and broke the tension, smiling at the sound of her tinkling laughter.

"I don't have a clue. I'm not exactly the queen of social graces," Leigh conceded with a warm giggle. "But the least you could've done was tell her in person."

"I know. Springing the news over the phone was pretty gutless, but it was the only way I could tell her. I just couldn't bear seeing the look on her face. What did she say about it?"

"None ya, big guy. You know our girl talks are none of your business."

"Then why are you calling me?"

"I called to bitch you to the ground," Leigh said, her voice softening as she relaxed, listening to the pleasant, melodic sound of his deep voice. She closed her eyes, picturing his rugged handsomeness in her mind. "How are you, Cam?" she asked lightly. She missed him like mad, yet was unwilling to admit it.

"I'm okay. Just staying busy and working late," Cameron answered casually, careful to keep his tone professional, never allowing one note of underlying emotion to creep into his voice. "Gotta earn a living, you know."

"When are you going to swallow your pride and live your life as the privileged prince you were born to be?"

"Hmm, I guess that would be the same day that you go back to Atlanta and grant your parents forgiveness for ignoring you all your life."

"Well, won't that be a cold day in hell," Leigh growled. "Touché, Carson. You got me, but you know that wasn't very nice."

"And what you said was?"

Cameron goaded her, doing or saying anything to keep her talking, and Leigh let him, arguing every point with him until late in the night. They sat on opposite ends of the line, each clinging to the sound of the other, yearning frantically for the slightest touch, but neither willing to be the first to let on.

And when they hung up, neither felt any better for having remained silent.

Andie returned to her hotel room, dejected and alone, feeling as though her trip to Georgia had been fruitless. *Maybe I approached this all wrong,* she thought, replaying her visit to Cameron in her mind as she changed into her cotton nightshirt, distractedly hanging her suit on its hanger and returning it to the garment bag hooked over the bathroom door. *But what else could I have done?*

She didn't know what she had expected to happen. She certainly hadn't expected Cameron to ask her to join the family circle, but she hadn't counted on him pushing her away altogether. He clearly viewed her as a threat and, in his position, rightly so.

She turned back the thin generic sheets and climbed into bed, wiggling around to find a comfortable spot on the lumpy mattress. She lay back against the pillows, deep in thought, her racing thoughts jumbled. "I don't know how I'm going to get any sleep!" she grumbled, flopping onto her side and yanking the covers over her shoulders. "I'll never be able to shut my eyes. I might as well drive home tonight."

The loud jingling of the telephone startled her and she rolled over, reaching for the receiver. "Hello?"

"Ms. LaRue?" Andie immediately recognized the deep voice of Cameron Carson and scrambled up, leaning back against the hard wooden headboard of the rickety bed, perking up with hope that he had good news.

"Mr. Carson, what can I do for you?" she asked, somehow managing to keep her voice calm and professional sounding.

"I called to let you know that I told Zoë about our meeting this afternoon, so the ball's in her court now, not mine. I wash my hands of it."

Andie's heart sang with joy, and she had to pinch herself to stay grounded. "Did you tell her how to reach me?" she asked, her voice tinged with jubilant laughter.

"No," Cameron answered curtly, letting some of the wind out of her sails. "She didn't ask and I didn't volunteer, but I'll tell her if she wants to know." He popped a Tums in his mouth and sucked it broodingly, hating that he was having any part of the conversation. He felt like a traitor, a turncoat to his own family, betraying his aunt Diane for some woman he didn't even know and certainly didn't trust.

"Should I extend my visit?" Andie asked tentatively, hoping for some clue to Zoë's reaction.

"I don't care what you do," he snapped. "I told you, I'm done with this. However, I'll offer one small piece of very good advice: I wouldn't waste my time hanging around here waiting, if I were you. I'm far from being my cousin's keeper, but I have a feeling it'll be a long time before she contacts you, if she ever does."

"I understand. Thank you, Mr. Carson."

"Do not thank me. There's no guarantee you'll ever hear from her, and personally, I hope you never do. I just wanted you to know I'd done my part."

"I appreciate that," Andie said warmly, sensing what a big sacrifice it had been for him. "And I do understand that you're no longer involved, but would you mind terribly if I ask you one last question?"

"Shoot."

"What does she look like?" She had to know, just to satisfy her own curiosity.

She heard his sigh echo over the line — heavy, frustrated and sober. "She looks like you, Ms. LaRue," he answered in an abrupt, clipped tone. "My cousin Zoë is the spitting image of you."

He slammed down the phone and Andie squealed, hugging her pillow to her chest in anticipation. It wasn't what she had hoped for, but at least it was the first step — the first big step to meeting Shannon.

She arrived back in Biloxi late Friday afternoon, not at all surprised to find Cole's white sports utility vehicle parked in the drive. She pulled her car in beside it, cutting the engine, attempting to wipe the let down look off her face as she stared at her cozy little home. Unsuccessful and still feeling blue, she walked slowly toward the front door, using the thought of seeing Cole to lift her spirits.

She found him in the kitchen in jean shorts and Doc Marten sandals, chopping vegetables on a cutting board with Estelle at his feet. He glanced up as she breezed through the doorway, his face lighting with a glad smile to welcome her home.

"Hey Andie," he said, setting his knife on the countertop and stepping over Estelle's thumping tail to take her by the shoulders. He kissed her warmly. "How was your trip?"

Andie returned his kiss and beamed up at him, tossing her handbag onto the tile-topped table in the center of the dining room. "Fine," she answered, forcing a light-hearted tone.

"Where'd you go? Dell said that you were away on a business trip, but she was pretty vague," Cole questioned her casually, returning to his dinner preparations.

Andie leaned against the countertop, feeling like a heel for having kept something so important from him. "Well, I was in Georgia, although I wouldn't exactly say that I was on a business trip," she said, meeting his interested gaze as he looked back at her in surprise.

"What kind of trip then?"

"You might say that I was away taking advantage of an engagement present from Bill."

Cole smiled expansively, his bright gray eyes twinkling with laughter. "Bill, huh? What'd he do, get you an all-expense-paid trip to a spa or something? That'd be just like him. I'm surprised he didn't go along for the ride."

The joyful look on his face made her even bluer, and Andie wished desperately that she had something more positive to reveal. All the way to Columbus she had imagined this moment, envisioning the ecstatic expression that would appear on Cole's face when she told him about Zoë. She had hoped to return to Biloxi having met their daughter, even fantasizing so much as to imagine Zoë happily accompanying her back to Mississippi to meet her biological father. But her vision was sadly unrealized, and Andie had returned to Biloxi empty-handed, bringing with her only the news of being so close, yet so far away.

She was aware of his eyes upon her, his brow wrinkled in bewilderment over her hesitation to answer. She lifted her eyes, smiling haltingly. "No, Cole, it's much, much more than that."

She approached him and wrapped her arms around his neck, gazing deeply into his handsome face. "Cole," she spoke softly, pacing herself, knowing he would be overjoyed at her next words. "Bill found Shannon. She's in Georgia, and I went there to meet her."

Cole's jaw dropped in surprise, and he stared at her, a flush of jubilation spreading rapidly over his face. He gripped her shoulders in exhilaration, the thrill in his eyes reflected in his euphoric voice. "How did Bill find her?" he asked, wide-eyed, guiding Andie to the living room sofa as he chattered excitedly. "Never mind, never mind. We'll cover that later. Tell me about her, Andie. What's she like? Is she beautiful? Was she happy to see you? Give me the details, hon, and don't leave anything out." He sat facing Andie with his arm along the back of the couch, fidgeting anxiously, barely able to sit still.

Andie placed a gentle hand on his forearm, shaking her head slightly and displaying a long face. "I said that I went to meet her, not that I did meet her," she said, casting her eyes downward in sorrow. "I only met her cousin, who said that he would tell her about me."

"And did he?"

"He said he did, when he called my hotel that evening. He said that he relayed the message, so I waited, all night and all the next day, to hear from her."

Andie's eyes misted over, her bottom lip trembling with the threat of discouraged sobs. "But I didn't hear one word from her. Not one. I went to Georgia expecting a happy reunion, but I got nothing, not even a phone call." She broke down, her face pressed against his firm chest, her voice cracking as scalding tears cascaded down her cheeks, puddling in salty pools at her chin. "I guess she doesn't care to meet me or want anything to do with me, for that matter. I was foolish to hope so in the first place."

She wept openly, and Cole lifted his hand, stroking her hair gently as she cried, his own bitter disappointment welling inside him. For three years, he and Andie had searched, praying that one day they would be reunited with their child and now they knew where she was, but still could not see her. *I'm not sure if that's good or not,* he thought dismally. It would almost be better not to know.

He leaned his head back against the couch, closing his eyes, suddenly weary. Andie's news tore at his heart, his very soul mangled by an unseen, twisting force. *I can only imagine what Andie must be feeling,* he thought grimly. *Shannon's rejection must be sheer hell for her.* He pulled her close and embraced her tightly, tenderly kissing the top of her head.

"Andie, darling, shh," he said, comforting her softly with his gentle, pleasing voice. "It's a setback, honey. A small setback, that's all. Give the girl some time to think about it. I'm sure she must be in shock. She may come around after giving it some thought. We have to believe that some day she might contact us."

Andie raised her head, looking up at him with grateful eyes, forcing a smile for his consoling pep talk. "You're right, of course," she said, wiping her tears away with her sleeve. "We'll just have to remain optimistic and think that some day she'll miraculously appear on our doorstep."

"That's my girl," Cole stroked her cheek tenderly and lifted her chin, kissing her softly on the lips. "Andie, baby, let's not let this spoil the happiness we've found together." He rubbed her shoulders enthusiastically, hoping to cheer her with his energetic grin. "Let's quit putting it off and set a date. What do you say?"

Andie nodded, hiccupping quietly, closing her eyes as she rested her head against his chest. "I think that's a great idea," she conceded, her bright tone a façade of glee. She relaxed in his arms, pretending to be at peace, but inside she was shattered, her heart broken into a thousand tiny pieces. For as long she could remember, her dream had been Shannon. And now that dream had been crushed.

*I thought that finding Shannon would heal all the old wounds,* she thought dejectedly, fighting back renewed tears. *But I was wrong. The old wounds will never heal — and finding her like this has only opened new ones.*

# 15

Zoë took a couple days off from the clinic and headed for Eden Glen, using her driving time to reflect on the events of the past twenty-four hours. She hadn't yet recovered from the shock of learning about Andrea LaRue's visit to Cameron and needed time away from Columbus to clear her head and arrange her chaotic thoughts. She hadn't informed anyone of her travel plans, not even Cam. She planned to see Lois before she saw anyone else, hoping to catch some private time alone to explain her confusing dilemma and ask for some much-needed advice.

She reached the family estate mid-afternoon on Thursday and pulled into the circle drive in front of Carson House, climbing out of her car into the warmth of a sunny spring afternoon. She shielded her eyes and gazed out at the pond, sparkling like a jewel in the sunlight, thinking of Cameron and Leigh and many long summer days of cane pole fishing. Smiling nostalgically, she climbed the steps to the welcoming veranda.

Lois flung open the front door, an astonished grin on her face. "Well, looky here what the cat dragged in!" she exclaimed, rushing to embrace her granddaughter, giving her a resounding kiss on the cheek. "Here you are, sneaking home on a weekday like this, and Diane didn't even tell me that you were coming. I saw her just this morning, and she didn't even mention it."

"She didn't tell you because she didn't know," Zoë informed her, throwing an affectionate arm around Lois as they strolled across the porch. They paused by twin rockers, taking opposite chairs and relaxing together in the warm rays of afternoon sun.

"How about a cold glass of raspberry tea and some warm peach cobbler?" Lois asked with a grin. "Tressa's on her way out here with some right now."

"Raspberry tea and cobbler sound great."

Lois made her way to the door, bellowing inside for Tressa. "Tressa! Better make that a double! Zoë's here."

As Lois ambled back toward her, Zoë studied her, taking in her slow-moving form with worried eyes. There was definitely something different about her. She was feisty enough and her green eyes shone brightly, still burning passionately with the exuberant fire of youth, yet she seemed a little frail, notably more sluggish in pace and her complexion appeared to be an odd shade of pale gray.

*I suppose it is time that Lois began to show her age. After all, she is pushing eighty,* Zoë reasoned uneasily, trying to justify her grandmother's changing appearance and reassure herself that everything was as it should be, but finding it an impossible task. It was hard to think of Lois growing old. In her mind, Lois should remain forever youthful and healthy, going ninety-to-nothing with no remote possibility of her ever leaving them to join Palmer senior.

Lois noticed her peculiar expression and halted mid-gait, throwing her hands on her hips. "What's the matter with you?" she demanded sternly. "Are you sick? You look absolutely nauseous."

"What?" Zoë startled guiltily.

"I said you look absolutely nauseous. You aren't pregnant, are you?" Lois bent forward, inspecting her suspiciously.

"No! I'm not pregnant!" Zoë giggled, taken completely by surprise. "Although Eli would be in hog heaven if I was. That would be the only way that I might consent to marry him," she grinned, giving Lois a reassuring pat on the shoulder. "I'm fine, Lois. Must be the heat."

"The heat?" Lois studied her doubtfully, easing stiffly into her waiting rocker. "Good lord, Zoë! It's a perfectly balmy eighty-two degrees. You must be spending way too much time inside that clinic if you can't tolerate this," she laughed, beaming happily as she reached over to squeeze Zoë's hand. "I'm glad you're home. I've been missing you."

"I've been missing you too," Zoë replied, shaking off her morbid thoughts, giving Lois an obligatory smile. "I can never stay away too long, you know that. I get too homesick."

"Hi there, baby! Welcome home," Zoë looked up to find Tressa standing before her, her wrinkled face lit by a merry smile and her hands gripping a wicker tray overflowing with frosted tea glasses and huge bowls of steaming cobbler.

Zoë jumped out of her chair, reaching for the tray. "Here, Tressa," she said. "Let me get that for you."

"You'll do no such thing," Tressa scolded, her expression playfully offended. "You sit yourself right back down in that chair and visit with your grandmother."

Zoë gratefully accepted the tall glass of raspberry tea she offered, crinkling her nose good-naturedly as Tressa yanked the end of her ponytail. She quickly drained her glass, gulping it thirstily, and held it out for a refill, taking a heaping bowl of peach cobbler with her free hand. She set it carefully on her lap, inhaling deeply the luscious aroma of Tressa's world-famous dessert as she watched her walk away.

"Is Tressa ever going to retire?" she asked curiously, observing how difficult it was for her to get around, her arthritic hands working hard to pull open the door. "She's got to be close to seventy-five, if not older. I would think that she is getting pretty tired."

"Retire?" Lois asked incredulously, shooting Zoë a skeptical look. "Whatever for? I don't think she has any desire. She stays because she wants to, Zoë, not because I require it. Besides, where would she go? She's been with us a hundred years. She's practically part of the family. I'm sure Tressa will be at Carson House until the day she dies."

"Okay, okay. I got it. Sorry I asked," Zoë grinned, digging into the bowl of sweet cobbler. "Where's Mother?" she asked between mouthfuls, licking her spoon clean with childlike delight.

"She went into Savannah to meet your daddy for dinner, so we have the evening all to ourselves, just to catch up." Lois smiled and sipped her tea, watching her granddaughter with happy eyes. "How's your job at the clinic?"

"Just fine. I love it. The people are great and my work is fulfilling — and not a total waste of time as *some people* would like to believe. Has he ever gotten over my being a social worker?"

"Palmer? Heavens no! Would you expect him to?"

"No. If Palm ever approved of anything I did, I think I'd die of shock." Zoë laughed. "Speaking of dear Palmer, how's the law practice? I'm sure he's added just the right blend of arrogance to the firm."

"That goes without saying. You have to give Palmer credit. He's a law firm's dream: A chronic workaholic and vicious litigator, with an all-knowing, self-righteous attitude to boot. All in all, I'd say he's had a very profitable year. You know he's been seeing Senator Riley's daughter, Susan?"

Zoë shook her head. "No! I hadn't heard that yet," she admitted, cutting her eyes slyly to Lois. "But then again, I haven't read the social pages in a while. Have they been seeing each other long?"

"Long enough for me to suspect that Susan Riley may become Mrs. Geoffrey Palmer Carson III."

"Palm's in love? Now there's a concept. I never thought he was capable of loving anyone but himself."

"When did you hear me mention anything about love?" Lois cackled mischievously. "Trust me, Zoë. Nothing's changed. Palmer only sees true love when he looks in the mirror. Not that I think love really matters to him anyway. You know his philosophy: Why marry for love when you can marry for position?"

"So typically Palmer," Zoë smirked, sipping her tea thoughtfully, biding her time until she could bring up Andrea LaRue.

"How are Cameron and Leigh?" Lois asked about her favorites, beaming radiantly as she mentioned their names.

"Same as they were the last time I saw you, stubbornly resisting their feelings for one another and playing a hopeless game of hard to get. They're pathetic."

"I hope they don't waste too much time being pig-headed," Lois declared. "I should like to see some great-grandchildren out of them before I die."

"What are you talking about, dying? You're not going anywhere, Lois. You're going to live forever."

"I don't know about that. The old ticker's not what it used to be," Lois smiled regretfully, reclining in her chair, rocking back and forth as she stared candidly into Zoë's dismayed face. "Now don't be looking like that, little missy. My Papa died young, as did your great aunt Nicole. It is inevitable that my day will come as well. In fact, Ol' Doc Brown says it's only a matter of time."

"Which only goes to show you how much he knows," Zoë scowled with displeasure. "Old Doc Brown has never been much of a rocket scientist. Besides that, he's older than the hills. Why don't you get a new doctor?"

"I like Bartholomew Brown just fine, thank you. He happens to be a very intelligent man and, old or not, I trust him with my life. I don't need a new doctor."

"You're going to be sorry," Zoë teased in a singsong voice, laughing softly at her annoyed expression.

"C'est la vie," Lois frowned, dismissing Zoë's worries with a flippant wave of her hand, transforming her facial expression into one of casual nonchalance. "I know you didn't come all this way to discuss Cameron and Leigh, pompous Palmer or my miserably failing health," she said, squinting at Zoë suspiciously. "What's on your mind, child?"

Zoë deposited her tea glass on the table, raking her slender fingers nervously through her hair as she cleared her throat, carefully avoiding Lois' probing stare. "Cameron had the most interesting visitor this week," she said, her faint voice quivering slightly with excitement and concealed anxiety.

Lois lifted an intrigued brow. "Anyone I know?"

"No, at least I don't think so." Zoë drew a deep breath. "My birth mother came to see him."

"Oh, did she now?" Lois leaned forward keenly, without flinching or showing emotion. She kept her composure, regarding Zoë with interested eyes. "And what was her business with Cameron?"

"Now, Lois," Zoë rewarded her with a condescending look for playing dumb. "You have a pretty good idea what she wanted."

"Of course, I do, chère. She wants to meet you," Lois stated frankly, holding Zoë with a level stare, her wise eyes dipping deep into her soul. "And what do you think about that?"

Zoë rose from her chair, leaning against one of the tall columns, her hands tucked apprehensively behind her back. "I'm not sure what I think."

"You want to meet her?"

"I don't know. Part of me is curious, of course. You know, just to see what she looks like and all."

"Just as I would expect you to be. That's a perfectly natural response," Lois acknowledged with an encouraging nod, her gaze still fixed on Zoë's wistful expression. "And the other part of you?"

"The other part," Zoë looked out over the front lawn, her eyes lingering on the thick grove of live oaks, host to many a tree house during her childhood, a half-smile poised on her lips as she spoke. "The other part of me is afraid," she said. "Afraid to meet her, to know who she is, to open a door that, once it's opened, can never be closed again. Maybe it's fear of the unknown, or maybe it's just fear of Mother's reaction to it all," she chuckled lightly, tossing her blond ponytail over her shoulder as she glanced back at Lois.

"Diane had to know this day might come. If you really want to meet this woman, you can't let Diane stop you."

"But I would feel so disloyal. Diane is the only mother I've ever known. She's always been there for me. She was the one who fed me, bathed me, rocked me and loved me, no matter what. Andrea LaRue certainly hasn't done anything for me."

"That's her name? Andrea LaRue?"

"So says Cameron."

"Ah yes, Cameron. For a short moment, I forgot he was involved. And what does he have to say about all this?"

"Believe it or not, he didn't really say much. He only told me that she had been to see him and said that if I wanted to meet her, it would be my decision to make and not Mother's."

"That's pretty subdued, especially for Cameron. I can't imagine him not having an opinion about all this."

"Oh, I'm sure he has an opinion. He just hasn't chosen to express it, yet."

"So, what made you come to me?"

"Why wouldn't I?" Zoë asked, moving forward to kneel at her feet, placing a soft hand on her grandmother's knee. "I trust your opinion above all others."

Lois chuckled in appreciation. "You might as well trust it — you knew I'd give it."

"That's what I was counting on anyway," Zoë took Lois' hand, squeezing it tightly for security, looking up at her with uncertain eyes. "Okay, Lois, now I'm asking you. What do I do?"

"Zoanne, you know I can't make this decision for you," Lois chided her gently. "I will, however, offer my point of view." She smiled tenderly, looking into Zoë's face with eyes full of love. "Zoë, you belong to us. You're every bit as much a Carson as the rest of us are, even as much as Palmer is, no matter what he thinks. Nevertheless, every living soul has the right to know where they came from, and for you, Andrea LaRue holds the key. Naturally, you have to be curious about her, and if you want to meet her, if only for nothing more than to satisfy your curiosity, then I say more power to you, my dear."

"But what about Mother and Daddy?"

"I think Jay will be just fine about it. Your father is the very epitome of self-confidence," Lois said, ruffling Zoë's hair with a grin. "And your mother? Well, just leave Diane to me."

Zoë nodded thoughtfully, still queasy with indecision. "I'll think about it," she murmured timidly.

"You do that," Lois smiled, tweaking her nose fondly. "You make the decision when you're ready. I know you'll do the right thing."

They spent the evening on the veranda, reminiscing and catching up, dining on ham sandwiches and potato salad provided by Tressa. Just after nine, Diane's Lincoln pulled through the gates of the estate, skidding to a halt in front of Carson House when she spied Zoë's car.

"Zoë!" she sprang from the driver's side, her face bright with a radiant smile. She dashed up the stairs, flinging her arms around Zoë in a joyful embrace. "Why didn't you tell me you were coming? I would've stayed home."

"If I'd told you I was coming, it wouldn't have been a surprise," Zoë responded, her eyes twinkling at Diane fondly. She peered over her shoulder, searching the empty lane. "Where's Daddy?"

"He's coming," Diane replied with a casual wave, gesturing in the direction of town. "He ran into the opposing counsel on one of his cases, and stayed at the restaurant for a minute to chat. He'll be along shortly."

They hooked arms and strolled along, chattering excitedly, each tripping over words of the other as they tried to make up for lost time. Lois looked on pensively, contemplating the days to come. "Be happy now, my daughter," she whispered sadly, rocking back and forth in her chair. "Be happy now and savor the moment, because soon you won't be quite so cheerful. Your content little world is about to change."

With Zoë safely on the road to Columbus, Lois spilled the beans on Sunday afternoon, pandemonium quickly taking over as, one by one, she broke the devastating news to each family member. What remained of the Carson clan descended swiftly upon Carson House, gathering around the dining table, heatedly discussing the appearance of the birth mother over a dinner of beef stroganoff.

"You've known for three days, and you're just now telling us?" Diane stared at Lois in disbelief, clearly hurt by her betrayal.

"Diane, I wasn't about to shoot off my mouth while Zoë was here," Lois informed her defensively. "I figured if she wanted to discuss it, she would have told you herself."

"You had no right to keep this from me!" Diane glared, dismissing her explanation angrily, her voice quivering with rage.

"I had every right," Lois peered down her nose authoritatively, her words clipped and defiant. "Zoë told me in confidence. It wasn't my place to say anything."

"So why are you opening your mouth now?" Geoff asked scornfully, arching a skeptical brow. "I could have easily made it through the rest of the weekend without having to deal with this."

"It wasn't my place to tell you while she was here," Lois repeated, stressing the latter part of her statement. "However, I am gracious enough to save you all from being side-swiped by it in the future. There will come a day when Zoë goes to meet this woman, and I don't want anyone to act insulted or surprised."

"I just can't believe this is happening," Diane shook her head pitifully, glancing at Jay, wordless and slumped in his chair, his strong jaw set grimly.

"All I want to know is how the hell did that woman find us?" Geoff asked indignantly, pounding his fist and glaring around the table, studying each solemn face with livid brown eyes, demanding an explanation or suggestion from the rest of them. "This is not supposed to happen, especially not to us."

"Well, it's happened," Lois remarked dryly, throwing him an impatient smirk.

"Am I mistaken in saying that those records are supposed to be sealed and protected? I seem to recall that we went to great lengths to make sure Zoë couldn't be traced. We greased a lot of palms to destroy the paper trail. In fact, I'm surprised there are records left at all," Geoff glowered, his facial expression furious. "No one could *just stumble* onto her adoption file. This has to be an inside job, and I'll have someone's head over it. If I ever track down the person who leaked all this, there'll be hell to pay."

Already late for his date with Susan Riley, Palmer lounged in the doorway in his black tuxedo, regarding his father with a lofty roll of his eyes, sniffing haughtily as he lifted his wine glass to his lips. "I don't see what all the commotion is about," he stated disdainfully, glancing at the long faces around the table. "It's not really that big a deal. This can be taken care of easily. In fact, I happen to have the perfect solution," he smiled devilishly, his eyes bright as the family looked at him, awaiting his answer.

"Let's just give her back," he suggested cleverly, chuckling as he drained his glass, earning a warning glance from his mother, a look of extreme irritation from his grandmother and a scathing glare from Jay. Diane frowned and stared down at her hands, too numb over learning about Andrea LaRue to have the strength to reprimand him.

"Whatever would possess Cameron to tell Zoë about that woman in the first place?" Geoff ignored Palmer's snide remark and continued ranting, eyeing Lois inquisitively. "Has the boy no family loyalty whatsoever? Spoiled rotten kid! Give him the world and he betrays you."

"Once a black sheep, always a black sheep." Palmer set his empty glass on the table, grinning wickedly as he left the room.

"If I live to be a hundred, I'll never understand you people! Don't try putting all this off on Cameron," Lois said sternly, pointing a defensive finger in Geoff's direction. "The boy only did what he thought was right. You should be proud of him."

"Proud? Proud that he would stab his family in the back without so much as an inkling of regret?"

"No — proud that he managed to grow up with some sense of morals and values, although I'm not quite sure how, coming from this family. Zoë deserved to know about his meeting with her mother, and she has every right to meet her if she so chooses."

"Thanks for the support, Mother," Diane said, offended. "You're the last person I thought would turn on me."

"I'm not turning on you. I'm only pointing out that Zoë is old enough to make her own decisions."

"I think I have to agree with your mother, Diane," Jay said, clearing his throat, hit with the full brunt of Diane's appalled expression. "Honey, maybe Lois is right. Let Zoë meet this woman if she wants to. It'll be a good experience for her."

Diane offered him an icy stare. "You wouldn't be quite so secure in your position if it was her *father* she was meeting," she said resentfully, a fountain of tears replacing the wrath in her eyes. She threw her linen napkin onto her untouched plate, retreating from the dining room and up the staircase, making her way to the second floor and into Zoë's childhood bedroom. She flung her body onto the pristine bed, making a nest among Zoë's stuffed animals, weeping brokenheartedly as she mourned the possible loss of another child.

She couldn't remember the last time she had felt so utterly helpless and devastated, unless it was around the time of her father's untimely passing and the death of the last child she and Jay had conceived together. "That was an awful time," she sobbed, her heart aching with the release of old memories. "I had almost forgotten how much it hurt."

Losing her father had been horrible. Losing her baby had been worse, and now she was faced with losing Zoë, the very light of her life, to the woman who brought her into the world.

She had spent the first years of Zoë's life fearing the woman's unwanted appearance, but soon let go of her anxiety as Zoë's childhood passed smoothly, without so much as a peep from anyone. She thought she was safe, yet the hellish nightmare had come true, slapping her in the face while her guard was down. She wept inconsolably against the neck of Zoë's brown teddy bear, hugging him tightly to her chest as if he could alleviate some of her pain.

Lois tapped lightly on the bedroom door and joined her, sitting on the edge of the bed, stroking Diane's hair. "Now, Diane. Don't cry, chère," she said soothingly, running her hand down the length of her daughter's flaming locks. "This is not the end of the world."

"So says you," Diane lashed out, facedown on the bed. "You don't know what it's like to lose a child."

"Sometimes I wish I did," Lois said, chuckling as Diane lifted her head, glaring irately. "Lighten up, Diane. It was a joke. I'm just trying to lift your spirits a little. You need to relax. You haven't lost her."

"I will though. I'm sure of it." Diane sat up, hugging her knees to her chest. "I'm sure this is what Zoë has waited for her entire life — the day when her *real* mother would waltz back into her life, apologize for giving her away, and the two of them would ride off into the sunset together without so much as a look back."

"Don't be ridiculous," Lois rolled her eyes, carefully fighting her irritation. "You're blowing this way out of proportion."

"I don't understand how you and Jay can be so indifferent about this."

"We are not being indifferent. Jay may be sitting downstairs, pretending all is okay, but his heart is breaking. He may not show it, but it is. And me? I guess I just handle it better, or maybe I'm just not quite so insecure."

Diane stuck her chin out defiantly at Lois' laughter, blinking back scalding tears. "How can you be so callous? I think you couldn't care less what happens."

"You think I don't love her? That this isn't tearing me apart?" Lois sputtered, her eyes flashing passionately. "I'll have you know that I love that child every bit as much as you do."

"You don't act like it."

"Why, because I'm not screaming, wailing and showing my butt? I do love Zoë, Diane — enough to bite my tongue, offer good advice and let her do what she needs to do." Lois took Diane by the shoulders, curbing the overwhelming urge to shake some sense into her. "Listen to me. Zoë is not a baby in diapers, void of emotion, waiting to be stolen away by some woman with a claim. She's an adult, with adult feelings. She knows who she loves and who her family is, and as far as Zoë's concerned, you're her mother, and she loves you."

"But that other woman is Zoë's flesh-and-blood mother."

"You know what?" Lois reached out, lifting Diane's chin with the gentle touch of her hand. "In this case, flesh and blood doesn't matter, least of all to Zoë. You may not be her flesh-and-blood mother, but you're the mother in her heart and the one who really matters."

Diane gazed at her gratefully, throwing her arms around Lois' neck in a show of tender emotion. "Thank you, Mother," she whispered softly. "I know you're right about this, although I never expected you to express it quite so eloquently."

"Of course I'm right, Diane. I always am," Lois chuckled cleverly as she rose from the bed, stopping short as a spasm of discomfort stabbed at her chest. Keeping her expression purposely blasé, she waited until the spasm passed, exhaling deeply with relief, and straightened to a standing position. "Now, enough of this foolishness. Come back downstairs with me. I need some fresh air. All this unpleasantness is giving me one hell of a case of indigestion."

They descended the stairs, shoulder to shoulder, Diane sniffling and dabbing at her puffy eyes with a Kleenex. She glanced at Lois, a reluctant smile on her face. "Do you really think it's going to be okay?"

"Of course I do," Lois reassured her, taking her arm as they reached the landing. "Do you honestly think that I'd encourage Zoë if I thought it would ruin your life?"

Diane cut her eyes skeptically. "Maybe."

"Diane please," Lois huffed, shaking her head in exasperation. "For once in your life, trust me. I know what I'm talking about. It's going to work out fine."

"I do trust you, Mother," Diane replied as they reached the bottom of the staircase. "Unfortunately, you're not the one I'm worried about."

# 16

After a long and trying Labor Day weekend, Zoë shoved Eli out the door of her apartment, handing him his overnight bag and giving him a chaste peck on the cheek. "Out you go, Eli," she said with a weary smile. "You'd better hit the road to Atlanta. Tomorrow's a work day and you wouldn't want to be late in the morning."

"That's one of the advantages of being the boss, Zoë," Eli reminded her with a smug grin. "I can be late if I want to." He dropped his bag to the floor, gripping her shoulders tightly and kissing her enthusiastically on the lips. "Come on, Zoë. Just let me stay one more night. I don't want to leave you, not yet."

Zoë sighed and wriggled out of his embrace, pushing him away with a firm hand to his chest. "Eli, it's really best if you go back tonight. I'm exhausted, and I'd really like to get a good night's sleep. The clinic is bound to be a zoo tomorrow, being the day after the holiday and all."

"You are still planning to take me along to Eden Glen for Palmer's wedding next weekend, aren't you?"

"Only if you go home now."

Eli huffed in exasperation, reaching down for his bag. "Fine, I'll go," he said, retreating down the corridor with an irritated scowl on his face, turning to look back at her as he reached the stairwell door. "You know, Zoë, you've proven your point. I do see you as an independent woman, and I do respect you. Why don't you just give in and marry me so that we can end this foolishness?"

"Good night, Eli," Zoë sang out her farewell, giving him a silly wave before stepping inside her apartment. She leaned against the door, slapping her palm to her forehead, shaking her head slowly in frustration as she rubbed her throbbing temples and muttered obscenities under her breath.

Eli was right. It was time to put an end to the foolishness, the sooner the better as far as she was concerned. His frequent unannounced visits and constant badgering about matrimony were not only smothering her but were also putting a definite cramp in her style. She knew that she would never marry him. Life as Mrs. Elijah Feinstein was definitely not in her plans. The time had come to make a clean break, and she would do so the very next time he arrived unwanted on her doorstep.

She snapped off the living room lamp, trudging tiredly to the bedroom of her rented flat, pulling back the covers of her bed and flopping with welcome relief onto the soft mattress. She had barely dozed off when an insistent pounding on the front door jolted her from her light slumber. With a growl, she threw back the covers and stomped down the hallway grumpily, convinced that Eli had returned, ready to give him a piece of her mind. Reaching the front door, she slid the chain lock free and unfastened the deadbolt with an angry jerk of her hand. She flung the door open with the wrath of God on her lips, but instead of finding Eli standing before her, she came face to face with a glum-looking Cameron.

"Cam, what are you doing here?" she asked, standing aside as he pushed his way into the apartment. "Do you have any idea what time it is?"

"I couldn't sleep," he shrugged. "I knew you'd be awake."

"I wasn't awake."

"You are now," he trudged into the kitchen, swinging open the refrigerator door. "Got any beer?"

"Look on the bottom shelf," she stifled a yawn and shuffled to the couch, picking a corner to curl up in.

Cameron sauntered in from his beer search, holding an open bottle in his hand. "Jeez, Zoë. This is the good stuff," he remarked, reading the label on the imported brew. "Don't you ever drink domestic?"

"That's Eli's," she answered, looking slightly annoyed.

"Ah, the wonderful Mr. Feinstein. I gather he was here again this weekend?"

"He was. He just left around midnight."

"Why don't you dump him? You don't even really like him."

"Cameron, why are you here?" she snapped with a scowl, pulling her legs snuggly under her nightshirt and leaning her head on her knees. "It's one-freaking-thirty in the morning. State your business and be on your way."

"I told you — I couldn't sleep. I've been thinking about Leigh." A melancholy shadow crossed his eyes as he took a sip of beer and then another, until he finally tipped the bottle back, draining it dry.

"Why don't you call her?"

"Because I don't want her thinking I still have a thing for her."

"Don't you?"

"Hell, yes. But I don't want her knowing it."

"I think she already knows it."

"No, she doesn't — not unless you told her."

"I told her nothing."

"Good," Cameron marched back into the kitchen, returning with another beer. "Let's change the subject."

"Fine," Zoë declared, eyeing the bottle in his hand. "If you're going to keep me awake, the least you could do is bring me a beer."

"I thought you'd never ask," Cameron said, his voice trailing off as he walked back to the refrigerator. "You know how I hate to drink alone."

"So, you are going home for Palmer's wedding next Saturday, aren't you?" Zoë quizzed him as she twisted the cap off her beer.

"I don't know," he growled, rolling his eyes, rolling his bottle between his hands. "I haven't decided yet."

"Well, you better decide. He's expecting you to be best man."

"I don't know why. We aren't exactly on the best of terms."

"So, what else is new? I can't remember a time when you were on good terms. You're still his brother, and he expects you to stand up for him."

"Crap! I guess I can't get out of it then, can I?" he grumbled, draining another brew and slapping his bottle down on the coffee table with a bang. "I'm not very well prepared for this shindig. I don't even have a date."

"What about Clydesdale?"

"Kelly? Lord, Zoë. I don't know. Bleach-blondes aren't exactly high-society material."

"Neither are you," Zoë retorted mockingly. "Bring Kelly."

"Whatever. I'll call her tomorrow," he yawned, stretching his arms above his head. "Can I spend the night?"

"Yeah, sure. Whatever. Let me get you some covers." Zoë gathered the empty beer bottles and tossed him a blanket, then moved down the hall to retrieve a pillow.

She padded back down the hallway, hearing his exhausted snore. "Good night, Cam," she whispered, grinning at the already-slumbering figure stretched out on the sofa. She slid the pillow beneath his curly head and softly kissed his cheek, snapping off the light. "Sweet dreams."

They convoyed home for the wedding: Eli and Zoë in his Jaguar, followed closely by Cameron and Kelly Clinesdale bringing up the rear in his soft-top Jeep Wrangler. "She's a pretty girl," Eli remarked, glancing back at the car behind them in the rearview mirror.

"She's all right," Zoë shrugged, deeply engrossed in *The New York Times*.

"Don't you like her, honey?"

"I like her just fine. She's just not Leigh," Zoë replied abruptly. "And stop calling me honey."

"Touchy, touchy," Eli remarked condescendingly. "What's wrong with you, Zoë?"

"Nothing," Zoë gritted her teeth, pulling the paper closer to her face. *I'll be so damn glad when we get there,* she thought irritably. *If I have to ride in this car with him much longer, I'm going to choke the life out of him.*

They arrived in Eden Glen just in time for rehearsal, meeting up with everyone at the church. Palmer glanced up as they burst through the doors of the chapel, lifting his wrist to tap the crystal of his watch. "So glad you could join us, Cameron," he taunted, his rich voice reverberating through the sanctuary. "I was beginning to wonder if I had a best man."

"Dear God, he's as pretentious as his father," Diane remarked in passing, winking and giving Zoë a welcoming hug.

"Why don't you just go to hell?" Cameron muttered under his breath, glaring at Palmer, earning a slap on the arm from Zoë and an enamored giggle from his blonde companion. He sauntered down the aisle and took his place at Palmer's side, shaking off his father's attempted handshake. "All right, I'm here," he snarled. "Let's get this show on the road."

"Cameron's in rare form tonight," Lois commented, walking up behind Zoë. "What's wrong with him?"

"Nothing that hasn't been wrong with him for years," Zoë shrugged, "You know how he is, Lois. Cam's just mad at the world."

"Hello, Mrs. Carson!" Eli called out, waving and schmoozing his way through the crowd.

"He doesn't know he just burned his bridges with me, does he?" Lois turned to Zoë, clearly annoyed.

"Nope," Zoë shook her head solemnly, cringing as Eli drew closer, "but he's really bad at reading signs. He wouldn't know it if you had a skywriter emboss it in black smoke above his head."

Lois smiled broadly, pinching Zoë's cheek. "You are truly my granddaughter," she cackled, smoothing the lapels of Zoë's jacket with her hands. "I've taught you well, and there's not a thing your mother can do about it."

The Carson-Riley nuptials went off as planned, taking place in a packed cathedral, with the reception crowd at Carson House swelling to more than eight hundred. The new Mrs. Palmer Carson was a classic beauty in a simple white sheath and flowing veil with a single strand of pearls adorning her swan-like neck, poised gracefully on Palmer's arm like a fairy princess. Zoë admired her from afar, determined to avoid the receiving line.

"I'll just stay here by the punch bowl," she said as Eli suggested they congratulate the bride and groom. But Eli wouldn't take no for an answer, insisting that she come along.

"It would be rude not to deliver your cousin best wishes," he informed her disapprovingly, taking the crystal cup from her hand as he dragged her across the floor.

"It would be even ruder to greet him in my current mood," Zoë replied scathingly, wrenching her wrist free from his zealous hold. "Palmer has been a perfect jerk all weekend. If he makes one more snide remark, I promise — wedding or no wedding — I'll take a swing at him."

"Eli!" Palmer was beside himself with joy, clasping Eli's hand and patting his back warmly. "So glad you could make it to our little soirée."

"I wouldn't have missed meeting your lovely bride for the world," Eli gushed, lifting Susan's hand to his lips. "I've never seen two people more meant for each other."

"Except," Palmer countered, sliding a pseudo-affectionate arm around Zoë's shoulder, "for you and my dear cousin Zoanne. When should Susan and I expect to attend one of these for you?"

Zoë rolled her eyes and looked away in disgust. *I think I'm going to be ill,* she thought. *Forget me and Susan. Eli and Palmer are the ones meant for each other.*

"As soon as your dear cousin finally says yes," Eli smiled, gazing at Zoë with adoring eyes.

"That should be a cold day in hell," Cameron's voice rang softly in Zoë's ear and she glanced back at him gratefully, glad that he was next in line. "Dump him, Zoë," he whispered tauntingly, terrorizing her and making her giggle. "Dump him now and run for your life! Hurry, before you catch the bouquet. I'm sure Eli has already paid Susan to knock you out cold with it."

"I wouldn't be so concerned about Eli, if I were you," Zoë shot back wickedly. "You had better look out for old Clydesdale. I see her out there, skirting the ballroom, jockeying for a prime nosegay-catching position next to the staircase."

"I'm not too worried," Cameron laughed jovially. "Kelly's not real coordinated. On the off chance it comes anywhere near her, she'll just miss it."

"Then I'm sure she'll fight somebody for it. Now, that's something I'd like to see — Championship Bouquet Wrestling in Carson House," Zoë giggled and glanced around for Eli, finding that he was deeply engrossed in conversation with Susan's father, Senator Riley. She used the opportunity to make a swift getaway, grabbing Cameron's arm and pulling him toward the kitchen. "Hurry, Cam — before he notices that I'm gone."

At the end of an impossibly long evening, Susan and Palmer left for their honeymoon, escaping through a blizzard of birdseed. Zoë leaned against the front wall of the house, removing her pumps, flexing her cramped toes tiredly. "Jeez, what a night," she sighed, ready to keel over.

"And where, pray tell, is the Feinstein boy?" Zoë lifted her eyes, finding Lois standing before her, high heels in one hand, the other on her hip, looking at Zoë expectantly.

"Drinking brandy and smoking cigars in the study with Daddy, Uncle Geoff and the other dignitaries," Zoë answered curtly, straightening and stretching her sore back with a groan.

"Good!" Lois declared, breathing a great sigh of relief. "That'll keep him out of my hair for a while. I swear that boy's a brown-noser."

"I'm glad someone around here finally noticed," Zoë sighed. "Palmer still thinks he's the finest thing since sliced bread."

"Palmer's never been known for having good taste," Lois remarked dryly, her amused laughter echoing down the length of the veranda. "Susan's the first move he's ever made that I've approved of."

"She seems pretty sweet," Zoë responded pleasantly, glancing at Lois and they locked eyes, grinning ear to ear as they sang out in unison: "What in God's name does she see in Palmer?"

They shared a giggle and hooked arms, strolling down the porch toward the swing. "Where's Cameron?" Lois asked, beaming happily, thoroughly enjoying herself, her cheerful face illuminated by silver streaks of moonlight.

"Umm, I believe he took Kelly out for a drive," Zoë replied. "Showing her his old stomping grounds, I suppose."

"Is that the blonde girl he brought with him from Columbus?"

"Yes, Lois."

"Well, I didn't know. I never caught her name," Lois snapped, her brow creased in exasperation. "She looks like a tart."

"Kelly? No, she's okay."

"Is she after his money?"

"I doubt it. To be honest, before this weekend I don't think she knew he had any."

"She knew," Lois countered confidently, her tone sarcastic, rolling her eyes disdainfully as she settled onto the swing. "They all know."

Zoë shook her head in disbelief. "What makes you so cynical?" she asked laughingly and plopped down next to her, swinging her legs in childlike abandon.

"I'm old, Zoë — all old people are cynical."

"Well, stop it. Kelly's okay."

"She's not Leigh."

"No," Zoë agreed with a regretful smile. "She's not Leigh."

They sat in comfortable silence, moving back and forth, a light breeze cutting mercifully through the humidity. Zoë stifled a yawn, resting her head against Lois' shoulder, reveling in the peace of the moment. Lois lifted her hand, stroking her silky hair, leaving a fond kiss on her forehead. "You staying here tonight, baby?" she asked affectionately. "Your old room is still open."

"Yeah, I think so," Zoë answered, forcing her weary body erect. "I don't imagine Mother will mind too terribly, since she farmed my room at home out to Susan's relatives."

"And where is Mr. Feinstein sleeping?" Lois inquired, raising a quizzical brow. "Do I need to stand guard outside your door?"

Zoë grinned, indulging her grandmother's humor. "Eli is bunking with Cam, so you needn't worry. I'm sure Cameron still remembers how to use the old baseball bat, so my virtue is safe — for tonight anyway." She stood, extending her arms lazily above her head. "I'm going to turn in. Are you coming up?"

"In a bit," Lois stretched her legs across the swing, resting her head against the chain, an amused smile on her lips. "I think I'll stay out here for a while, just in case I need to go break up the party," she indicated the rising noise level inside the study with a nod of her head, grinning as if the men inside were naughty children.

"I feel for them, I really do."

"As you should," Lois chuckled, her eyes sparkling with mirth. "I'll tell you what. Why don't we get up early in the morning and go for a ride before you head back to Columbus?" she suggested brightly.

"On horses?" Zoë asked, glancing at her questioningly.

"Of course, on horses. What did you think I meant?"

Zoë stared at her, her mouth dropping open in protest. "I can't believe you! You're not still riding, are you?"

"Sure, I am. Nearly every day, if I can get away with it. I just can't let Diane catch me."

Zoë shook her head incredulously. "You're going to be really sorry when you fall off one day and break a hip," she scolded, bending down to kiss Lois' cheek.

"Don't you be worrying about me, little missy," Lois retorted. "You have your hands full enough with the old brown-noser in there. The agony of a broken hip is nothing compared to him."

Zoë giggled, retrieving her shoes from the deck. "And on that note, I'm going to bed," she said, tossing her grandmother a teasing smile. "Good night, Lois. I love you."

"I love you too, baby," Lois bade her goodnight, shooing her away with a wave. "Sweet dreams."

Zoë was exhausted. It had been a very strenuous weekend. "Putting up with Eli alone is draining," she muttered as she climbed into bed, "but putting up with both Eli and Palmer is enough to kill you."

She pulled up the soft bedcovers and extinguished the light, falling asleep before her head hit the pillow. She felt like she had just closed her eyes when all of a sudden, Cameron was there, standing by the bed, still in his tuxedo, shaking her awake. "Zoë! Zoë, wake up!" Out of breath and frantic, he jiggled her shoulder insistently, jarring her to the teeth.

Her eyes flew open and she sat up with a start. "This had better be good, Cam," she mumbled sleepily, glaring at him through bleary eyes. "I was sleeping good."

"Zoë," he stammered and she suddenly noticed how pale he was — and how very, very frightened.

She threw back the covers and leapt from the bed, her blond hair standing on end. "Cam, what is it!" she clutched his arm in panic, her wide eyes searching his face. "Tell me."

"It's Lois," Cameron faltered, gripping the bedpost for support. "We found her outside, unconscious on the swing."

Zoë recoiled in horror. "That can't be!" she gasped, her heart hammering, feeling an instant rush of heat flood her face. "I just left her not an hour ago, and she was fine!" Her eyes swam in terrified tears, and she slid numbly to the floor, her knees buckling as she dissolved into sobs.

"No, Zoë. Don't lose it on me now." Cameron crawled across the floor, pulling her up by the arms. "We've got to go. You have to get some clothes on so we can go to the hospital. The ambulance is on its way."

In the distance, the sirens sounded, growing louder and louder as the ambulance raced into the drive, paramedics leaping out of the rear double-doors before it came to a complete stop. Zoë forgot everything and dashed from the room, bounding down the stairs in her pajamas with Cameron at her heels, shrieking hysterically as they lifted Lois onto the stretcher and began to wheel her across the lawn.

"No, no! Lois wait!" Zoë burst out the front door and ran after them, wailing frantically, seeing her mother and the wounded expression on Diane's face as she climbed into the vehicle behind the stretcher. "Don't leave me!" Zoë screeched, her feet leaving the ground as she hurdled the front steps.

Jay caught her around the waist, halting her before she reached the street, and Zoë wrestled in his arms, struggling wildly to break free.

"No, Daddy! No! Don't let her leave me! Don't let her leave me," she broke down, falling against him as the ambulance streaked away, sirens blaring. He enfolded her tightly in his arms, stroking her hair soothingly, even as she beat him desperately with her fists.

Zoë collected herself and got dressed, riding with a stony and silent Cameron into Savannah. They arrived at the hospital to find the rest of the family gathered outside the emergency room, wearing grim faces and talking soberly amongst themselves. Geoff looked mildly surprised at their timely appearance. "You made it here much more quickly than I anticipated," he told them, glancing down at his watch. "But, then again," he gave his younger son a withering look, "I'm sure Cameron drove like a maniac."

Cameron didn't reply, thinking it was neither the time nor the place to argue, and turned his back on his father, his face hardening as he crossed the room to stand next to Patricia. Zoë sought out her mother and tenderly kissed her cheek, looking into her red, swollen eyes with much-too-genuine sympathy. Without a word, she sat down next to her on the old vinyl couch, taking her limp hand and holding on to it tightly, resting her head on Diane's shoulder.

Eli and Kelly showed up at sunrise, meek and mild out of respect for the grieving family. Kelly quickly offered to run to the cafeteria for coffee, grateful to have something to keep her busy. Eli located Zoë next to a wall of windows, staring out at the city soberly, her face ashen and dark circles deepening beneath her tired gray eyes.

"Zoë, darling. What can I do for you?" he asked gently, massaging her shoulders with the heels of his hands.

"There's nothing you can do," Zoë told him in a wooden voice, having no strength left for emotion. She lowered her head and pressed it to the glass. *I wish I could just close my eyes and this would all go away,* she thought desolately, too drained even for tears.

"Really, baby," Eli persisted, resting his head against hers, his breath just behind her ear. "Just say the word," he whispered. "I'll do anything. Fly in specialists, medi-flight her to another hospital, whatever you want."

"I told you! There's nothing," Zoë shrugged him away, spitting angrily as she spun around, drawing startled looks from the silent waiting area. She was instantly sorry and placed an apologetic hand on his forearm, kicking herself for the crushed look on his face. "Eli, I'm sorry," she murmured humbly, her quivering voice solemn and sad. "I didn't mean to snap at you that way. Please forgive me."

"Zoë, please. Don't apologize," he began, his dark eyes full of sympathy.

"Eli, can I talk to you for a minute?" Cameron interrupted, appearing beside them, drawing Eli to the other side of the room. "Listen, man," he said soberly. "Things are going to be pretty rough around here for the next several days, to say the least, and Zoë is not going to be herself at all. Do me a big favor. If you want to be helpful, go back to Atlanta — and drop Kelly off in Columbus on your way."

"Are you trying to get rid of me?" Eli asked distrustfully, his eyes flashing with subdued anger.

"I'm trying to spare you some grief. If you stick around, you're going to end up getting your feelings hurt, along with your inflated pride. Zoë needs her family right now, not you."

"If that's the case, then I'm staying. I am family, Cameron. Zoë and I are as good as married."

"Quit fooling yourself, man," Cameron issued a short laugh and smiled mockingly, feeling almost sorry for him. "You're about as close to being family as Kelly is." He returned to Zoë's side, putting an arm around her and pulling her close, leaving Eli staring after him in offended disbelief.

Kelly and Eli left town at noon, right after the doctor on call pronounced Lois stable, passing Susan and Palmer on their way in from the airport. "Palmer! What are you doing here?" Patricia called out, moving from her chair as she saw them come off the elevator. She rushed forward, throwing her arms around him, offering Susan a grateful smile. "You two are supposed to be on your honeymoon."

"We caught the first plane back from New York as soon as we received word," Palmer explained, loosening his tie as he took a chair next to his mother. "We can do Paris any time. Family comes first."

"I hope it's your bride you're trying to impress," Cameron spoke up from the corner where he lounged, trying futilely to catch a catnap. "Because your words are wasted on me. You don't care about family. I know damn good and well the only reason you ran back here was to make sure we didn't divvy up your part of the inheritance while you were gone."

"Charles Cameron!" Diane took it upon herself to be the disciplinarian, too weary to put up with any arguing. "Save it," she advised him harshly, the fiery look in her eyes forbidding him to continue.

Later that afternoon, Lois was transferred to a private suite of rooms. Diane and Jay were the first to be admitted. Zoë paced up and down the corridor, waiting for an update and fearing the worst, hurrying over to Jay as he came out. "How is she, Daddy?" she whispered apprehensively, her eyes round with fear.

"Stronger than you would think, given the circumstances," Jay said, stroking her cheek consolingly and offering her a gentle smile. "Go see for yourself."

Zoë entered the room timidly, unsure of the condition in which she would find her beloved grandmother. She was pleasantly surprised to find Lois propped up in bed on fluffy pillows, pale yet regal in an orchid bed jacket, her silver hair piled high upon her head and an air of rich indignation in her voice.

"I will not stay in this hospital," she said, glaring impatiently at Dr. Bartholomew Brown as he stood at her bedside, taking her pulse while receiving a scathing reprimand from his star patient. "I'm not going to get any better sitting here in this wretched hospital than I would at home, lying comfortably in my own bed."

Lois paused, spying Zoë standing hesitantly in the doorway. She smiled cheerfully, beckoning her into the room with a gesture of her blue-veined hand. "It doesn't take a rocket scientist to figure that one out; just ask my granddaughter," she added with a coy wink to Zoë.

"Is that a fact?" Dr. Brown turned his head, regarding Zoë critically. "Practicing medicine these days, Zoanne?" he asked, his condescending tone laced with disapproval.

Zoë flushed with embarrassment, shooting Lois a perturbed look. "No sir," she answered sheepishly. "As usual, my grandmother is just taking something I said and twisting it to her advantage."

"Why does that not surprise me?" he chuckled dryly and leaned against the rail of Lois' bed, towering above her, his eyes dark and stern. "Lois Carson, I've known you for forty-seven years. Do you think I don't know there's not a snowball's chance in hell that I can keep you in this hospital?"

Lois grinned. "I know you know, Bart," she acknowledged gruffly, lifting a weak hand to touch his arm. "Sometimes you just have to be reminded."

Against his wishes, Dr. Brown released Lois home to Carson House the following afternoon, settling her into her spacious room on the third floor. As he conducted a thorough examination, the family assembled in the parlor, sharing a box of tissues as they discussed the situation.

"Dr. Brown says that Mother's lungs are full of fluid, and he doesn't expect her to get any better. Her heart is failing so rapidly that it could be only a matter of days — a few weeks at most — before she passes away," Geoff updated them in a solemn tone, the grief he felt at the thought of losing his mother apparent on his weary face. He slumped unhappily on the piano bench beside Patricia, his eyes downcast as he reached clumsily for her hand. She gazed at him sorrowfully, giving his hand a hard squeeze, praying her touch would provide the comfort he so desperately needed.

"Do we have to talk about this right now?" Diane sniffled loudly from her place on the sofa, her face drawn and puffy as she yanked a tissue from the community box on the coffee table and dabbed daintily at her crimson nose.

"I know this isn't pleasant, Diane, but I'm only preparing us for the inevitable."

Cameron leaned against the wall, blocking them out, his arms crossed tightly against his chest. He gazed broodingly out the window, looking like a forlorn little boy as he reflected on his grandmother's faltering health. It didn't seem possible to be contemplating Lois' death. Lois was invincible; nothing could take her away from him, not even a miserably failing heart.

From his position across the room, Palmer studied his brother, his eyes gleaming wickedly, almost delirious at finding an opportunity to kick Cameron while he was down. "What about you, Cameron? Since you're gracing us with your presence, are you going to stick around and act like one of the family until Grandmother passes on? Or are you going to run back to Columbus and that insignificant little newspaper job and await the funeral there?"

"Of course we're staying," Zoë spoke up, darting forward to step between Cameron's ready fist and Palmer's smug, arrogantly set jaw. She grabbed Cameron's clenched hand and held it tightly, pleading with him to keep the peace, if only out of love for Lois. Through furious eyes, Cameron caught her beseeching gaze and relaxed, nodding slightly, conceding to her wishes by lowering his fists obediently to his side.

"In fact," Zoë continued, satisfied that she had successfully delayed the first Carson brother altercation, "I should go call the clinic and tell them I'll be away indefinitely." She crossed the parlor, heading in the direction of the phone.

"I don't understand why you just don't go ahead and resign from that job, Zoanne," Palmer said, shooting her a look of disdain. "God knows between us and Eli Feinstein, you don't need the money, and it's not much of a job anyway."

Zoë stopped dead in her tracks, tossing a withering glance over her shoulder. "Palmer, you're such an ass."

Palmer's mouth stretched into a cynical smirk, and he laughed in appreciation as he watched her stride angrily from the room. "Well, it's nice to see that sending her to college wasn't a totally wasted effort," he declared. "If nothing else, she did manage to develop a little backbone."

"You are really pushing me," Cameron snarled, pointing a finger in Palmer's face, the rest of his threat going unspoken.

Overhearing Palmer's insulting remark, Zoë closed her eyes and shook her head in aggravation then moved quickly down the hall, electing to use the telephone in the kitchen. Cameron followed her, touching her arm as she picked up the receiver to dial. "While you're phoning, you better call Leigh," he said soberly. "She'll want to tell Lois goodbye."

After Dr. Brown left, Diane sent Jay home, then crept upstairs to check on Lois. She slipped silently into the room, taking the cozy wing chair next to the bed, peering anxiously into the pale face of her sleeping mother.

Lois was dying. It didn't seem possible. It was beyond all comprehension that her feisty mother, afraid of nothing and intimidated by no one, could be reduced to this frail, ailing creature, gasping for every breath. Diane leaned forward, gripping her feeble hand, squeezing it softly, choking back the sobs rising in her throat.

"If you think I'm going to let you sit by my bed and cry, you are sadly mistaken," Lois said, lifting an eyelid to peer at Diane sternly. "For God's sake, Diane. Cheer up. You look pathetic."

Diane rolled her eyes, hastily wiping her salty tears with the back of her hand. "Oh hush, Mother. I'll cry if I want to."

"I hope you don't behave this way at my funeral. I've always hated swooning, squalling women falling all over the casket."

"I promise not to swoon on your coffin, Mother, whenever the time comes. But that's a long time away. You're not going to die."

"I might paint a rosy picture for the grandchildren, Diane, but that's only because I can't bear to see their tears."

"What about my tears?"

"You're an adult and tears or no tears, with you I'll play it straight. There's no way to tap-dance around it. I'm going to die, Diane. That's all there is to it."

"But I don't want you to die."

"Whether you want it or not, it's going to happen. This is one thing I can't get out of. Death is mighty hard to cheat."

"Mother, not now. I need you. You can't just die and leave me with all this."

Lois raised a quizzical brow. "What 'all this'?"

"You know 'what all this'," Diane sighed heavily, throwing her body against the back of her chair. "*This* house, *this* family, not to mention Zoë's birth mother lurking in the shadows with her fangs exposed."

Lois laughed, an especially hearty laugh given her weakened condition, and reached out to clasp Diane's hand. "This house isn't something that you're really going to have to worry about. Geoff and Palmer have already staked their claim on it, homesteading it the way they have for all these years. Aside from that, this family isn't all that bad. I've handled them for years. And as for Zoë's birth mother, I'm not worried. If I had to place bets on it, my money would be on you."

"Meaning?"

"Meaning you're strong enough to handle whatever comes of it. You're my daughter, Diane, feisty and tough. No one will ever be able to take you down."

"I thought I was a mealy-mouthed little debutante."

"Did I say that?" Lois asked, wrinkling her brow and frowning. "Yes, I suppose I did, on more than one occasion, I seem to recall," she patted Diane's shoulder apologetically. "Well, I was wrong. There's not a weak bone in your body. You're one hell of a fine woman, Diane Carson, and I'm proud of you. I could've never asked for a better daughter," Lois smiled, the dimples in her once-rosy cheeks finding their way from beneath the deep wrinkles in her face. She lifted her arms to Diane, who fell into her mother's warm embrace, hot tears spilling from her eyes.

"I love you, Mother."

Lois closed her eyes and pressed her lips to the top of Diane's chestnut head, holding her tightly. "I love you too, Diane, and I'll miss you more than you'll ever know."

"Then don't go. Stay here with us."

"Good Lord, don't start that again," Lois said irritably, holding Diane at arms' length, glaring at her with clear annoyance, their tender moment broken. "I can't stay, Diane. I've had enough. Besides," her look softened and she smiled in anticipation, "your daddy's waiting for me, up in heaven with Sadie and Jasper, ready to go for a long ride through the clouds."

The next day Lois appeared to be stronger. Dr. Brown's early morning visit found her propped up in bed smiling, with more color in her face than she'd had in weeks. Dr. Brown checked her over completely before pulling Diane away from her ceaseless bedside vigil, taking her downstairs to join Geoff in the privacy of the study for an update on Lois' condition.

Seeing that his Aunt Diane had left her post, Cameron bounded up the two flights of stairs to his grandmother's room, hoping to catch five minutes alone with her. He found Palmer lurking outside her door, pacing up and down the hallway with a pensive expression on his face.

"What are you doing out here, Palmer?" he asked, raising a skeptical brow at his older brother's unusual show of concern for a family member. "I thought you'd be down in your room, packing up your things for the big move into the master suite."

Palmer glared at him caustically, clearly offended. "If you must know, I was waiting until Grandmother recovered from Dr. Brown's visit before I went in to see her."

Cameron chuckled sarcastically, finding Palmer's feeble attempt at sincerity highly amusing. "Bullshit, Palmer," he said. "You were out here with a tape measure, making sure your bedroom furniture would fit through the door."

"Will you boys quit loitering outside my room, brawling over my personal effects?" Lois barked out from her bed, craning her neck to get a look at their faces. "You're boring me. Save your bickering for the reading of my will. Cameron, come in here and close the door. I want to talk to you. Hurry up, boy, before Diane gets back and shoos everyone away."

Cameron sauntered confidently over the threshold into Lois' suite, offering Palmer a smug, shit-eating grin as he pushed closed the solid double doors. He crossed the room with casual strides, sitting on the edge of the bed beside his grandmother, inspecting her face with affectionate eyes. "You're looking good this morning, Lois," he said jovially. "How do you feel?"

"I feel just dreadful. How would you expect me to feel?" Lois said, scowling at him irritably. "I try not to think about it. I just wish you people would quit asking me about it."

"Okay, okay. I'm sorry I asked," Cameron grinned at her, giving her a fond kiss on her wrinkled cheek. "You're a little testy this morning, old girl. But I love you anyway."

"I love you too, Cameron. You've been one of the true joys of my life," she replied sentimentally, reaching up to softly finger the chestnut hair curling around his ear. Her jade eyes glowed lovingly as she surveyed his handsome face. "Did I ever tell you that you look just like your grandfather?"

"Thanks, Lois. I consider that a great compliment."

"As you should," Lois said, struggling weakly to push herself higher in the bed. Cameron took her gently by the shoulders and lifted her effortlessly into her desired position, fluffing her pillows and tucking her soft blanket snuggly around her thin legs.

"Thank you, darlin'," Lois smiled up at him warmly, waiting for him to settle back in his spot. "Are you happy with your life, Cameron?" she asked solemnly.

Blinking in surprise at what seemed a silly question, Cameron shrugged nonchalantly. "Sure, Lois. I'm happy enough. Why wouldn't I be? I've got a good job, money if I want it, lots of dates with hot chicks. What more could a guy ask for?"

"What about Leigh? You do still love her, don't you?"

"That's off limits, Lois."

"What do you mean, off limits? Son, I'm dying. Nothing's off limits."

"That is," Cameron eased himself from the bed, moving to the French doors leading out onto Lois' balcony, catching sight of a bright yellow taxi pulling into the circle drive in front of the house. Intrigued, he slipped out onto the terrace, his heart in his throat as she stepped from the cab, stylishly attired in an outfit right out of *Vogue*, removing her wide-brimmed hat and shaking out her ebony chin-length hair, looking up at the house with a soft smile.

Leigh had come to Carson House, arriving straight from the airport in Savannah. Cameron stared as she climbed the front steps to the veranda, washed over by a tide of joy, unable to tear his eyes from her face. She was so beautiful and his love for her so deep that he could scarcely catch his breath. "I'll be damned," he marveled, "she's here." He exhaled, his heart soaring as he bolted back into the room, unable to wait one second longer to be near her.

"Excuse me, Lois. I'll be right back."

"What is it, Cameron?" Lois called after him as he rushed from the suite, her mouth twisting into a perplexed grin as she watched him skid around the banister at the top of the stairs and bound down the first flight at break-neck speed.

He slowed on the landing, catching his breath, and proceeded at a leisurely pace down the second flight of stairs into the entryway, arriving just in time to see Tressa admit Leigh through the front door, welcoming her with a warm embrace of her chubby arms. "It's so good to see you, Miss Leigh," she said, taking Leigh's hat and bag. "I just wish it didn't have to be under these circumstances."

"I agree, Tressa," Leigh murmured gravely. "Where's everyone?"

"Hello Leigh," Cameron spoke softly from his position on the stairs, his stomach contracting into a tight knot. Leigh glanced up, her face aglow as she caught his eyes, locking them with hers in an unguarded gaze that spoke volumes. Tressa viewed them with a veiled smile, discreetly exiting the entry hall to give them some much-needed privacy.

"Hello Cam," Leigh said, breaking the trance, finally able to stabilize the erratic beating of her heart. "I came as soon as Zoë called. How's Lois?"

"Better today than yesterday, but still not great," Cameron answered soberly, taking her by the arm as she joined him on the steps. "She's going to be so thrilled to see you."

The familiar electricity that surged through Leigh's body at his touch was unsettling, and it was all she could do to maintain control. *Well, staying away for a year certainly didn't help*, she grumbled inwardly, squelching the overwhelming urge to throw her arms around him with wild abandon. She had hoped that not seeing him would help ease her desire. Clearly, it had not. Her well-thought-out plan had backfired. Her heart still melted into a puddle at the sight of him, and his touch still left her quivering like Jell-O. It was hopeless and she knew it. *Just my luck*, she thought, cutting her eyes at him discreetly. *I guess I'm stuck loving Cameron Carson until the day I die.*

Cameron guided her upstairs, sticking his head through the crack between Lois' doors. "I've got a surprise for you, Lois," he called out in a singsong voice, his effort rewarded by Lois' annoyed frown.

"I don't like surprises, boy. I've got a bad heart, haven't you heard?"

"You'll like this one. I promise," Cameron winked at her and pulled Leigh into the room, smiling broadly at Lois' squeal of delight.

"Leigh, come here and give me a kiss, you darling, darling girl." Lois hugged Leigh to her bony chest, touching her hair and kissing the top of her dark head with great affection. "How'd they get you here? What did they do, lie to you and tell you I was dying?"

"I knew that was just a vicious rumor," Leigh shot back, taking Lois' hand as she perched on the edge of the mattress beside her. "You're way too mean to die."

Cameron leaned against the doorframe, watching their happy reunion with a look of satisfaction. Feeling his stare, Lois glanced up, shooing him away with a majestic wave of her hand. "What are you hanging around for? Get out of here, Cameron, and let us girl-talk in private."

With a mocking bow, Cameron backed out of the room, throwing a grin to Leigh as he closed the double doors. Leigh giggled, her cheeks rosy, remembering how much she enjoyed his wry sense of humor. Checking her laughter, she turned to Lois, offering a sympathetic smile. "Can I get you anything, Lois?"

"All this heart-to-heart, last wishes garbage has left me a little parched," Lois admitted. "Will you bring me a glass of water from that pitcher over there?"

She watched Leigh pad lightly across the room, pouring ice water from the crystal pitcher on the dresser with a steady hand. *Cool as a cucumber*, Lois thought admiringly. *That's my Leigh, the sensible one of the two.*

"Hey, I hear I missed quite a wedding," Leigh chattered vivaciously, making cheerful small talk as she filled Lois' glass.

"Oh yes," Lois snarled with a lofty roll of her eyes. "Another glorious Carson wedding, complete with Southern royalty." She relaxed, reliving some of the more pleasant moments of the nuptials, a whimsical smile spreading over her face. "It was a nice wedding, really, as Carson weddings go. I only wish I had lived to see yours."

"Lois, what's with this defeatist talk? It's so unlike you."

"Will you be quiet and let me speak? It's an effort as it is, without having to talk over you."

"Then go right ahead. You've got my undivided attention."

"I didn't know which one of you I'd say this to. Since Cameron ran out of the room when I tried to discuss it with him, I'll just discuss it with you. Not that I think for one minute that it'll do any good. You're both so damn stubborn."

With water glass in hand, Leigh spun around, offering Lois a cool smile. "Cussing on your deathbed, Lois? How very unladylike."

"So, you're going to play games too, are you?" Lois snapped in exasperation. "I don't have time to be wasting while you and Cameron dance around the issue like a couple of fools. Leigh, are you going to listen to me, or am I going to have to bust you in the chops?"

"I'm listening, Lois," Leigh said with an amused giggle, handing Lois the glass of water and settling into the wing chair beside the bed. "What did you want to say?"

"Make me happy and marry my grandson."

"Ah ha! So that's what this is all about!" Leigh exclaimed, shaking her head apathetically. "Lois, we've been through all this. I can't marry Cameron."

"You still love him, don't you?"

"Even if I did, it still wouldn't work. Cameron wants to stay in the South and I have a great job that I love in New York. The logistics of it all are just piss-poor."

"Cameron just thinks he wants to stay in the South, but what does he know?" Lois scoffed. "I know for a fact he'll never come back to Eden Glen to live as a bona-fide member of the Carson family, and I'm glad. He'd never be happy here. He thinks he's happy in Columbus with that newspaper job and his fluff-for-brains little girlfriends. But he's wrong. I know better than he does, Leigh, and I know he's not happy. He could never be happy anywhere without you."

Leigh considered Lois' statement thoughtfully. "So what do you suggest that I do?" she asked.

"Marry Cameron and take him to New York. I still have a little influence left, even on my deathbed. I'll make some calls and get him a job at *The Times*."

"You had better not let Cameron hear you say that. He'd rather die than know that the Carson name was used to pull strings for him."

"Who said anything about the Carsons?" Lois shot back indignantly. "I'll have you know the LeJeune name still carries a little weight in high society. I'll just call them up, let them know who I am and tell them to give my grandson a job."

"Thanks for the offer, Lois, but no thanks. If Cameron comes to New York, he can make it on his own."

"Independence! That's my girl," Lois exclaimed, her eyes dancing brightly. "That's what I've loved about you most." She pinched her cheek, regarding her speculatively. "So what's it gonna be?"

Leigh rolled her eyes, clucking her tongue chidingly. "I can't believe you're wasting your last breath on this. Wouldn't you rather spend the time composing some sort of offensive speech to be read as your eulogy? Talk about getting in the last word."

"You two have pussyfooted around long enough to prevent me from seeing your children," Lois barked, shooting Leigh a withering look. "Could you at least do me the courtesy of assuring me that you'll marry him?"

Leigh bent forward, kissing her paper-thin cheek, her violet eyes twinkling playfully. "I could never deny you anything," she smiled. "I'll see what I can do."

Leigh found Cameron on the pier with his bare feet dangling in the murky water and an old cane pole in his hand, pretending to be fishing but actually lost in deep thought. She slipped off her pumps and tossed them carelessly into the tall grass on the bank, then tiptoed in her stocking feet down the long dock, sneaking up behind him and sliding into the spot beside him on the wooden planks. He looked so down and out that it broke her heart, and Leigh reached out to him, encircling his muscular arm with her own. "Fish biting?" she asked in a sunny voice, hoping to cheer him up, if only a little.

"They might be if I bothered to bait the hook," he said, turning to Leigh, his expression serious. "You just leave Lois?"

"Yeah, I did," Leigh said dismally, her chest aching with remorse. She rested her head against his shoulder, her violet eyes full of tears. "I can't believe she's dying, Cam. I thought Lois would outlive us all."

"How'd she seem to you?"

"Weak, but spunky as ever. Dying sure hasn't made her any less outspoken, that's for sure."

"What did she say?"

"Lots of things," Leigh said, sitting upright and shrugging uncomfortably, suddenly uneasy with his line of questioning. "You know, Cam, just more of Lois' usual lecture about living life to its fullest."

"C'mon, Leigh, don't hold out on me," Cameron said, regarding her shrewdly. "I know Lois, and she had something important to say, much more important than telling you to live life to its fullest. She's making her last stand, making the most of her last chance to express her unadulterated opinion. Now tell me, what'd she say?"

Leigh stared down at her hands, feeling his eyes search her face. She bit her lip, struggling to conceal a mischievous smile. "She didn't really *say* anything," she said coyly, peeking up at him from beneath her lashes. "Although, she did make one simple little request."

"Which was?"

She lifted her eyes, staring at him candidly. "Lois asked me to marry you and take you to New York."

Cameron threw his head back, laughing heartily, his white teeth flashing brilliantly in the light of the early autumn afternoon. "That figures," he said. "Matchmaking up until the very end. What did you tell her?"

"I told her that I'd love to, but you wouldn't be interested."

Cameron shot her an incredulous look, his mouth gaping wide in disagreement. "Who says I'm not interested?" he grinned broadly, losing his grip on the cane pole and letting it fall with a splash into the water as he took her into his arms, pulling her tightly against his chest. His lips found hers, and Cameron kissed her, his passion rising, making up for the endless days and nights without her, silently thanking Lois for using one of her precious last wishes to bring them back together.

Zoë watched Cameron and Leigh through a slit in the drapes, giving Lois a play by play of the action on the pier. "He's kissing her now, Lois. I guess that means she popped the question."

"Fine, at least that's settled," Lois said. She patted the spot next to her on the bed, gesturing for Zoë to leave the window and join her. "What about you? Are you going to marry that Feinstein boy?"

"Oh, I hardly think so," Zoë said with a doubtful laugh. "Eli's not really my type."

"Good! Glad you finally came to your senses. That boy's nothing but a weasel. Besides, you're way too good for those Feinstein people anyway," Lois gave her a pleased smile, patting her leg affectionately. "And what about the other?" she asked, eyeing her inquisitively.

"You mean going to Mississippi?"

"You know I do."

"I don't know, Lois," Zoë confessed uneasily. "I got her address from Cam, but I really haven't decided yet."

"Do it, Zoë," Lois grabbed her hand, urging her in a voice suddenly full of energy and passion. "Do it for yourself. Don't be afraid of what it might do to the Carsons or even to Diane. We know that you love us. You're one of us, Zoë, just as much as you would be if you came from Diane's womb. Remember, child. It's not the blood that runs through our veins that makes us family — it's the love in our hearts."

Zoë did remember. She remembered it well as she stood solemnly between Jay and Diane at Lois' grave, knowing it to be true as they lowered Lois' casket into the ground, feeling as if her heart was being ripped from her chest. Lois was gone, her spunk and wisdom gone with her, and they all grieved her, especially Zoë, who felt like she had lost part of her soul.

# 17

Zoë returned to Columbus a different woman. She made the final break with Eli and resigned from her job, then began packing up her apartment for a move back to Eden Glen. Upon hearing that she was returning home, Cameron was livid. He drove across town like a mad man, screeching his Jeep to a halt in front of her apartment building. He bolted up three flights of stairs and burst through the door, grabbing her by the shoulders, accusing her loudly of giving in to the Carsons.

"Lois has been gone less than a month, and you're already selling out, letting them suck you right back in!" he scolded as he paced around the living room.

"I'm not selling out," she reassured him calmly, then resumed packing, carefully wrapping her treasured keepsakes in white tissue paper before placing them into an empty moving box. "Why shouldn't I go back? With you moving to New York with Leigh, there's really nothing to keep me here."

"Then come with us."

Zoë eyed his determined expression, giving him a wry smile. "Cam, be realistic. I can't tag along with you and Leigh forever. I'm going to Eden Glen. With Lois gone, Mother is lonely, so I thought I'd go home for a while and keep her company."

"What about your work? Are you going to turn your back on the very thing that you love most, all for the sake of family?"

"I don't intend to give up my work. If I wanted to turn my back and leave it all behind, I would've married Eli."

"What if you can't find a job?"

"Cam, please. Go to New York and be happy. Stop worrying about me."

Cameron sighed loudly, shaking his curly head, and plopped down among the cardboard boxes, looking up at her with a growl. "I do worry about you. If you don't find something constructive to do with your time, they'll have you crocheting afghans and hosting afternoon teas."

"I hardly think so," Zoë laughed, taping shut the overflowing box. "I was going to surprise you, but since you're being so nosy, I might as well go ahead and tell you. Mother is not the only reason I'm going home. I decided to put the Carson money to work at something useful. I'm going to use my inheritance from Lois to open a clinic."

"In Eden Glen?" He eyed her skeptically.

"Or Savannah. I'm sure there's as much need for free medical care there as there is here."

Cameron displayed the first smile he had given Zoë all evening — a broad, satisfied smile that brightened his entire face. "I can live with that," he said, his mood significantly lighter. "As long as there's good motive behind your madness, I can live with you going back to Eden Glen. Just be sure you don't let them corrupt you."

"I won't," she promised, tossing down the tissue paper to give him a big hug. "You've taught me well," she said, giving him an affectionate kiss. "Trust me. The influence of one Cameron Carson can undermine the pressure of a thousand Palmers."

A week later, Zoë dropped Cameron at the airport and drove to Eden Glen, moving back into her childhood bedroom at Jay and Diane's.

"This is only temporary," she told them, observing the delighted expressions on their faces as she set her bags down in her room. "As soon as I get my affairs in order, I'm getting a place of my own."

"I hardly see the need in that," Diane began, gearing up to protest.

"I do," Zoë said firmly, putting her foot down before things got out of hand. "I'm a grown woman, Mother, and very used to being on my own. There will come a time — and probably much sooner than you think — that I will need my space." She smiled at Diane's putout expression, linking arms with her as she led her back downstairs. "Until then, let's just make the most of it and enjoy our time under the same roof while we are still on speaking terms."

"You make it sound so dismal," Diane remarked disapprovingly as they descended into the living room. "We've never had a problem living under the same roof before."

"That was before I became old and set in my ways."

"Too many years of living with Leigh and Cameron?"

"You got it. Four years with the two of them taught me that sometimes you're better off alone."

With the help of Jay and Geoff, she located a building in midtown Savannah that she deemed perfect for her clinic. It was a rundown little building, all but forgotten by its former owners, a fact reflected in its awful state of disrepair.

"Oh baby, I don't know," Jay said, stroking his chin as he gazed doubtfully at the building's ramshackle exterior, taking in the broken windows and peeling paint. "Let's take a look at a few others before you make a decision."

"No," Zoë said, whirling around with a determined smile. "I like this one, Daddy. It's got a lot of potential."

"If you say so," Jay laughed, sliding an arm around her waist. He continued to squint at the structure in question, scrutinizing it without enthusiasm. "I think the only potential it has is to crumble into a pile of dust."

"I disagree," Zoë told him smugly, eyeing the building with rising intrigue. "It has wonderful potential and will be a great clinic."

"You're an eternal optimist, my dear."

Zoë glanced at him affectionately. "Only because I had one heck of a role model." She tiptoed, kissing him lightly on the lips. "I love you, Daddy."

"I love you too, honey — but don't think I don't know what you're up to." Jay's eyes twinkled comically.

"What?" Zoë asked, batting her eyes innocently.

"You're buttering me up to help you repair this monstrosity of condemnation, aren't you?"

She smiled victoriously. "However did you guess?"

After many trying months of painting, papering and small-scale remodeling, the clinic was finally ready. Zoë then set about the task of recruiting a staff.

The first to enlist in the cause was Diane. With Auntie Cee, Daisy and Lois gone, Diane was lonely and bored, having very little to do to fill her days.

"Let me help you, Zoë," she said, trailing her through the empty building, paintbrush in hand, taking a break from putting the final touches on the reception area to beg for a job. "I have nothing to do at home. I'm not like Patricia. I'm not content to hang out at Carson House, day after day, preening myself for lifelong duty as an armpiece."

"Mother, that's not very nice," Zoë chided her, her teeth clamped firmly around the row of nails she held in her mouth, removing one to hang a picture. "You shouldn't say nasty things about Aunt Patricia."

"Nice or not, it's true," Diane said. "I like Patricia, I always have, but she lives and breathes for Geoff. I'd smother your father to death if I acted that way." She followed Zoë into her office, standing with both feet planted firmly in front of her desk. "Give me a job, Zoë," she repeated, leaning against her palms and peering into Zoë's face. "I know I have no medical training, but I'm a hard worker. There has to be something that I can do."

Diane's persistence paid off, and Zoë put her to work manning the reception area and later answering the busy switchboard. Diane blossomed, finding her work immensely fulfilling.

Diane in turn enlisted the aid of her lengthy list of contacts, finding just the right applicants to suit their needs. They hired Trudy, a matronly head nurse, Steve, an ultra-feminine file clerk, and Zelda, a physician's assistant who moonlighted as a prison guard. Overall, Zoë was very pleased.

"A very eclectic group," she said to Diane. "You've done well."

"See! I turned out to be much more useful than you thought I would," Diane beamed proudly.

"Don't get too big for your britches, Mother," Zoë advised her smugly, her head down as she pored over a dwindling roster of potential physicians. "We're not up and running yet."

The rest of the staff had fallen quickly into place, but locating a doctor was no easy task. It was difficult to find a qualified physician willing to work long hours for very little pay. "This is turning out to be much harder than I anticipated," Zoë grumbled, chewing the end of her pencil as she scanned the names remaining on a very short list. "I may never find the right person for this job."

"Try offering more money, Zoanne," Palmer recommended snidely, making a rare appearance at the clinic over his two-hour lunch break. He stepped gingerly around a scaffold in his silk suit, striving to keep his balance as his tasseled loafers came dangerously close to tipping a paint can. "Paying the going rate may be enticement enough for someone to seriously consider working in this armpit of human suffering."

He trailed his fingers along the wall, and then frowned, lifting his fingertips disdainfully, holding them away from his body as if he had been exposed to the plague.

"Palmer, you big sissy," Zoë said, rolling her eyes in exasperation. "Put your hands down. You haven't contracted any dreaded disease. We haven't even seen patients yet."

"Like that really matters," he sniffed, giving her a dry smile. "I'm sure the bacteria and vermin are swarming, gathering in the back alley as we speak, crouched and ready to spread infection."

He inspected the room judgmentally, his gaze lingering on Zoë, dowdy in stained overalls, her arms and face speckled with smudges of paint. "Just look at you, Zoë," he remarked with a sneer. "Reduced to looking like the poor urchin you were born to be. Why do you want to do this? You could've had the world on a platter. You could be married to Eli, cruising the Mediterranean on his yacht. Instead, you're here, squandering your inheritance and working like a dog, all for the sake of strangers who will never appreciate one thing you've done for them."

"Palmer, if you love Eli so much, why don't you marry him?" Zoë suggested coolly. "I'm sure Susan would be more than happy to let you go."

"Obviously, you don't know Susan."

"No, but I know you — and you're no prize." Zoë laid down her paint roller and turned, pointing emphatically to the door. "For the time being, just get out. You're not being helpful and certainly have nothing constructive to say, so hit the road. Go back to your office and terrorize your secretary. At least she gets paid to listen to you."

"Fine. I'll leave," Palmer retorted haughtily, picking his way around assorted hardware, pausing in his retreat to issue a warning. "But mark my words, little cousin. You're making a grave mistake. This will be the worst thing you've ever done."

The doctor dilemma was solved when Sean Murphy arrived for duty in early September, recruited from Boston by an extremely influential

Jay. He breezed through the front door of the clinic attired in a lab coat and blue scrubs, carrying a battered briefcase in one hand and a Styrofoam cup of coffee in the other. Zoë glanced up from Diane's desk in the reception area, casting a curious gaze at the tall man, his large frame filling the doorway, with one lock of his jet-black hair falling recklessly over the rim of his round Ralph Lauren glasses. *Wow,* she breathed, swiveling in her chair to get a better view. *I bet he's what they had in mind when they came up with the phrase, 'I'm not a doctor — I just play one on TV.'*

He was devilishly handsome with panther-like grace, looking more like an actor than a doctor. She knew from his bio that he was thirty-four, but his boyish appearance suggested otherwise. She didn't know what she'd thought a Harvard grad was supposed to look like, but Sean wasn't at all what she had expected.

She rose from her chair and scooted around the desk, extending her hand in welcome. "Dr. Murphy?" she asked pleasantly. He hastily stuck his coffee cup between his teeth and gripped her small hand. "Hi, I'm Zoë Forest, the patient advocate here."

"Nice to meet you, Zoë," Dr. Murphy said, his speech muffled, smiling enthusiastically as he pumped her hand. He removed the cup from his teeth and set it on the desk. "Call me Sean."

"We're glad to have you," she beamed, taking him by the arm. "Let me show you around."

She gave him the twenty-five-cent tour before showing him to his tiny office at the back of the clinic, leaving him to settle in. She passed Diane and Trudy in the hallway, stopping when Diane touched her arm.

"Was that Dr. Murphy with you, Zoë?" she asked curiously, craning her neck as if she could see through his office door. "Did you ask for his I.D.?"

"Of course not. Why would I? Did we have a sudden barrage of men showing up here impersonating doctors? "

"In this neighborhood, anything's possible," Trudy snorted. "That boy with you didn't look old enough to shave, much less practice medicine."

"And isn't he good-looking?" Diane commented, wiggling her eyebrows comically.

"He can look good all he wants to," Trudy replied, shaking her head doubtfully. "Just as long as he can doctor. Good looks don't count for nothin' if you don't know what you're doing."

"I'm sure he'll be just fine," Zoë said and continued down the long corridor to the file room. She pulled some patient charts, flashing Steve a happy smile. "We have ourselves a doctor," she told him, finally satisfied that they were on their way.

Dr. Murphy settled in and went right to work, and Zoë quickly discovered that she liked him immensely. He was a terrific doctor, wonderful and friendly, with a great sense of humor and an incredible bedside manner. He was down to earth and jovial, and his cheerful disposition instantly set at ease even the most timid patients. His robust laughter filled the clinic, bringing a smile to Zoë's face each time she heard it. He was kind, caring, and most of all competent, making friends with his patients as he gained their trust. Soon their little clinic was bursting at the seams with off-the-street visitors and clientele.

"So, how is it that you ended up here?" she asked him curiously, relaxing against her desk with an armful of patient files, pausing in her task as he wandered into the room. "With your background, why aren't you at the Mayo Clinic, or somewhere equally as prestigious, instead of hanging out here in this Podunk little clinic, making practically nothing caring for the indigent of southeast Georgia?"

Sean glanced at her with a grin, revealing a deep dimple she had not noticed before. "Quite a polished little speech, Ms. Forest," he said, taking a seat on the edge of the copier, his white leather tennis shoes dangling above the floor and his shiny stethoscope peeking out from beneath his rumpled lab coat. "Although your question isn't all that far-fetched. Why am I not somewhere more prestigious? Hmm, surprisingly enough, at one time I was headed straight in that direction.

"You see, I come from a large family, four brothers and three sisters to be exact. I'm the baby and the only doctor, making me the apple of my mother's eye." He winked at her charmingly. "My family's nothing outstanding, mostly blue collar — not that that's a bad thing," he assured her proudly. "We weren't destitute. We just didn't have any spare change. I worked my way through college waiting tables and stocking grocery stores shelves and then mortgaged myself to the hilt to pay for medical school.

"Things were great. I sailed through school and got on as a resident at one of Boston's finest hospitals, practicing with the best of the best. I was larger than life. I sincerely didn't think it could get any better. Then along came Miss Lauren O'Reilly."

He paused and Zoë studied his solemn face. There was no mistaking it: The change in tone, the soft smile, the distracted look shadowed by a faraway twinkle. This Lauren O'Reilly meant a great deal to him.

"She was something else," Sean murmured, giving his head a quick shake, striving to get a grip on his emotions. Feeling Zoë's speculative stare, he looked up, flashing a sheepish smile. "I met her on rounds one night. Lauren was a pediatric resident with one heck of a bright future and the first time I saw her, I was hooked. She was perfect, tall, dark-haired and smart as a whip. She was even Catholic. I think my mother loved her more than I did."

"So what happened?"

Sean folded his arms, looking down as he stubbed the edge of the desk with the toe of his shoe. "We finished our residencies and got engaged. Man, did the future look promising. I had it all: A stunning fiancée from a good family, a comfortable position in family practice and the opportunity to make gazillions of dollars. Lauren got on as head of pediatrics at a children's hospital and began to plan our wedding. Everything started falling right into place. It couldn't have been more ideal."

He lifted his head, gazing at Zoë with candid blue eyes. "But I was smothered, Zoë, absolutely claustrophobic. If I hadn't gotten out of Boston when I did, I would've gone completely nuts. The pressure of the job and the pressure from my family — it was more than I could take. Everyone demanded perfection — as a doctor, as a son, as a person. Even Lauren began to expect it. Your father's ad for the clinic was like a gift from above. The minute I saw it, I knew it was the right move. I took the job, packed my gear and ran for my life."

"I see," Zoë cleared her throat, placing her stack of files down on the desk. She glanced at him curiously. "What about Lauren?"

"I broke up with Lauren before I left town," he said soberly, shoving his hands deep into the pockets of his coat. "Hardest thing I ever did really, but it was for the best. It would be unfair of me to ask her to wait until I decided what to do with my life. Lauren deserves more."

"So what are you going to do with your life?"

Sean slid off the copier, flashing her an uncertain grin. "I don't know," he shrugged. "I'm still working on it. See ya, Zoë."

"Later," Zoë murmured as he strolled from the room, head down in his own thoughts, her gaze lingering on him until he was out of sight. *What a lucky lady,* she thought. *If Dr. O'Reilly was really smart, she'd drop that job and follow him to the ends of the earth. Why would anyone with a brain let a man like that get away?*

Zoë invited Sean to Leigh and Cameron's December wedding, introducing him to the happy bride and groom and receiving Cameron's glowing seal of approval.

"I like him," Cameron said devilishly, drawing Zoë to the side during the reception. He eyed Sean chatting with Jay and Geoff at the champagne fountain, nodding in satisfaction as Zoë told him the whole story. "Pissed away his entire future to work in a free clinic. You gotta love it," he chuckled heartily, shooting her a sidelong glance, his jade eyes dancing slyly. "You did well, Zoë. Hang onto this one, Cuz. He's not at all what a Carson should marry."

"Marry?" Zoë's jaw dropped. "We didn't hire Dr. Murphy so I could marry him, Cam. We're not seeing one another! Is that what you thought?"

"Well, what did you expect me to think? You did bring him here to meet the family."

"I didn't bring him to meet the family. I brought him to your wedding!" Diane heard Zoë's impassioned outburst from across the ballroom and snapped her head around, scolding her with a stern frown. Embarrassed, Zoë lowered her voice. "Sean's new in town, and I just brought him along so he could meet some people," she hissed. "That's all."

"If you say so," Cameron snickered. "I should've known it anyway. If there's a good man around, you'll be sure and let him get away. Keep that up, and you *will* end up married to someone like Palmer."

"Over my dead body!" Leigh bellowed, overhearing Cameron. She lifted the full skirts of her wedding gown and dashed over, her long veil flying in her wake. "She most certainly will not marry anyone like Palmer," she exclaimed. "I'll shoot her first."

"Glad you both have so much confidence in my taste," Zoë grumbled, pushing her lip out in a pout.

"Well Zoey-bear, your track record's not that great. Take a look at Eli."

"Eli wasn't so bad."

"Maybe not at first glance, but I guess you don't remember all that begging, pleading, and following you around."

"You exaggerate."

"Oh yeah? Well, you're in denial." Leigh hooked her arm through Zoë's, dragging her out onto the veranda to pose for a photo. "You could do much worse, Zoë," she murmured, lowering gracefully to the top step, arranging her silk skirt around her in a becoming fashion. She looked over her shoulder and stared into the house at Sean, fanning her glowing face with her hands. "Have you taken a really good look at him? My God, Zoë! He's incredible. He's so classically handsome he takes my breath away." She chuckled and raised her heavy bouquet of creamy roses, lifting her face to the photographer with a radiant smile. "He's almost too good to be true."

Zoë frowned, receiving a scolding cluck of the tongue from the woman waiting patiently to snap their pose. "Don't try it, Leigh," she advised sternly, giving her a huffy look.

"Try what?" Leigh asked, batting her eyelashes innocently.

"The matchmaking. That's something right up Lois' alley and it's not going to work."

"But Zoë! He's wonderful."

"Forget about it, Leigh," Zoë sighed, forcing a bright smile for the camera. "The good doctor's in love, but certainly not with me."

The clinic progressed nicely and Zoë was pleased, but couldn't shake her nagging conscience, reminding her that there was still something left undone. Lois' dying words continued to haunt her, urging her to settle the matter of meeting her birth mother. *"Do it, Zoë. Do it for yourself,"* Lois' voice echoed constantly, never letting her rest.

In marrying Leigh and moving to New York, Cameron had upheld his end of the bargain with Lois, and now it was time for Zoë to uphold hers.

She made up her mind in the spring, electing to take a week off from work, and made up an acceptable story for Diane and Jay. Late on Thursday afternoon, she cleared her desk and made ready for the trip, her chest heavy, already feeling guilty for her deceit. "I feel like such a heel," she groaned, laying her head on her desk. "I've never lied to my parents, ever, not about anything, and this is killing me. Why can't I just tell them the truth?"

*The truth?* she thought. *Please!* The idea was ridiculous. *Daddy might be supportive, but Mother would never understand. No, it's really better this way, deception and all.*

The sound of footsteps, accompanied by the loud rustle of paper caught her attention, and she slipped from her chair, padding softly to her office door. She stuck her head out in the hallway, catching sight of fluorescent light shining from Sean's office. With an inquisitive smile, she snuck down the corridor, stopping just outside his door, watching him work diligently at his desk, his brow etched in concentration, his dark hair spilling into his face.

"What's the matter, Doctor? No hot date?" she asked in a teasing voice, lounging against the doorframe with a playful grin on her face.

Startled, Sean looked up, surprised to see her. "Hello Zoë," he said with an easy smile, leaning back in his chair. "I could ask you the same thing. What are you doing here so late?"

"Just tying up some loose ends," she explained, stepping inside. "I just thought I should let you know that I'm leaving town tomorrow and will probably be gone several days."

Sean removed his glasses, eyeing her curiously. "Going somewhere fun, I hope?" he asked light-heartedly.

Zoë shrugged. "That depends. The official story is that I'm going to New York to visit Cam and Leigh."

"And the real story?"

"The real story is that I'm going to Mississippi," she came forward, taking the beat-up metal chair opposite Sean's desk. "To Biloxi, actually, to meet my birth mother." She confided in Sean, telling him the whole story and explaining her dilemma. "So, no matter what, I made a promise to Lois, and I'm making good on it," she sighed, propping her elbows on the edge of the desk and leaning her chin in her hands.

Sean watched her, chewing the end of his glasses as he studied her pensive expression. "Is that the real reason you're going?" he asked softly.

Zoë lifted her eyes, meeting his inquiring gaze. "That, and to satisfy my own curiosity. It's been eating me alive ever since Cameron called me with the news. I'm dying for a peek at her, to see what she looks like, to know who she is and who I am."

She caught Sean's puzzled look and offered him an apologetic smile. "Sorry to run on that way," she said. "I guess you really wouldn't understand." She straightened, squaring her shoulders. "So, will you cover for me?"

"I'll cover for you, but I don't understand why you're being so secretive. Diane's pretty level-headed. Why not just come clean? I bet she'd understand."

"I seriously doubt that," Zoë laughed doubtfully and rose from her chair. "Mother tends to be a little insecure where Andrea LaRue is concerned."

"So you're never going to tell her?"

"I'll tell her when the time is right."

"Whatever you say — you're the boss." Sean watched her stroll determinedly toward the door. "Zoë?"

She paused, glancing over her shoulder. "Yes?"

"Have a safe trip and hurry back," his gaze softened. "Trudy and Zelda are good, but things just won't be the same around here without you."

Zoë gave him a shy smile, her face lighting with delight. "Thanks, Sean. See you soon."

Zoë traveled alone to Biloxi, pulling her car up in front of the gingerbread cottage overlooking the sea. She studied the house anxiously, debating her sanity before exiting the car and climbing the steps to the front door. Hesitantly, she lifted her hand, almost changing her mind, then drew a deep breath and tapped lightly against the stenciled glass. She waited, holding her breath, her heart pounding erratically in her chest, ready to face the woman who had brought her into the world.

The door opened to reveal a beautiful young woman with long, shining ebony hair and dark eyes, wide and flashing with shock and angry disbelief. Zoë met the girl's stare reluctantly, feeling her cheeks flush under such livid scrutiny.

"Hello," she began uncertainly, searching for the right introduction. "I was looking for Andrea LaRue."

"Well, you certainly don't have to tell me who you are," the girl said, squaring her jaw defiantly. "You're Zoanne, Andie's precious firstborn. It figures that you'd look just like her. You couldn't look any more like her if you were her clone." *Except for the eyes,* Dana noted, taking a slow, appraising inventory of her half-sister. Zoanne Carson-Forest had her father's eyes: The same clear, honest gray eyes of Cole Dewberry.

"I'm sorry," Zoë said shyly, taking a step backward. "I'm afraid you've caught me at quite a disadvantage. At the risk of sounding rude, I have to tell you, I have no idea who you are."

"Of course you wouldn't," Dana said with a mocking laugh. "I doubt very seriously that you've ever heard of me. I'm Dana LaRue, the other daughter, the second in line, the legitimate one."

"Which would make you my half-sister?"

"I guess that's one way of looking at it," Dana scoffed, shrugging indifferently. She wanted to continue hating the young woman before her, but found it almost impossible. She was so damn likable, even though she'd only been there a few moments, making her seem even more like Andie.

"You really should've called before you came over," she told Zoë in a scolding voice. "She's not here. She's gone to New Orleans for the day."

"Perhaps I should wait at my hotel."

"No, I wouldn't want Andie to accuse me of being a poor hostess in addition to being a poor sport." Dana moved to the side, opening the door wide to allow Zoë to enter. "By all means, come in and make yourself at home. You are, after all, the prodigal daughter."

They waited two hours together in Andie's living room: Two sisters, seated on opposite sides of the room, sizing one another up, attempting polite conversation and small talk, each praying desperately for Andie's quick return. Finally, the sound of slamming car doors alerted them, and Zoë stood, too nervous to remain seated yet too anxious to run to the front door. Dana remained curled in the corner of the sofa, her stomach churning, dreading having to witness Andie's jubilant reaction to Zoanne's presence.

The door burst open, followed by the appearance of a large Black Lab. Estelle came bounding into the room, leaping onto the couch and bouncing into Dana's lap, licking her face with obvious affection. Dana laughed, her pretty face transformed by the first genuine smile Zoë had seen since her arrival.

*So she isn't a totally unpleasant shrew*, Zoë thought with relief. That was nice to know. She ripped her eyes from Dana and Estelle's playful reunion, focusing on the door, waiting apprehensively for her first glimpse of her birth mother.

Andie entered the room with her arms full of shopping bags, grinning happily at Dana and Estelle. "You should've come with us,

Dana," she said with a factitious French accent. "The market was full of bargains today, chère."

"Mother, I don't believe you've met our guest," Dana said coolly, gesturing toward Zoë with a grand sweep of her hand.

Andie gave her a curious look, wrinkling her brow at Dana's unusually formal manner, and turned her head, looking in the direction Dana indicated. Seeing Zoë, her eyes widened and she stared at the tall, slender blonde standing beneath the living room window. Realizing who she must be, Andie gave a startled gasp, dropping her packages and clutching her chest.

"Zoë?" she asked in a quivering voice, so faint that she could barely be heard above Estelle's excited panting. "Is it really you?"

Zoë nodded, unable to find her voice, feeling a lump rise in her throat and the odd sensation of joyful tears welling in her eyes. *This is my mother*, she thought dizzily, her mind buzzing, caught up in an eerie still frame of euphoric disbelief.

Andie rushed across the room, first taking Zoë's hands into her own and squeezing them tightly, staring at her through sparkling tears, then threw her arms around Zoë with wild abandon, sobbing happily as she embraced her lost child. "I can't believe it," she said. Her hands were trembling. "You're so beautiful, and you're here. I just can't believe it!"

Zoë closed her eyes, relaxing in Andie's warm embrace, unable to explain the undeniable bond she felt with the woman, who up until seconds before had been a total stranger. She was drawn to Andie, feeling that it was only natural to be in her arms.

Cole breezed through the doorway and came to an abrupt halt, looking in bewilderment from Andie to Zoë, and then to Dana, who answered his questioning gaze with a shrug and a pouting smirk. He heard the sounds of Andie's sobs, then considered the young woman in her arms curiously, until it dawned on him, jarring him to the bone. *She had to be Zoë, this girl wrapped in Andie's tight embrace. She had to be the daughter Andie had given up for adoption — dear Zoë, his only child.* Shaking, he gripped the arm of the sofa to steady himself, taking a seat beside Dana, and reached out to scratch Estelle's ears, welcoming something to calm his turbulent emotions while he waited for Andie to acknowledge him.

Andie opened her eyes, looking happily over Zoë's shoulder to Cole, her face shining radiantly. *It's her, Cole*, her thoughts rang out to him. *This beautiful girl is our daughter, the one we thought we'd never find, and she's here with us, standing in the middle of our living room.*

"Zoë, I want you to meet someone," Andie said, and Zoë turned, smiling pleasantly as Andie introduced her to Cole. "This is my husband, Cole Dewberry. Cole, meet Zoë Forest."

Cole stood eagerly, observing a mirror image of his own eyes in his daughter's face as he shook her hand.

"I was just going to whip up some shrimp salad for dinner," Andie said after settling Zoë comfortably into a chair and fetching a pitcher of lemonade. "You'll stay for dinner, won't you?"

"I'm going out for a while," Dana announced brusquely, her eyes blazing as she bolted from the sofa and headed to the door, grabbing her purse from the coat rack.

"Out?" Andie stared after her, her eyes round with surprise. "What about dinner?" she asked, puzzled by Dana's sudden decision to leave.

Dana threw her a curt look. "I'm not hungry," she snarled and flew out of the house, slamming the door behind her.

Andie and Zoë chattered excitedly over dinner, exchanging life stories and comparing notes, attempting to cram twenty-four years into twenty-four minutes of mealtime conversation.

Cole observed Zoë in awed silence, taking in her beauty, fascinated by her uncanny resemblance to Andie. He listened intently as she told about her childhood, finding her articulate, bright and funny, with an air of grace that could only come from good breeding. Cole felt an extraordinary sense of pride when he looked at her, amazed that he and Andie had created someone so remarkable, and sorry that he had missed her growing into the terrific young woman she was. By dinner's end, he adored her, profusely grateful to the family that had loved and reared her for doing such a fine job. She was wonderful, and he was thankful for the chance to get to know her.

As it grew late, Zoë glanced regretfully at her watch, sliding from her place at the table. "I should get back to my hotel before it gets any later," she said almost apologetically, hating to end their pleasant evening.

"You could stay here," Andie rushed to offer, reluctant to let her long-lost child out of her sight.

"That's kind of you to offer," Zoë began, and Cole had to smile again at her flawless manners.

"I'm sure Zoë would be more comfortable sleeping in neutral surroundings for the time being, Andie," he interjected, saving both mother and daughter from an awkward situation.

"Of course you're right." Andie beamed at Cole, grateful for his timing. She leaned across, giving Zoë a soft peck on the cheek. "Thank you for coming, Zoë. You have no idea how much this means to me."

"Good night, Andie." Zoë reached out to squeeze her hand, smiling brightly as she made her way to the door. "I'll see you all tomorrow."

Zoë left the house, meeting Dana on the front porch, seated in the shadows, the red glow from the end of her cigarette giving her away. "You like her, don't you?" Dana spoke first, flicking her cigarette over the porch rail, approaching Zoë with her arms folded tightly across her chest.

"Yes, I do," Zoë said matter-of-factly. "She's great."

"You spend a few hours with her, and you think you know her," Dana sniffed disdainfully. "I've got news for you, Miss Zoanne Carson-Forest from Savannah, Georgia. You don't know her. You don't know her at all. She hasn't always been so wonderful. Mom is a totally different woman from the mother I grew up with. Growing up with Andie was like living through a train wreck."

"I bet that was tough. I'm sorry," Zoë said uncomfortably, looking down as she scuffed her sandal against the wooden porch. "I suppose we all have our problems."

Dana stared at her incredulously, her dark eyes flashing. "Problems?" she said acidly, mockingly clutching her chest. "What do you know about problems? What's the worst problem you ever had, other than having to decide which little white dress to wear to your coming out?"

"That's not fair."

"Not fair, Zoë? You want to hear about what's not fair? Take my childhood, for instance. That wasn't fair. Life with Andie as a mother was no barrel of monkeys. Losing you caused an earthquake. I had to live with the aftershocks. I had to deal with her depression, her rejection. She didn't love me. She only loved you, and I was the one who was there for her. Now, that's not fair."

Dana stomped down the front steps, stalking off into the darkness, leaving Zoë staring after her in confusion.

"Don't take what she says to heart." Cole appeared beside her from the shadows, his hands shoved deeply into the pockets of his jeans.

"Dana did have a hard time growing up, but sometimes she tends to be a bit of a martyr."

"I'm sorry," Zoë said, looking down at her hands.

"Don't be sorry," Cole said, taking a seat in one of the Adirondacks, offering the other to Zoë with a generous gesture. "We're glad you came — ecstatic even. Don't worry about Dana. She'll snap out of it."

Zoë rested her head against the back of the chair, completely relaxed, inhaling the salt air and listening to the sound of the surf drifting from the nearby beach. "You're awfully nice to cheer me up this way," she said, rolling her head to the side, smiling at Cole.

"You're pretty easy to be nice to."

"Do you mind if I ask you something?"

"Ask away."

"Do you know anything about my father?"

Her question caught Cole off guard, and he shifted uneasily in his chair, hoping he could keep a straight face. "A little bit," he replied cautiously.

"Did he want Andie to give me up for adoption?"

"He didn't know about you, Zoë." Cole paused, choosing his words carefully. "Your father loved your mother very much and would've never allowed her to give you away had he known anything at all about your existence."

Zoë examined his distant expression with a keen eye, wondering how he knew so much about it. "You sound as if you knew him well. Were you friends?"

Cole grew quiet, struggling indecisively over whether now was the right time to reveal the truth. *Like it's not already written all over my face*, he thought ironically. She'd had an emotional day already, just from meeting Andie, not to mention having to deal with Dana's animosity. He wasn't certain if she could handle the shock of meeting both biological parents in one afternoon.

"Cole? Are you okay?" Zoë's voice jerked him back to reality, and he met her bewildered gaze. He coerced a brilliant smile, unselfishly choosing not to reveal his identity, and reached over to pat her hand. "Sure, sweetie. I'm fine. Just a little tired from all the excitement," his eyes sparkled with humor. "I am an old man, you know."

"Yeah, right," Zoë laughed. "All old men should look so good."

Cole chuckled good-naturedly. "You are a charmer," he said. "You definitely get that from your mother."

Cole stepped back inside the house as Zoë drove away, finding Andie at the window, watching from behind the lace drape, an exhilarated expression coloring her face. She glanced at Cole as he closed the door, a joyful smile lighting her lips. "She's wonderful, isn't she?" she asked softly, rushing to clasp his hands.

"She's pretty terrific," Cole agreed with a nod, pulling out a chair at the kitchen table for her.

Andie sat, propping her feet in the adjacent chair. "It's weird," she said quietly, her face still cheerful. "She's nothing like I expected, yet everything I've ever dreamed."

"What did you expect?"

"I don't know," Andie laughed pleasantly, "but she's better." She peered out the window, a worried crease in her brow. "Have you seen Dana?"

"Yeah. She was out on the porch with Zoë when I went out earlier."

"Uh-oh. Was she ugly?"

"A little."

"What did Zoë say?"

"Nothing really. She's just like her old man. She took it all in stride, rolled with the punches and went on."

"Uh-huh. If she was so unfazed, what were you talking about so long out there?"

"Nosy," Cole teased, winking at her playfully. "Actually," he said, his face sobering, "she was asking me about her father."

"Really?" Andie looked over in surprise, chewing her lip. "What did you tell her? Did you tell her it was you?"

"No." Cole got out of his chair, going to the window, and pushed back the curtain to stare out at the dark sea.

Andie considered his reply, puzzled. "Don't you want her to know?"

"Of course, I do," he glanced over his shoulder, the look on his face oddly melancholy. "But not now. The timing's all wrong. Let her get used to you and Dana, Andie. God knows, I'm the easy one."

"How can you stand it, having her here right in front of you and not being able to tell her?"

"It's not easy, trust me." He dropped the curtain, coming forward to rub Andie's shoulders. "Nevertheless, I have no doubt that the appropriate occasion will present itself eventually, and when it does, you better believe that I won't hesitate to spill my guts." He bent down, kissing her neck warmly. "Zoë's a great gal and I can't wait to let her know that I had something to do with it."

It was a confusing weekend for them all — a weekend of laughter and bewildering emotions, all linked by an undeniable bond that could not be explained. For Zoë, it was especially weird. She felt like a stranger, yet felt she belonged, seeing habits and mannerisms in Andie that mimicked her own. She was comfortable with Cole, sharing his dry sense of humor, and found herself giggling most of the weekend away. The only one she didn't feel relaxed with was Dana.

"Will you be back, or will I now have to live with your gilded memory?" Dana asked sarcastically, traipsing through the living room on her way back to Tulane, going back a day early to escape Zoë's presence.

Zoë glanced up at her, meeting her acidic glare evenly, a slow smile spreading over her face. "I don't know," she replied casually. "I'll just surprise you."

"Oh, good," Dana muttered, tilting her cheek upward for Andie to kiss.

"Behave yourself," Andie teased as she escorted her to the door.

Dana offered her an irritated stare. "Like you would care," she huffed, flinging open the door with a flourish and letting the screen slam in her wake.

Andie turned, leaning against the door, shaking her head with a heavy sigh. "Hard-headed kid." She smiled apologetically to Zoë. "She gets that from her father."

"The hell she does," Cole laughed, winking at Zoë. "Freddie LaRue is a very nice man. She gets it from her mother. Andie is the most stubborn woman on the face of the earth."

"That's okay," Zoë smiled, her mind drifting to another stubborn woman in her life. "I've dealt with my share of stubborn women. I actually prefer them."

"It's a good thing," Cole said, flashing Andie a naughty grin. "Because that's all there is around here."

Zoë left on Sunday, walking out to her car with Cole and Andie just as the sun was peeking over the horizon. "I wish you didn't have to rush off so soon," Andie said, embracing her tightly. "We were having so much fun getting to know you."

"I know," Zoë said regretfully as she turned to Cole and shyly hugged his neck. "But I really have to get back. I am glad that I came though."

"We are too," Cole said, opening her car door for her, gazing at his only child with fond, thoughtful eyes.

Zoë tossed her bag into the back seat and slid into the driver's seat. "Tell Dana bye for me," she told Andie with a smile.

Andie shook her head sadly. "I don't know what's gotten into her," she fibbed, knowing exactly what Dana's problem was. "Maybe next time she'll stick around long enough to get to know you."

"That may or may not be a good thing," Zoë giggled, throwing the car into drive, "for either of us."

Zoë pulled out of Biloxi and flew down the interstate, anxious to get back to Eden Glen. She felt good about the weekend, glad that she had honored Lois' wish and made the trip to meet Andie. She was an incredible lady. Meeting Cole was an added bonus. They both were terrific people. "What happened to Dana?" she laughed aloud, reaching over to tune in a radio station.

She was lost in recollection when her car phone rang, making her jump. She leaned forward to retrieve it from where it had fallen under the front seat, keeping her eyes on the road while feeling blindly for the jingling object. Finally, she seized it, lifting it to her ear and punching the call button to say hello.

"The next time you're going to use me as an alibi, at least give me a little warning," Cameron's irritated voice rang loud and clear in her ear.

"What are you talking about?"

"Your cover's blown, Cuz. Whatever you were up to this weekend, the cat's out of the bag. Aunt Diane knows you weren't with me."

"Oh great, Cameron!" she exploded, her stomach churning sickly. "What kind of investigative reporter are you?"

"What's that got to do with anything?"

"Can't you think on your feet? Couldn't you have pretended that you forgot I was there and that I had stepped out to the store?"

"Give me a break!" Cameron growled sarcastically. " 'Oh yeah, Aunt Diane. Zoë is here. I forgot — she ran to Macy's with Leigh.' That would've gone over well. Aunt Diane's a sweet lady, and sometimes a little naïve, but she ain't stupid."

"Shut up, Cam," Zoë snapped, racking her brain, frantically trying to decide what to do.

"So, where were you?" he asked slyly. "Hope it was somewhere amoral and decadent."

"Not quite. I was in Biloxi."

The line grew silent, save for the crackling of their poor connection. "Great," Cameron said finally, snarling unhappily. "Thanks for sharing. I would've covered for your ass. Not willingly, but I would've done it to avoid what's going to happen when you get home."

"Well, it's a little late for that now, isn't it?" Zoë clicked the phone off, not inclined to listen to one of his lectures. "Good lord," she shook her head in disbelief, unable to believe that Cameron had inadvertently spilled the beans. "This should make for a lovely evening."

After a long anxious day on the road, Zoë stole into the house, hoping to make it safely to the sanctuary of her bedroom without being discovered. *Please, God. Just let me have time to practice my speech before I see her.*

She didn't get her wish. Diane was waiting for her, spying her as she eased open the front door and tiptoed across the entryway, allowing her to get to the bottom of the staircase before she called out to her from the den.

"Is that you, Zoë? How was New York?" Her voice was light and cheerful, yet coated with an underlying note of suspicion.

*Thank you, Cam, for the warning,* Zoë thought in silent relief. *At least I'm not being set up for the kill.*

With sweaty palms, she deposited her bags on the bottom step and backtracked into the den, lingering just inside the doorway. "Hi," she said, offering Diane her most brilliant smile.

"Hi," Diane replied, observing her quizzically from the couch, patiently waiting to hear what she had to say.

"Actually, I didn't go to New York," Zoë said, looking Diane straight in the eye, extremely proud of herself for not flinching.

"I know. Cameron called from Kentucky. He and Leigh were covering the horse races. I'll never understand how that boy could grow up in this household and still lie so poorly." Diane laughed softly and relaxed her hands calmly in her lap, eyeing Zoë smugly. "So, where've you been, and why did you think you had to lie about it? What was it? An erotic weekend getaway with a man that you just couldn't bring yourself to tell your old parents about?"

"Is that wishful thinking on your part?" Zoë asked kiddingly.

"Maybe on mine," Diane joked. "But certainly not on your father's."

"Well, set Daddy's mind at ease. I haven't been on an erotic getaway. I've been in Mississippi — Biloxi, actually." Zoë paused as the color drained from Diane's face. She knew she had to tell her mother the truth, but desperately wanted to soften the blow. She simply couldn't think of a way to do it. "I went to meet Andrea LaRue."

"Oh, I see," Diane stammered. "That's not what I expected at all." She was visibly shaken, her face growing ashen as she stared numbly at Zoë. She leaned her head to one side, surveying Zoë with carefully suppressed anger. "Biloxi. Is that right, Zoanne? To meet Andrea LaRue?"

Zoë nodded solemnly. "Yes."

"And did you like her?"

"I did," Zoë answered softly, moving slowly toward Diane. She sat next to her on the sofa, searching her white face with gentle eyes as she attempted to take her hand. "I'd be lying if I said I didn't."

"So, should I be expecting to share you on holidays now? Or will you be packing up your things to move closer to her?" Diane jerked her hand away and moved to the window, turning her back, her arms folded tightly across her heart, symbolically protecting it from the harsh impact of Zoë's words.

*Suck it up, Diane!* She could hear Lois' voice berating her from the great beyond, but she didn't care.

"Mom, don't be this way." Zoë joined Diane at the window, wrapping her arms around her mother's waist. "I said I liked her. That's all. Andie may have given me life, but she's not my mother. You are. You're the only mother I'll ever have. Please don't be upset."

"How can I not be upset?" Diane muttered, resting her forehead against the windowpane. Her heart ached so badly she thought it would burst. "Why did you do it, Zoë? Why did you have to meet her?"

"I was curious. I have been since Cam first gave me the news."

"If you were only curious, we could've hired an investigator and gotten all the information about her you wanted."

"It wouldn't have been the same." Zoë sank to the window seat, drawing her knees tightly into her chest. "I wanted to see her, to hear her voice, to know what she is like. You can't get all that from a snapshot and some biographical facts printed out on computer paper."

"I suppose I can sympathize with that," Diane admitted stiffly. She kept her face pressed to the glass and stared out at the setting sun, unwilling to look into Zoë's face. "I'm not as upset about you meeting her as I am about you going behind my back to do it."

"I couldn't tell you before I went. I knew it would break your heart."

"And you thought telling me after the fact wouldn't?" Diane whirled around, her eyes flashing with poorly concealed anger. "I guess I really shouldn't be upset, should I? The fact that my only daughter, the one I've spent my entire adult life loving and protecting from harm, ran behind my back to the woman who tossed her to the wind shouldn't upset me in the least."

"Mom, I never meant to hurt you," Zoë sighed heavily, holding her head in her hands. "I promised Lois that I would go, and I had to uphold my end of the bargain."

"You promised Lois!" Diane lashed out at her, whirling around lividly. "Lois is gone — her feelings no longer matter! What about my feelings, Zoë? Aren't my feelings important?"

"Yes, of course they are."

"Then why are you sneaking behind my back to meet that woman and keeping things from me?"

"I met her because that's what I needed to do, for me, but I'd never keep anything from you. I'll tell you anything about her that you want to know, but I won't tell you unless you ask because I don't know how much you want to know."

Diane glared at her with steely eyes. Her stare was as cold as her voice. "I don't want to know anything," she said and stalked from the room, leaving Zoë staring after her.

Diane found Jay in their bedroom and ran to him, allowing the hot tears to come as she sobbed against his shoulder. "I always knew this would happen!" she wailed, her voice strangled by sobs. "She's found her mother, and now she's going to leave us."

Jay stroked her hair soothingly. "Ah c'mon now, Sis. Aren't you blowing this a tad bit out of proportion?"

Diane looked up at him, her eyes flashing with insult. "I don't think so."

Jay grinned at her. "Well, I do," he said. "Think of how you sound, Diane. What would Lois say?"

"Why does that matter now? Mother is dead."

"Diane," he said chidingly.

"Oh, all right," Diane snapped in irritation, her tone cynically singsong. "Mother would say that I'm being mealy-mouthed and silly, and that I should just keep my mouth shut and let the chips fall where they may."

"And Lois would be right. She also warned us that Zoë would eventually go to meet this woman, and that none of us should act insulted or shocked. Remember that?"

"I remember."

"And how are you acting?"

Diane glanced at him sheepishly. "Shocked and insulted."

"See." Jay took her in his arms, smiling kindly into her sullen face. "Honey, you're being crazy. Zoë's not going anywhere, I promise you that. She's just being inquisitive, exploring her family roots. That's only natural. I don't find a thing wrong with it. Wouldn't you want to do the same?"

"Not if it meant breaking Mother's heart." Diane pushed him away and paced the room, not wanting to hear anything else he had to say. *Natural or not, I don't like it, not one little bit.* She turned, staring at him pointedly. "Put yourself in my place, Jay. How would you feel if it were her father?"

"Calm, cool and collected," Jay replied, his eyes dancing. "And very secure in my position."

"Sure," Diane scoffed as she moved forward, tapping her finger against his smug chin, smiling reluctantly at his attempt to cheer her up. "You would be shaking in your shoes, feeling exactly as I do at the moment."

"Maybe," Jay grinned, placing his hands on her shoulders and giving them a gentle squeeze. "But we'll never know, now will we?"

"If we're lucky," Diane sniffed, allowing him to guide her through the French doors to the backyard hammock. "If we're really lucky, we'll only have one biological parent to deal with."

She climbed into the hammock and lay next to him, inhaling deeply, the smell of fragrant roses and blooming honeysuckle lingering in her nose. She sighed, nuzzling her head against his chest. "It's just not fair, Jay. I raised her. I shouldn't have to share her."

"Life is not always fair, precious. Haven't you heard?" Jay glanced down at her, his face shining with good humor. "All we know for certain is that Zoë loves us. As for the rest of it," he shrugged, enfolding her tightly into reassuring embrace, "we'll just have to bide our time and see what tomorrow brings."

The subject of Andie LaRue did not come up between Zoë and Diane again. Diane didn't ask for details because it hurt too much to know, and Zoë didn't bring it up, afraid of causing further damage to a relationship that had already been fractured. With Jay's blessing, she moved into Auntie Cee's house next door, asserting a little independence and putting some much-needed space between herself and her mother until things blew over.

Auntie Cee's house was a single-story dwelling of white stucco, with black-shuttered windows and a quaint gazebo in the back yard. "Much too big for one person," Zoë sighed sadly as she unpacked her many boxes. There were three large bedrooms and Zoë settled into the master with its mahogany canopy bed and private sitting area, intermingling her lifetime of treasures with Auntie Cee's. It felt strange living there alone, next door to her family home, her own parents a stone's throw away. It felt even stranger to have a strained relationship with Diane.

"We've never been on bad terms," she revealed to Sean, surprising him at the clinic late one evening with Chinese take-out. She unloaded the generic white cartons of food on his desk, spilling her guts on his sympathetic ear. "We were never like other mothers and daughters. We never fought, never disagreed. We've always been close, and this estrangement is killing me."

"Give it time to sink in, Zoë," Sean advised wisely as he offered her a fortune cookie. "Give Diane a little time to realize that nothing has changed between the two of you. It'll all be okay."

"I hope you're right," Zoë sighed, ripping into the plastic wrapper and breaking open her cookie. She grinned as she read her fortune: "Your family is a jewel in your life of many riches."

"Couldn't have said it better myself," she murmured, handing the scrap of paper to Sean.

He read it and smiled. "Right on the money," he replied, "although mine was better."

Zoë craned her neck, peering to see the tiny slip of paper he shielded in his hand. "What's it say?"

"Nothing doing," he chuckled, rolling it up and sticking it in his pocket. "It's about my love life, and I always keep that private."

"Speaking of, how is the grand Dr. O'Reilly?"

"The same," Sean replied nonchalantly, his face decisively indifferent. "Still a VIP and still begging me to come home."

"Then why don't you go?"

"And leave all this?" he questioned incredulously, gesturing to the organized chaos piled high around them. "You're kidding, right?"

"You miss her, don't you?"

"Sure I miss her, but I'm not going back. I'm acclimated now and I happen to like Savannah. The way I see it, if Lauren O'Reilly wants me, she can come here."

"Ooh, let's hope she does," Zoë said, putting a positive spin on the discussion as she scraped the last grains of chicken-fried rice out of the carton. "We could use a good pediatrician."

# 18

After Zoë's visit, the summer passed peacefully, almost post-climactic after such an incredible surprise. Andie took life in stride, going about her day to day, looking back on Zoë's stay with great happiness and wishing that she could see her again.

"There's still so much to catch up on," she said to Cole, snuggled in his embrace, the cast of summer moonbeams filtering through the lace curtains on the bedroom window. "I want to know everything there is to know about her, to see the person she's become. I just can't wait to see her again."

"Believe me, Andie. I know exactly how you feel." Cole smiled down at her, his handsome face reflective. He was still getting used to the idea that Zoë was his child. "I'd kill or die to live a little bit closer to her so I could see where she lives and occasionally 'accidentally on purpose' run into her. I would love to plan a trip to Savannah to see her, but I don't think that's such a good idea right now."

"No, I don't think so either," Andie agreed sadly. "Zoë said her mother was none too pleased about her trip here last spring."

"I guess we'll just have to wait our turn," Cole said with resignation, pulling her more tightly against him, "and hope that it will be really soon."

Dana returned to Tulane for her final semester of college and could not wait to get through. "I'm practically standing on my head to graduate," she told Andie over the phone, laying flat on her back on the hard mattress of her bunk, tossing her pillow over her head with glee. "I'm so antsy my skin is crawling. I'm glad you suggested that I go to summer school. Getting out of here six months early is a godsend."

"What do you think you'll do when you graduate?" Andie asked.

"I don't know, but I'm sure it will have something to do with food. Between you and Daddy, I don't stand a chance. I'm doomed to cook somewhere. I was kinda thinking of flipping burgers."

"Dana!" Andie objected with a chuckle, protesting her declaration in a scolding tone.

Dana laughed gruffly. "Jeez, Mom, I'm only kidding. Lighten up, will ya? Can't you take a joke?"

"With you I never know what's a joke and what is serious."

"Well, like I said, I'm sure I'll go into some type of food service. Claudette and I were tossing around the idea of opening up a restaurant."

"Really?" Andie sounded disappointed. "I was hoping that you would come to work with me."

"Me? Move to Biloxi? Wouldn't that be kind of close for comfort?"

"Not as far as I'm concerned," Andie answered brightly. "Dell and I would love to have you at Crème de la Crème. God knows we could use the help. We're so swamped we can barely catch our breath."

"Hmm," Dana considered the offer thoughtfully, her heart singing with delight. "I'll sleep on it and let you know."

"You do that, sweetie — and the sooner the better. We could really use you and would be thrilled to have you on board."

*Although any set of hands would do at the moment,* Andie thought wearily, surveying the cluttered kitchen as she hung up the phone. She and Dell had more late summer parties and weddings than they could handle, and although they had already hired one new helper, they could really use three more.

"I pitched Dana the offer," she told Dell, glancing across the kitchen to where she was busily rolling out pastry dough.

Dell wiped her brow and looked up, her chef's hat askew and her face dotted with flour as she gave Andie an encouraged smile. "Let's hope that she takes it," she said. "Not only do we need her, but it would also do you a world of good to have her near."

"Don't tell her that," Andie warned comically. "She'll never come."

The bell at the delivery door buzzed, grabbing their attention. "I'll go," Dell said, wiping her hands on a towel as she dashed for the door. "I hope it's that order of boneless chicken I've been expecting. You know as well as I do that Bill is expecting Hawaiian Chicken."

Andie giggled and bent forward to check on the cheesecake tarts baking in the bottom oven, becoming suddenly dizzy as she peeked in the door. She stood upright, her head swimming nauseatingly as the room spun. She closed her eyes and gripped the countertop, swaying unsteadily.

"Hello Sunshine!" Bill's voice rang in her ears as he sprang through the galley door. "I just came by to see how preparations were coming for my Labor Day extravaganza. You know I'm counting on your famous Hawaiian Chicken. It's..." he trailed off, inspecting her colorless face, taking special note of the beads of cold sweat on her upper lip. He rushed forward, taking her by the elbow. "Andie, honey — are you all right?" he asked worriedly.

"I don't know," she answered weakly, opening her eyes reluctantly as she fought the rise of bile in her throat. "I'm just so sick — and dizzy. I..." she faltered as her knees buckled and Bill caught her, grabbing her under the arms just before she hit the floor.

"Thank God, it was the chicken," Dell strolled back into the kitchen, wearing a happy smile that instantly faded when she saw Andie crumpled in Bill's arms. "What happened?" she asked shrilly, running across the room to the sink. She wet a paper towel and hurried over, pushing back Andie's hair to apply it to her forehead.

"I don't know," Bill stammered, for the first time in his life at a loss for words. "I just walked in the door, said two words to her, and she passed out."

"Do you always have such a profound effect on women?"

"Dell," Bill glowered at her sharply. "Now is not the time for your warped sense of humor. Where's Dewberry?"

"New Orleans."

"Of course he is. Why should he stick around, just because his wife is sick?" Bill snarled unpleasantly. "Who's her doctor?"

"Sabrina Pittman."

"Well, get her on the phone, darlin', and tell her we're on the way."

Andie awoke in the doctor's exam room, lying flat on her back on a table. She rolled her head to the side, focusing her blurry eyes on Dell sitting in a vinyl chair in the corner. "Hey," she managed weakly. "What are we doing here?"

"You passed out, and Bill insisted on bringing you in."

"It was nice of Dr. Pittman to work me in."

"Like I had a choice in the matter," Dr. Sabrina Pittman eased into the room, catching the end of Andie's remark. "You have awfully influential friends, Andie. Had I even been inclined to refuse, I doubt very seriously that Mr. Fairgate would have taken no for an answer."

"He usually doesn't." Andie attempted a smile. "So what's wrong with me?"

"I don't know for sure yet," Dr. Pittman replied. "I talked to your husband on his way in from New Orleans, and he gave permission for us to draw blood and run some tests."

Cole arrived just after the test results, coming face to face with Bill in the waiting room. "Is she okay?" he asked, his face etched with deep concern.

"Like you would care," Bill said testily. "Running off to New Orleans and leaving her sick that way."

Cole crimped his mouth in annoyance. "She wasn't sick this morning. She was fine. Otherwise, I wouldn't have left her."

Dell slipped out into the reception area, a slight smile on her face as she studied their worried expressions. "Test results are back," she said casually, taking a seat in the chair next to Cole.

"What'd they say? Can I go back there?" Cole asked, grasping her arm.

"Just stay put. She's getting dressed and will be right out — after she gets over the shock."

Cole sank in his chair, the anguished look on his face mimicking Bill's. "Oh God," he stuttered. "Is it bad?"

"That depends."

"On what?"

"I'll just let Andie tell you."

A few minutes later, Andie emerged, looking a little better, although she was still pale, and her expression was frozen in disbelief. She sank numbly into a chair. Bill and Cole instantly leaned forward, staring into her huge, unseeing eyes.

"Honey?" Cole questioned hesitantly.

"What's the prognosis, Sugar?" Bill asked. "Whatever it is, sweetheart, we'll fight it — we'll go after it with both guns loaded."

"I'm pregnant," she said in a wooden monotone.

Cole and Bill fell back in stunned silence, neither able to utter a word. Dell giggled, her hands clasped in delight, looking in amusement from face to face. "Come on, you guys!" she urged cheerfully. "This is not the end of the world."

"Not by a long shot," Bill recovered and flashed a grin, reaching over to pat Andie's leg. "Dewberry may be unhappy about it, but I think it's just great, Cupcake. Just great."

Cole glanced over at him, giving him an irritated scowl. "I am not unhappy about it," he snarled. "I wish you would quit putting words in my mouth and learn to mind your own business."

He slid from his chair and kneeled in front of Andie, gazing into her eyes with elation. "Andie," he whispered, his mouth stretching into a delighted smile. "Do you realize this is the first time anyone has ever told me that I'm going to be a father?"

Andie's expression softened, and she encircled his neck with her long slender arms, running her fingers through his thick dark hair. "I know," she replied quietly, searching his face, her voice oddly melancholy. "I'm so sorry, Cole — sorry that I didn't share this news the first time around. Look how many years we missed with Zoë, all because of me."

Cole cuddled her head against his chest, gently kissing the top of her head. "Don't apologize, Andie, and please don't be sad. This is a wonderful moment — we're going to be parents! We've been given another miracle to celebrate."

He pulled her to her feet and put his arm around her shoulder, guiding her ecstatically toward the exit. "So what if we're old enough to be grandparents," he kidded her as he opened the door. "God has given us a second blessing."

Bill frowned as he watched them stroll down the corridor, their heads nestled together in astonished bliss. "Go figure," he muttered to Dell, linking arms with her as they left the office. "I'm the one responsible for getting her to the doctor and he gets all the credit."

"Well, Bill," Dell suppressed a laugh, "I think he had a little bit more to do with her condition than you did."

"Did I ask for your opinion?" Bill demanded, growling at her as he punched the down button by the elevator. "I know he had more to do with Andie's pregnancy than I did. Do I look like an idiot?" He pointed a finger at her entertained face, wagging it warningly. "Don't answer that."

The elevator opened and they stepped inside, taking opposite sides of the car. Bill surveyed the numbers above the door, the thought of what had transpired finally crossing his mind. "Andie's gonna be a mama," he declared with a pleased chuckle, giving Dell a comical wink. "Well, darlin'," he drawled as he moved to stand next to her, flinging a chummy arm around her small shoulders. "Looks like me and you are gonna be planning one heck of a baby shower."

"Looks like it."

"Why don't we start discussing it now — say over dinner?"

Dell glanced up at him, gazing shyly into his twinkling eyes. "I think that sounds swell," she said with a soft smile.

"All right then," Bill grinned happily and squeezed her shoulder. He looked down into her pretty face, beaming in friendship, only to be pleasantly surprised by the spastic flutter of his heart.

Dana took the news much better than Andie expected. She arrived in Biloxi on Friday evening, three days after Andie had been given the news. She bounded through the front door, skidding to a halt to pet Estelle, then searched the room until she found Andie curled up on the couch, eating crackers and sipping ginger ale.

"Good God, Mom. What's wrong with you?" she asked brusquely, flopping on to the opposite end of the couch. "You look awful."

"Thanks," Andie mumbled tiredly, reaching into the box for another saltine.

"Jeez, if I didn't know better I'd swear you have morning sickness," Dana chuckled, amused by the idea.

"I do." Andie waited quietly for the other shoe to fall.

"You do?" Dana gawked at her, her eyes roaming from her pasty complexion to her swollen breasts. "My God, you do!" She leapt from the sofa, throwing her hands in the air. "You're pregnant? Do you know how old you are? Are you nuts?"

"I'm very aware of my age, Dana," Andie answered dryly, giving her a thin smile. "These things do happen, you know."

Dana sank to the ground, sitting Indian style on the braided rug. "I'm graduating from college, and my mother is pregnant. Wow — what a concept." She shook her head, rubbing her temples in a daze.

Andie relaxed against the cushions, resting her head on the armrest of the sofa, watching her daughter's face apprehensively. *This is the test,* she thought guardedly. *The first of Cole's children didn't ruin our relationship. Will the second?* She cleared her throat, raking her fingers anxiously through her hair. "So what do you think, Dana?"

Dana raised her head, eyeing her warily. "What do I think?" she asked blandly. "I think it's a darn good thing that I came here to accept your job offer, because you're going to need all the help you can get."

Intense relief flooded Andie's weary body, and she offered Dana a grateful smile. "Welcome aboard," she said cheerfully. "Crème de la Crème will never again be the same."

"Gee thanks, Mom."

"It will only get better," Andie added softly, sitting up to accept Dana's congratulatory hug.

"I think it's great news about the baby," Dana whispered, leaning her head against Andie's shoulder. "I know how much you and Cole love each other and how much this baby will mean to you both."

"Thank you, sweetie."

"I just hope it's a girl. I've already been through Jerry, and having Cole around is about as much testosterone as I can stand."

Andie laughed softly and stroked her hair, emotional tears trickling down her cheek. She heard Cole's key rattle in the lock, and she raised her head just in time to see him come through the door, her heart fluttering ecstatically at the sight of him.

He surveyed the two women on the couch and quickly took inventory of Andie's happy smile, then dropped his briefcase by the door to join them in a group hug. "What fun!" he declared playfully. "Two beautiful women in my arms at the same time. What more can a man ask for?"

Dana lifted her head, her dark eyes sparkling naughtily. "Hey, did you bring me a cigar?" she asked, relaying congratulations with her mischievous grin.

"Not yet," Cole replied easily. "I'm saving it — you know, for when the fat lady sings."

"Would the fat lady be Mom?" Dana asked wickedly, winking at Cole with good humor.

"I think so," Cole replied jovially, tickling Andie gently in the ribs.

"Hey!" Andie protested. "You two aren't going to spend the next nine months ganging up on me, are you?"

"Would we do that?" Cole asked innocently.

"You better believe it," Dana answered for them both, returning Cole's conspiratorial grin. "I bet between the two of us, Cole and I know enough fat lady jokes to fill a book."

"Great," Andie moaned, concealing her good-natured smile as she rolled her eyes for their benefit. *Thank you, Lord,* she praised silently, lifting her eyes upward. *For once in my life, everything's going to work out for the best.*

# 19

Winter flowed into spring, and spring progressed without another earth-shattering event cropping up to disturb Zoë's increasingly stressful life. Diane had not mentioned Zoë's visit to Mississippi nor asked anything about Andie, but Zoë could sense her bitterness and see the hurt she tried to hide. Things between them were strained, even though Diane tried to pretend they were not. Because of the underlying tension, Zoë spent her days at the clinic and most of her evenings with Sean Murphy, their friendship blossoming into something more.

She thought often of her trip to Biloxi, thinking of Andie and Cole and even Dana. She and Andie had begun to keep in touch by letter and e-mail and had even exchanged a few phone calls. The news of her late-in-life pregnancy came as a pleasant surprise, and one that Zoë welcomed. "A baby brother or sister!" she marveled to Andie with delight. "How grand!" It was the happiest news she had received in months.

Zoë felt like she was getting to know Andie, yet there was still so much she wanted to ask. *I want to know about her family, her childhood, her life up to now. And most of all, I want to know about my father.* Andie had never mentioned him, and no matter how badly she wanted to know, Zoë couldn't bring herself to ask. Their relationship was still too new, and Zoë certainly didn't want to overstep her bounds.

In mid-March, she sat at her desk, shuffling through a mountain of health department paperwork, thinking she was the only one left working late. "Ye gods, where is that silly file?" she grumbled, leaning back in her chair and rubbing her tight neck muscles. She glanced up at the clock. "Eek, seven o'clock. Where has this day gone?"

Sean appeared in the doorway in jeans and hunter-green oxford, bouncing on the toes of his sneakers excitedly. "Hey, you ready to go?" he asked.

Zoë glanced up, offering him a pleasant smile. "Where to?"

Sean's mouth fell open, his face glazed in mock disbelief. "Where to? To drink beer, of course! It's St. Paddy's day, love." He sauntered into the office, grabbing Zoë's jacket off the peg behind her door, and tossed it over her shoulders. "Where've you been? The entire town's out celebrating and you act like you didn't even know what day it is. In fact, I should pinch you for not wearing green."

"I know precisely what day it is, and I am wearing green," Zoë said, cutting her eyes flirtatiously. "You just can't see it."

Sean did a double-take, staring wide-eyed at her, his face turning bright red and lighting with good humor. "Thanks for the enticing visual," he grinned, chuckling as she flounced past him with a giggle and raced him for the car.

Arm in arm they entered an Irish pub on River Street and navigated their way through the crowd, miraculously finding two empty stools at the bar. Sean lifted his hand to catch the bartender's attention and ordered a pitcher of green beer.

Zoë giggled as Sean filled her glass with the Kelly-green brew, lifting her frosty mug and gulping with pleasure. "Is it true that this will make you pee green?" she asked, lowering her glass and wiping away her frothy mustache with the edge of her sleeve.

"Among other things," Sean replied with a mischievous grin, jerking his head around as a cheer went up in the bar. He lifted his mug and looked up at the television set. "All right! Basketball!" he whooped, pointing excitedly and sloshing beer on the counter. "Look Zoë! It's the Celtics."

"Good! That ought to keep you out of trouble, for a few minutes anyway," Zoë smirked, draining her glass. Out of curiosity, she glanced at the other television, catching sight of Eli Feinstein's face on the screen. She set her glass down with a bang and strained her ears to hear over the noise.

*"Perhaps one of America's youngest corporate executives, today Eli Feinstein vaulted into one of this country's most coveted hot seats, being named Vice President of Feinstein Foods, second in line to CEO."*

Zoë smiled softly at the reporter's words, her heart skipping as she studied Eli's face with nostalgic affection. *Eli, Eli, sometimes I really miss you,* she thought, her gaze transfixed, completely engrossed by his image. *Even if you did get on my nerves.*

Her face glowed as she remembered their time together. *Did I really make the right decision in pushing him away?* Sometimes she still had to question her sanity, almost as much as Palmer did. She sighed, her eyes still glued to the set, a wistful expression coming over her face.

"So he's the competition," Sean observed dryly, turning from the game and catching the look on Zoë's face. "The infamous Eli Feinstein," he remarked, reading the news caption and inspecting the man on the screen. He shrugged, unaffected. "He's not at all what I pictured. Somehow, I thought he'd be a little more grandiose."

"Don't let his looks deceive you," Zoë laughed distractedly. "He is extremely grandiose." She tore her eyes from Eli and stared curiously at Sean. "Competition?" she asked. "For what?"

"For you."

Zoë flinched, flabbergasted, until she caught the teasing twinkle in his bright blue eyes. She smiled and shook her head soberly. "Nope, Eli Feinstein is not the competition — for anything or anybody," she retorted lightly, fingering the bowl of mixed nuts before her, a faraway look in her eyes. "It's been over between me and Eli for quite some time now."

"That's good to know," Sean said heartily, lifting his mug for another drink. "I'd like to know that I still stand a chance of catching your eye, Miss Zoanne Annette Carson-Forest." He ignored the astonished look on her face and scooted his barstool closer. "I know we were supposed to keep this relationship completely platonic, but I can't help myself. I have to confess I'm completely taken in. In my whole life, I've never met anyone like you."

Zoë laughed, her expression light-hearted. "It's the beer talking, Doctor," she said casually. "I refuse to take anything you say seriously. Tomorrow you'll be singing a different tune, and you'll be awfully sorry that I was around to hear anything you said."

To prove her wrong, Sean reached into his coat pocket, pulling out a dazzling diamond solitaire, holding it between his thumb and forefinger as Zoë gawked. "I hadn't really planned it this way, but hey, why not? It's St. Paddy's Day, my favorite day of the year, and that's reason enough for me."

He slid off the barstool and got down on one knee, attracting the attention of everyone around them. "Marry me, Zoë Forest," he said with a jaunty grin, holding his arms open wide.

"Sean, what are you doing? Get up off the floor."

"What do you mean, what am I doing? Gee, Zoë — you act like you've never seen a man propose before."

Zoë reeled in astonishment, tingling all the way to her toes. "Are you for real?" she asked, her eyes widening in alarm.

"Would I be embarrassing myself in front of two hundred people if I weren't?"

"But I don't know what to say," she stammered, her face growing red and warm.

"Women!" the bartender interjected humorously, his face lit in scornful amusement. "They never know what to say when it's important."

"Say yes, girlie!" urged an inebriated patron, yelling loudly and slapping Zoë hard across the back.

"Yeah!" the rest of the crowd joined in, starting a drunken chant that began at the bar and traveled in waves around the tavern. "Say yes, say yes," they pounded their fists on the tables and crowed at the top of their lungs, obnoxiously goading Zoë to accept Sean's proposal.

Zoë's eyes darted around the room as she searched for an escape. She glanced back at Sean, her expression pleading. "Sean," she said.

He read her thoughts and rose to his feet, holding a hand up to silence the multitude. "Hey now," he said with a friendly grin. "I don't expect the girl to be influenced by a bunch of drunken losers like you," he joked, receiving thunderous applause and shouts of approval. He turned to Zoë, taking her hand. "Let's get out of here."

They left the bar and went out on the crowded street. St. Paddy revelers were still in rare form. Pushing through the throng, they picked their way along the cobbled road, ending up on a somewhat secluded bench overlooking the Savannah River. Zoë stared numbly into the distance, too astonished to speak, her ears still ringing from the shouting and his impromptu proposal. Sean cast a sidelong glance at her, studying her quietly.

"Okay, so I was wrong to pop the question in a bar full of drunks," he finally said, grinning sheepishly. "I know you're shocked. I'm sorry."

"Shocked? That's an understatement," Zoë replied, shooting him an incredulous look. "I've seen some men do some crazy things in my lifetime, but this takes the cake. How did you think I was going to react? You proposed to me, Sean — where did that come from? We aren't even dating."

"Not in an official capacity," Sean objected, "but we've been going out together almost every night for months."

"You know what I mean," she sighed in exasperation, tapping her feet impatiently on the sidewalk. "I don't know what you want me to say. What about Lauren O'Reilly?"

"Well, don't say anything until you hear me out," Sean appealed to her, gathering his thoughts as he watched a grand paddleboat float past on the river, returning to the dock after a moonlight dinner cruise. "When I went back to Boston over the holidays to visit the family, I called Lauren. We met on Christmas Day at a park not far from the house. She was so beautiful, everything that I remembered, and I should have been just thrilled. There she was, in the flesh, arms open wide, ready to take me back," he paused, looking at her, his blue eyes penetrating Zoë's soul. "It just wasn't the same. Everything had changed — and that's when I knew. I looked at her, and all I could think of was you."

Zoë looked down in stunned silence, unable to form a reply. Sean gazed at her, his eyes dancing happily as he reached for her hand.

"I don't know what came over me, Zoë. I certainly didn't intend to do this tonight. I just picked up the ring today. I had planned to make it official, to start seeing you romantically and pop the question at a later date, but sitting in that bar next to you, seeing your face, I just couldn't help myself. Maybe it was the beer — or maybe it was just my heart. I'm crazy nuts about you, Zoë. Don't you feel the same?"

"I don't know what I feel," she answered quietly, her face flushed and her heart pounding uncertainly, feeling like a heel when she saw the crushed look on his face.

"I see," he said and withdrew his hand, his long face revealing his disappointment. "I guess I was hoping for a better response."

"Hey Doc," she touched his arm, her soft voice pleading for understanding. "Don't take that the wrong way. I really like you and think you're wonderful, and under ordinary circumstances I would be jumping for joy over your marriage proposal. But right now, my life is in such turmoil. I just can't take on anything else."

Sean looked over at her, his expression shining with relief. "Knowing what I know, I can certainly understand. I don't expect an answer tonight," he said in a low voice, searching her face for some clue to her thoughts. He reached down and slipped the ring on her finger, then pressed her hand to his lips, meeting her astonished gaze. "Think it over and let me know when you're ready. And just keep the ring. You can return it if you say no."

"So much to think about," Zoë sighed, pressing her forehead against the pane of her living room window, staring bleakly into the darkness. It was well past midnight and she wandered the length of her house, unable to rest, too agitated and confused to get a good night's sleep. "I remember when life used to be simple," she mumbled unhappily, massaging her aching brow. "Now everything is so complicated. First Mother and Andie, and now Sean." She groaned, thumping her head rhythmically against the glass. "Maybe I should've just married Eli or moved to New York with Cam and Leigh."

"And that will be enough of that!"

Zoë turned slowly, a cold chill running up her spine as she focused on the vision before her. A shadowy image of her grandmother lounged in the corner of the living room sofa, attired in a flowing white gown, her silver hair piled atop her head in tranquil waves. Zoë shook her head in disbelief. *Great*, she thought cynically. *Now, I'm hallucinating.*

"Don't you be back-pedaling on me, Zoanne," Lois barked sternly, wagging a disapproving finger. "You don't belong in New York. It's too big and too crowded. And as for Eli," she glared at Zoë, rolling her eyes extravagantly, "you made the right decision about that weasel while I was still here."

"Lois, what are you doing here?" Zoë asked, dropping to a chair in amazement. "You're supposed to be dead."

"I am, missy — dead and buried. But how in the world do you expect me to rest in peace with you down here crying and fretting? Do you want to tell me just what the problem is?"

Zoë twirled the end of her ponytail, too distracted to find it odd that she was having a midnight discussion with her deceased grandmother. "Well, first of all, Sean Murphy wants me to marry him."

"Well, of that I approve!" Lois cackled. "That's hardly what I call a problem. I like him so much better than I ever liked that Feinstein boy."

"Oh, how would you know? You don't even know him. I didn't meet Sean until after you were gone."

"You think I don't know exactly what's going on down here? You may not see me, but I'm around. I've got too much at stake not to keep tabs on my family."

"If you know so much, then why are you asking me what the problem is?"

"Because, that's the only way I can find out what's on your mind."

"Then I suppose you know I've been to Mississippi."

"I do."

"What do you think?"

"You know what I think," Lois answered, peering at her with wise eyes. "You still want to know more about Andrea LaRue, and you should. That's your right."

"I do want to know more about her, Lois. I can't explain it. I'm drawn to her like a magnet. I try not to think about it, but it's always there in the back of my mind, that little voice egging me on. I wasn't really ready to leave when I came home last spring, but I did, out of obligation to the family. I just don't want to make any more waves."

She leaned forward in her chair, staring down at her hands, running her thumb along the smooth polish of her nails. "I feel like there's so much more I need to learn, like there's something left unsaid or undone. I just can't let it go." Zoë paused, gazing up at Lois wistfully. "Nevertheless, no matter how badly I want it, I can't possibly pursue a relationship with Andie without alienating Mother more than I already have."

"And like I told you before — Diane will get over it."

"I want to go back to Biloxi, but it would break Mother's heart, not to mention the uproar it would cause with the rest of the family."

"Oh, to hell with them!" Lois burst out emphatically, her fist clenched tightly above her head as she cheered Zoë on. "Go!"

"You know, for an angel, you sure have a vulgar vocabulary."

"Oh Zoë, lighten up. Even God has a sense of humor."

"Obviously. He let you in, didn't he?"

"And Beatrice," Lois grimaced, shaking her head sadly. "Can you believe it? After everything she said and did, she still managed to squeeze her frigid butt through those pearly gates." She sighed and gave Zoë a smile, caressing her with soft eyes. "You do what you need to do, Zoë. I'll always be around to back you up."

Zoë woke up on the couch, curled in a ball, her terrycloth robe wrapped tightly around her and a blanket covering her feet. She looked around the room, finding herself completely alone. "It had to be a dream." She shook her head, smiling foolishly. "Or a nightmare, depending on how you look at it. There's no way she was really here."

She rose stiffly from the sofa, staggering across the room to make some coffee. "I better not rock the boat," she decided wearily, pushing open the door to the kitchen. "I have enough to deal with as it is. I'll just stay put and leave things alone."

A gust of wind came out of nowhere, ruffling the kitchen drapes, blowing over a picture of Lois setting on the top shelf of the baker's rack. Zoë startled, staring wide-eyed at the overturned frame.

"Okay! I'll go!" she said, glaring defiantly. "Jeez, Lois! Will you ever stay out of my life?"

She procrastinated for weeks but finally made up her mind to go again in late April, the tug of the yet-unexplained propelling her into action. She made her travel plans, and then broke the news, telling only those who mattered most.

She saved Sean for the last minute, popping her head into an exam room on Thursday afternoon. "Hey," she sang out cheerfully and nodded to Sean, giving his pediatric patient a silly wave. "How are you, Bobby?"

"Fine," Bobby giggled and hid his face, peeking out at Zoë as he stole the stethoscope from around Sean's neck.

"What's up?" Sean asked, glancing back at her, his eyes dancing with affection.

"Not much," Zoë answered flippantly. "Just wanted to say hi," she pivoted and started out the door. "Oh, by the way — I'm leaving," she said over her shoulder and continued her stroll down the corridor.

Sean and Bobby exchanged a curious look, and Sean wrinkled his brow. "I'll be right back," he said, patting Bobby on the shoulder, then hurried out into the hall, spotting Zoë near the exit. "By the way, you're leaving?" he called out, sprinting to catch up with her. He skidded to a stop by the door and leaned against the wall. "Should I take that as a farewell? Where are you going?"

"Oh, I thought I'd head over to Biloxi for a while," Zoë answered with a shrug.

"Oh really? And just how long will you be gone?"

"I don't know," Zoë replied, her face alive with excitement. "A few weeks, I would expect. Maybe more, depending on how it goes."

"I see. That's a helluva lengthy vacation, Ms. Forest," Sean kidded, keeping his tone pleasant as he gave her a playful wink. "And just who do you think is going to run the show around here while you're off horsing around?"

"I think I'm leaving it in pretty good hands. Trudy and Zelda can probably keep it under control, not to mention my mom, and I've located an extra pair of hands to help pick up the slack."

Sean lowered his head, his hands in his pockets, and scuffed the carpet with the toe of his tennis shoe. "What about me?" he asked, glancing up soberly. "Who's going to watch over me while you're away?"

"Oh," Zoë smiled mischievously, lifting her hand to stroke his cheek. "I'm sure there are a lot of willing women who will gladly fill in for me."

"You think? And what happens if I find one I like better?"

"Then I suppose I'll have to forfeit the ring. It's one size fits all, right?"

"You bet. Adjustable — right out of the gumball machine," Sean grinned, taking her by the arm as he escorted her from the clinic, "although, no one else could wear it quite the way you do."

"Hey," Zoë stopped walking. "Thanks for being on my side. I need to get away for a while. I've got a lot on my mind and need to sort it all out."

"And may I be so bold to assume that some of that sorting out includes me?" Pausing by her car, Sean enfolded her in a warm embrace, his mouth against her ear. "I support you in what you feel you have to do, Zoë," he whispered softly, "but I'll miss you."

"I'll be back before you know I'm gone," Zoë murmured, cringing with pleasure as his warm lips brushed her neck.

"I seriously doubt that," he chuckled, pulling away, regarding her with affection. "I'll know you're gone. It just doesn't feel the same without you."

Early the next morning she left her house, stepping into the gray shadows just before dawn, the air still thick with dew. She packed her car, her nerves jangling uneasily as she anticipated sharing her travel plans with Diane and Jay. She craned her neck and peeked around the house into the kitchen next door, seeing her parents sipping coffee together over the breakfast table, viewing them apprehensively. She hated to drop the bomb, knowing from experience what kind of uproar her announcement would bring. *Maybe I'll just fib*, she decided. *It might be for the best. A little white lie never hurt anyone. I'll clue Cam in this time and get him to cover for me.*

"Chicken!" she scolded herself and pushed her bag into the trunk. "This is ridiculous. I'm an adult. I can leave town any time I want, and go see anyone I want. There's no reason why I can't just march myself over there and tell them the truth."

As she reached up to slam the lid, her mind drifted back to the tense altercation following her first trip to see Andie, remembering the look on Diane's face and the hurt in her voice.

"I can't do it," she said, dashing around to the driver's side and jumping inside. "I just can't do it. I know what telling her will be like and I can't go through that today."

She started the engine, thankful for its soft purr, and put the car into reverse, backing stealthily out of her driveway without turning on the lights. "I think I'll just leave Cam out of this altogether," she decided. "I'll call Sean when I get on the road and beg him to tell them. He's a neutral third party so he's safe. Mother is much too refined to lose it on him."

She sped south down Interstate 95, stopping in Jacksonville for breakfast and in Tallahassee for gas. Fed and refueled, she got back on I-10 for the last leg of the trip. "Getting closer," she said, tapping her fingers nervously on the steering wheel. *Closer to finding answers, to resolving issues, to finding closure and moving on with my life.*

Her cell phone let out a shrill ring, startling her. "Oh great," she muttered with dread. "Good news travels fast." She answered cautiously, reluctant to see who was on the other end.

"What the hell are you doing?" Cameron's gruff voice barked in her ear, aggravation raising it a couple octaves.

"What do you mean, what am I doing?" she asked, hardly in the mood to defend her actions.

"Just what I said. What the hell do you think you're doing? I called home this morning, just to check in, and the whole place was in an uproar. Aunt Diane was locked in one of the bedrooms, crying her eyes out, and Uncle Jay was beside himself, blowing off work and drinking Bloody Marys. Dad was highly agitated, as was Mom. Hell, even Palmer was upset."

"Oh, I'm sure he was."

"Okay, so maybe I lied," Cameron admitted gruffly. "I can't believe you're doing this."

"Why not, Cam? What about the evils of selling out and the importance of being my own person? Didn't you give me countless lectures on that?"

"Yeah, but I never meant like this! I never told you to be your own person by deserting your family."

"I'm not deserting anyone! I'm going to Mississippi to spend a few days with Andie and get to know her a little better. Why is it that you're only concerned with the family when it pertains to you?"

"Because I've finally come to realize that — like it or not — I'm still one of them and I don't want to see anybody get hurt."

"I'm not out to hurt anyone."

"You're making a mistake, Zoë."

"Maybe, but how will I know if I don't go?"

"All I know is you're making me really sorry I ever told you about Andrea LaRue."

"But you did, so it's too late to start spouting regrets, isn't it?"

"I never thought you would turn out to be such a rebel."

"I'm not being a rebel. I'm trying to get my life together. I wish everyone would just stay out of it and leave me alone, including you."

"Will you give me that phone!"

Zoë heard Leigh in the background and listened in amusement as she and Cameron tussled over the receiver. Apparently, Leigh won the battle because her voice was the next one Zoë heard.

"Killjoy," Leigh scoffed at Cameron, and then spoke pleasantly into the phone. "Don't pay any attention to him, Zoey-bear," she said loyally. "You know how he is. He tries to take the fun out of everything. Just go to Biloxi and have a good time. Everything will work itself out. Just do me one favor."

"For you, anything," Zoë giggled with relief.

"Promise me you won't forget about the good doctor while you're there. My, my, but he's a cute thing. Just to die for."

"I promise," Zoë said. "Thanks, Leigh."

"Any time, Zoey-Anne. I'm always on your side."

Zoë pulled in to Biloxi mid-afternoon and, after finding no one at Andie's house, made her way to Crème de la Crème. The reception area was empty, so she padded down the long corridor, finding her way to the kitchen. She stopped at the door, dismayed. *Great*, she thought. *Of all the people to welcome me to Biloxi, it would have to be her.*

Dana stood at the stove, stirring the contents of a large Dutch oven with a wooden spoon, her dark hair hanging in moist tendrils around her face. Zoë leaned in the doorway, watching her, enjoying the fact that she had not yet been discovered.

Sensing her presence, Dana looked up. Seeing Zoë standing there, her mouth dropped open in shock. "Good God!" she growled, rolling her eyes. "What are you doing here?"

"I could ask the same of you," Zoë replied matter-of-factly, taking a step into the room. "I thought you were in college."

"I was," Dana said, laying her spoon on the rest and wiping her hands on her apron. "I graduated, with honors I might add. Now I'm in business with Mom and Dell." She eyed Zoë warily. "What's your excuse?"

"I came to see Andie and stay until the baby comes."

"Oh great! That could be weeks. Don't you have anything better to do?"

"Not really."

"Where are you staying?" Dana asked, her eyes narrowing. "Surely you don't think you're staying with us."

"You're living with Andie and Cole?"

"For the time being, until I get enough money in the bank to get my own place." Dana perched on the edge of the counter, swinging her legs, sneering smugly. "So, you see, there's really no room at the house for you."

"Well, I certainly didn't intend to barge in anyway," Zoë covered, unwilling to let Dana believe she had the upper hand. "I thought I'd just stay at a hotel."

"But of course," Dana's voice dripped with sarcasm. "A luxury one, no doubt. Our quaint little abode isn't near good enough for you, is it Your Highness?"

"I thought you said there wasn't room for me."

"Well, even if there was, you wouldn't stay there. You're way too important for such ordinary accommodations."

Zoë exhaled in aggravation, running a weary hand through her hair. "I can't do anything that pleases you, can I?"

"Sure you can," Dana laughed, an evil gleam in her eye. "Try going home."

"Zoë!" Andie waddled into the kitchen, her pregnancy well into its last stages. She held her arms out, giving Zoë a big hug. "What a nice, nice surprise! Why didn't you tell us you were coming?"

"Yeah, warning us would've been good," Dana piped up, surveying their embrace jealously. "That way, we could've evacuated."

"Dana," Andie shot her a warning. She turned back to Zoë, her smile warm and welcoming. "What would you like for dinner? You are hungry, aren't you?"

"Famished."

"Good! Let's go on to the house and get dinner started while Dana finishes up here."

Zoë glanced at her watch. "I thought I'd drop my stuff at my hotel first, then come by."

"Hotel!" Andie objected. "I won't hear of it. No daughter of mine is staying in a hotel when we've got more than enough room at the house."

"Well," Zoë began sheepishly, not really wanting to be a tattletale. *But on second thought,* she decided wickedly, *it might be fun to get Dana in trouble.* "Dana tells me that she's staying with you right now."

"So?" Andie pivoted, giving Dana a harsh look. "That doesn't mean anything. We still have room for you. In fact, you can bunk with Dana. That'll give you two a chance to get to know one another."

"Oh good!" Dana bellowed loudly, leaping from the counter and stomping toward the door. She left the kitchen, looking back to give Zoë and Andie one last glare, then marched down the hall, slamming out the front door with a bang.

Zoë glanced at Andie uncertainly. "She'll get over it," Andie assured her with a smirk, laughing softly. *When opportunity comes knocking,* she thought devilishly. Whatever she had just done by throwing them into a room together, they both definitely deserved it.

After dinner, Cole enlisted Dana to help with the dishes, Andie went to bed and Zoë took a hot bath, letting a long soak in the tub ease her road-weary muscles. She eased out of the bathtub, patted dry with a soft towel, then donned her favorite rose-covered pajamas.

Feeling refreshed, she glided out of the bathroom, a happy tune on her lips, halting in her tracks when she discovered Dana sitting on the end of the bed, Zoë's overnight case in her hand, appearing deceptively angelic in white baby doll pajamas.

"If you're going to stay in here," she said menacingly, looking up and flashing Zoë a sarcastic smile, "you're gonna have to learn to keep your shit on your side of the room." With one easy motion, she tossed Zoë's case across the room, aiming for the daybed beneath the window. Missing the bed by a foot, it crashed soundly into the wall, falling open, spilling its contents all over the floor. She smiled, satisfied with her work, then picked up a bottle of red fingernail polish and nonchalantly began to polish her toenails.

Zoë furrowed her brow, biting her tongue, determined not to lose her temper. Ignoring Dana's infuriating smirk, she crossed the room, kneeling to gather her scattered cosmetics. "I've never seen such a conniving, spoiled-rotten brat in my whole life," she grumbled quietly, using her hands to rake compacts and eye pencils across the floor.

"What's that?" Dana stopped polishing, lifting her laughing eyes to survey Zoë. "I'm sorry. Were you talking to me? I can't understand you when you mumble like that."

Zoë sat back on her heels. "What is your problem?" she demanded.

Dana lifted a hand to her chest, answering in a mocking tone, "Problem? I don't know what you mean. No one else seems to think I have a problem. Maybe the problem is yours."

"Why don't you grow up?"

Dana smirked, lifting the polish bottle, moving the brush up and down repeatedly. "Look, Zoanne. If you don't like the way I'm acting, you can get out. This is my room."

"Oh, then this must belong to you!" Zoë reached behind her, flinging a large down pillow high into the air.

It landed on the other side of the room and hit Dana squarely in the face, startling her and knocking the nail polish from her hand. Before she could stop it, the gooey liquid spilled down the front of her pajamas, staining them crimson, giving her the appearance of a badly injured accident victim.

Zoë froze, wincing at the damage. Seeing her shocked expression, Dana looked down at her pajamas then back at Zoë, her eyes and mouth forming identical O's. "Now look what you've done!" she yelled, her voice high and hysterical, then let out a guttural scream. "What is wrong with you, throwing a pillow like that! These are my favorite pajamas."

"Not anymore." Zoë burst into sidesplitting laughter, finding the look on Dana's face hilarious. She rolled on the floor, clutching her side, giggling until she couldn't catch her breath.

"I'm gonna get you for this!" Dana threw down the empty polish bottle and leapt from the bed, landing on top of Zoë, punching her arms and pulling her hair.

"Hey! That hurts!" Zoë screamed, fighting back, kicking Dana in the shin.

"It's supposed to, idiot!" Dana rolled her eyes, shoving Zoë with all her might and sending her skidding across the hardwood floor. She didn't give her a chance to recover. She rolled until she was beside her, reaching out to scratch her face. They tussled on the floor, screaming, yelling profanities and calling each other deplorable names.

"Hey!" Suddenly Cole was beside them, pulling them apart, lifting Dana off the floor, her legs kicking frantically in the air. "What the hell is going on here?"

"She started it!" Dana panted, pointing her finger at Zoë.

Zoë sat up, leaning against her palms as she labored to catch her breath. "No I didn't," she said, shaking her head. "You did, when you threw my stuff all over the room."

"Na ah!" Dana glared at her.

"I don't care who started it," Cole broke in, looking in disbelief from Dana to Zoë. "This has got to stop. You're supposed to be grown women."

"Well, one of us is," Zoë said. Dana narrowed her eyes, sticking out her tongue.

"I can't believe I'm having to do this!" Cole exclaimed. "I did not sign up to referee."

"I hate to interrupt the fun," Andie stood in the middle of the room, her face white, clutching her abdomen and grimacing with discomfort. "But I wondered if I could get a lift to the hospital?"

Cole blinked in astonishment. "Is it time?" he asked in a nervous voice.

"Oh man," Dana moaned, shooting him a perturbed look. "Couldn't you have come up with a more original line?"

Andie didn't seem to notice. She nodded solemnly, her face grim with pain. "I think so," she said anxiously.

Cole dropped Dana and grabbed Andie by the arm, pulling her out of the room toward the front entry.

Dana jumped up, her eyes wide as she collided with Zoë, each of them scrambling for their clothes. Zoë donned a white T-shirt and jeans, while Dana threw an old sweatshirt and ragged shorts over her soiled pajamas. She seized Zoë's hand, yanking her out of the bedroom. "Let's go!"

Forgetting their brawl, they squealed together in excitement, running frantically from the house, diving into the back seat of Cole's vehicle as he backed out of the driveway.

Andie was in labor for what seemed like an eternity. Cole stayed at her side, feeding her ice chips and counting contractions, his face animated by excitement and elated wonder.

Dell ran in and out of the room, chattering on her cell phone, spreading the news to close friends and clients. "Bill will be here in the morning," she told Andie as she rested between contractions. "He wanted to come up tonight, but I wouldn't let him. The last thing you need is him around holding your hand and giving you pep talks."

"Thanks, Dell," Andie smiled briefly before being overtaken by another sharp pain. She winced and squeezed her eyes shut tightly as she gripped Cole's hand.

Dell eyed her watch, counting the seconds and yelling out encouragement. "C'mon, Andie. You can do it. This one's almost over."

Andie fell back against the pillows, panting and catching her breath. "Dell, I'll be so glad when you get to do this," she snapped irritably.

Dell blushed and looked down at the floor. "Don't hold your breath," she said lightly, stubbing the tile with her sandal. "It'll probably be a while."

Andie chuckled softly, giving her a knowing smirk. "Don't think I don't know exactly what's been going on. I might've been pregnant, but I am not stupid."

"I have no idea what you're talking about," Dell stammered, dashing to the door. "I think I'll go check on the girls." She hurried out, leaving Cole and Andie grinning after her, glancing at one another and exchanging an amused look.

The relative silence of the hospital was shattered by the midnight arrival of Tammy. She skidded into the room, appearing frazzled with her sable curls disheveled and a tattered Army duffel bag slung over her shoulder.

"I know, I know," she said as she noted the look on Cole's face. "I came as soon as you called, but it's not as easy to get here sometimes as you think. I left Pine Prairie like a bat out of hell, and somehow managed to catch the last flight out of Dallas. But there's practically nothing flying into Gulfport after dark! I had to fly in to New Orleans, then rent a car." She threw herself into a chair, glancing at them expectantly. "Did I miss anything?"

"Just a few contractions and a little breaking of the water," Andie answered, trying to remain pleasant as she faced another round of excruciating agony.

"Well, good." Tammy eased out of the chair and approached, wearing a jaunty grin. "If you're going to be stupid enough to have a baby at this stage in life, I damn sure wanted to be here." She sat on the edge of Andie's bed and looked around curiously. "Where's the rest of your fan club?"

"Dell ran down to the cafeteria, and Dana and Zoë are in the lobby."

Tammy's eyes grew round. "Zoë?" she asked incredulously. "Your Zoë?"

"How many Zoës do you know?" Andie asked teasingly.

Tammy flew across the room, flinging open the door, and looked down the hall to the waiting room. She spied dark-haired Dana and grinned. "Dana's looking good," she remarked over her shoulder. "It's hard to believe she's officially grown-up."

"That's debatable," Cole said with a gruff chuckle. "Although she has been known to display a mature moment every now and then."

Tammy stuck her head back into the corridor and squinted, spotting a slender blonde lounging in the chair next to Dana. "Oh my God," she gasped. "That's got to be her."

Cole moved next to her, peeking out the door. "Yep, that's her," he confirmed proudly.

"Oh Cole," Tammy said, taking his hands. She kissed his cheek, beaming at him with delight. "She's gorgeous. You and Andie must be thrilled."

"It's pretty wonderful."

"What does she think about gaining a second set of parents?"

"She and Andie have a great relationship, but she doesn't know about me yet."

"What!" Tammy shrieked, staring indignantly. "You haven't told Zoë that you're her father? Why not? Are you crazy?"

"When we first met, it didn't seem appropriate."

"What about now?"

"I'm going to tell her, Tammy," Cole said, becoming annoyed. "The time just hasn't been right."

"What are you waiting for? Hell to freeze?"

"I'll tell her when I think she's ready," he replied firmly. "I don't want to scare her off."

"From you?" Tammy offered him a dubious frown. "You've got to be kidding. I'd love to be told I had a father like you. It'd be like hearing your father was Harrison Ford or Mel Gibson."

"More like Elmer Fudd," Cole laughed.

"Arrgghh!" Andie screamed out in agony, lifting her head to glare at them. "Damn it, Cole! Are you here for me, or are you here for her?" she demanded scathingly, her features distorted by pain.

"Touchy, touchy," Tammy said, closing the door to join Cole at her side. "I bet you're really making Cole glad he missed this the first time around."

"Tammy, sit down and shut up, or I'm replacing you with Dell," Andie snapped, slapping her on the arm.

Tammy laughed, rubbing her arm as she plopped on the fold-out sofa next to the bed. "Okay, you've convinced me. I'm staying celibate," she announced. "I damn sure never want to go through anything like this."

"That's it! Get out," Andie said, collapsing exhaustedly against the mattress. "I cannot do this and put up with you."

"Okay, fine," Tammy said agreeably, sauntering toward the door. "I'll just go down to the waiting room — with the girls."

"Tammy. Keep your mouth shut," Cole warned.

Tammy tossed him an entertained grin. "Don't worry," she taunted as she left the room. "Far be it from me to spill the beans. It's certainly not my place to tell."

"So you say," Cole replied doubtfully. "Just be sure you keep that in mind."


Throughout the long evening, Zoë and Dana took turns visiting Andie's bedside, then ended up together in the waiting room, sipping coffee from paper cups as they lounged in uncomfortable orange vinyl chairs. Dell lounged nearby on an equally hard sofa, resting with her eyes closed and cell phone in her lap.

"Where'd you get that ring?" Dana asked, eyeing the pear-shaped diamond on Zoë's finger.

Zoë jumped in surprise, then remembered, looking down at the ring. "Oh, from a guy," she said, shrugging nonchalantly.

Dana lifted a skeptical brow. "From a guy?" she repeated mockingly. "That's one helluva way to refer to your fiancé."

"Well," Zoë hedged, scratching her head, "he's not actually my fiancé."

"What do you mean? You got a ring, don't you?"

"It's not official. I'm still thinking about it."

"What's to think about? Don't you love him?"

"I think so, but I'm not sure. Sean's a great guy, and I really care about him…"

"Wait! What's he do?"

"He's a doctor."

"Okay, that answers the social position question. So, what's the hold up? A doctor is pretty impressive. What's the matter? Doesn't he have enough money to live up to your standards?"

"Will you cut that out?" Zoë jerked her head around, her eyes ablaze with anger. "I've spent most of my life fighting that stereotype. Just because my family's wealthy doesn't mean all I care about is money."

"I should have such problems."

Zoë closed her eyes, sighing and shaking her head in frustration. *Why on earth did I think she'd possibly understand?* she mused. *I'll never be able to make her get it. This discussion is getting me nowhere.*

Wisely ignoring Dana's sarcasm, she opened her eyes, using another ploy, hoping for an intelligent conversation with her half-sister. "What about you? Do you have a man in your life?"

Dana beamed, flushing bright pink. "Well, as a matter of fact, I do," she said. "And he's a babe — probably ten times better looking than that doctor of yours."

"Well, tell me about him."

"His name is Greg and he's a chef, a *gourmet* chef at one of the casinos."

"Really? Then you have something in common — you're both great cooks."

Dana's expression softened and she offered Zoë a shy smile. "You think I'm a good cook?" she asked, almost timidly.

"Of course I do!" Zoë replied enthusiastically, reaching over to deposit her empty cup in the trash receptacle. "And that makes you one up on me. I've yet to master toast."

Dana laughed, accepting her compliment with an easy grin. She glanced down the hall toward Andie's room, spotting a familiar figure with sable curls strolling down the corridor. "Aunt Tammy!" she cried out happily, rushing to meet her as she entered the waiting area. "When did you sneak in?"

"I've been here about an hour," Tammy said, accepting Dana's fond embrace. "How are ya, kid?"

"Great!" Dana said, leading her by the arm to meet Zoë. "Zoë, this is Aunt Tammy," she said.

"Aunt Tammy?" Zoë asked, wrinkling her brow in confusion. "I thought Andie only had a brother. Or is this your father's sister?"

"Neither," Tammy said, taking the seat next to Zoë as she extended her hand. "I'm Honorary Aunt Tammy, loyal family friend. I grew up in Texas with your mom and da — Cole." Tammy recovered nicely from her slip, flushing slightly. *Jeez, Cole. I'm sorry!* she thought. *I promised you I'd keep my mouth shut, and I almost spilled the beans on introduction. What a ditz!* She lifted her paper cup, sipping Coca-Cola pensively.

"How's Mom?" Dana asked, leaning casually against the wall.

"Grouchy," Tammy replied, her eyes sparkling devilishly. "She kicked me out a long time ago."

Suddenly, Cole skidded into the waiting room, adorned in green scrubs and shoe covers, his head covered with what looked like a shower cap. "Hey, girls!" he said, standing before them, bouncing on his toes with excitement. "Come meet your new baby brother!" He did an abrupt about-face and sprinted from the room, beckoning them to follow.

Side by side, they entered Andie's room with Tammy and Dell close behind, clutching arms with building anticipation. They tiptoed to Andie's bedside, taking in her tired yet elated face, then peered over the top of the blanket, getting their first glimpse of the infant she held tightly in her arms.

"Oh!" Dana clasped her hands and clutched them to her chest, happy tears flooding her eyes. "He's so pretty."

"Let me see," Zoë said gently and moved her aside, leaning forward to get a look.

"Better yet, both of you move and let me get a look," Tammy said, attempting to elbow her way in.

Andie smiled serenely, ignoring Tammy, thrilled to see her two girls together. "Would you like to hold him?" she asked, looking first to Dana.

Dana recoiled, horrified at the idea. "Oh, no!" she gasped, staring down at the tiny baby. "He's too little. What if I dropped him?"

Andie laughed. "You won't drop him. Here, take him."

Dana adamantly shook her head, stepping back and gesturing to Zoë. "Let her hold him."

Andie handed the baby to Zoë, watching as she skillfully cradled him in the crook of her arm and padded gracefully to the rocker in the corner. Dana trailed her, mesmerized, her huge eyes following her every move. Zoë sat in the chair, moving back and forth with Dana hanging over her shoulder, cooing and giving the baby her pinkie to hold.

"What are you going to name him?" Zoë addressed the proud parents, tearing her gaze momentarily away from the beautiful baby boy.

"We're going to call him Jake, after Andie's father." Cole answered, his chest swelling with pride as he studied the pair in the rocker. For so long, he was childless. Now he had two — actually four, counting Dana and Jerry. He was beside himself with joy. *If only I could tell Zoë,* he thought wistfully. *Then everything would perfect.*

The nurse came in, bearing a bouquet of flowers. "Here," Tammy jumped off the bed, taking the vase from her. "Let me take those." She placed them on a table by the window and removed the card, laughing aloud as she read it. "Hey! What do ya know?" she said. "David sent flowers. Only goes to show you that wonders never cease."

The nurse remained at Andie's side to take her vital signs, distracting everyone from the trio in the corner. Tired of standing, Dana pulled up a footstool, sitting at Zoë's feet, studying her face as she played with Jake.

"He's just gorgeous, isn't he?" Zoë gushed, looking over at Dana as she leaned down to kiss the baby's forehead.

"He's not too bad," Dana shrugged. "For a boy."

"Not too bad?" Zoë teased. "Don't be silly. He's just perfect." She cuddled Jake tightly, an adoring smile on her face.

Dana watched her thoughtfully, impressed by such an unconditional display of love. *Maybe she's not so bad, after all,* she decided, allowing herself a slight smile. Witnessing the way Zoë was with Jake, Dana's heart swelled, melting what remained of the icy barrier she had thrown up against her sister. She relaxed, reaching out to touch Zoë's hand. Feeling Dana's touch, Zoë glanced up, meeting her gaze cautiously.

"You know, I've always wanted a sister," Dana admitted, then bit her lip and looked away.

"Me too," Zoë said. "And now I have one." She squeezed Dana's hand tightly and Dana glanced back at her with a grin.

"Pretty cool, ain't it?" she said, her eyes locking with Zoë's.

"Yeah," Zoë nodded, returning Dana's smile. "It's pretty cool."

Cole interrupted their ceasefire, urging Dana to accompany him to the cafeteria. "Having this baby has left me starving!" he declared.

"Yes, Cole, by all means," Tammy spoke up cheerfully. "You've worked so hard. Please go get something to eat so you can regain your strength."

Jake began to fuss as soon as Dana and Cole left the room. Zoë pushed out of the rocker and returned him to Andie, hanging out beside the bed as she fed him.

Sensing that they might need a moment alone, Tammy got to her feet, yanking Dell off the sofa with her. "We're going down to the nursery," she announced, pulling an objecting Dell toward the door. "We're going to see the other babies — you know, size up Jake's competition."

When they were gone, Zoë studied Andie's blissful expression and the adoring glow in her eyes as she looked down into Jake's face, feeling the need to pose one of her remaining questions.

"How did you feel when I was born?" she asked timidly, taking a seat on the edge of Andie's bed.

Andie gazed up at her, her eyes swimming in sentimental tears. "I thought you were the most beautiful baby I had ever seen," she said, her voice quivering with emotion. "I held you in my arms and fell deeply in love, vowing to never let you go."

She sighed heavily and took Zoë's hand, bittersweet tears cascading down her cheeks. "But then they came and took you — before I even had the strength to fight them. By the time I was released from the hospital, it was too late. You were with your adoptive family. I wanted to appeal the adoption, to get you back and raise you myself, but my brother David talked me out of it."

Zoë's eyes misted over, her heart aching for Andie's loss. "I'm so sorry," she said quietly.

"Oh sweetie, don't be sorry," Andie said, wiping her eyes with the sleeve of her gown. "It all turned out for the best. You had a family who loved you like no other could. Look at you — Jay and Diane Forest nurtured you into an amazing young woman. I couldn't have done better myself. I'm proud of you, Zoë, and I'm so glad that we have this kind of relationship. It's helped to make my life complete."

Cole and Dana slipped in from the cafeteria, bearing a plastic tray in each hand, followed closely by Tammy and Dell. "Look!" Cole sang out. "Nutrition for everybody."

He settled in the chair next to Andie's bed and handed Zoë her plate. "Here girl," he said. "Take, eat."

"No," Zoë sat the plate in front of Andie, smiling as she traded it for the baby. "Let Andie eat. She needs it worse than I do. I'll just play with Jake."

Mealtime was interrupted by the thud of the door, slamming against wall as it was pushed hurriedly open. "Well, well, well! Look who's had a baby!" Bill Fairgate's brassy voice filled the room. He laughed heartily and strode to Andie, bending down to kiss her cheek. "Look at you, Mommy," he praised. "All propped up eating, like it was nothing at all."

"Hello Bill," Andie said, her face aglow as his lips brushed her cheek.

"Hello, Cupcake," he smiled, taking both her hands. "Congratulations."

"Thank you," she said softly, peeking up at him from beneath her thick lashes.

Watching them, Dana shook her head, elbowing Zoë sharply in the ribs. "Would you look at that," she whispered. "He's making a move on her in her hospital bed. I still say there was something going on with those two."

Zoë was completely baffled by the presence of the boisterous man. "Who is he?" she asked curiously.

Before Dana could reply, Bill whirled around, scanning the room for signs of the newborn, zeroing in on the rocking chair and the swaddling blanket of pale blue.

"Ah! There's the youngster. Let me just get a look at him." He sauntered over, swooping the baby out of Zoë's arms, and held him tightly against his broad chest, peering down at his tiny face.

"What a great-looking kid!" he exclaimed, grinning at Andie. "And I do believe he looks like you, Dewberry." He acknowledged Cole with a friendly nod and gave him a genuine smile, finally offering his blessing.

"Here you go, darlin'," Bill handed the baby to Dana, plopping him into her arms, ignoring the protesting look on her face. "Now, Andie, I want you to hurry back to work, you hear?"

"Can I take a couple of days off to recuperate?" Andie asked jokingly.

"I guess you can have a couple," he replied generously. "But not much more. I need you to oversee my Memorial Day fish fry. Not that I don't love Dell and Dana here, but only you can add that extra special touch." He came forward and touched Andie's face, his undying affection revealed in his expansive smile. "Gotta go," he said abruptly. "I've got to get Dell home to bed."

"Whose bed?" Andie asked tongue-in-cheek, batting her eyelashes playfully.

"An-die!" Dell squealed, her face turning bright red as she slid down the chair cushion in embarrassment.

Bill recovered from the surprise of Andie's insinuation, his mouth breaking into a huge smile. "Why, mine of course, if she would let me," he drawled, glancing fondly at Dell. "I've never dated a woman with morals before."

"Ah ha!" Andie pointed an excited finger at them. "So, you are dating."

"Yeah, we're dating. For the last six months, as a matter of fact," Bill said proudly. "Why else would I have been so deficit in striptease barbecues and girls jumping out of cakes?"

"That should have been my first clue," Andie conceded with a giggle. She turned to Dell, her dancing eyes conveying congratulations.

Bill turned to leave, collecting Dell from her seat. "Come on, Baby Doll," he said tenderly, taking her by the elbow. "You look exhausted."

He strolled with her toward the door, then suddenly noticed Zoë sitting in the corner and stopped dead in his tracks. He studied her face, cocking his head to one side, raising an intrigued eyebrow as he approached her.

"Zoanne Carson-Forest, as I live and breathe," he declared, extending his hand for a firm handshake. He took in the uncanny resemblance and shot Andie a delighted smile.

Zoë appeared perplexed, scrutinizing his strong features in bewilderment. "Yes, that's me — but how did you know? Have we met?"

"Not hardly, honey," Bill chuckled robustly and threw a friendly arm around her shoulder. "But I'd know you anywhere, sweetheart. I probably know more about you than you know yourself." He pulled her from the chair and moved with her to the door, intent on leading her to a spot where they could speak in private.

"Where are we going?" Zoë asked. "I thought you had to get Dell home to bed."

"Oh honey, I can wait," Dell interjected cheerfully. "Visit with Bill. That's more important. Besides, it'll give me a few more minutes to play with Jake."

Bill guided Zoë out into the corridor, holding her attention with his engaging smile. "See, darlin', my name's Bill Fairgate," he said charmingly, "and Andie and I go back a long way. I also knew your grandfather Palmer and your Uncle Geoff, and let me tell you one thing: You, Jelly Bean, are exceptional — just like your mother."

His voice trailed off as they traveled down the hall, Zoë listening in fascination and Bill grinning ear to ear, pleased to finally meet the girl he was responsible for finding. *Yep,* he decided as he glanced over at her, *finding her for Andie was definitely worth it all.*

Tammy and Cole stayed at the hospital but sent the girls home in the car, shooing them from the room in the wee hours of the morning. They arrived at the cottage just as the sun was coming up and stumbled into the house in an exhausted stupor.

Zoë made her way to the daybed in Dana's room and turned back the comforter in a zombie-like daze, pausing when she heard Dana's voice.

"Hey, Zoë. Take the real bed."

"Are you sure?" Zoë asked suspiciously.

Dana grinned. "Sure, I'm sure. I'll sleep in Mom's bed."

Zoë fell across the bed and crashed, not moving a muscle until she heard the vague ringing of the telephone. She sat up, rubbing her eyes sleepily as Dana stuck her head in the door.

"Hey Zoë," she said. "It's the doctor."

"Andie's doctor?" Zoë asked groggily.

"No, dummy. Your doctor," Dana laughed. "Says his name's Sean Murphy, and he's got a real sexy voice. Man, if you don't want him, I'll take him, sight unseen. Anybody with a voice like that can talk dirty to me any time."

Zoë rolled out of bed and stumbled to the phone, stubbing her toe on Dana's discarded loafers. "Ouch!" she moaned and then lifted the receiver from where Dana had let it drop to the floor.

"Sean?" she asked tentatively.

"Hello Zoë." His warm voice caressed her ear, making her smile.

"Hi, Sean. How did you find me?"

He laughed pleasantly. "Never let it be said that I'm not resourceful."

"How are things at the clinic?"

"Manageable."

"How are my folks?"

"Your father pops in daily for lunch. He seems to be doing okay. Your mother, on the other hand, has been better. But, she's okay too."

"How are you?"

"Lonely." His solemn answer melted Zoë's heart. "So," he covered, changing the subject, "are you finding your place in the world out there?"

"I think so," Zoë said. "It's weird and hard to explain, but I feel like I belong. I miss you though, and my parents too."

"We miss you too. When are you coming home?"

"I don't know," Zoë answered uncomfortably, wishing she could give him a better answer. "Why? Do you want the ring back?" she teased.

"Are you saying no?"

"No."

"Then no, I don't want it back. Keep the ring. I can wait."

"Until you find an acceptable replacement?"

"At least that long. Finding a replacement for you could take a lifetime."

Zoë held onto the receiver long after they hung up, homesickness gnawing at her insides. *I can't go yet,* she told herself stubbornly. *I still don't know all I want to know.*

She replaced the receiver and wandered into the living room, looking for Dana. She spotted her bouncing around the kitchen, her pretty face unusually cheerful. "What are you doing?" Zoë asked, peeking into the room.

"Making coffee," Dana replied, flashing a humorous grin at Zoë's sleepy face. "You drink that stuff, don't you?"

"Religiously."

"Well, go sit down. I'll bring you some when it's done." The happy lilt in her voice took Zoë by surprise.

"I'd never figure you for a morning person," she remarked as she retreated to the living room and flopped wearily on the sofa, yawning and closing her eyes.

Dana stuck her head out of the kitchen, observing Zoë stretched out for a catnap. "There are a lot of things about me that might surprise you," she said.

The doorbell sounded, and Zoë lifted a heavy eyelid. "You want me to get that?" she asked.

"I've got it!" Dana flew by her in a flash, flinging open the front door. "Jerry!"

Zoë sat up, peeking around Dana to view the tall man standing in the doorway. He was stocky and handsome with dark hair and dark eyes, showing a white-toothed grin as he bent down to kiss Dana's cheek.

"Hey Sis," he said, his deep voice drifting pleasantly into the room.

"Hey Jer," Dana replied, stepping aside to let him to pass. "When did you get here?"

Jerry stopped in the foyer, dropping the heavy backpack he carried by the door. "Early this morning," he said. "I hopped on the first plane out of Nashville as soon as you called."

"It's about time you learned to come when I call," Dana kidded, giving his shoulder a light punch. "How long are you staying?"

"Just until tomorrow afternoon. I have to get back to school."

"Have you been by the hospital?"

"But of course," he grinned. "I had to see the new bambino — although I had to fight Aunt Tammy to get a peek at him. Jeez, that woman's abrasive."

"What'd you think?"

"He's a cute little bruiser. I'm just glad he's a boy," Jerry said, reaching out to pinch her cheek. "I need another male on my side."

"You guys still don't stand a chance. I can take both of you with one hand tied behind my back."

"I don't doubt that," Jerry laughed, holding Dana's hand as they strolled together into the living room.

"Although, there's really no need for that anymore. I have a helper." Dana acknowledged Zoë with a nod.

Jerry glanced over in surprise. "Hey, I'm Jerry," he said, coming forward with an outstretched hand.

"I'm Zoë." She flashed a congenial smile and shook his hand firmly.

Jerry wrinkled his brow questioningly, glancing back at Dana. "Shannon," Dana affirmed hastily, sliding in next to Zoë on the sofa.

"Oh," Jerry plopped into a chair, appraising Zoë with enlightened eyes. "I should've known. You look just like her."

"So I've been told," Zoë responded with a soft giggle. "Where do you go to school?"

"Vanderbilt," he said. "I'm finishing up pre-med."

"Then on to medical school?"

Jerry nodded optimistically. "Hopefully," he said.

"Zoë dates a doctor," Dana said, "and a darn sexy sounding one at that."

"Is that right?" Jerry asked interestedly. "What kind?"

"His specialty is family practice," Zoë said. "Although right now, he's kind of a jack of all trades."

"You know what? I'm starving," Dana announced, slapping her bare legs and jumping from her seat. "What do you say I whip us up some breakfast? Maybe a little French toast and scrambled eggs?"

"Sounds like a deal to me," Jerry agreed enthusiastically. "All I've had today so far was honey-roasted peanuts and a microscopic package of stale pretzels on the plane."

Dana went into the kitchen and began rattling pots and pans, humming to herself as she made breakfast. Jerry glanced at Zoë expectantly. "So, are you here for a visit?"

Zoë nodded. "Yeah," she said. "I thought I hang out for a while and get to know the family better."

"How do you like Mom and Cole?"

"They're great."

"And Dana?"

Zoë glanced over her shoulder into the kitchen. "Dana's getting better," she admitted with a chuckle.

Jerry laughed. "Funny," he said. "She's said the very same thing about you."

"I'm not at all surprised."

"How long do you plan on staying?"

"A few weeks. Long enough for a nice visit and a few trips to the beach. I'd also like to find out some things about my background."

"From Mom?"

"Preferably."

"Good luck," Jerry sighed, giving Zoë a sympathetic look. "If you can get anything really deep out of Mom, you're a better man than I am. A better bet might be Aunt Tammy. She'd tell you everything you want to know."

Andie and Jake came home the next morning, chauffeured by an extremely proud Cole. Jerry glided down the front steps, meeting the car in the drive. He opened Andie's door and helped her out, escorting her toward the house, immediately engaging her in happy small talk.

Cole retrieved the baby from his car seat, cradling him tightly in his arms like an old pro. Tammy, Zoë and Dana watched from the front porch, wearing identical grins. "He's a terrific father," Zoë observed, her gaze locked on Cole and the baby. "It's amazing that Jake is his first child."

"Yeah," Dana agreed, carefully concealing her guilty expression. *If you only knew,* she thought, turning her head so Zoë couldn't see the uncomfortable flicker in her eyes.

Tammy dropped her gaze, frowning in aggravation. It wasn't right that Andie and Cole continued to hide Zoë's paternity. It wasn't fair to Zoë. *If one of them doesn't hurry up and tell her,* she thought crossly, *I'm going to tell her myself.*

stifling a gasp, her eyes widening incredulously. "I thought you were going straight to the office," she sputtered.

Jay glanced over, spying her on the stairs. "I was," he replied cheerfully, "but I had to come back by for a file." He took another step and spotted her bags, eyeing them curiously. "Going somewhere?"

Diane looked up at him, blinking innocently. "Why, yes," she said, smiling like a saint. "I decided to take a little trip to the beach."

"Is this kind of sudden, or did I miss something?"

"Pretty spur of the moment, actually. I decided in the shower. I was going to call you when I got there."

"Okay, Diane. Which is it — mid-life or menopause?"

"I beg your pardon?"

"Well, first you cut off all your hair, and now you're running off on your own, taking cross country trips without warning. Either it's an aging crisis or this thing with Zoë has sent you into quite a tizzy. "

Diane ran a nervous hand through her newly shorn locks, praying the hot flush of her face wasn't giving her away. "It's not cross country, darling — it's just Florida."

She moved forward, sliding her arms around his neck. "I just decided to get away for a few days, take some time to get over my anger and anxiety." She batted her eyelashes, horrified that she could lie so smoothly to the man she loved. *But these aren't ordinary circumstances,* she reasoned. *This is about Zoë, and I'll do what I need to do to keep my family together — even if it means lying to Jay.*

He rested his forehead against hers. "You want me to come with you?"

Diane panicked. *What do I say now?* "No, that's okay, honey," she said sweetly, fingering his lapel. "I'll be just fine at the condo."

"Can I at least drive you out to the plane?"

On cue, Geoff pulled up, laying on the horn. "I thought you would be in court," she said, kissing Jay's cheek as she pulled away to grab her bags. "I already asked Geoff to take me."

"See! I knew it," Jay exclaimed, kidding her as he took the suitcase from her hand. "Going somewhere voluntarily with Geoff? It is mid-life if you're trying to make peace with your brother. That's all the proof I need."

He opened the front door and escorted her to the car, missing the stunned expression on Geoff's face. "Jay! I thought you were in court," he said, hurrying around to open the trunk.

Diane shot him a scorching look, warning him to shut up. Jay looked from his wife to his brother-in-law with a cynical smile. "The two of you are awfully concerned about my whereabouts this morning. If I didn't know better, I'd swear this was some sort of conspiracy."

"Diane and I work together on something? Hardly," Geoff scoffed, recovering nicely. "I just hate having to take time out of my busy day to shuttle my dear sister to the airport."

"I can still take her," Jay offered, pausing as he prepared to hoist Diane's bag into the car.

"No," Geoff scowled, taking the suitcase from Jay and giving it an emphatic shove into the trunk. "I'm here now. I might as well take her."

He sauntered back to the driver's door, giving Diane a relieved grimace. Diane turned to Jay, lifting her face for his farewell kiss. "Bye, sweetheart," she said. "I'll call you tonight."

Jay slid his arms around her waist, kissing her tenderly. "Take care, Sis," he whispered. "I'll sure miss you."

Diane glanced at him, smiling as they strolled arm in arm to the front of the car. "Sure you will," she teased, reaching up to tweak his cheek. "You'll be in hog heaven without me here nagging you."

"I doubt that," Jay said as he settled her into the passenger's seat. "I've never wished for a day without you in almost thirty years. I don't know why I'd start now." He kissed her again and closed the door, pounding the roof of the car with his palm.

With a brusque nod, Geoff gunned the engine, waving out the window as they sped away. "Whew!" he said, mopping his brow. "That was close."

"Tell me about it," Diane said, her stomach churning queasily.

"How did you manage to get out of the house without having to spill your guts?"

"I lied," she said, quickly noting his amazed expression. "Oh don't act so surprised," she snapped. "I do know how to lie. I've watched you and Palmer do it for years."

"So I guess that means you learned from the best, huh?"

"You don't have to sound so pleased. That's not really an exemplary attribute."

"I don't know about that. It really depends on the circumstances."

Diane sighed and stared out the window, focusing on the blooming azaleas lining their path to the main road. "I feel so guilty and deceitful," she said.

"You're not being deceitful, Diane. You're being resourceful."

Diane eyed him warily. "Can you always come up with a way to justify anything?"

"Usually," Geoff said with a grin. "It's a family trait."

"Do you really think I'm doing the right thing?"

"Of course I do. You're investigating the enemy, seeing what you're up against, staking your claim. I think it's marvelous." He looked at her with a frown. "You're not backing out on me, are you?"

"No," Diane said, squaring her shoulders. "I'm not backing out. Did you make all my arrangements?"

"I did. I've got you booked on a flight going into Gulfport, although I am sad to say all I could get you on is one of the god-awful prop planes. Are you sure you won't take the company jet?"

"Like my destination wouldn't get back to Jay? 'Oh, Mr. Forest — we just dropped your wife off in Mississippi'."

"Oh, I don't know. I think a few Ben Franklins might buy a little silence."

"Please, Geoff. I'm not paying off the pilot. I want the least amount of people involved in this as possible. I'll take the prop plane. What else have you got?"

"I booked a rental car."

"What kind?"

"A Lexus."

"You got me a Lexus?"

"Well, yes. Is something wrong with that?"

"I'm supposed to be inconspicuous."

"Look, Diane," he said, dismissing her annoyed glare. "It's bad enough that you're flying commercial. I guess you wanted me to put you in an economy car too?"

"Never mind," Diane sighed. "I'll deal with it when I get there. Where am I staying?"

"Beau Rivage."

"Under what name?"

"Lois LeJeune," he laughed, seeing her amazed smile. "I'm not stupid, Diane. I know better than to reserve the room in your real name."

"Anything else?"

"Yes. Most importantly, I have a file on Ms. Andrea LaRue Dewberry." He reached behind the seat, placing a manila envelope in her lap. She fingered the edges, dying to open it, but held off, wanting to view it in privacy.

They arrived at the airport just in time for Diane to check her bags and board the plane. "Thanks, Geoff," she said, giving him a quick hug before going through the security check.

"You're welcome." Geoff sent her off with an embrace, feeling unusually close to her for the first time in years. "Good luck, little sister."

He watched her walk out the sliding glass doors and board the plane, admiring her stunning beauty and determined gait. "A true Carson if there ever was one," he murmured proudly.

Diane landed in Gulfport just after noon, welcomed by a pleasant ocean breeze blowing through her hair as she stepped off the plane. She collected her luggage from baggage claim and retrieved her rental car, trading in the Lexus for something more modest. She drove down Highway 90 into Biloxi, taking in, but not truly seeing the coastal scenery. Her nervousness effectively blocked her view.

She checked in to her room at Beau Rivage and removed the file on Andrea LaRue Dewberry from her carry-on bag. She spread it out on the coffee table and reviewed its contents meticulously, studying the names and addresses as if memorizing them for an exam. "Okay," she said finally, sitting up to stretch her stiff neck muscles. "I know where she lives, what she does and where she works. All I have to do now is observe."

She watched them for two days, first finding them on the beach across the street from Andie's seaside cottage. She viewed Andie resentfully, staring in bitter astonishment the first time she got a good look at her. "There's no doubt about it," she muttered, gawking at the tall blond. "She's definitely Zoë's mother."

She followed them as closely as she could, staring out the car window, taking in their laughter as they shopped, dined and walked along the beach, her heart stabbed repeatedly by jealous rage.

*They look so happy together*, she thought sadly as she watched the identical fair-haired beauties sharing a playful chat over a picnic lunch on the boardwalk. *As if they are genetically destined to get along perfectly*. She pounded her hand on the steering wheel. "It's just not fair," she choked angrily. "There's simply no way to compete with that."

The morning of the third day, she donned her straw hat and dark sunglasses, looking extremely glamorous — more like a Hollywood starlet than an undercover mom from southeast Georgia. She strolled through the lobby of Beau Rivage, receiving admiring stares, and took the elevator to the parking garage to retrieve her rental car.

She drove past the cottage, arriving just as the little red Mustang was pulling out. Keeping a safe distance, she followed them to the pier and parked on the far side of the lot, peering through her binoculars as Zoë and the dark-haired girl boarded a sailboat.

"Well, isn't this just pathetic?"

Diane gulped, her arms blossoming with tiny goosebumps at the sound of the voice. She trembled, her skin growing cold and clammy. *It can't be,* she thought hysterically. She slowly turned her head, her mind reeling, almost in a dreamlike state. Sure enough, it was Lois, sitting next to her in the passenger's seat, her brow arched in disapproval.

"Oh, good lord!" Diane exclaimed, clutching her chest in relief. "Mother! You scared me. What are you doing here? Why aren't you somewhere resting in peace?"

"Resting in peace?" Lois scoffed, glaring at Diane. "Now there's a novel concept. I'm never going to get to rest in peace, Diane. I am destined to roam the earth forever, all because you people need a constant chaperone."

"I see you're still as dramatic as ever."

"Well, miss. Dramatic though I am, I have put up with your bad-mouthing, saying that I deserted you in your time of need and all that other boloney, but this Dick Tracy business is the very last straw. What the hell do you think you're doing?" Lois demanded, indicating Diane's get-up with an indignant wave. "Have you lost your mind?"

"What does it look like I'm doing, Mother? I'm protecting my interests."

"Protecting your interests?"

"Yes. I thought you'd be proud of me for taking a stand."

"Not like this. Not by deceiving your husband and stalking your child like some kind of homicidal maniac. What are you thinking, Diane?"

"Geoff knows what I'm doing, and he doesn't have a problem with it."

"Oh, so that makes it okay, because Geoff doesn't have a problem with it." Lois exhaled heavily, shaking her head. "You really are in dire straits if you consider Geoff's judgment sound."

"Fine! If my way is so wrong, what would you do?"

"I wouldn't do this," Lois said firmly, her jade eyes leaping with fire. "You're better than this, Diane. If you have one brain cell left in that addled head of yours, you will go back to your hotel, get your things and take the first plane out of town. Go home, Diane — and start behaving like the class act you are."

"But what will my going home solve?"

"What will staying here?"

Diane stared, her chest heavy as Lois' harsh words brought her to her senses. She looked down at her hands, her lip quivering as her eyes flooded with tears. "You're right," she admitted quietly. "I have no business being here, doing what I'm doing. I was just so desperate. I didn't know what else to do."

"I know," Lois acknowledged kindly, her voice tender and soothing. "I still say you have nothing to worry about. Zoë will come around."

"Have you seen her, Mother? That LaRue woman? She's stunning, dynamic, a successful businesswoman. What about me can possibly compare?"

"You have things that she will never have. You have memories of Zoë as a baby, melting our hearts with that silly toothless smile. You have remembrances of a sunny toddler and a ballet-dancing preschooler, a giggly schoolgirl and an independent college student. You have the love Zoë has given you all her life and the love you've given her in return. Those are the real treasures, Diane. Not physical beauty, status or money. It's love — above all things — that will win out in the end."

"How do you always know exactly the right thing to say?"

"I don't know. It certainly never came from being gracious, I'll tell you that much right now."

Diane raised her eyes, her expression pleading and pitiful. "Can't you just stay with me, Mother? I need your support."

Lois gazed at her regretfully, her face shining with love. "I would love to, Diane. But you know I can't."

"But I need you! I can't make rational decisions without you."

"Yes, you can," Lois laughed gently. "I have faith in you. Now, just get back home where you belong and start using the good sense God gave you."

And as quickly as she appeared, she was gone — the only trace of her being a soft wisp of air that brushed Diane's cheek.

Diane started the car and drove back to the hotel, methodically loading her clothes back into her suitcase. She called the airport and made reservations, then toted her luggage to the elevator. "I'm going to turn in my key and grab a good dinner, then get out of town as fast as I can, before I get into any more trouble."

She checked out and drove toward Gulfport, ducking into a seaside restaurant along the way. She took a corner table and dined alone, staring out the window toward the beach as she ate, lost in thought.

She missed Zoë coming in the door with Andie and Dana, their faces sun-kissed and their hair glazed lightly with sand and salt. Chattering excitedly, they followed the hostess, taking a booth near the door.

"That was so much fun!" Zoë declared, sliding in next to Andie. "Do you think Bill will take us out on the boat again before I go back home?"

"Maybe — if you're really sweet," Andie said. "Although I've never known him to refuse a pretty girl yet."

"I'm sorry you couldn't go out with us. You missed quite a ride."

"Next time," Andie promised. "Next time I will be on the water, instead of marooned on the beach missing all the fun."

"I'm starving!" Zoë said, reaching for a menu. "What is it about fresh air that makes you want to eat everything in sight?"

"It's a plot," Dana commented cynically. "Someone's bright idea to undermine all attempts at weight loss through physical exercise." She took the menu Zoë offered, flipping it open to view the selections. "What are you having?" she asked.

"I don't have a clue," Zoë answered from behind her menu, her eyes roving up and down the page. "Everything looks good."

"I'm having the usual," Andie said. "Grilled shrimp with fresh vegetables."

She folded her menu and set it aside, then gazed around the room, engaging in her favorite sport of people-watching. Her eyes jumped from table to table, lingering briefly on each face as she looked for anything unusual or interesting. A slight movement caught her attention and she turned her head, spotting an attractive redhead next to the window.

Andie inspected her, perplexed, taking in her sculpted cheekbones, flawless skin and wide brown eyes, feeling there was something oddly familiar about her. *What was it?* There was something about her coloring, her features. Two words instantly leapt to mind. *Cameron Carson. That's it!* She grinned in satisfaction as she solved the mystery, swiftly remembering his handsome face. She kept her eyes on the table and elbowed Zoë, nodding toward her as the woman rose to pay her check.

"Look at that lady over there, Zoë," Andie said cheerfully. "She could be one of your relatives."

Zoë snapped her head around, her mouth falling open when she saw Diane. *Oh my God.* Her breath caught in her throat and she turned to Andie, her eyes wide with horror. "Could be?" she remarked skeptically. "Not could be, Andie. She *is* one of my relatives."

Ignoring the looks of astonishment plastered across Andie's and Dana's faces, Zoë bolted from the booth and rushed across the room, grabbing Diane's arm just as she prepared to leave.

"Mother!" she hissed shrilly. "What are you doing here?"

Diane spun around, her cheeks burning as she stared into Zoë's outraged face. "Zoë!" she stammered. "You startled me. Where did you come from?"

"I asked you first," Zoë replied.

"I was just passing through and stopped for dinner," Diane offered lamely, spouting the first thing that came to mind.

"Passing through? From where?"

"New Orleans." *Oh, how smoothly you rolled that out, Diane. Bravo!* Diane suppressed a pleased smile.

Zoë suddenly became aware of two pairs of probing eyes from the booth across the restaurant and hastily took Diane by the elbow. "Let's go outside," she said, pushing open the glass door leading to the covered veranda.

They stood side by side against the railing with the salty wind blowing through their hair, eyeing each other in silence. Zoë was sullen and her expression stony, suspecting what Diane was up to, even if she wouldn't admit it.

Diane, in turn, was mortified. *I can't believe I've been here for three days, following her every move, and I got caught on my way out of town. What kind of justice is that?*

"Where's Daddy?" Zoë asked.

"Eden Glen."

"So, you went to New Orleans alone? Why do I find that a little hard to swallow?"

"Oh all right!" Diane cried out in frustration. "I was not in New Orleans, or anywhere else for that matter. I've been in Biloxi the entire week. I came here to spy on you."

Zoë gawked in disbelief. "I can't believe you would actually own up to it! Spying on me? Mother! What's gotten into you?"

"I don't know," Diane confessed. "I guess I just wanted to gauge my odds — you know, see what I was up against."

"Up against! This isn't some sort of competition."

"It seems like it to me. I feel like I have to compete for your affection. Every day that goes by I see you slipping farther and farther away."

Zoë looked at her, feeling a hard tug at her heart as she noted Diane's glistening tears. "Look, Mom. Nothing has changed. I am not slipping away, and as harsh as this may sound, this trip to Biloxi is not about you. It's about me. There are things I need to know, things I need to learn to satisfy my own curiosity. I didn't come here looking for a family or a place to live. I came here looking for answers."

"I can respect that," Diane said with a sigh, glancing down at her watch. "Listen, my plane leaves in an hour. Why don't you come back with me? We'll send for your car later. Or better yet, we'll just leave it here and buy you a new one. What do you say?"

Zoë giggled, entertained by Diane's intense expression. "Spoken like a true Carson," she grinned, squeezing her mother's hand playfully. "Thanks for the offer, but no matter how tempting, I'm going to have to pass. I'm not ready to go home, not yet. Andie just had a baby, and I'm having a ball playing with him.

"Andie had a baby?" Diane asked incredulously. "At her age?" *How lovely that she can keep reproducing,* she thought bitterly. *I wonder how many she's given away?*

"Hey," Zoë grabbed her arm, excited by a sudden thought. "Why don't you come back inside and meet her? It'll make your trip worthwhile."

Diane looked offended. "My trip has already been worthwhile — I'm standing here talking to you, aren't I?"

"I'd love for you to meet her."

"I don't want to meet her. She'll think I'm a fool, coming all the way to Biloxi to check up on you."

"Too late," Zoë sang out softly. "She's heading this way." Zoë watched as Andie glided down the length of the deck and smiled loyally at Diane, stretching her hand out to stop her fidgeting. "Don't worry — I'll cover for you."

"Andie," she called out, motioning her to join them, then cut her eyes to Diane, winking discreetly.

Andie strolled up, her light hair bouncing on her shoulders, flashing a cheery smile as she removed her sunglasses. "Hi," she said, regarding Diane with curiosity.

"Andie Dewberry," Zoë took her hand. "I'd like you to meet my mother, Diane Forest."

"Your mother!" Andie exclaimed in amazement as she stared at Diane. "I didn't even know she was here."

"Neither did I!" Zoë giggled. "She's just passing through on her way from New Orleans and stopped to grab a bite to eat. Isn't that the weirdest thing?"

"What an incredible coincidence," Andie said, extending her hand. "It must be fate. I'm honored, Diane. I've been wanting to meet you for quite some time."

Diane nodded, suddenly shy as she reluctantly accepted the enthusiastic hand Andie offered. "Is that a fact?" she replied coolly, wishing she weren't at such a disadvantage so she could say what she really thought.

"Yes," Andie paused, digging into the pocket of her shorts for a tissue, suddenly teary-eyed. "I wanted to thank you," she explained, her voice faltering, overcome with emotion. "I wanted to thank you for taking my child and loving her and doing such a fine job."

Zoë backed away slowly, giving them some space, praying this meeting between the mothers would help to ease some of the tension. She slipped back inside the restaurant and stood next to the glass, peering out.

Dana joined her, looking out at the two women on the deck, her eyes glued to their faces. "What do you think is going on out there?" she asked Zoë.

"Reconciliation and clearing of the air, I hope," Zoë replied, "along with a whole lot of getting acquainted."

Dana considered the pretty redhead giving Andie hell. "Your mother?"

Zoë nodded solemnly. "Yeah."

"Pretty cool."

Diane stared off in the distance, watching the waves ripple against the sand, finding it impossible to ignore Andie's presence. "For so long, I've wanted to hate you," she said solemnly. "I wanted to hate you for finding Zoë and waltzing back into her life and for trying to take over and act like the mother you never were. I've spent the last couple of years despising you for thinking you could replace me without so much as a fight."

She glanced at Andie, regarding her soberly. "You'll never understand how I feel. I know you gave birth to her, but in my mind, Zoë is my child and you have no right to her." Diane looked away, issuing an ironic sigh, her voice so hushed that Andie had to strain to hear it. "I only wish you weren't so nice. It makes my animosity seem almost unjustified."

"I wouldn't say it's unjustified," Andie replied softly. "I can't imagine how I would feel in your shoes. Just let me say this and hope it will put your mind at ease: I could never replace you, nor would I even try. I only want to be her friend."

Diane met her steadfast gaze. "I wish I could accept that."

"I wish you could too. You might still, over time." Andie took a step closer and reached out her hand, placing it gently on Diane's shoulder. "I'm sorry I upset you when I found Zoë," she whispered, her eyes brimming with sentimental tears. "That wasn't my intention. I could never be to Zoë what you have been, nor could I have done as well with her as you have. I'm just grateful for the opportunity to get to know her and celebrate all that she's become."

Diane wiped her eyes and glanced down at her watch. "Hey! You know what — I've got a plane to catch." She extended her hand boldly. "Andie, it's been a pleasure."

Andie took her hand, clasping it tightly. "No, Diane. The pleasure was all mine. You're an incredible lady. At least now I know where Zoë gets it. She's wonderful, and it's all because of you."

Zoë walked with Diane to her car, enfolding her in an embrace and tenderly kissing her cheek. "I'll be home soon," she promised with a smile. She closed the door and blew another kiss, then turned to join Andie by the front entrance of the restaurant.

Diane waved as she drove away, her eyes shielded by her dark glasses. Her smile faded as she turned onto the highway, and she spent the entire trip to the airport wiping away searing tears, exhausting her supply of tissue.

"I was so foolish," she sobbed miserably. "I humiliated myself in front of Andie LaRue and for what? I gained absolutely nothing. Zoë is still there, living under her roof, and I have to go back to Eden Glen alone to face the music. I have to come clean and answer to Jay, and then somehow think of a way to pass the time until the day Zoë finally decides to return home."

Andie watched her taillights fade on the horizon, and gave Zoë a sidelong glance, considering her thoughtfully. "Your mother's a nice lady," she said.

Zoë nodded wistfully. "Yeah, she is."

"And very pretty."

"Yes," Zoë agreed. "She's a classic beauty, all right — much more beautiful than me."

"I wouldn't go that far," Andie said with a giggle, slinging an arm around Zoë's shoulder. "You're an awfully good-looking kid."

They moved toward the entrance to collect Dana, finding her by the giant aquarium near the bar. "What a weird stroke of luck, running into her here as she was passing through Biloxi," Andie commented, holding open the door to the restaurant as Zoë went in.

Zoë glanced back at her with a meek smile. "She wasn't passing through, Andie."

"I know," Andie confessed. "It's okay, Zoë. Her coming here speaks volumes. It shows she cares enough to be concerned."

Dana sauntered over to them, annoyed. "Are y'all ready to go yet?" she mumbled, stifling an exhausted yawn. "I need to check in on Dell, and I'm ready for a nap. All this excitement has worn me slick."

# 21

That afternoon Andie napped while Dana went to check on Crème de la Crème, taking her role as new business partner very seriously. Cole arrived home from New Orleans and peeked in on Andie, then looked around for the baby, finding him in the rocking chair with Zoë, their blond heads snuggled closely together. He paused in the doorway, watching them, tears springing into his eyes. *My children,* he thought, his chest swelling with pride.

Zoë looked up, her eyes sparkling warmly when she saw him. "Hi, Cole," she whispered.

Cole quickly wiped his eyes, rubbing them with his fists to feign a pollen problem. "Hey Miss Zoë," he said. "Baby sleeping?"

Zoë leaned her head back, peering down her nose to view Jake's cherubic face. "Yeah, he is," she said in a dreamy voice, her gaze fixed on his rosy cheeks. "He's such a sweet baby," she said, hugging him to her chest.

Cole stepped into the nursery, taking a seat on the toy chest. "How was sailing with Bill?" he asked.

"Exhilarating," Zoë said. "Although not nearly as exciting as the unexpected lunch date with both my mothers. Did Andie tell you?"

Cole nodded. "Yeah, she filled me in — right before she started snoring. She said your mother was extremely gracious."

"Andie exaggerates," Zoë giggled. "I think my mother was very well behaved, all things considered. She's much too reserved to exhibit her true feelings in such a public setting."

Cole studied her cheerful expression with doubtful eyes. "Are you okay?"

"Yeah, actually. In fact, I'm somewhat relieved. Maybe their meeting was the closure I've been seeking."

"Maybe," Cole said, nodding toward his sleeping son. "How'd you end up babysitting?"

"Just got roped into it, I guess."

"See! I knew if you hung around long enough Andie would put you to work."

"Please! This is not work." Zoë glanced down at Jake, bending to kiss his cheek. "This is a joy. Jake is a darling, darling baby."

"You're pretty crazy about him, aren't you?"

"Oh yes," Zoë beamed. "I just love him. I couldn't love him any more if he were my brother."

"That's good," Cole smiled, "because he is."

"Is what?"

"Jake is your brother."

"Half-brother," Zoë corrected him. "We have the same mother."

"No. Full brother," Cole said softly. "You also have the same father."

"What?" Zoë jerked her head up, stunned.

"Jake is your brother, Zoë, because I'm your father." He watched Zoë's eyes flicker in disbelief, her pretty face growing pale as she realized he wasn't playing around.

"You're kidding right?" she stammered uncertainly, unwilling to risk jumping to false conclusions.

"I would never kid about something like that."

Zoë stared at him incredulously, her jaw dropping in shock. "Why didn't you tell me before?" she sputtered. "Why did you wait until now?"

Cole took the slumbering baby from her arms and placed him gently in his crib. "Come on," he said, pulling her up gently by the arm. "Andie will hear him if he cries. Let's get out of here so we can talk."

In zombie-like slow motion, Zoë threw on her beach hat and stepped into her flip-flops before leaving the house with Cole, walking beside him uncertainly as they crossed to the beach. Her head was spinning, dizzy with the idea of her paternity.

*I can't believe it,* she marveled. *Cole Dewberry's my father, the one I've been seeking, the answer to the question I've been dying to ask. And he's been right here, under my nose all along.*

They strolled along in tense silence, the salty wind stinging their faces, neither willing to be the first to speak. Zoë was still too flabbergasted and Cole still too unsure of what to say.

"I wanted to tell you," Cole said suddenly, shattering the silence. "I wanted to tell you the very first night I met you, but you'd already had a full day meeting Andie, and then Dana showed her butt. I thought you'd had enough to handle."

"But I asked you about my father," Zoë said, her eyes flashing accusingly. "We talked about it out on the porch, and you pretended he was someone else!"

"And it took everything I had to bite my tongue, not to tell you then and there that it was me. I just couldn't run the risk of overwhelming you and scaring you away." Cole stopped on the sand, taking her by the shoulders, his expression sincere. "But the rest of it was true, I promise you, Zoë. I didn't know about you until you were nineteen years old, and the minute I found out, I started searching. Andie and I hunted high and low for you, turning up nothing. It was like you just disappeared. Thank God for Bill Fairgate. If it weren't for him, I wouldn't be standing here, having the great privilege of addressing my only daughter."

His eyes filled with tears and he embraced her, tenderly kissing the top of her head. "I didn't know you existed until it was almost too late, but let me tell you what. I've never known a more powerful moment than when I walked into the house and saw you standing there." His voice cracked with emotion. "I am so proud of you — and so very grateful to your parents. Andie and I couldn't have done a finer job of raising you."

Zoë gazed up at him, her eyes round with wonder. "My parents are wonderful people," she whispered.

Cole nodded. "That's obvious. Look how you've turned out. You're a fine young woman, Zoanne Carson-Forest. I'm only sorry that I missed you growing up."

Zoë studied him thoughtfully. "We've got a lot to catch up on, don't we?"

Cole smiled and took her outstretched hand, squeezing it tightly. "Yes, we do," he agreed, swinging hands with her as they walked back to the house. "And I plan to spend the rest of my days making up for lost time."

Over the days that followed, Andie began feeling a little more spry. By the time Jake was two weeks old, she actually felt like a person again. He was a good baby and had good nights, sleeping through most of them.

"Thank goodness," Andie remarked as she stood in front of the bathroom mirror, inspecting the dark circles under her eyes. "If he wasn't such a good baby, I'd never live through this. I'm getting way too old for stuff like this."

She ventured out onto the porch, finding Zoë and Dana sitting side by side in deck chairs, sharing orange juice and laughter. *What a difference* a *couple of weeks make*, she thought, pausing beside the screen door to watch them. *I'm so glad they've finally decided to be friends.*

Nevertheless, as she observed Dana and Zoë together, instead of reveling in the joy of their thriving relationship, she was haunted by Diane Forest, remembering the hurt in her eyes and the anguish on her face. And she felt guilty.

*But I love having her here,* she thought, gazing affectionately at her stunning blond daughter. *I just found her — I'm not ready to give her back.*

Arguing with her conscience did no good. For as much as she cared for Zoë and as thrilled as she was at having her in Biloxi, Andie could not forget the woman who had really raised her. Andie's intrusion into their lives had created nothing but chaos, straining a tight-knit family. *All the tension between them is because of me,* she acknowledged dismally. *And as much as I hate it, it just isn't right.*

She wrestled with her inner demons and selfish thoughts, looking for the opportune time to make things right. *It's my duty to mend their fences. I owe the Forests that much, if not more.*

Another week went by, and Zoë was still there, seeming more content with each passing day. She fed Jake breakfast and grabbed a quick shower before joining Andie and Cole on the front stoop.

"Hey," she greeted them brightly, donning a pair of neon-colored shades, a glittery headband with spring-held antennae bobbing on her head. "You like?" she asked with a grin.

"I like," Andie nodded, giggling at her comical appearance. "Where on earth did you get those?"

"Dana and I found them while I was souvenir shopping at Sharkhead's." She pulled down the glasses, directing her cheerful gaze toward Cole. "Don't you have a job?" she asked.

Cole chuckled. "I think so, yes. I'm playing hooky today, though. I wanted to spend some time with my boy. He's getting all the attention, and I'm getting jealous."

"Can't handle the competition, huh?" Zoë kidded, punching his arm teasingly.

Andie studied her laughing face pensively. "Have you talked to your folks?" she asked.

Zoë's smile faded and she looked down, studying her fingernails. "I talked to Daddy last night," she said with a heavy sigh, "but Mother refused to come to the phone. I don't know whether she's mad or embarrassed."

"Maybe it's time for you to go home and check on her."

"Or maybe I'll just stay here where it's safe," Zoë said, then quickly changed the subject. "I think I'll take another week off from the clinic. No one would even miss me. The place practically runs itself."

The moment had presented itself. Andie looked over at Cole, guilt-stricken as she examined his unsuspecting face, knowing what she was about to say would break his heart. She hated tearing apart the bond he was trying to build with Zoë, but she had to do it.

"No, Zoë. I don't think that's such a good idea," she said softly, avoiding Cole's baffled stare. He leaned forward, wearing a dark frown as he elbowed her sharply in the ribs.

"Why not?" Zoë asked, her eyes dancing merrily. "Are you tired of me already?"

"If I lived to be a hundred, I could never get tired of you," Andie said, swallowing hard to fight back tears. "But you don't belong here, honey." She reached out, placing a gentle hand on Zoë's arm, their eyes locking in understanding. "Go home, Zoë. You have a mother."

Zoë stared, her expression flooded with relief. "Are you sure?" she asked timidly.

Andie nodded, feeling Cole's eyes like twin daggers in her back. "I'm sure."

With a subdued, yet excited smile, Zoë dashed inside to pack, and Andie remained on the steps, her face twisted in sorrow, a dull empty ache already beginning to gnaw at her soul.

Cole leapt from the stoop and glared at her, pacing up and down the veranda, his fists balled tightly against his sides. "I can't believe you just did that," he snapped, his voice trembling with anger. "After all the years we searched for her, after all Bill's hard work, we finally find our daughter, and you just told her to leave. You may be tired of her, Andie, but I'm not. I was just getting to know her. You could have at least consulted me before sending her away without a second thought. I guess my feelings aren't any more important now than they were the first time around."

"How dare you?" Andie whirled around to face him, her eyes smoldering. "How dare you say I did what I did lightly, without giving it a second thought? Right now, I'm dying inside."

She marched across the porch and leaned into him, poking him hard in the chest. "Let me tell you something, Cole Dewberry! You've only known about Zoë for a few years, but I've known about her for twenty-five and sending her away again is just about the hardest thing I've ever done."

She stomped down the stairs, rushing out to the street, and crossed to the beach, blinded by tears as she stumbled over the sand. She sank to the ground at the water's edge, sitting with her arms crossed tightly, letting the wind whip through her hair as she shook with anger. *How dare he accuse me of not caring!* she thought bitterly.

"I wasn't finished talking to you yet." Cole appeared beside her, out of breath from running, his eyes still blazing with indignation.

"I don't care," Andie said, gritting her teeth defiantly. "I've said all I have to say."

"I still can't believe you did that."

"Cole, I feel no obligation to keep explaining my actions. Regardless of what you think, I did the right thing. You weren't there to meet Diane Forest. You didn't see the devastated look on her face. She loves Zoë too and this separation has almost destroyed her, so much that she traveled nearly five hundred miles to make sure she was all right."

She turned, staring unwaveringly into his face. "You ask why I did what I did? I did it because I'm a mother — and I understand."

She scrambled from the sand, wiping her hands on her shorts and stalked down the beach, getting as far away from him as she could before she said something she would regret. Soon she felt him come up behind her and slide his arms around her waist, bringing her to an abrupt halt. He pulled her against him and pressed his chin into her shoulder, kissing her softly on the nape of the neck.

"I'm sorry, Andie," he said, his voice husky with emotion. "I know in my heart that you're doing the right thing. I didn't mean to hurt you. It's just that I love Zoë and can't bear the thought of her leaving again."

Andie turned slowly, slipping her arms around his neck in a comforting embrace, salt-water droplets sliding down her face as she tenderly kissed his cheek. "I know exactly how you feel," she whispered hoarsely. "It's so hard to let her go. But you have to understand. Zoë doesn't belong here. Biologically, she's ours, and we needed to find her. Now that we've seen her, and know she's all right, our souls can be at ease. We'll always be her friends, but Zoë has a family, and she belongs with them."

The next morning, Dana sat on the end of the bed, swinging her legs, her lips pursed in frustration as she watched Zoë snap her bag closed. "I can't believe you're leaving," she grumbled unhappily. "I was just starting to tolerate you."

Zoë glanced up, her face reflecting great empathy as she swung the heavy suitcase to the floor. "I know, Dana. But it's time for me to go. I've got some things to take care of."

"What, did you find out what you needed to know and now you don't need us anymore?" Dana demanded, her eyes flashing irately. "Is that it?"

"No, that's not it." Zoë sat on the bed, sliding an arm around Dana's shoulders. "I've had a terrific visit, and as most good visits go, it has been much too short. But," she added with a smile, "I've been away from home a long time, and I need to go check on the doc."

"Oh! Why didn't you say so? Seeing about the doc I can understand. I would definitely miss that sexy voice." Dana nodded in satisfaction, accepting her explanation. "Are you ever coming back?"

"Of course, I'm coming back, goose," Zoë replied with a laugh. "I've got too much invested here not to come back."

"Such as?"

"A mother, a father, a brother, great friends that I love, and a mean little sister that I think the world of."

"Yeah, well," Dana stammered in embarrassment, suppressing a grin. "Me too, I guess. It'll be kind of weird here without you."

"I'll tell you what," Zoë said, rising from the bed to collect her bag. She stuck her hat on her head and pushed on her neon shades, laughing at Dana's entertained expression. "Let's start planning now and take a trip together next spring. Just you and me. What do you say?"

"Really?" Dana asked, leaping from the bed in excitement. "Ooh, Zoë! I like that. Let's go somewhere really fun, like Bermuda or the Bahamas."

"You got a deal." Zoë took her hand and walked with her outside, stopping where Andie and Cole waited on the porch. "Well, I guess this is goodbye, for now," she said, holding her bag in her hands.

Andie put up a brave front, offering the most radiant of smiles. "I'm so glad you came. It's been fun."

"It has been fun," Zoë agreed cheerfully. "And I'm already planning my next visit. I thought I'd come back over Jerry's next semester break, if that's okay."

Andie's heart soared. "That would be great," she said. "We would love it, and so would Jerry. I know he'd like to see you again."

"I'd like to see him again too, plus I have to come check up on Jake and see how much he's grown. He'll probably be so big I won't recognize him."

"Don't worry about that," Andie laughed. "You'll recognize him. We'll send you plenty of pictures."

Zoë dropped her bag, throwing her arms around Andie's neck in a tight embrace. "I'm so thankful that Bill Fairgate is such a persistent bulldog and finally brought us together," she whispered. She pulled away, smiling up at Andie through misty eyes. "You're a great lady, Andrea Dewberry, and I wouldn't have missed meeting you for the world."

Andie took her hands, squeezing them tenderly. "You're everything I ever hoped for and more," she said, her voice cracking as she gave in to her tears. "I love you, Zoë dear, and I hope this is only the beginning of a very long and special relationship."

Unwilling to let Zoë see the deep sadness in his eyes, Cole picked up her suitcase and headed down the steps in the direction of her car. He set the bag on the ground and lifted the hood, hiding his sorrow by checking the oil.

Zoë followed and slipped up next to him, tiptoeing to kiss his cheek. "Hey, Cole," she said, noting the grim expression on his face. "Cheer up! You should be happy to see me go. You'll have a little less estrogen to contend with."

He offered her a thin smile. "You haven't been too terribly tough to put up with," he said gruffly.

"Sure, you can say that now," she said teasingly, "but just wait until I've been here a few times. Then you'll be singing a different song." She gave him a hug, resting her head against his shoulder. "Thanks for telling me the truth, Cole," she added quietly, gazing up at him with familiar gray eyes. "I'm very honored to know you're my father."

Cole caught her arm as she turned to go, pulling her into a tight embrace. "Not half as honored as I am," he said softly, holding her at arms' length. "See you soon, okay?"

"You can count on it." She grinned broadly and walked to the steps, punching Dana's shoulder as she said goodbye. "See ya, Butthead," she growled playfully.

"Later, Your Highness," Dana retorted, unable to hold back her wide smile.

Cole and Andie stood together in front of the house, arms linked and waving as they watched Zoë drive away. "Think she'll really be back?" Cole asked.

Andie squinted in the early morning sunlight, staring after the disappearing taillights of Zoë's car. "Yeah," she nodded with a smile. "Yeah, honey. I think she'll be back."

Andie's life had come full circle. She had Cole, her one true love, after believing for years that she had lost him forever. Their affection and trust were even stronger now than twenty-five years before, and they had been blessed with their son, Jake — an unexpected miracle conceived in love.

But Jake wasn't her only miracle. All of her children were miraculous, in their own ways. Jerry was a miracle. Undeserving though she might be, Andie was blessed with Jerry's unwavering love, finding his ever-present faith in her so amazing. He had never given up on her, even when she had given up on herself.

She was equally blessed to finally have the kind of relationship she'd always longed for with Dana. Dana's love had been earned, hard won after years of mistrust. Because of their early years together, Dana grew up determined, hard-nosed and not easily swayed, but at the same time, she was bright and funny, with an incredible enthusiasm and a zest for life. She didn't take any flack from anyone, and Andie admired her. Dana was her hero.

And at last, Andie had found her Shannon. In all the years she had yearned for her lost child, Shannon had been only a dream, one so impossible to achieve it hurt. However, Zoë was a reality — a jubilant reality, more beautiful and wondrous than Andie could have imagined. To have Zoë in her life was the answer to her prayers.

She kissed the top of Jake's head and lifted him in the air, marveling at his happy laughter and the joyful baby smile on his handsome little face. *Yes,* she thought blissfully, *I am truly, truly blessed.* After two and a half agonizing decades of heartache, at long last Andie's life was complete.

Zoë drove home, her heart light, filled with an overwhelming sense of relief, spending most of her travel time reflecting. She had finally learned the truth about her biological parents and gained a sense of where she came from. No longer did she feel torn between two families. She loved Cole and Andie, and they would always share a special connection, but she also knew exactly where she belonged.

She reached Savannah late in the afternoon and drove through rush-hour traffic toward the clinic, in no great hurry to reach Carson House. She pulled in, finding Sean's car in the lot, just as she'd known it would be.

Entering the building, she padded softly down the dimly lit corridor in search of him, finding him in the tiny kitchen at the back of the clinic. Still attired in bright green scrubs, he sat at a small, round table in the center of the room, staring into space, stirring his heavily creamed coffee with a plastic spoon.

She leaned in the doorway. "Hey Sean," she said, giggling softly as he glanced up with a start.

"Why Zoë, you're back," he said, leaning back in his chair, a wide smile stretching across his face. "I was beginning to think you ran away with Eli Feinstein."

"Fat chance of that happening," she said, slinging her purse over her shoulder. "Eli Feinstein is hardly my type." She moved into the room, her eyes sparkling with laughter. "Did you really think I wasn't coming back?"

"I didn't know. You were a little unclear."

"Well, I've had a lot of time to think things over and everything's crystal clear to me now." She slid into his lap, wrapping her arms tightly around his neck, kissing him with irrefutable affection. "I missed you, Sean," she said breathlessly. "I could never stay away from you for very long."

Sean opened his eyes, peering happily at her flushed features. "This is a much better homecoming than I was anticipating," he said. "I notice you're still wearing that ring. Does that mean I still have a fiancée?"

"If you still want one."

"You know I do." He studied her inquisitively. "Should I take that as a yes?"

"Now, I don't know about that," Zoë kidded, twirling the end of her hair with her finger. "Why is it again that I should marry you?"

"Because I'm absolutely wonderful!" Sean joked, chuckling when she rolled her eyes in bogus irritation.

"Not even," she drawled.

Sean slipped her arms from around his neck, balancing her on his knee, and gazed into her face. "Zoë, look. Seriously, I know I don't have much to offer. I'm not Eli Feinstein. I'm not influential or worldly, nor do I come from a long line of money or hold a prestigious position on a board of directors.

"I'm just a self-made man who has worked his entire life to become a doctor, hoping he could help change the world. I don't have wealth or power, but I do have goals and dreams." He took her hands, his expression sincere. "And I want you by my side. I love you, Zoanne Annette Carson-Forest. You're beautiful and amazing, and the only woman I've ever met who sees things the way I do. I was miserable when you went away, and I never want to go through that again."

"Ooh, Dr. Murphy — you are quite the speechmaker. Maybe you should go into politics."

"Zoë!" he frowned. "I thought we were having a serious discussion."

"We are," Zoë said, wiping the smirk off her face. "It appears to me, Doctor, that we make a great team. Maybe I should marry you."

The muscles in Sean's arms tightened involuntarily, and he gave her a questioning look. "Should I take *that* as a yes?"

"Yes," Zoë nodded emphatically. "You may take that as a very definite yes."

"Finally," he grinned and lowered his mouth onto hers, kissing her deeply. Zoë dissolved at his touch, a hot wave of desire searing through her body as she relaxed against him. She closed her eyes, savoring the taste of his lips.

"Wow!" she breathed as he lifted his head, his deep blue eyes staring intensely into hers. "Why did you stop?"

"It's not that I was crazy about the idea," Sean replied, his voice ragged with passion," but you really should go say hello to your mother."

"She's here?" Zoë hurriedly sat up, smoothing down her disheveled hair. "What's she doing here so late?"

"She's been here late quite a bit in the past few weeks," Sean revealed with a wink. "She says she likes being at the clinic because it makes her feel closer to you. However, I think she stays down here because she's in the doghouse with your dad — you know, over the Biloxi stunt."

Zoë grinned wryly. "Daddy was pretty upset with her, huh?"

Sean nodded soberly. "Oh, yeah. He was pretty pissed."

"Let me go say hi then," Zoë said, climbing out of his lap. She turned back, tweaking his cheek playfully. "But don't you go anywhere, Doc. When I come back, I want to take up right where we left off."

"No problem, Ms. Forest," Sean beamed cheerfully, reclining comfortably to await her return. "I'm not going anywhere as long as you're here."

Zoë found Diane at her desk, head down, diligently scribbling away on paperwork, her brow creased in concentration. She tiptoed into the office and relaxed against the wall, smiling as she watched Diane work.

"Hi, Mom," she said softly, breaking the silence.

Diane stopped writing and looked up, uncertainty and surprise lighting her face. "So, you've decided to come back," she stated blandly, lifting her eyes to meet Zoë's. She looked so tired, so emotionally drained and weary, that Zoë was instantly overcome by guilt. "How was the rest of your trip?" she asked, biting her lip to force back tears.

"It was fine," Zoë said, strolling over to take a chair.

"Zoë, I'm really sorry about Biloxi. I don't know what I was thinking."

"Don't worry about it, Mom. It's not that big a deal. In fact, I was really glad to see you."

"You were? Even though I embarrassed you by acting like an amateur detective?"

"You didn't embarrass me," Zoë laughed. "I'm glad you got to meet Andie."

Diane's face fell at the mention of her name. "She seems very nice," she acknowledged brusquely.

"She is very nice — she and Cole both."

They shared a moment of tense silence, neither knowing quite what to say. Diane studied Zoë's face nervously. *There are so many things I want to ask, so many things I just have to know, but I can't bring myself to say the words. I don't dare risk ruining this surprisingly pleasant reunion.*

Zoë waited for the other shoe to fall, idly fingering the pencils in the penholder on Diane's desk, squishing the rubbery pink erasers between her thumb and forefinger to avoid Diane's stare.

"Did you find what you were looking for?" Diane finally blurted out, then instantly regretted it, almost terrified to hear Zoë's answer.

Zoë sighed, staring into space, scratching her head distractedly as she tried to think of a way to explain. "I told you I went to Mississippi in search of answers, to learn more about my family and discover my heritage. I did have a lovely time in Biloxi, and enjoyed being with Andie and Cole. They couldn't be more wonderful, and I really learned a lot."

"How very nice," Diane's tone was bitter.

"But," Zoë continued, "to answer your question: Yes, I did find what I was looking for. I went to Biloxi in search of my heritage, and I found it."

She paused, giving Diane a soft smile. "Don't get me wrong. I love Andie and Cole, and will always love them, but I belong here — right here in Eden Glen with you and Daddy.

"You are my heritage, Mom — you and Daddy, Uncle Geoff, Cam and, God forbid, even Palmer. My heritage is you. You're my family. Andie gave me life, but you and Daddy gave me the world."

Suddenly, the tiny office seemed illuminated, and Diane felt the heavy weight lift from her shoulders. She stared at Zoë, her eyes round and sparkling in jubilant amazement. She flew out of her chair, sending it sailing across the floor.

"That's the best news I've heard all year!" she declared gleefully, filling the room with relieved and delirious laughter. She threw her arms around Zoë, holding her tight, her face streaked with tears. "Of course, I wasn't worried," she sniffled lightheartedly. "I never doubted that you would come back."

Zoë pulled back, eyeing her doubtfully. "Now who's not being honest?" she teased.

"Well, maybe I was just a little worried," Diane admitted sheepishly, tweaking Zoë's cheek as she slipped an arm around her waist. "Whatever the case, I'm glad you're back. Welcome home."

"Oh, by the way," Zoë said slyly as they walked together toward the office door. "While I was in Biloxi, I also met my father. You can tell Daddy if you want to. You know, use it against him to put him in his place."

Diane gave her a sidelong glance, her brown eyes gleaming devilishly. "Oh no," she said lightly as she guided Zoë down the hall. "I think I'll keep that information to myself, thank you. I'll save it for one day when he's feeling particularly cocky and then spring it on him, unexpected like. Now, that would really put him in his place."

She caught Zoë's entertained look and flashed a naughty smile, linking arms and sharing a laugh with her as they retrieved Sean from the break room and stepped outside the clinic to their waiting cars.

Zoë married Sean Murphy the following summer in Diane's Danielle Laurent gown and a veil of Irish lace, promising to love and cherish him forever.

She sent an invitation to Andie, Cole and Dana, sincerely hoping that they would attend. Andie called when she received the invitation, not to accept, but to respectfully decline. "No, Zoë," she said firmly. "This day belongs to your family. Cole and I won't be there in person, but we'll be there in spirit, wishing you and Sean all the happiness in the world."

"I'll be there," Dana teased, taking the phone from Andie. "I'll be there with bells on, hidden in the balcony — just in case you back out at the last minute. I want to be the next in line with dibs on the doc."

The Murphy-Forest nuptials were a social event, as was any Carson wedding, and to Zoë, the elaborate preparations were dizzying, closely resembling a three-ring circus. But somehow, it all came together, and before the ceremony, Zoë congregated with Diane and Leigh in the bride's room, letting her mother fuss over her.

Attired in a bridesmaid's frock of pale iris, Leigh unzipped the garment bag holding Zoë's dress, pulling out the hanger and surveying the gown with disdain. "You could've had a Vera Wang," she lamented, rolling her violet eyes pathetically. "Why is it again that you're wearing your mother's thirty-year-old dress?

"Tradition, Leigh," Zoë replied pointedly, meeting Diane's eyes. "It's very important."

"Yes, Leigh," Diane agreed as she crossed the room and reached out to squeeze Zoë's hand. "Any decent Southern woman should have a dress to pass on to her daughter."

The wedding was lovely, held in the garden at Carson House with the usual elite on hand. Palmer surveyed the affair from his position by the altar with the other groomsmen, shaking his head in pompous astonishment.

"It's amazing this shindig turned out as well as it did," he remarked to Susan as they retreated down the aisle behind Zoë and Sean. "And I actually approve of the groom. He'll never be Eli Feinstein, of course, but given Zoë's taste, she could've done so much worse."

Cameron approached Zoë in the receiving line, shooting her a scornful look, lifting her hand to view the diamond wedding band. "A doctor's wife, Zoë," he said jokingly, sneaking a peek at his new cousin-in-law. "Talk about the ultimate sellout."

Zoë brushed aside her veil and rolled her eyes. "Don't you ever give up?" she asked.

"Oh Cam, will you shut up already?" Leigh pushed to the head of the line, elbowing Cameron out of her way, and embraced Zoë with all her might. "Why can't you behave? It's her wedding day, for heaven's sake. And sellout or not, of the doc I approve — one hundred percent. He is perfect for her. I don't know what your problem is."

Cameron grinned at Zoë, his jade eyes dancing, amused by his wife's indignant outburst. "Zoë knows I'm kidding, Leigh," he said. "Besides, she doesn't need me to tell her anything. Zoë's perfectly capable of taking care of herself."

Zoë clutched her chest, feigning shock at his confession. "I can't believe I heard you say that," she said. "It's about time you figured it out."

Cameron leaned forward, giving her a tender kiss. "Congratulations, Cuz," he said softly. "I'm happy for you."

Zoë gazed up at him and smiled. "Thanks, Cam," she said, reaching for Sean's outstretched hand.

"I only hope Sean knows what kind of screwed-up family he's getting into," Cameron couldn't resist and chuckled heartily as he walked away, stealing a mischievous look at Zoë over his shoulder.

Zoë danced first with her new husband, then glided gracefully into Jay's arms, sharing a waltz with her father, feeling Diane's adoring smile as she watched them from the sidelines. Zoë rested her bouquet on Jay's shoulder and glanced up, catching the tender gleam in his eye. "I love you, Daddy," she said, her gray eyes shining happily.

Jay gazed into his daughter's face, taking in her rosy cheeks and upswept hair, remembering the beautiful baby, the impish toddler and the vivacious teenager as he studied the incredible woman before him. "You know, Zoë, I've loved you all your life," he said, his voice faltering as he stared at her through misty eyes. "And even though I've loved you deeply, I've never loved you quite as much as I do right at this moment."

Zoë and Sean left the reception in a horse-drawn carriage, running through a throng of cheering guests lining the long veranda. Zoë found her mother at the bottom of the steps and stopped in front of her, reaching down to take her hands. "Hey, see you in a week," she said.

Diane beamed at her, almost blinded by joyful tears. "I won't even have time to miss you — you'll be back before I know it," she said, giving her hand a tight squeeze. "I love you, baby."

Zoë bent forward, leaving her a tender kiss. "Love you too, Mom. You're the best." She let go of Diane's hands and took Sean's arm, continuing down the sidewalk to the buggy.

"Don't do anything I wouldn't do!" Cameron belted out, flashing an obnoxious grin.

Zoë lifted her skirt and climbed into the carriage, looking back at him with a wicked smile. "Well, that doesn't really eliminate anything at all, now does it?" she said, settling onto the seat next to her groom.

The driver cracked the whip, setting the grand roan stallion into motion, and he trotted briskly down the drive. Zoë and Sean leaned over the seat, waving goodbye to the well-wishers through a steady rain of birdseed.

"Well, I guess the party's over now, Zoë," Sean said as they traveled down the oak-lined path leading to the main road, his eyes leaping mischievously as he pulled out a chilled bottle of champagne stashed beneath the seat.

Zoë giggled and lifted the crystal goblets she had tucked neatly within the folds of her silk dress. "Oh no, dear doctor," she corrected him. "The party's only just begun."

As she spoke, the late afternoon sun broke through the clouds, shining brilliantly on the retreating carriage, filling Zoë with an overwhelming sense of warmth. She gazed up into the clear blue skies, certain that the sudden luminous rays of sunlight were a sign. "You just had to be here, didn't you?" she asked slyly, ignoring Sean's startled look.

In that moment, the sun seemed to shine even brighter, and Zoë laughed, leaning forward to give her groom a warm kiss. "In case you didn't notice," she murmured, "our union has officially been blessed."

She raised her eyes to heaven and offered a big grin, her eyes sparkling with glee, knowing that Lois was smiling down on them.